MORE BOOKS FROM THE SAGER GROUP

The Swamp: Deceit and Corruption in the CIA
An Elizabeth Petrov Thriller (Book 1)
by Jeff Grant

Chains of Nobility:
Brotherhood of the Mamluks (Book 1-3)
by Brad Graft

Meeting Mozart:
A Novel Drawn from the Secret Diaries of Lorenzo Da Ponte
by Howard Jay Smith

Death Came Swiftly:
A Novel About the Tay Bridge Disaster of 1879
by Bill Abrams

A Boy and His Dog in Hell: And Other Stories
by Mike Sager

Miss Havilland: A Novel
by Gay Daly

The Orphan's Daughter: A Novel
by Jan Cherubin

Lifeboat No. 8: Surviving the Titanic
by Elizabeth Kaye

Hunting Marlon Brand
A True Story
by Mike Sager

D1444401

See our entire library at TheSagerGroup.net

iNTO THE RiVER of ANGELS

A Novel

George R. Wolfe

Published in the United States of America.

Cover and Interior Designed by Siori Kitajima, PatternBased.com

Cataloging-in-Publication data for this book is available from the Library of Congress

ISBN-13:
eBook: 978-1-950154-94-4
Paperback: 978-1-958861-02-8

Published by The Sager Group LLC
(TheSagerGroup.net)

Maryellen —

4/1/24

Congratulations on being a WIN<u>NE</u>R *of this Goodreads Giveaway! I'm honored. I hope you enjoy the book!*

George Wolfe

iNTO THE RiVER OF ANGELS

A Novel

George R. Wolfe

THE SAGER GROUP

Artifex Te Adiuva

To Zaha and Omi
—and Jed Schipper

CONTENTS

Section 1

THE LAUNCH

Seek the river's source and take it where you will, watching destinies and mysteries unfold around each bend.

—Sam Hawkins, November 11, 2015

i. THE SOURCE

Remember how they said, *In the beginning was the word?* I always thought that was cool because, well, it was true: A person's word either rings true or stinks pretty badly—and, as you'll see, I've never been a fan of gray areas. Sometimes all you've *got* is your word; you go against it for too long, you become alienated. At that point in my life, choosing my words more carefully became important, plus sticking to them long enough to see where they took me. It was like a little experiment.

So let's start there. That was me, Sam, about seven years ago, the summer before my senior year of high school, 2008. There was a vague sense that everything was about to change, that there'd be no turning back. That turned out to be true, just not in the ways I'd imagined.

And then there was the L.A. River. Of course, there's the stuff you've seen in the movies, like the one where the Terminator and the boy are on a motorcycle, being chased down the dry cement riverbed by a humongous truck. Sure, that was stretching the truth, but it was okay because the rule we all agreed to was that it was in the land of make-believe. I identified with that movie because it had two sides fighting it out, and a kid stuck in the middle.

Being bounced between parents who were divorcing and who tended to stretch the truth, I'd had enough of all the fork-tongued, two-faced half-truths that a seventeen-year-old kid could bear. Or any kid. It was my Land of Fake-Believe, 'cause all the agreements and trust were shot and everyone was trying hard to believe it wasn't happening, that it hadn't all gotten so bad. Apart from my little wordy experiment, that was another reason for me to get on the river: to get some distance for a change.

Then again, there was our resident jerk, Ronnie McMasters, dogging and hunting me all around the neighborhood, practicing his bullying skills. And then my dad laying into me, literally, around home. They say to turn the other cheek, but how does that work when you're getting hit from both sides? I still don't know.

On the simpler side of things, I wanted to impress a girl: Zoe Shapiro. Things had been heating up between us for a year or so. But we'll get to her a little later.

Where was I? Oh yeah, being cynical—some things never change. It always got me into trouble. I didn't mean to be so cynical, it just came naturally. Adults hated it when they heard a cynical kid, and I figured it was because a lot of them felt cynical themselves, after so many years of living without much of a purpose. Turns out I was spot on. It seemed to jab at something deep inside them to be faced with a bitter little reflection of themselves. It was fun for me to see the way it got under an adult's skin; I'd imagine smoke escaping from their ears, like in those old cartoons. Kids got a rise out of it, adults called it attitude; kids got in trouble, got forgiven, and it all started up again—that was the game. Anyway, that's only one of my many theories.

Forgive me ahead of time: Thinking too much is one of my issues. My therapist calls it my thinking problem (and she's right). In fact, she's the one who, after hearing me blab on about my experiences on the river, suggested I jot down some thoughts about it on paper to see if it brought back any memories to discuss. Classic case of *careful what you ask for.* Those thoughts sort of blew up into this larger story—good thing I like to write. Now that she's been reading some of these memories, she's convinced I'm having my quarter-life crisis.

But back to that whole thinking thing. It just seemed like kids were either too much into their own heads or too concerned with what was going on in other kids' heads. Either way you couldn't win. Adults are always talking about kids having disorders or whatever—they said that about my best friend, Ian Wang. Sure, he could be obsessed with his own inventive tinkering and didn't always hit his social cues, but what boy that age ever did? Not anyone I cared to hang out with. Speaking of Ian, I had just dodged Ronnie on my way to meet up with Ian over at the river, near Balboa Park.

I lived in the San Fernando Valley, in a neighborhood called Canoga Park. *Canoga* was Native American for *canoe*. Way back when the L.A. River was a real river, that made sense; now, not a chance. At some point Canoga Park was designated an All-American City, whatever *that* meant. Still, it sounded great—that is, if you can put aside America's worst nuclear disaster that happened just a bit north of town and polluted the air above and water beneath the Valley starting in the 1950s. Lovely little legacy—how's that for all-American?

But there I was, on the overpass at Owensmouth Avenue where two streams, Bell Creek and Arroyo Calabasas, came together to form the headwaters of our glorious river, right near my old high school. To say those are still creeks or streams is definitely a stretch—they're these ugly concrete canyons boxed in by twenty-five-foot vertical walls, topped off by chain-link fences and barbed wire. Nice piece of design! Even *I* could've designed something easier on the eye that still kept the city from being washed away.

Anyway, right behind this spot was Canoga Park High School. I was near there when I texted Ian on my way to our hideout in the basin, telling him about how I narrowly avoided Ronnie.

It was rare that Ian and I got out of the house and did stuff. For one thing, there was the hot weather. Then again, there were favorite shows to be watched and video games to be played. Besides, we didn't have the same freedom our parents had, when kids could wander all day without adults hovering over them. Kids only came home when they got hungry or maybe broke an arm, and moms didn't care if you changed your underwear or took a shower. Making a mess of yourself was a sign of pride and character; it showed you had real experiences. But at the time that could simply be bought: We got "distressed" jeans from the mall, tattered and dirtied, so we didn't have to go out and get our feet wet doing stuff. I was so tired of all the fake stuff, facades, strip malls, you know. I craved something authentic. Well, anything really, anything *else* but my regular life at that point.

I rolled along the bike path that ran beside the river's narrow channel along a ridge. I was like that kid in *The Terminator*, riding fast like there's no tomorrow. But the truth was that, apart from Ronnie, I was chased by my own thoughts about why I felt so out of touch with everything around me—a subject that, inevitably, led back to parents.

My mom said video games were to blame for kids being checked out, but I didn't buy that. My theory was deep down, their generation was jealous 'cause they only had lame games like Asteroids, Pac-Man, and Pong, so naturally they're upset. We grew up with awesome games, and so they were always trying to get back at us by assigning endless chores and making us practice classical music against our will.

I was almost at the rendezvous spot and thinking of stuff my dad used to say. My dad, when he wasn't busy putting me down, was usually harping on how easy our generation had it. Okay, so maybe he had a paper route as a boy and got up before the crack of dawn to ride his rickety, rusty bike and toss a few lousy newspapers on driveways—give the guy a medal. But before I even *got* to school in the mornings, whether I was at Mom's or Dad's place, there were, like, *ten* things to do: mindless repetitive stuff like emptying the dishwasher or taking out the trash and recycling. That doesn't build character, it only dumbs you down.

But adults could never let go of stuff like that—they kept reminding you, constantly repeating worn-out sound bites, forgetting that they'd already guilt-tripped you with the same tired points at least a dozen times before. And if you tried to argue with them, they'd pull out crap like "Oh, you'll understand some day." Granted, there's truth in that, but we don't need to go into it.

See now, talk about distractions and attention deficits— no one ever labeled *adults* as having trouble staying focused and on task. But one look at dads and you know what I mean—their minds are so elsewhere.

Anyway, with my bike I had to stop and work my way awkwardly through the hole in the fence. I finally got through and was zooming again along the path at the top of the concrete riverbank, getting closer to Ian.

Below and up ahead, in the riverbed beyond the vast concrete stretch, there was the oasis of the dirt-bottomed part of the river—trees and shrubs, with angled concrete still coming up and out of the river to form the sides. Swooping down along the angled concrete before dropping back onto the flat part again, I got to the bottom and picked up the winding, worn-down, sandy dirt trail next to a lush part of the river that we used to call Skanky Springs—'cause the water was stopped up there and it had this gassy, obnoxious smell. I got to the turnoff at the Boysenberry Patch—our special place where we could find a sliver of peace.

There was still no sign of Ian. So I stashed my bike in the dense brush, propping it up against the skeleton of a prehistoric, rusty shopping cart, then walked down to the river's edge—finally, this part looked like a real river, even a nice one: Everywhere there were willows, sycamores, and cottonwood trees along muddy riverside banks. I looked out, scanning for signs of life, waiting for Ian.

ii. THE BOYSENBERRY PATCH

I hadn't been at the meeting spot for more than two minutes when I spotted Ian through the trees, poised on the cusp of the riverbank. Before he dropped down, he reached forward to his specially rigged, very old whistle attached to the handlebars of his tricked-out bike. That whistle was his trademark gadget: something that he and his brother ordered. They and their nerdy pals were into the whole steampunk thing. He pulled the string, and that airy, dull sound was released into the air like he was a steamboat captain. More and more he wore those damn aeronaut goggles and a pair of leather riding gloves from like a hundred years ago—that and his long black jacket stuck through with a bunch of brass grommets.

Ian could be such a dork! It beats me why he didn't get picked on more often. If bullies like Ronnie knew how to label him exactly, they'd have a stronger case for getting hassled, but they were so dumbfounded with Ian that they never knew where to start. Besides, apart from being smart and resourceful, he had a disarming charm, like a cute baby possum that's good at playing dead. It's like he was too much work for lazy evil jerks to get worked up about. I wasn't so lucky—all my acting-out made me an easy target.

Ian's front wheel rolled over the edge of the embankment and soon he was barreling down the incline. He built up speed and hit one of the jumps we sculpted out of earth and junk. He landed it squarely, kicking up a cloud of dirt and screeching to a halt. He dumped his bike next to mine, and we were off to our secret meeting spot.

During middle school especially, we used to take walks along the soft-bottomed Sepulveda Basin Recreation Area, a sprawling park—sort of like L.A.'s version of New York City's Central Park. The river there is only a few miles long, but that's plenty for two boys to get lost in; besides, we mostly explored only the upper half of it and didn't know much of anything past Balboa Boulevard. Beyond that it was a no-man's land—in the old explorer maps they'd mark it like *There Be Dragons*.

But when some kids we didn't like started hanging out in our area, drinking and smoking after school, we realized we needed a place to hide away. Eventually, we discovered this berry thicket, which offered us protection.

So we created our boysenberry hideaway 'cause we could be hidden within it and no one else dared go near because the stems have long, sharp thorns. But before we managed to sculpt a better entryway, we came home totally scratched up, like we'd picked a fight with Wolverine. Eventually we got smart and took a couple of shears and garden gloves with us and cut a small tunnel through it, creating a nook that was cozy and protected; then we cut another tunnel that went about twenty yards down to the river. We stuck cool-looking garbage from the river onto the thorns and the inside and outside walls to camouflage us more. Once we were inside our little fort, no one could see us. Whenever we left, we were always careful to close our thorny, makeshift door. Sometimes I'd even go there alone when I needed to get away. Every teenager needs their own safe space like that, with something prickly on the outside that sends a clear message to the world to stay away.

One day a couple of old chairs floated by, so we fished them out, cleaned them off, and propped them up on the riverbank so we could sit by the river, have our chats, and eat as many boysenberries as we could stomach.

You wouldn't believe the crazy stuff we've seen: baseballs, soccer balls, life preservers, baby dolls, stuffed animals, dead fish, broken umbrellas, garden hoses, dead birds, dildos, down parkas, women's bras, crutches, beer coolers, men's underwear, even a whole mattress once! And because there used to be a bunch of natural springs that bubbled up right around our spot, we dubbed that part of the river Mattress Springs.

So we sat there, like we'd done before, watching the floating museum pass us by, just thinking about stuff.

"What are we gonna *do* all summer," I asked, intending it as much for me as him.

Ian considered this a while. "I thought you were going to be a counselor at that camp thing."

"Yeah, but that's just a few days here and there, usually just filling in if someone's sick or on vacation. My mom signed me up, mostly so she can feel like she's got me properly taken care of. I get it though: Between her work and the divorce, she's got her hands full."

We both threw sticks into the water, then launched pebbles and stones at them like they were ships under attack. I looked across to the other side where there were dozens of white plastic bags like crazy big fruit caught up in a cottonwood tree, fluttering in the hot breeze. Suddenly, it was like two of those bags morphed into huge wings as a great blue heron with a five-foot wingspan sprang from the tree, flapping its way downriver.

"You know what's cool about rivers?" He shrugged. "They're never the same twice, even though it always *looks* the same. It's brand-new water every second coming through."

"Huh. Yeah, I guess," he said, not particularly impressed. "Except water is always recycled. All this will evaporate, rain down again someday and pass by here over and over—so it's maybe not as new as you think."

"Well, yeah," I countered begrudgingly, "but come on, not for like a bazillion years."

"Maybe sooner. What if it rained here tomorrow?"

"Oh, come on, dude, you know what I meant! The point is: Where's *our* different water that's supposed to be flowing, you know? We need something new to go with *our* flow. Things are too predictable. I'm tired of the same old stuff. Let's come up with something fresh, something outrageous."

"You mean like if we got season passes to Hurricane Harbor," Ian proposed, "and hung out there all summer?"

"That's actually not bad. Sure, that'd be fun, but expensive. Plus, I feel like we're at a crossroads that demands something *more*. Something with *meaning*. You know, like at the end of French this year we learned the phrase *raison d'être*: reason for existing. That's cool—let's find *that*. Let's shake things up, find ... what if we started up a business? Maybe sell some of that stuff you and your brother make in your garage, or we invent a new gadget, or learn to program and we create a new game. We should do it, make a bunch of money, buy whatever we want and get outta here, maybe go on an extended road trip, like along Route 66, with your brother. Or to Vegas, Joshua Tree, Tijuana ..."

"Yeah, if only we had our own car. And real driver's licenses."

"Well, hell, I don't know."

"How about shooting a bunch of short videos, posting them on YouTube, see if we can make them catch on?"

"I don't know. Maybe. But yeah, that's more like it."

"Or what if we formed a band," he added, "and practiced in our garage ..."

"But we don't play real instruments."

"I know guitar."

"You know *about* guitars."

"I can sing a little."

"You'd need to sing a lot, or at least better."

"True. That's a potential problem."

"No, that's an *actual* problem, a dealbreaker."

"Well, damn, don't be so negative," he said.

We stared out at the river. I envied *it* for the places it would go. *How pathetic!* I thought to myself. *I'm jealous of a river. Lame.*

I complained how my parents' situation was getting me down lately, and when was I was going to get to start my own life, and then it hit me.

It was one of those *Aha!* moments.

"Yeah, what?" Ian said, sitting up on the edge of his raggedy lounge chair as he saw the glint in my eye.

"We said road trip, right?" He nodded, looking skeptical already. "Okay, so we can't drive or fly or whatever, but a river, it's like a road that moves."

"Yeah, so?"

"What if we hopped on it and took it from here all the way to the end of the line?"

"Which is *where* exactly?"

"I don't know. Santa Monica Bay, Marina del Rey, San Pedro, Huntington Beach? What does it matter? It goes to the ocean eventually. We'll work out the details. Plus, we don't need permission from anyone."

Long pause.

"You're joking, right?" He searched for my familiar grin but didn't find it—which worried him.

"I'm totally serious! Why not?"

"Let's see," he said, "um, okay, take your pick: a) we don't have a boat; b) we don't know how to row a boat; c) it's summer and there's not enough *water* to float a boat; d) you're not allowed to actually *be* on the river; and e) our parents would never allow us to do it."

"That's all you got?"

"No, I could go on but didn't want to rain on your parade."

"Don't worry," I argued back. "Look, we could a) find a boat; b) learn to paddle a boat (and you row a *row*boat, dude); c) okay, so water depth could be a problem, but, hey, at least not right here (we'll research that); d) yeah, maybe we're not *allowed* to, but it doesn't mean we *can't*. And e) What if this is, like, *destiny* calling? Are we just going to let it go to voicemail?"

"Yeah, maybe," he said. "But what if it's, like, a spammy *bad idea* calling?"

"Look, someone's always got to test the boundaries. Maybe that's us. And besides, we obviously don't tell our parents. Right?"

Ian sighed and rolled his eyes, calculating the trouble he could get in. I could see him glancing at the other side of the river, wincing, looking for more excuses.

Without much else to find, he finally resorted to, "You're crazy. I'll bet we couldn't even make it from here to over there," pointing to the muddy bank about fifty feet away.

"What?! Are you kidding me? Piece of cake!"

More eye-rolling, sighs, and foot shuffling.

"I'll take that as a bet," I said, looking around us. I calculated. "Here's the deal: We make it over there and you have to at least seriously consider my idea." I held out my hand as he considered his escape options.

He nodded with a sense of resignation. He knew that once I got an idea in my head, I wouldn't let it go. I knew he'd cave if I kept at him. And he knew that I knew he always balked when it came to taking a risk—usually 'cause I won. Ian's a hedger, always doing damage assessment and control, looking for ways to weasel out of anything that might spell trouble. Me? I tend to believe you need to learn to trip before you can walk.

Finally, ever so faintly, he sort of mumbled: "Fine."

So we started gathering junk to use for an improvised little raft. We figured a bunch of those big plastic soda bottles and jugs would give us buoyancy. Then we found ratty old pieces of twine and nearby vines and tied stuff together. We held our noses and strapped the plastic bottles to broken-up pieces of hard-fiberglass insulation and found a big chunk of Styrofoam and combined them with a few crosspieces made of tree limbs and stray lumber and chicken wire and shoved in a few partially deflated soccer balls and footballs to help it float.

It couldn't have been more than an hour or so before we had ourselves a rough prototype—a junky raft, for sure, but still a raft!

"See?" I could see his hesitation. Suddenly, the other side looked twice as far.

I knew that once Ian commits, he usually does okay. It helps that he likes building things. We're good for each other: He keeps me alive by stopping me from doing *really* stupid stuff, and I show him cool things every now and then to get him out of his shell.

"It's time for the maiden voyage," I announced proudly.

I'd like to say that it felt super sturdy when we tried to get in, but it didn't at all. Still, I didn't want Ian to freak out, so I got on it slowly and carefully. I didn't let on how tippy it felt. After getting settled, I nodded for him to get in, too. "It'll be fine."

It got wobblier with Ian on board, and before we could adjust our positions, I lost my grip on the shrub and we scooted away from shore. Whoops. Ian tried to grab hold of some other twiggy plant, but it snapped and broke off. Like it or not, our humble garbage barge had launched.

"Hey, stay still!" he said, as it lurched from side to side as we adjusted our positions.

"It's not me. It's shifting!!"

Looking warily into the dark, murky water, I delicately raised a broom, which served as our paddle and demonstrated my best impression of paddling. After a few strokes I offered it to Ian, but he didn't want any part of it. He wanted stability; he was frozen there like a cat. Still, we were moving—granted, in circles. We crossed, in fits and starts, but somehow, miraculously, we were scooting across the surface of the water.

Ian started to grin with confidence as we crossed the halfway mark. But his grin quickly faded as, one by one, our various parts began to fail and move away from us. We started to simply sink down into the water.

There was nothing we could do.

I tried not to think of what was beneath us in the water. There could be the remains of woolly mammoths that got trapped in this same slop way back in the Ice Age or whatever. Or maybe bodies—*human* bodies. It was hard not to think about stuff like that. But the more I tried to push those thoughts away, the more they got stuck in my head.

Ian clawed his way up to my side of the raft, which was the last to go under.

"We're going down, Sam!" Eventually, we had no choice but to abandon ship. We made sure to keep our heads above water as we swam the twenty-five-or-so feet to shore, cursing the whole time. We crawled our way up the muddy bank, slipping and sliding. We finally managed to stand on solid ground again. We looked at each other, in shock.

I'd never quite seen that particular look on Ian's face before. He didn't look too thrilled, but then again, finally, as if he didn't know what else he could do, he burst out in laughter. It was a deep, gut-busting laugh that wouldn't stop. In turn, it got me going, too, and in no time we were like two foolish lunatics, a couple of bizarre mud people.

Actually, it felt great! We felt totally—what was it?— *alive*. We staggered around and then tossed mudballs at each other for a while.

At the end of it all, we both collapsed.

Ian confessed, "If this is failure, Sam, then I'm in. Let's do it."

I nodded. Then, finally, we sought out a sunny spot nearby to dry off and warm ourselves, simply gazing up at the sky, thinking.

iii. A VESSEL

After Ian and I baked like a weird couple of cups in a kiln, we were faced with the problem of clothing—that is, unless we wanted to trudge through our neighborhoods half naked and fully caked in mud. We'd get laughed out of town!

We found ourselves crouched beside the backyard fence of a house near the river. We spied a clothesline with stuff drying. So we cranked up our nerve and made a dash: up and over, then bolting and grabbing whatever we could, then back to the fence, where we tossed the clothes over. We were trying to climb up when we saw a lady coming out her back door, cussing. We made it over, landed, scooped the clothes, and took off, back to the safety of the river.

We hid in a grove of willow trees and caught our breath. We washed off as much mud as possible. Then we changed into our new clothes. We drew sticks and Ian won, so he got first dibs on clothing. He ended up with a sort of toga made from a floral-patterned curtain with a tassel tied around his waist. On his head was some sort of kooky, bleached-white tennis hat. But at least he could pull down the brim and no one would recognize him.

I wasn't so lucky—ended up with a damn dress! As far as dresses go, it could've been worse, but still, there was no way around the fact of it. He said I looked "shockingly natural" in it. All I could think was, if we ran into Ronnie we were dead meat.

The truth was, even though we were dressed, it was only marginally better for us than being all-out mud people. We still needed a place to get real clothes and cleaned up before going home. At least now we could pass ourselves off as a very odd couple—and if we biked fast enough, we figured that maybe no one would identify us. This was the kind of thing that could totally destroy what was left of our already-tenuous high school reputations.

"*Now* where do we go?" Ian asked.

"We can't go to my house—my mom'll be home soon. What about your house?"

"Too many siblings," he figured. "They'd rat us out, if they didn't first die laughing. What about Billy?"

"No, his mom and mine are too tight."

"What about Zoe? She's nearby."

"Yeah, but, well," I stammered, "we don't know if she's home, and what if her parents are there?"

"But they don't know any of our parents, so if they saw us like this it'd only be embarrassing."

He was right, except that Zoe lived with her mom and Zoe's brother. Did I want to risk having Zoe see me like this? The truth was I liked her, and I'm pretty sure she liked me, too, but it's not like we ever did anything about it—not 'cause we didn't want to, just, I don't know. So there was this tension. Through doing something idiotic, would I jeopardize any future possibility with her? Finally, I figured that if she couldn't accept me as I was, dress and all, then chances were slim she'd ever accept me for being my regular self. At least that was my twisted logic at the time.

"All right," I conceded, "to Zoe's."

We got up to her neighborhood pretty quickly and slunk along the side of her house and into her backyard. First we looked through the windows. Part of me was hoping her mom would be there and she'd tell us to scram, thinking we were a couple of homeless people. And that would be the end of it.

Seeing no one on the first floor though, we took up a few pebbles and pitched them at her bedroom window. Nothing. Phew. We were set to explore other options when the upstairs bedroom curtains suddenly parted and there was a long awkward pause. It was Zoe. Big gulp.

She opened up the window to get a better look and see who it was. It took a while. She looked around cautiously, as if it were a prank. Then she put her hand up to her mouth and started giggling. She definitely knew who we were. She disappeared from the window altogether.

She appeared again at the sliding glass door on the first floor, frantically gesturing at us. We hurried over. "Come on in," she said, trying to contain her laughter. "But *ssssh*— Mom's working in her office."

She practically pulled us up the stairs. We tried our best to tiptoe and not track mud on the beige wall-to-wall carpeting. We scurried into the master bedroom and then into the master bathroom. She locked the door behind us, and we burst out with nervous laughter.

"Oh my God, what the?!" she said.

"We had an incident. Don't ask," I said. "Look, we need a change of clothes."

"Yeah, no shit, Sherlock."

She strategized quickly. "Okay, here's the plan. Ian, you take this shower here. Sam, you come with me. Down the hall there's another bathroom. I'll get you both some of my brother's extra clothes. When you're done, gather up your ... whatever and meet in my room at the end of the hall. Got it?"

We weren't about to argue.

Ian unlocked the door. Zoe and I scampered out and headed down the hallway and zipped into the other bathroom halfway. Zoe and I scampered out after him and headed down the hallway and zipped into the other bathroom halfway. We were both giddy with the excitement of being on the verge of trouble.

She shut the door behind us, turned on the shower, and started getting towels. The room started to steam up pretty quickly. I turned around to say something and, wham—there she was, right up in my face.

Time slowed, like they say. She planted a soft kiss on my lips that left me stunned. My eyes were still closed by the time I heard her jostling the doorknob and, through the steam, she gave an unforgettable, coy little wink as she closed the door on her misty way out.

After Ian and I got cleaned up, we met down the long hall, in Zoe's bedroom. Ian darted glances at me—he could tell *something* was up. But I didn't have time to tell him.

It was a relief that Zoe's room wasn't girled up with pinks and purples; it was tastefully done, with blowups of artsy, gritty photos she'd taken herself around the Valley. I already knew she had a good eye for photography and design. You could see it in how she dressed, too.

We shifted the conversation to our trial run on the river and then the harebrained idea of going down the whole river. She didn't laugh at it outright, but she didn't exactly gush over it either. In the end, she started coming around to the idea and eventually volunteered to help plan it. Suddenly, her room shifted into a bona fide situation room.

She started by addressing the same question Ian had raised: "You and what water?"

"Well," I hemmed, "let's look it up."

Being the modern tech-savvy, semi-geeky gal that she was, she had a Mac laptop covered with cool stickers. We huddled around it while she googled. In a few seconds she'd pulled up the main questions we had and scrolled down until she got to an answer she liked.

"The fifty-one miles of the river are fed by three water-treatment plants that provide a steady year-round flow of water."

"See?" I bragged to Ian. "No problem."

"Hey, a water fountain has steady flow," countered Ian, "but that doesn't mean you should float a boat on it."

"I never said it would be easy."

"What about those signs that say we could be fined, like, a thousand bucks!?" said Ian.

"That's only to scare people off."

"Yeah, well it's working."

I turned to Zoe, who was already surfing other pages. "And so where does it end up?"

"Looks like Long Beach," she said. "Right next to the Queen Mary." She showed us the satellite view of the old-timey ocean liner anchored in the harbor, across the expansive mouth of the river from a fake lighthouse, a sprawling park, and a marina.

"See!" I told Ian. "The Pacific Ocean."

"You didn't say Long Beach."

"Well I was close."

"*Close* isn't going to get us there. Whatever. I suppose we're going to build another garbage boat?"

"A what?" said Zoe.

"We need a kayak, or rowboat, or ..."

"How 'bout a canoe?" she asked. We both shrugged and nodded. "Well, why didn't you just say so? My dad left behind an old canoe in the garage. It's been there for years. Not fancy, but it should do the job."

On our way out, Zoe took us to the shed in the back of their property to take a peek at the canoe. It was aluminum, with dents and random metal patches and evidence of soldering. It was sketchy—like it had been over Niagara Falls a couple times. My first impression was that it wouldn't even float. But it had two seats, one in the front and one in the back, and on the middle part of the boat a metal cross-piece connected the two sides. On the side of the boat, a blue sticker read Grumman.

Right next to the canoe, there was an old shotgun and an assortment of used shotgun shells splayed out.

"Jeez," said Ian, "what the heck is this? Shoot much?"

"Actually, yeah, some."

"Seriously?" I said.

"Sure. Dad and I used to go to shooting ranges or shoot clays—you know, those little flying saucer things." She imitated the motion of tracking one and firing.

"Hey, look," Ian said.

Leaning against the wall like big smooth spoons were a couple of ancient wooden paddles. And beside those were a few life preservers. *Perfect.*

None of us said much. We gathered up all the random equipment and put it in the boat. Our minds raced with all kinds of thoughts. We stood there, a little stunned.

Finally, I broke the ice, touching Zoe gently on the arm: "Looks like we got ourselves a boat—now we just need a good alibi."

Ian gave me a sidelong glance, confirming his suspicions.

iV. ALiENATED

On the way home from Zoe's, when I wasn't answering questions from Ian about what happened with her, we had time to think about our alibi for the expedition, as we'd been calling it.

The best excuse we could come up with was an extended summer weekend holiday sleepover. We'd do it over the three-day Fourth of July weekend. Mom was taking a few extra days on a business trip to New York around then, so the timing was good. If we left Friday, that meant three nights and four days, coming back Monday evening, though we weren't sure we could do those fifty-plus miles in four days—we might need a Plan B for a little longer. Plus, doing it around the Independence Day had a nice ring to it, with the whole freedom thing.

Free the teens!

I'd tell my folks I was going to Ian's, and he'd tell his folks that he was spending the weekend at my dad's house. The challenge was how to keep any one of them from actually talking to another. Fortunately, we were old enough that they pretty much trusted us to be where we were supposed to be. They seemed to assume that as long as there was a computer or video game involved, we had no motive to do anything but that, as if the real world was something we'd sworn off in favor of our virtual realities. Usually they'd be right.

"What about phones?" Ian said.

"What about them?"

"We take our phones along or we completely unplug?"

That was a tough one. Lots of pros and cons. "Well, if our parents try to call to check in, we'd stay in control of the story. Or if there was an emergency, phones could definitely help."

"Yeah, but taking them along," Ian countered, "feels like it betrays the, you know, spirit of the whole adventure. Plus, where would we charge them?"

"I guess so."

"They could also fall out and get wet and ruined."

"True, yeah," I agreed.

Because we were walking and talking on our way home, we'd evidently lost track of our surroundings. We were taking a shortcut through a path behind the high school when suddenly, like out of nowhere, a voice—*that* voice— made me freeze in my tracks.

"Hey, Spam!" said Ronnie, putting his hand on my shoulder from behind. The guy was like a phantom: He had a knack for just appearing out of nowhere. "What're a couple of fags like you doing in a nice place like this?"

I took a deep breath and looked over at Ian, sighing at our painful miscalculation. *How could we have been so stupid to come this way?* I thought about just running, but it was too late. I already knew he was faster than us. Slowly, awkwardly, I turned to face him.

"You think you're so smart, Spam. How stupid d'you feel now?"

I thought about responding the way I usually did, to sort of shuffle apologetically, sheepishly, and mumble my way out of it. But coming straight from Zoe's and feeling surprisingly good, something in me shifted and I spoke up.

"Actually, I'm feeling all right. Thanks for asking, Ronnie."

"Really?" He sort of stammered, taken aback. "Well, smartass, how 'bout we change that?"

This was it. I knew guys like Ronnie were just wrecking balls who needed someone, anyone, to get their anger out. I didn't know why, and I didn't understand *why me*. Under other circumstances, I might've felt sorry for him.

But they say that getting that first punch in is your best chance. So as quickly as I could, my fist went up and ...

I found myself falling backward, just as quickly, with a stinging pain in the middle of my face. Then, nothing.

There was some sort of weird dream. My eyes slowly blinked open—I let them focus before turning on my side. My nose was running. Ian was crouching beside me. I reached up to wipe my nose and noticed the blood. I'd probably only been out for a second, but it felt much longer. Looking around, Ronnie was nowhere in sight.

As I tried to sit up, the pain started. My finger went to my lips, and I felt some swelling.

"Dude," said Ian, "You stood up to him."

"I did?"

"Yeah, man. That was awesome!"

"If I stood up, then why am I on the ground?"

"Well, sure, *literally* you fell down, but that's just a ... a footnote."

"It doesn't feel so awesome. It hurts."

"Don't worry. Come on, let me help you. Let's get you home."

We hobbled over to my house. As if to cheer myself up, I mumbled more about how things had been building with Zoe over the last year. Nearing Mom's house, I said I didn't want to talk about the "fight" with anyone, including my mom.

So we quietly changed back into our regular clothes. I got the first aid kit and started cleaning up my wounds.

Nothing broken but my pride—again. Fortunately or unfortunately, because he whacked me in the nose, I wouldn't get a noticeable black eye that would be up for discussion with Mom. Okay, so he sort of split my upper lip, but I'd gotten all too good at finding ways to hide stuff like that.

We raided the fridge for something to drink and some comfort food. I put a bag of frozen peas on my face as a cold compress. Later, we sat and squeezed in some video game time before Mom got home. I was awfully distracted—about the incident with Ronnie and the sudden kiss with Zoe but also about the canoe. Now more than ever, I wanted to get out of town, to get lost. I needed a full-on reset.

Eventually we heard the familiar sound of my mom's jangling keys searching for the lock in the front door. As usual, she came in on her headset, chatting up a storm and pecking away at her Blackberry. She gestured in our general direction without looking at us, as if to acknowledge us. There was always a drama going on with her business. She could put it aside, but she usually needed some transition time after she first came through the door.

And *she* was the one who was always telling us *we* were so addicted to technology!

Ian stayed for dinner, which basically meant he was witness to the complete interrogation of me from my mom.

"Did you empty the dishwasher?"

"Yes."

"Don't forget to empty the recycling."

"I won't."

"Did you water the plants?"

"Done." (Sort of.)

"Did you practice trombone?"

"Not yet."

"Do I need to take away screen time?"

"No."

"Is it too much to ask?"

"Yes, but I'll do it anyway."

"Don't eat so fast. Does he eat so fast at your house?"

"No. I don't believe so, ma'am."

"See how nicely Ian responds? Very civilized. I hope you're as polite at other people's houses. Is he, Ian?"

"Oh, yes. Sam's *very* respectable." Ian said, shooting smirky looks at me.

"Come on, Mom, that's not fair! He's totally playing you." On and on it went. Somewhere in between, I was able to slip in my own agenda.

"So, assuming I do my chores this week," I began, "would it be okay if I went over to Ian's this weekend for a sleepover? Billy's coming, too. There's an online video gaming tournament we want to be in. And Monday is a holiday, too, so there's no camp. Besides, aren't you going to be away anyway?"

She thought about it. "Hmm, yes, let's see," She pecked at her electronic calendar oracle before asking, "You sure you have nothing else going on?" I shook my head. "How do I know you won't just be sitting in front of a screen the whole weekend, playing video games?"

"Oh, you don't have to worry. I promise: We've got a bunch of ... hands-on activities planned, too. We *swear* we'll get enough outside time. Isn't that right, Ian?"

"Um, for sure."

Putting my hand over my heart, I gave her my best puppy dog eyes. "Besides, Ian's parents feel the same way. We'll get fresh air and sunshine and all that stuff."

We both turned to Ian, looking for further affirmation.

"Yeah, promise." Ian and I shook hands. "My parents like all that, too."

"Do I need to check up on you?"

"Mom, why don't you ever trust me? What do you want, a blood oath?" I picked up the wooden butter knife and pressed it against my thumb.

"Hey, don't joke about stuff like that, and don't roll your eyes."

"You trust I'll do my chores, but you don't trust me to make good choices otherwise? I get all the responsibility but none of the liberty, no equal rights for kids. That's not fair."

She pondered. "You're right. I'm sorry. I *do* trust that you make good choices." She pawed at her sacred device again. "All right, yes, so, I'll be out of town starting the first, and I return on the evening of the fourth, possibly the fifth if I need to deal with a few more things, depending on how it all goes. So I guess you're good."

"Sweet!" I said, rising to excuse myself and hugging her. She paused, steadied her gaze on me, and raised a finger. That always meant a lengthy monologue was coming. I froze.

"But before you run off, I have a question for both of you," she declared. "I was speaking with another mom today, and she was saying that her two kids felt, well, alienated. I mean, they didn't *use* that word, but, well, that's it. Do you two ever feel that way?"

We looked at each other, searching for the correct answer an adult would want to hear.

"I'm not sure what you mean exactly," said Ian.

"She means, like, were we ever probed by space aliens."

"All right, all right."

"Help, I'm being alienated!" I yelped, frothing dramatically at the mouth.

"Come on," she complained, "you're not taking this seriously!"

"Is this coming from another one of those parenting books?"

She sighed. "That's neither here nor there."

"Hah—I knew it!"

Ian's phone buzzed. "Would you excuse me? That's my mom."

"Of course, honey" she said, indicating to me about his manners.

"Mom, stop. I swear, you're so gullible."

After a while, Ian hung up and excused himself to go home. What a brownnoser! I can't blame him though—I did the same at his house. Why do we always appear perfect to other kids' parents but never so in the eyes of our own parents?

Anyway, as far as our venture was concerned, so far so good.

Bring on the next phase.

V. TRIALS AND ERRORS

The next morning Ian and I set into motion a training exercise that Zoe had planned, code-named The Trial, designed to get us more familiar with boating. The only problem was that I was supposed to be working at that camp.

Mom and I got up and ate breakfast like we always did. It was fairly civil—nothing like the previous night's existential interrogation. I felt guilty though, knowing how the morning was supposed to play out according to the plan Ian and I concocted, designed to trick her.

On our way driving over to camp, I told Mom she could drop me off a few blocks away so that it'd be convenient for her to get to where she was going (she was running late, as usual). The walk and the fresh air would do me good. Yeah, right. With perfect timing, her phone buzzed. So she gave me a peck on the cheek and a hug and reminded me to head over to Dad's for the next few nights.

"Yeah, I know."

She was already on the headset talking business by the time the car sped off. I meandered a couple blocks, biding my time. It wasn't like I minded the camp so much—I just had other plans. Plans with Ian. Plans for adventure.

Doubling back and heading over to Zoe's, I called camp and told them I was sick. They noted it and didn't seem to care one way or the other. They had no shortage of teen counselors.

Then I texted Ian: "OK, we're on."

"Got it. cu @ 9ish."

Zoe was waiting beside the open doors of her shed, as planned. We were both in our unspoken roles, like nothing had happened between us the previous day. To tell the truth, it was a relief when Ian showed up 'cause I didn't quite know what to say to her now, let alone how to *be* with her. I could've just been myself, but then I remembered that I didn't really know who that was.

The taxi came soon enough. Zoe had asked for a vehicle with a roof rack. The driver looked surprised that we were kids. They probably don't get too many calls from nonadults, and then not so much from nonadults with canoes.

The guy was nice and patient, and he didn't ask too many questions. That was exactly what we needed. As soon as adults started asking questions, it was over. The boat was lighter than I'd imagined, as the three of us lifted it up, slid it onto the rack, and strapped it down.

He took the side streets and went slowly. We got down to the river in no time. We got the boat off the car. We had scraped together some collective money that we called the Adventure Fund and gave it to Zoe for the fare there and back to her house. She had other stuff to do. We figured out a respectable tip for the guy being so patient and all.

But with only Ian and me, the boat seemed a lot heavier. It wasn't long before we were dragging it along the grass with the rope that was tied to the front, like it was a stubborn camel. When we got it to the top of the concrete riverbank, we dragged it down the incline. It made an awful sound: metal on concrete, like fingernails on chalkboard. At the bottom, we somehow carried the boat through the bushes and up and over a muddy bank.

We finally got to the actual water and scooted the boat into it. I steadied the canoe by holding the side as Ian carefully stepped into the boat and went to the other end. We remembered our experience from the day before and didn't care to repeat it. I could hear Ian muttering. When he was in position in the front seat, he took up a paddle and looked back at me.

I held tight to bushes while trying to step into the boat, but each time my legs split apart. Eventually I got the hang of it and got into the boat, but it was real shaky and we nearly tipped over as I gave a big push while jumping in.

Our trial run involved going around the deeper parts of the river, north of Balboa. We found a tall bamboo stick and kept it in the boat; every now and then we'd take it out and measure the depth. I estimated it was usually around four to eight feet—more than enough to drown in, but not so much that it was spooky and bottomless. Since we didn't know much in the way of steering, we zigzagged all over and ended up terrifying a few ducks foolish enough to get in our way. They scurried along, confident that we couldn't keep up with them, let alone follow them in a straight line (and they were right).

At a certain point we gave up on paddling and simply drifted. Lots of birds flew overhead, and an occasional fish would pop up and make a splash. After a while, we kicked back and floated, tracking the stray clouds that passed by. Time just evaporated. It was actually pretty nice.

"Piss and vinegar!" Ian blurted out.

"Huh? The smell?"

"No. My grandpa says that—it's sort of like 'go for it,' or to do something like you mean it. You're right, Sam. We could *do* this. I can see it."

It was good to hear him getting excited. And that's from a guy who doesn't usually let his emotions show.

We relaxed into the day, and it stretched out real long.

Being in an actual boat made it clear to us that it was a river after all. Growing up in the area, I only ever heard it called the wash, culvert, storm drain, ditch, or sewer. I was surprised how by shifting our thinking even a little, I saw there was a lot more to it.

After the basics of learning how to paddle without getting the other guy soaked, we didn't really speak much. But eventually, after thinking of dinner the night before, I asked Ian:

"Do you think I've become 'alienated' like my mom was saying?"

He thought about this for a bit. "No," he thought more, "but only because you have a naturally alienated personality to begin with. I don't think anybody *turned* you that way. And I don't mean that as a negative. It's not neurotic. It's sort of … you keep some distance from people, like an outsider. And you seem to sort of *like* that role, but it suits you, in a weird way."

"What about me?" he asked in return.

"Yeah, sure, but not like she meant. She thinks we're out of touch with the world. But you're only alienated from your*self*. No offense, dude, but that's my take. A lot of times you don't always know what you need or want, what's good for you."

"Huh. I see." But he didn't. How could he? He was too close to it. Same for me.

Still, we took in the information and stored it away somewhere deep inside our brains. We floated some more, until …

"Hey!" a deep voice shouted from a distance.

We popped our heads up out of the boat and looked to the side of the river. There was a guy in a brown and green uniform and sporting a curly silver mustache.

"What are you boys doing out there?" said a ranger dude adjusting his Smokey the Bear-like hat.

Ian and I looked at each other. Ian suddenly seemed very nervous.

I replied, "We lost something in the boat, and we were looking for it."

"Yeah, but where'd you get the boat?"

"What does it matter?"

"Look, kid, you're not supposed to have boats in here."

"Sorry. We didn't know." We were hoping he'd buzz off, but he kept on going. How very adult of him. We were comfortable out there, and I didn't want to move. So I decided not to cave just because the guy had a uniform. Girl Scouts have uniforms, too, but it doesn't mean we *have* to buy their cookies, right?

"So, I'm going to have to ask you boys to leave. You can't be on the river."

"But I've seen boats near here," I said, "on Lake Balboa."

"Well, yes. But that's a designated boating area."

"But it's all water," I argued. "Why isn't *this* a designated boating area? It's better than what they got there." The poor guy sighed loudly. He didn't look comfortable with kids making their own arguments, but he didn't know what else he could do. It's not like he was about to swim out and pull us back to shore.

"Look. Slowly come on in. It's unsafe."

Under my breath, I said to Ian: "Oh, so now it's about *safety*." Ian muttered, knowing full well where I was going with this.

"Sam, let's go in," whispered Ian. He started to pick up his paddle. But I stared him down and turned back to Ranger Rick.

"What's not safe about it?"

"What's not *safe*? Well, for starters, you could drown."

Rummaging for a good argument, I went deeper into a debate. "Well, a person could drown at the beach, too. Or in a pool, even a bathtub. Don't worry, we're both good swimmers."

"That's beside the point."

"Is it? I thought safety *was* the point."

"You should at least have life preservers, you know."

We reached into the boat and held up two square flotation cushions. "How's this?"

More sighs and rolled eyes. "Look—it's still dangerous."

Under my breath to Ian: "Classic adult logic—the old bait and switch. When you take it apart, there's nothing holding it together. But they're always big on authority, on being the deciders."

Then, to the guy: "With all due respect, sir, where does it say that we can't be out here?"

"Look," he groaned impatiently, glancing at his watch, "I've got to go, but I'm not leaving unless I know for sure that you're off the river."

"But," I pressed him, "you didn't answer my question. *Who* says we can't be out here?"

I was being a total pain in this guy's ass, but I didn't care. "The Army Corps of Engineers. Is that what you mean?"

"Yeah, for starters. Thanks. But who gave them that right to keep people out?"

"Look, son. I don't make the rules, I only enforce them."

Finally, an honest answer. Why is that so difficult for adults?

"I see. Thanks." I only wanted to reward this guy for being straight with me—not for trying to dodge questions or pull the adult authority card on us. So, picking up my paddle, I gave Ian the law-abiding nod he so desperately craved. Then we paddled back to shore.

When we got there, I could see that the guy was relieved. The ranger helped us out of the boat and also helped us carry the canoe up the riverbank. He left us there but made us promise not to take it back onto the river. He told us we could get fined for trespassing.

Yeah, right. I looked around: no fences and no signs in this area. Anyway, we did our best to look sorry, and promised we wouldn't simply turn right back around and go in again. Seemingly satisfied, the ranger moved on, making a call on his walkie-talkie as he walked back to his white pickup truck.

But secretly we knew we'd be back another day.

We brought the boat back to the boysenberry patch and stashed it inside the thorny cave.

We hopped a bus back to my dad's place before he got home, to rummage for supplies. As I looked out the window at the passing Valley, I imagined Ian and me cruising down the river, pausing to eat a ton of junk food and drink all kinds of drinks, all the while a balmy breeze helped us sail away into the sunset.

VI. To Long Beach

Ian and I arrived at Dad's place. He was in the living room, flopped on the couch, glued to his favorite news station, already surrounded by a whole weather system of cigarette smoke that wafted around the room and a bunch of empty beer bottles.

"Hey there, Dad."

"Oh, look who it is: the prodigal son. Where the hell've *you* been?"

"Just, you know, working at camp, and hangin' with Ian."

"Well, no, I *don't* know, actually, 'cause no one thinks to tell me. But I'm glad you finally decided to grace me with your presence."

I thought of responding with something clever but knew better—I quickly swallowed it. It was one of those lose-lose traps he was so good at setting.

"What? Too above it all to respond? You *seriously* gotta learn about respect. When someone asks you someth—"

"No. I mean, I understand. We were just on our way to the garage, to look for a few things."

"Well, be my guest. Have at it. Take, take, take—everyone's doin' it these days! All the rage, in fact—like mother, like son. Hey, get me another while you're up, would ya?"

I crossed to the kitchen, grabbed a beer from the fridge and handed it to him. He polished off the last of the other and grunted as he grabbed the new one.

"Aw, look at this bullshit!" he growled at the TV.

It was some show about "illegal aliens" coming into the U.S., with talking heads spouting off, plus surveillance imagery of groups of people with belongings strapped on their backs, forging a river.

"Ian, Ian, c'mere," he said, waiving him over eagerly, a little slurry. I looked over at Ian like, don't do it. But of course he didn't want to be rude—he'd do anything to avoid a confrontation. My dad sat Ian down beside him and started his lecture, putting his arm around Ian with force, making his feeble head wobble like a rag doll beside Dad's six foot two, barrel-chested frame.

"Now, you boys understand why people gotta come into the country in an orderly, lawful way, right?"

"Oh yeah, sure, sir."

"It's like, if someone at school decided to cut in the lunch line and then got rewarded by some teacher or administrator for cutting. How'd that make you feel, huh?"

"Not good, definitely."

"Damn straight. That'd suck! Assholes, coming into the country, taking our jobs—rape, pillage, plunder, they do it all, you know, these illegals. Poppin' out tons of babies, too. It's just a matter of time until the numbers shift. Hell ..."

"Yeah, *not* cool," Ian said, kissing up to him.

"All right," dad said, grabbing Ian by the scruff of the neck and squeezing hard, "you boys go do your thing." Then he sort of pushed Ian away, with all the subtleness of catch-and-release hunting. "Go on now," shifting into his glazed look as he returned to watching TV intently—as if we'd already left the room.

So we did.

In the garage, I apologized for my dad's gruff handling of him like that, making him uncomfortable.

"It's all right," Ian said. "I know he means well. He's just all, I don't know, cut off and living in his bubble. I mean, first your mom leaves, and with you going away after next year he probably sees the writing on the wall: He'll be all alone."

"He's alone already, the way he treats people."

"Well, don't be too hard on him."

"Are you actually *defending* him?"

"No, I just ... I mean, I know he's got that side to him and all. I ... I know he does it, don't get me wrong—that's wrong—uh, I'm just saying I've never *seen* it, er, he's always been nice to me."

"Really? That's rich," shaking my head. "And *that's* how they get away with it."

Ian got real quiet.

"Look," I said, after an awkward silence, "let's just not go down that road."

He nodded sheepishly, relieved.

We turned to the task of gearing up. We realized a main problem was that we didn't know what to take because we didn't know what to *expect*, and we didn't know what to expect 'cause we didn't know the full extent of what we didn't know.

After rummaging through Dad's garage, we ended up collecting some GI Joe-era water bottles, a bunch of camouflaged bandanas, a cool old compass, a fishing rod and tackle kit, and one of those multi-tool Swiss Army knives.

Oh, and we also found a bunch of my old rock-climbing equipment: ropes, carabiners, and other gadgets. I wrapped one length of rope around myself a few times, made a few knots and clipped a couple carabiners to it to create a makeshift belt buckle. Perfect fit. A *rope belt—sweet!*

We also found a bunch of old firecracker strips—perfect timing for the Fourth of July weekend. We added them into the mix—not that we had a practical use for them, but they seemed like a no-brainer to bring along. We didn't know how we'd use all these things, but there was still time to figure that out.

We debated the whole phone thing again. We finally agreed to leave all cell phones behind, just committing to the real deal: *cold turkey on tech*. Having the phones felt too much like cheating, like a crutch.

When we were done in the garage, we gathered our stash of stuff and went back out through the living room, nearly making it out the door before—

"Hooooold on a sec," Dad said, startling us 'cause we thought he'd nodded off.

"Um, yeah?"

"Your mom says you're comin' here for the weekend?"

"Oh, that actually changed. It's now a sleepover at Ian's, starting Friday. I thought she told you already. Is that okay?"

There was a long pause, followed by an equally long drag on his cigarette.

"Fffine."

"Thanks, Dad." I winked at Ian as I opened the door for him. "Okay, Ian. See you tomorrow."

I shut the door and turned back to the living room. I heard my dad starting to snore. I crossed to the sofa, took the cigarette out of his hand, and snuffed it out in the ashtray. I grabbed the nearby blanket, draped it over him, and went to my room.

The next morning I decided that Ian and I should go and finalize details about the trip. That is, *I* decided we were overdue for a rendezvous with Zoe. I passed my dad on the way out; it wasn't a pretty scene, but hey, at least the house didn't burn down and I didn't get hit.

We met up with her that afternoon, in her room. We were feeling pretty good about ourselves until she clued us into reality and how much prep work there was to get done—little things like: Where were we going and how the hell to get there?

Fortunately, she was good with logistics. She'd been busy and had printed a trip itinerary that highlighted the main things we could expect to encounter. She'd even mapped our whole journey online, marking with sticky notes the main neighborhoods we'd be going through: Van Nuys, Sherman Oaks, Burbank, Glendale, Atwater Village, Frogtown, Chinatown, Boyle Heights, Vernon, Bell, South Gate, Lynwood, Compton, and Long Beach (to name a few).

If some of the names sounded familiar, it was because they were famous for lots of stuff, sometimes notorious, or events, corruption, traffic, drive-bys, muggings, fires, homelessness, murder, mass rioting, and so on. The news and urban legends about this intimidated us and sounded so foreign to a couple of white-bread kids. Well, okay, so Ian's only half white, but being half Asian is nearly the same thing—kids who are more at home with whiteboards and computers, tucked away in comfy classrooms, than out in the wilds of L.A.'s hardcore streets.

Apart from the neighborhoods on the top half of the list, none of us had even driven through those other areas. The most we had to go on were urban legends sprung from a steady stream of sketchy local TV news broadcasts. We quickly changed the subject, not wanting to put a chill on our enthusiasm.

Still, we did our best to brush off that doom and gloom, choosing instead to stick to details of what we'd need in order to have a fun expedition. We showed Zoe our equipment so far: knives, flares, a tent, compass, maps, life preservers, fireworks, snacks, juice boxes, an old flip lighter, and bows and arrows.

"Really?" said Zoe. "What are you: Robin Hood and Little John? How about, say, a first aid kit? Maybe warm clothes? Drinking water? Pots and pans? A camping stove? Maybe a couple of sleeping bags or blankets?"

"Oh, yeah, true," Ian added, "but bows and arrows could help, no?"

"Sure. I guess. But it's not like ..."

"Hey, crazy people are *everywhere*."

"Look, guys," she said, laying down the law, "you aren't taking this seriously." She was right.

When we added up all her suggestions, we got depressed at the length of our new equipment list. After going back over it for an hour or so, finally Ian blurted, "We can't possibly take all this!"

"Yeah," I admitted, "well then, let's do a 180 and go John Muir and not take *any* food or supplies. Let's bring money and eat out along the way. I mean, it's only for a few days, right?"

Ian liked the bare-bones angle, but Zoe shook her head, seeing again that our planning was shaped not so much by reality, common sense, or survival tactics as it was by our latest impulses.

"You guys are pathetic," she said. "Look, I'm not the one going. It'll be *your* asses out there. You do what you want—I just don't want to see you two end up on the local news."

We laughed this off, but it stuck in both our minds. It didn't help with building morale. I could feel Ian tightening up the more we talked about all the things that could go wrong. And I had to admit that I wasn't exactly feeling too confident either. We found it easier to discuss and make fun of things than to cope with the realities of the trip.

In the end, we agreed to divide the latest list and gather as many of the items missing on it as each of us could find, and then we'd reassess once we could see it in one heap. Zoe agreed to help with the general management, despite her reservations about our sanity. She told us to look over the summary and maps she prepared from her research.

It occurred to me to ask if she wanted to come along for the ride, but I didn't know if that would be okay with

Ian—plus, I figured that if she wanted to join us, that she'd speak up and say so. She wasn't shy—she always said it like it was. That was one of the things I liked about her.

Our meeting broke up when Zoe's brother came home and we had to sneak out the bedroom window, using the foldout fire escape ladder stored in her closet.

I could tell by the looks I was getting from her that there were still a lot of feelings between us. I was still at a complete loss for how to be around her. I could've used a personal assistant for that alone. Girls still seemed as mysterious to me as most of those uncharted neighborhoods we were planning to explore.

Still, for all the mystery, Zoe's effect was clear: She always helped me understand myself better. She saw my restlessness and my wanting to prove stuff or test myself. But she didn't call it out in a way that made me defensive or feel exposed. She asked a lot of questions, which always got me thinking. She was like, "Who are you doing this for?" and "What do you really want to accomplish?" She sort of reflected back at me what I was thinking (but wasn't aware I was thinking).

She saw *me*. She never held back just to be polite. I had to admit I was really starting to like this girl. More and more this was done through talks about the trip, so even if I had my fears about going, I hid them from her. I didn't want her to think that I wasn't up for it, after the work she'd put into it, into me.

But those fears didn't mesh well with Ian's growing complaints about embarking on the journey. The more he thought about it, the more he pushed for delaying the trip; the more *I* thought about it, the more we absolutely *had* to go.

I called Zoe a few times to let her know what was going on. With Ian's back and forths, I secretly wanted her to step in and come on the trip. But she somehow knew the whole decision was symbolic for me—important in a way that I couldn't fully understand and which she didn't entirely understand either, but she sensed it was something I needed to figure out. That was something she couldn't do *for* me.

Zoe wasn't super book smart; she wasn't even street smart; but she had major common sense and emotional smarts about everything.

In the end, I called up Ian one afternoon and told him I was determined to go, that I *needed* to go. It had to be now; that is, it had to start Friday. Plus, with my mom possibly being gone a couple extra days, the holiday weekend was definitely shaping up to be our best window for the whole summer. It was pushing things, but there simply wasn't a better option later on.

Ian finally came out with it: he told me he couldn't do it.

"I feel horrible, but I can't, Sam. I've got too many things going on."

"Stop there," I said.

He stopped. "But I'll make it up to you—"

"Stop. Please, don't, it doesn't suit you." I knew that it wasn't about whether or not he could go, but that he *wouldn't* go. "You're *choosing* not to go. Can't you admit that?"

"Well, I, no, okay, yeah, um, I guess so, yeah, Sam. That's true."

"At least you're being honest—finally—even if you can't make up your mind. I wish you'd told me earlier. Now what am I gonna do? I'm scared, too, you know."

I tried to make the silence work its way into him. I could tell he felt bad, but he didn't budge. So I pressed him further.

"You think Lewis and Clark imagined their trip would be a picnic, with thousands of miles to trek through, in hostile Indian territory, and frothy uncharted rapids, and wildcats and bears, and deserts, and icy mountain ranges to cross?! You think Columbus and his crew didn't think they'd probably reach the edge of the ocean and go right over a point-of-no-return waterfall?! You think before the first astronauts went into space that they weren't barfing their guts out in fear of blowing up in a fiery ball of flames or suffocating to death out there in the cold darkness of outer space?! It's okay to be scared. Ian, how many times do you think you get chances like this?"

Final answer.

"Look, I'm sorry, I tried to wrap my head around it, I swear, but I can't. I mean, I won't ... I won't be joining you, Sam."

Long. Awkward. Silence. "Well," I sighed. "I guess that's it then."

"Yeah, I guess so. We'll do other adventures though. Don't worry."

"I'm worried, dude! I'm worried about *you*."

It was quiet for a while, each of us trying to find a positive spin, but there wasn't one.

"Look, I gotta run," I said, searching for a graceful way to end it.

"What'll you do, Sam?"

"I don't know," I told him honestly. "I need to think on it."

I hung up and sat down to take this in. I needed to take a walk and clear my head.

Eventually, I ended up over at the river, walking beside it for a while, losing myself in the brush and the quiet of the river, and the sound of birds.

Maybe Ian was right. *What a stupid idea!* What a dumpy river: I looked at the junk and thought how most of the river was wrapped in concrete and filled with other pollution. Miserable. I felt stupid. My old cynicism crept back in. Of *course* Ian didn't want to go. He's no fool. What a loser thing to do. I guess he'd been humoring me. Why would *anyone* in his right mind want to go along with this deranged idea?

As a matter of fact, Zoe was probably humoring me, too.

I found myself wandering back to check on the boat. Instead of planning for an adventure, I was thinking about how I was going to get the boat back to Zoe's house and what I'd tell her about what happened. She'd put so much work into this—on *some* level she must've believed in it.

The boat was still where we'd left it: the place Ian and I created, carved out of nothing, a secret place where we hid our secrets, something that was supposed to transport us to a world of excitement and promise. That was dashed now.

But I decided that, as long as I was there I'd take the canoe out for a final evening spin before turning it back over to Zoe. After all, I had the whole place to myself.

After a bunch of cuts and jabs, I got the canoe in the water and pushed off.

Paddling on my own was much trickier. I sat in the seat at the back of the canoe, but it made the boat too rear-heavy, like doing a wheelie—which also made it unstable. Moving up a bit and kneeling down helped and putting my butt on the crosspiece in the middle.

I paddled upriver, struggling to keep a straight line. Switching sides every now and then helped. I found a sunny spot out in the middle, then put down the paddle.

I imagined telling Zoe about scrapping the plan. I felt ashamed. I didn't much like the image of going back to her house with my tail between my legs, having to admit that I couldn't get my act together. I'd failed before I'd even begun. And if I was a failure at *this*, then why would a cute, smart girl like her want to date a guy like me? How sad was that? If she saw I couldn't do this, then why would she believe I could do anything else, like in a relationship? It's that *keeping your word* thing again. Damn!

Too restless to sit and ponder, I picked up the paddle again and tried to see how fast I could go. I cut angrily through the water and did okay for a while, but then the canoe got turned to the side and I gave up. The boat curved toward shore and rammed into a couple of bushes covered in spiderwebs before moving backward and drifting again.

Then, on the shaded side of the boat, something caught my eye, just beneath the surface. I squinted to see what it was. It turned out to be a fish, about a foot long, green gray with brownish-reddish colors around the edges and large silvery scales. It had a spiky spine. It looked like the dark-skinned, supersized cousin of a goldfish.

I remembered my dad, way back when, pointing out a dead one of these once: it was a *carp*.

And this fella wasn't alone—there was another. And then a third.

I traced their direction. They were going in a circle around me. What the hell!? Wherever my boat drifted, there they were, still in a perfect circle, joined by more of them. My eyes traced the circle until I counted a dozen or so in this humble little school.

Around they went in their aquatic merry-go-round. It was weird the way they calmly circled, like they had all the time in the world, and I didn't have a clue what they were thinking. They didn't seem to be afraid of me; I figured they thought I was some sort of giant alien mothership fish.

It reminded me of stories about old-time Indians going out into the woods on a solo quest and they'd run into their spirit animal—or something like that. I pondered if these guys were somehow *my* animals. They weren't the prettiest creatures in the world, but they'd have to do, at least for now.

Sure. Why not? Carp. Whatever. I felt strangely comforted by them. The more I watched them, the more hypnotized I became. I thought what it must feel like to be them, moved around by currents. I thought about the number of times I got pulled by a force in my own life, in a direction I never wanted to go. A lot!

In my leaning over the side while daydreaming, I lost my balance and nearly tipped over. I steadied myself and calmed down. When I peered back over the edge of the canoe, the fish were gone.

Did that actually happen? Was I daydreaming? I was, like, 95 percent positive it wasn't a daydream.

Right then and there, I had an epiphany. Not being a spiritual type of person, this was a strange position to be in. It was a real conflict to be faced with an experience that seemed to have special meaning. I'd swear there was a voice inside me that said: "Go!" But it was as clear as when Ian and I heard that ranger's voice yell to us.

Go?! That's it?

After a few stunned seconds, I felt like I needed to seize this moment, or whatever it was. It didn't offer any answers, only the chance to act. And there was an odd sense of surrender, and a quiet commitment. Then a soft breath came out of me: "All right then, I'll go to Long Beach!"

Vii. BON VOYAGE

I wanted to run to Ian and tell him what happened with the fish. But then I figured he might not appreciate it so much and think I was only using it to manipulate him into doing something, yet again, that he didn't feel comfortable doing. And most of the time, he'd be right.

So I decided to write him an old-fashioned snail mail letter instead, so he'd eventually know what happened but wouldn't feel the immediate pressure to join me. I figured I owed him at least that much.

Still, I needed to tell *someone* sooner, to get it off my chest. *Zoe.* I could always talk to her, even if I didn't understand her half the time. I gave her a call to see if she wanted to meet up for drinks at Starbucks. She said sure. I asked her to bring any other research she'd found about the trip.

I got there early, took a table in the back, and looked around. There was an old dude reading a newspaper, like some quaint scene out of the twentieth century. A mom was on her cell phone while her kid, under her seat, toyed with the electric socket, sticking wooden coffee stirrers into the holes.

There was another table that looked like a social club run by Tim Burton. Three women, each wrapped in various shades of black, were huddled together, elbows out awkwardly, arms moving, knitting. They didn't seem like your typical Starbucks crowd, and I didn't peg them as being from the area either. One of the women had a freaky white eye (I mean, the kind mostly without the color part in the middle) which wandered—it looked like that eye was staring at me the whole time. And each of the women had a small crumpled photo in front of them, as if they were making a Christmas scarf for a particular person—though it wasn't anytime near Christmas. Every so often one of them would hold up their knitting, as if to measure its length, then glance at the photo before returning to their work. They mumbled in a cryptic language—maybe Farsi or Arabic. When the eye-lady needed to measure though, she held it up in my direction (or so I imagined). Gave me the chills. I wanted Zoe to get there soon—I wasn't sure how much longer I could endure that eye's cold, constant gaze.

Zoe arrived wearing her usual Cali-casual, Coachella-like outfit, this time with her hempy hat, funky rose-tinted shades, a light blue scarfy thing, and a black-lace pair of those fingerless gloves to go with her black dress and silvery fingernail polish with orange polka dots.

I cleared my throat and cut to the chase: "Ian backed out of the trip. But hey, that's okay. I guess."

She gave me the once-over. "You don't have to put on a happy face, you know. Not with me."

I hated that she nailed things like that. "I mean, sure, it's not what I wanted. "But *I'm* going," I said, as boldly as I could manage, trying to keep my voice from wavering or cracking.

"When?"

"Tomorrow."

"Serious? No way!"

"No, *really*. I am."

"All right then," she said, staring at me for an uncomfortably long while. Then it was like a thought swept over her. "I mean, I'm happy for you, don't get me wrong." I sat there, mesmerized by her. "You sure you're okay?"

"Yeah, no, I'm a little edgy, nervous, about going, I guess, out there, alone, and guilty about not being straight with my folks. Stuff like that, that's all."

"Oh. Okay. I am, too."

"What, nervous? Why should *you* be?"

"I don't know. I … it's happening so fast, isn't it? The other day when you guys came over. And tomorrow, now you're leaving. But I think it's great you're, you know, going for it, jumping in. A lot of guys are afraid of that kind of … never mind. You're crazy," she laughed, "but then again, everyone knows that. For the record, I'd offer to come along, you know, except I've got my brother's birthday party to go to tomorrow, and I already made plans with my mom for the next day—like, in case you were wondering."

"Oh, yeah. I mean no, 'cause I *was* thinking of asking you, uh, to go out … er, on the outdoor trip, but I didn't know if you'd be into that sort of thing, and I didn't want to put you in a situation that might cause you any harm."

She looked at me hard. "Right. Actually, it sounds awesome. I mean, why should boys get to have all the fun? Besides, guys always get into trouble without girls saving their asses."

"Huh?"

"Sure. You think Lewis and Clark would've lasted one *week* in the wilderness without that sixteen-year-old Sacagawea leading the way? They would've been so ridiculously lost and helpless and, well, dead for sure."

I could never tell when she was joking. How did she know Lewis and Clark were on my mind? The girl was psychic, I swear. I took a chance and laughed, albeit nervously, and she laughed back. Then it got awkwardly quiet—or maybe it was the air-conditioning that just shut off.

"So," she finally declared, "are we like, together, or is this your way of trying to say goodbye?"

"Wha—?!" I grunted again. "No … I," a fur ball apparently stuck in my throat.

The girl could run me in circles like this all day long if she wanted. Then she said things, and I said things—I guess—but it was really all, honestly, a blur. In the end, I just remember that she gave me a kiss on the cheek and a soft squeeze of a hug. She smelled of sun-dried flowers, or maybe it was lavender, and some sort of candy, like gummy bears.

And then she was gone.

All I got from the conversation was a glimpse that it could be years, maybe a decade or more, before I could even *begin* to comprehend how girls thought. And by then she'd be a woman, and then I'd have to start over and figure out how *that* game went, too! Maybe I'd *never* be able to wrap my head around the female brain! I saw it in one sweeping vision, as a wave of anxiety hit me and washed over me.

I didn't even get to telling her about the whole fishy epiphany, which was my original thing. Somehow, now, it didn't seem to matter. I guess I really just needed to connect with someone. I guess we connected. I wasn't sure though.

I stumbled home in a daze, realizing I still had to do a bit more final research on the river, finish printing out a few more maps, and wrap up a few last bits of business. I also wanted to allow for hang time with Mom, more packing, writing that letter to Ian, and finding a way to get some shut-eye before the big day.

Dinner was quiet, with both me and Mom pretty distracted—she admitted she was thinking about her business trip the next day. I felt like I was secretly shipping out to Afghanistan or Iraq. And all the while, thinking about Zoe.

After excusing myself and giving Mom a big hug that left her slightly shocked, I went upstairs. I got to my room and pulled out a small backpack of trip stuff I'd been accumulating under my bed.

After finishing the packing, I sat down at my computer to write Ian that letter. I was timing the delivery of it so that I'd be two, maybe three days gone before it arrived at his house. I typed:

Dear Ian,

Sorry to push you so hard to join me. You made a choice, and that's okay, seriously (no sarcasm). By the time you get this, I'll be gone. Where the current takes me (hehe!) is anyone's guess. I realized that, for whatever reason, I had to do it. I figure we're defined by our actions, not our thoughts, plans, or promises. It's probably best not to question 'Why?' too much. The bottom line is: whatever I'm doing or whatever I think I'm doing with my life isn't getting me anywhere, and I'm tired of being yanked around. Anyway, I'll give you a call when I get to Long Beach (maybe you or your brother could give me a ride back home, eh?). Bon voyage!

Your pal forever,
Sam

I printed it out, shoved it in an envelope, addressed it, and slapped a stamp on it. How very antiquated! It occurred to me that I wasn't sure I'd ever written a real letter before (birthday cards and other special occasions aside). It felt very official and sort of surprisingly cool. I'd find a mailbox on my way to the river the next morning and trust that the ol' Pony Express would deliver it.

I was getting tired, so I flopped back into bed and tried to sleep. But I couldn't. I was too revved up. I tossed and turned, kicked off my sheets, then pulled them back on. Thoughts raced through my mind. Something was incomplete.

Ah—then it hit me: Didn't explorers do this thing before the first steps of their journeys into the Great Unknown? Duh.

I threw off the blankets, scampered over to the desk again, and clicked on the light. I got out a blank sheet of paper. This called for something more formal, more historic. I remembered the feathered pen my grandfather gave me way back when. I grabbed it from the dusty lower drawer. I pulled out his old inkwell, too. I dipped the pen in the ink, like they do in the movies—except my writing made a complete mess! At the top of the page, I scrawled (in cursive, with as many fancy doodles as I could manage): *Last Will and Testament.*

Even if I hadn't lived long yet, I had to write out my version of this, right? I thought hard. Nothing. I thought harder. Nothing still. Just when I was ready to give up, the words began to sputter out:

To Whom It May Concern,

I, Sam Hawkins, do hereby declare that my computer, online gaming accounts, video console, sporting equipment, books and toys should go to Ian Wang. All my financial assets ($137.46) are to go to Zoe Shapiro. All my pictures and personal belongings shall be split between my parents.

In the event of my untimely death, I'm okay with organ donation. I prefer cremation and that my ashes be spread over the Pacific Ocean.

— Sam B. Hawkins

Not bad—except for the puddles of ink splotches. I knew it probably wouldn't hold up in a court, but then again there wasn't a lot at stake. I guess it was mostly symbolic for me to go through. Plus, it was fun, in a twisted, melodramatic sort of way. Adulting 101. I put it in an envelope and left it on my desk. By then I was super exhausted and barely made it to the bed before I zonked out.

In the morning, I vaguely remember my mom kissing me goodbye before she took off for the airport.

Not too long after that, it began to get light. I remembered my resolve from the prior day and braced myself for an eventful day before I had the chance to talk myself out of it.

I got up and rechecked my equipment. I couldn't resist throwing in a few more comforts and gadgets at the last minute: Mom's bird binoculars, a childhood slingshot, popcorn, a pan, marshmallows, and gorp (at least that's what *we* always called it: M&Ms, raisins and nuts). So much for self-discipline and low-impact camping.

I called that same taxi dude (the one who drove the canoe to the river a week ago) to take me to the water.

Then I turned off my phone and put it in my desk drawer, just how Ian and I had discussed—the great unplugging. I just did it cold turkey and walked away to my ride.

I was officially off the grid.

The taxi guy arrived. It was nice to see a familiar face, even if he wasn't a close friend.

We got to the parking lot near the river. I paid him and he patted me on the back, as if he understood more than what I figured he knew.

"Good luck, son, wherever you're headed." I nodded back at him stoically and mustered up a nervous smile.

When I got down to the river itself, I set myself to the task of getting the boat into the water. Somehow I pushed and pulled and slid the damned thing until it dropped in. It nearly floated away, but I grabbed the rope just in time.

I loaded it up pretty quickly and paused to snap a few mental pictures. Apart from some crows, there wasn't a soul to see me off. This wasn't the image I had in mind when we first conceived of the expedition.

So much for the grand send-off. I guess I had imagined a bunch of close friends doing the fanfare thing: gathered around, tossing little bits of confetti, clinking glasses, or some other sappy scene.

Whatever. *If a boat launches in a river and no one is there to witness it, did it actually happen?*

Out on the water in the early dawn hours, the front of the canoe parted the murky water of the Sepulveda Basin as the sunrise segued into the heat of the day and a mostly clear blue sky (smog not included).

One of those great blue herons took off from the side of the river, then kept flying low in front of me that whole first stretch. I imagined it was there to keep me company.

Section 2

CATCHING THE CURRENT

There's something about rivers that truly beckons:
They're seared into landscapes and people's hearts
... indelible, immovable, incorrigible.

— Sam Hawkins, January 8, 2016

i. Alone

There was no mistaking it was just me, myself, and I. Still, I took some comfort in at least sticking to my word, taking action, and trying to carve out my own identity. It was one of those small things to claim some control over, even if just clinging to it somewhat clumsily in this beat-up aluminum canoe. Ronnie could only be dodged for so long— *not* out of the woods yet!

I'd been up and down these banks before but going through it from this perspective—from the river's point of view—was totally different. It was like in one of those postapocalyptic movies where you see the junk we've left behind. It was depressing to see the waste laid out so bare. Imagining it all slowly making its way to that swirling garbage patch the size of Texas in the north Pacific, it was painfully and ironically clear that if we didn't change our ways we'd all someday die of consumption.

In a setting like this, it didn't take much to make a person cynical: Given that I was already cynical, it just made me mad. Swearing to be on the lookout for anybody dumping their crap in the river, I vowed to not just complain about it but to do something.

There must've been an agency charged with cleaning that mess up, but judging by the lousy job they were doing it was probably those same people who ordered the "No Trespassing—$1,000 Fine" signs. So they put resources toward blocking off and padlocking a river, but they don't put a penny toward improving it? Great.

I'd heard of rivers back east that were so filthy they'd sometimes catch fire. It was tempting to want to try that out now, to burn up this river and start over with a fresh chance to get it right. I resisted the urge.

I passed under a large, bare tree where three sleek black birds with long snaky necks were chilling, drying in the morning sun with their wings outstretched awkwardly, as if frozen in that position.

Not far down from there I cruised silently beneath Balboa Bridge, with the tree limbs jammed from the winter floods into the underside like crazy-huge pterodactyl nests (not that I'd ever seen one, but you get the idea).

And below that was the jumping-off point between the known and the unknown worlds—at least in my own little universe. It's not that there was any big obstacle, it's that it just got to be too far from home after that. It was a place we called Cattail Chute, 'cause there was a bunch of those grassy plants with long, brown, hot dog-like tails on the ends. There was a small chute of rapids that curved its way through the cattails and over a few rocks.

When I got up to it, I dug my paddle into the river bottom and pushed off. The boat slid down and knocked into the rocks like a rickety old roller coaster. After a bunch of pushing and shoving and getting in and out a few times, I got through the chute okay.

At the end of it, I took another breather, chugging a juice box from my stash.

But when I tried to get back in the boat, my foot sank into the muck. And I mean deep. It was like quicksand; the more I moved to get my foot out, the more it seemed to get stuck, with my weight pushing the shoe still deeper. It was gross. Panicking slightly as I tried to get my foot back, I somehow managed to slowly work it upward. But when it got to the surface, there was no shoe left on the end of my foot.

Reaching down into the muck with my hand, I winced, trying to keep my head above water. My hand couldn't get down far enough. I must've spent fifteen minutes trying to find that stupid thing. And when that didn't work, I tried to stick my bare foot back down into the muck to grope around with my toes, to try to feel where it had gone. In the end, it was like the river had swallowed it up!

Great—how was I supposed to go anywhere with only one shoe? But I couldn't just stay there all day either, so I pushed on with one bare foot.

Later, up ahead, I saw an obstruction of some sort across the river. A blue heron floated ahead of me, perched atop whatever the obstacle was, straight ahead.

Up close it looked like a dead end; the edge of the earth just sort of dropped off into nothingness. On second look, I could see it was a rocky ledge that stretched across the fifty-foot-wide river. Who put these damn boulders there anyway—a couple of giants?!

Water gushed between the rocks, and the whole ledge dropped about ten or fifteen feet, until the next flatwater section picked up again below. I pulled out my maps, but nothing like this showed up on them. When we mapped it online, we hadn't zoomed in close enough. If my maps already proved unreliable, then I was screwed—what *else* was out there that I wouldn't be able to anticipate?

If I stayed in the boat and pushed my way over it, I'd topple out and crack my head open. Not cool. And it would be a major pain to haul the boat around, on land, through the thick bushes and trees. I could pick up ticks and die of some disease or maybe get a bad case of poison oak. The only real option was to pull the boat, little by little, over the rocks without getting hit by the canoe.

I didn't exactly get hit, but in watching out for the canoe I sometimes had to take my eyes off where I was stepping. I took a fall and scraped against the rocks and nearly twisted my ankle. My wet feet made the dry moss or algae on the top of the rocks become super slippery. I ended up sliding down the sides of rocks, losing my balance, and taking a tumble. One time I fell *into* the canoe.

Somehow I maneuvered my way over the ledge without killing myself. I was sweating like crazy already, too, so I took out another juice box and sucked it down in about two seconds. Then another. *Pace yourself!* It couldn't have been more than eleven a.m. and already it felt only slightly cooler than a pizza oven.

I had the foresight to pack sandwiches and other food (cigar pretzels, apples, and some trail mix) but decided to wait until lunchtime before indulging. I had to discipline myself and do things right.

I got back in the boat and pushed off.

I was glad to be in the boat again, but it wasn't long before I started hitting sandbars and the boat would grind to a halt. It was annoying and time-consuming, having to scoot with my body and push off the bottom with the paddle again. When that didn't work, I'd get out and rock the boat back and forth until it was freed or sometimes pull on the rope that was tied to the front in order to get it off a sandbar. Then I'd jump back in and continue.

Constantly looking ahead for obstacles to navigate around, I started to get a sense of where there was shallow water and where there was deeper water. It was learning to *read the water.*

Pretty soon there was yet another ledge with a drop-off. This one wasn't quite as steep, but there was a short set of rocky rapids. In the next flat section below there were two very elegant white birds hunting in the sandy shallows: *egrets*, I'd learned from Zoe.

Doing the same-old, getting-in-and-out-of-the-boat routine and scooting over precarious rocks and rusty jagged things (like steel rebar sticking out of old blocks of concrete), I was getting pretty tired—sloppy, too. I figured I knew the routine, so I put my brain on autopilot. Just then, of course, the canoe bounced off one rock with a loud metallic clang and came back and knocked into me. Toppling over and falling hard against the skeleton of an old shopping cart, I felt a sharp pain along my right shin.

I lay there for a few seconds, feeling the dull heat of idiotic pain, then spotting blood. As if that weren't bad enough, I'd poked myself on a rusty metal shard of that shopping cart. I realized I could get an infection. I imagined my leg getting gangrene and dropping off.

I took a breath and collected myself again, hobbled down the rest of the ledge, pulling on the rope at the front of the boat. I pulled it and cursed at it. It was as if it had a mind of its own and had knocked me down intentionally. I had to train it to understand what I wanted and how to behave; if it didn't respond, then I had to beat it into submission.

Angry and muttering, I limped ashore to assess the damage.

Fortunately, I'd brought along a first aid kit; unfortunately, it was in the bottom of the boat, which had gotten pretty sopped. A lot of the stuff inside the kit was wrapped in waterproof sandwich bags; unfortunately again, the gauze bandages were not among the bagged items.

Damn. I dashed some iodine onto the wound and worked it in with my less-than-sterile fingers, then squirted antibiotic cream on it, too, for double protection. But without a clean dressing, it was definitely sketchy. When was the last time I had a tetanus shot?

I wasn't thinking straight. I chocked it up to the heat, which felt about 105 degrees. I wondered how likely it was for a kid my age to die of heat stroke under these conditions. I drank another two juice boxes and looked around for my food bag.

Whoops. What a fool! Floating there along with the first aid kit, in the bottom of the boat, was my lunch, with the sandwiches still wrapped in plastic baggies, but I guess I'd stepped on them 'cause they were open and the river water had gotten into them—*all* of them. At first I thought I could salvage one, but no way.

I wasn't sure I'd ever been so hungry before. *Don't be so dramatic.*

ii. A LEAK

I figured one way to get my hunger under control was to keep busy. That first meant scooping up the soggy garbage from the bottom of the boat and putting it into a single larger plastic bag and tying it tightly together so it could be tossed in a garbage can—if and whenever one appeared.

It was tempting to leave it beside the river with the rest of the garbage; no one would ever know the difference. Then I gave myself a swift kick in the brain for even having such a white-trash thought. *No, think with integrity.* It was important to act according to what was *right.* My vow to keep others from dumping crap into the river meant nothing if I just turned around and did the same thing. This was the prime time to develop my principles, my ethics, something to live by—in short, respect for my word. Lose that, or compromise it, if just for the sake of lazy convenience, and everything was lost—my moral compass would have no true north.

After paddling again for a bit, it wasn't long before it felt like the boat was moving in slow motion. At first I thought it was from being half starved and operating under faulty senses, but more and more it seemed like something else. I looked in the water to see if it was stuck on something.

Nothing. I felt for a breeze—maybe it was about going against the wind.

Nope. Every time I got back into the boat, I brought in water—but not *this* much. There was water in the boat that was about two inches deep!

I stopped paddling and inspected the boat. Shuffling my belongings around the canoe, the culprit finally showed itself: up at the front-left part of the boat was a hole. It wasn't that big, but I thought I would've noticed it earlier. It must've opened up with the dragging, dropping, and smashing on those ledges.

I tried hard to pull over, but it was difficult. It felt like trying to steer a waterbed with a teaspoon. I had time to contemplate that the water streaming into the boat felt like the accumulation of all my nonstop cravings and comforts left behind, a great burden: the constant gaming, the infinite web time, texting, cell phones, the bottomless amounts of food and drink—and at the end of the day, a nice, fat, cushy bed.

After what seemed an eternity of confronting the full depth of my unchecked consumerism footprint, I made it to the side of the river. Phew!

I schlepped my belongings out of the boat and laid them in the sun to dry before taking a closer look at the hole in the boat. But first the water had to be emptied. I tried but couldn't budge it. The canoe just sort of lay there like a beached orca whale—no way I could even turn it over.

I went and got a big piece of wood and stuck it under the boat to create some leverage. But after two or three heaves of pushing down on it, the wood broke and I fell backward onto the muddy riverbank. A second, bigger branch of a tree also failed; I just didn't have enough weight to budge it.

Eventually, I gave up and flopped down and rested against my pathetic pile of drying supplies. I must've dozed off.

I awoke to the sound of whistling.

I could've been asleep for either a couple of seconds or a couple of hours. It dawned on me that time was becoming

unglued, already. And with the stifling heat, I felt disori-
ented (and sunburned). Okay, so I brought sunscreen, but
did I actually think to *use* it much? Duh. And even though
my baseball cap should've provided shade, how much does it
help when you're asleep and facing the sun? Duh. A stinging
red burn started coming on fast, and I was convinced that
I'd napped closer to two hours than two seconds. My leg felt
worse now, too—it looked like it had festered while it, too,
had fallen asleep.

I sat up and looked across the riverbank and downriver.
There was a Hispanic guy, maybe in his late teens or early
twenties, spritely and determined, like a leprechaun. He
whistled while attending to the details of fishing, but not
any method I'd ever seen before. He didn't notice me, so I
limped closer to watch.

It was hard to imagine someone who was mentally
disturbed as being a regular whistler, so I felt like he was
a good bet to help me empty out the water in the boat,
without him going postal on me. This guy was fairly short,
maybe five foot five. He hopped lightly along the edge of
the river, a dirty green fleece jacket tied around his waist.
He looked intently down into the water, very animated but
carefully and quietly monitoring something, using the trees
and bushes to hide behind, then popping out to adjust his
lines, then hiding again. I didn't see how any of it was going
to help him catch anything, but I was curious to see how he
fared. He put bait on a line, crossed himself, kissed the hook,
then tossed the line, real stealthy-like, into a shady part of
the river, about five feet from the muddy riverbank. Then he
tied off his end to a tree and retreated to observe.

He reached beside himself and grabbed some sort of net.
It looked like it could've been made from junk pulled out of
the river: different colors of twine, plastic six-pack holders,
including what looked like the stringy part of an old tennis
racket, and a shredded basketball net.

He was creeping back toward the fishing spot when he spotted me. He froze—not for fear, but almost like he couldn't believe that he hadn't seen me watching him. He smiled, ever so slightly—no way to be sure what he meant by it.

I limped closer, seeing that he had the kind of eyes that crinkle up when a person smiles, making crow's feet at the corners of his eyes. He had chestnut brown eyes to go with his dark, scraggly hair and one of those thin, peach-fuzz mustaches. He gave the slightest curious tilt of his head to acknowledge my presence, then continued on with his business, as if I were gone.

When he got back over to his fishing spot, back in the shade, he took up the line and was doing some sort of jiggling and tugging movements. I felt like I shouldn't bother the guy in the middle of his fishing, but then again I didn't want to wait all afternoon to get help only to see him catch a bucket of zilch. But within a minute his line started moving back and forth like crazy!

That was no rubber tire at the end of his hook. I found myself shuffling closer. He reeled it in, hand over hand, then crouched down to the level of the water, grabbed his ragtag net, and pulled up the line, revealing one of those carp fish, and a large one, too—maybe a foot and a half long!

He calmly unhooked it and put it in his bucket, where there was suddenly a lot of splashing and flopping—a real fighter. I could now see other tails flapping around in the bucket, too.

He looked straight up at me, flashing a wide, uninhibited grin, and shouted, "We eat good tonight, eh, *amigo?*!"

Over my dead body.

I searched my mental Spanish dictionary for something to say. I did a couple years of it in middle school and could still pick up bits and pieces.

"*Si*, uh, *felicitations. Muy bueno, el* um ... *pescado!*" I said, murdering the language all over the place. "Say, *tu* help me, uh, empty boat ... *bote* ... *aquí?*"

iii. PERV?

So that whistling impish guy hopped across a bunch of rocks, coming toward me to see what the problem was with the boat.

He took note of my stuff splayed out. He gave me the once-over, as if trying to figure me out, cocking his head again. It was weird: I felt like he was some sort of hybrid—part kid, part adult—and I wasn't immediately certain what that meant.

He gave the boat a once-over. He nodded as he walked around it, like a used-car salesman. At one point he reached into a shirt pocket, took out a few strawberries and started popping them in his mouth as he thought. I tried not to stare at the strawberries or drool, but that's all I could see. He couldn't help but notice.

"Take, *por favor*, please," he said, holding out a few. But I just sort of froze.

Then he quickly wiped his hand on his pants leg and stuck out his hand. "Ignazio."

We shook.

"Sam."

"What you do here, Sam?"

"Well," I began proudly, "I'm going down the river, uh, *el río*."

He took this in, processed it somehow, and looked at me inquisitively. "Down ... river? Why? Where?"

"Does it matter?" He looked at me blankly, but I didn't want to explain it to a stranger—I wanted him to magically appreciate the endeavor and its merits. He mulled over the info casually and pursed his lips nonchalantly. His silence made me uneasy, so I asked again. "Look, can you help me get this ... *agua*, you know, out?"

He smiled, sensing my anxiety. Then he went and squatted beside the canoe. He ran his hand along the sides of the boat until he felt something. He looked closer. He felt for the same spot on the inside. He found a leak and pointed it out to me. He chuckled.

"I know. Yes, a leak. I dropped it."

Then he kept on going and spotted a second leak. He looked around a bit more but didn't find anything else. Again, he contemplated the situation. He got up and stood back and took out a piece of gum, offering some to me.

"No, thanks." But that didn't stop him from shoving a couple more pieces in his mouth. He chewed for a bit and looked around, like he had all the time in the world. He chewed more. I was beginning to think maybe he did this to try my patience and be annoying, or maybe he was a bit mental. Finally, he turned to me:

"Okay, *amigo*, let us do this thing." I didn't know what that meant exactly.

With the boat parallel to shore, partly in the water, he put one foot on the side of the boat. He hoisted himself up, straddling the middle part of the canoe, with his feet resting on one side and grabbing the other side with his hands. Now on top of it, he started rocking the boat, very slowly at first. Before long though, he'd built up momentum. The water started sloshing from side to side, sometimes splashing clear out of the boat, as he increased the rocking. I stood there, sort of surprised at his unorthodox method, until he stared me down:

"When you want to help, iz okay for me."

"Right, sure, yes, *si, si,*" I said as I grabbed the boat like him and joined in his rhythm, letting the weight of the water help us. We rocked it back and forth, timing my heave with his ho. Each time the boat leaned to one side or the other, water sloshed out of it. The boat was getting easier to move. But it was hard work. After about five minutes of this, I was exhausted and started to ease up, ready to collapse.

"No, do not stop! Almost!" he yelled. "*Vamos*, come on— *poco a poco*—little by little. We count!"

"One, two, three," in unison.

And on the count of ten, the boat leaned over enough so that, in one big whoosh, it reached a critical mass, and we were able to flop it all the way over. The guy hopped off gracefully, barely getting wet at all. I stood there, panting, watching the water gush over me, the riverbank, and then back into the river.

He surveyed the scene, again casually taking out a few sticks of gum and shoving them in his mouth.

"You want me to do all?!!" he said, rolling his eyes, dramatic and exasperated. "Fine."

"*Gracias*," I offered, "*por* you know, helping out." I felt awkward now that we didn't have a common task to distract me from the fact that I didn't really know who this guy was. As far as I knew, his name wasn't even Ignazio.

He raised a finger, as if he was checking for wind. Then he inspected the leak again. He took his shirt ends and dried off the area around the leaks, inside and out. When that was done, he took out the glob of gum. He smiled coyly at me. He divided the gum into four big globs and stuck them on a few fingertips. He stuck one piece of gum on the outside of one leak and another on the inside. He pressed them together and worked them hard for fifteen seconds before stepping away. Then he repeated the process with the second leak.

"Okey dokey. You good to go," he said proudly. Then he looked down and pointed to my cut, "Oh, but *that*," pointing to the dirty gash with blood running down my shin. "*No es bueno.*"

"I'll be all right."

"I help."

"What are you, *el doctoro*? How old are you anyway?"

"Huh?"

"*Cuántos*, uh, *años tiene?*"

"Twenty. *Por qué?*"

I shrugged.

He looked over at my leg, then back at me. "I can see?"

Reluctantly, I stuck it out. He looked it over, sort of like he'd done with inspecting the boat. Then he got up.

"Wait," and he skipped back across a few rocks at a shallow part of the river and over to the other side. He grabbed a bag from his meager belongings and came back over with it.

It turned out it was an actual first aid kit (granted, a very homemade looking one, in a colorful little woven sack, like it was put together by his grandmother). There was a lot of stuff in it that I didn't recognize.

He took my leg and propped it up on his knee so that he could see what he was doing. He took my leg in his hands. That made me feel uneasy. He was gentle enough with the wound, but every time I tried to pull my leg away in protest, he'd pull it back forcefully and indicate for me to calm down.

My parents—and maybe a handful of doctors and nurses—were the only ones who ever worked on me like this. I wasn't accustomed to a complete stranger doing it. It occurred to me: What if he was a perv? The word came up a lot in school and online. I'd never met one firsthand. He smiled in sort of a knowing way—not good. He was very enthusiastic, friendly, and charming—but almost *too* much. He didn't seem to have any barriers about being touchy-feely and making physical contact—again, not good. I thought back to how, even in elementary school, there was a "no physical contact" rule for both students and teachers. And here was this guy, assuming it was okay to be so hands-on.

Despite my occasional but weak protests, I had to admit that, in the end, he cleaned up the wound and wrapped it nicely. Maybe I *was* overreacting.

Still, the whole situation, combined with the thoughts that I couldn't prevent from entering my head, made me awfully uncomfortable. There was something about that super-friendly grin of his. I figured he must've picked up that I was suspicious or at least hesitant.

"Well, I guess I'd better be pushing on."

"*Qué?*"

"*Yo dejo*, dude," I remembered from joking around in Spanish with my friends. "I have to go."

"Ah, okay," he said, as if he got the nuance. "Then go—go!"

I went over to the boat, like I needed to do something important, then futzed around, checking the gum in the holes (which started to feel harder already, having baked in the sun).

"You think it'll really hold?"

He didn't take his eyes off me but nodded. Piercing—that's how he looked. I went over to my mound of random drying belongings and felt the stuff. I nodded.

"Like I said, *mucho gusto por la* help," as I started putting my junk back in the boat, making sure to stay on the far side so I always faced him.

While I gathered my stuff, he didn't say a thing. He observed me, like he could see my thoughts. I didn't want to be a jerk, but I figured it couldn't hurt to be cautious around him (or any other strangers, for that matter).

I pretended to be cool and relaxed but knew he could see my nervousness.

After a bunch of fussing, I got into the boat and pushed off.

But I wasn't ten feet from shore before I realized that, in my haste, I'd left the paddle. *What an idiot.*

The guy matter-of-factly went and picked it up off the ground and walked it to the shoreline. I grabbed a branch and pulled myself back toward him, smiling awkwardly. The boat cruised up beside him. He extended the paddle, and when I grabbed hold, he pressed his hand over my hand and pulled the boat in close to him.

I couldn't get my hand out. If he'd wanted to, he could've pulled down and tipped the boat over, or with a rock in his other hand, whacked me over the head and run away with all my stuff. My heart was pounding, and I was getting ready to thrash about to free my hand or yell if necessary, when suddenly he whispers,

"If you can't trust *me*, you up shit creek, buddy, *rio de mierda!*"

And as quickly as he'd grabbed me, he let go again.

Flustered and confused, I backpaddled slowly, keeping my eyes on him. Weirdo. I didn't need all those mind games.

Without that extra water, it was easy to turn the boat around. I paddled forward, turning back occasionally, until I couldn't see him anymore.

iV. A NEW LEAf

I pretended like the incident with the Hispanic dude didn't bother me, but it was gnawing at me—which reminded me of food again. Damn!

I savored the taste of those strawberries he'd shared. What a jerk I'd been. Then again, some pervs use bait, like candy, to lure kids. Was it wrong to be cautious? Hell, I wasn't sure of anything. If I was going to get down the river, I probably *did* need people who could watch my back sometimes.

The river seemed to be getting a bit calmer and flatter now. No more annoying ledges, just lots of thick trees and bushes along the muddy riverbank. This part was pretty sweet, actually, with no concrete at all. I dipped my paddle down in the water to tell the depth: maybe five or six feet. No roads or bridges but still lots of birds. There was one I took a liking to that was hunched over, with red beady eyes and a black-feathered cap, like something out of an Edgar Allan Poe story. Sometimes there was the occasional splash in the shallows and a ripple spreading outward from something beneath the surface.

Apart from nature's sounds, it was quiet. But I knew I was surrounded by millions of people in L.A. It was bizarre. Despite being a bit beat-up already, this was more like how I'd imagined the venture would go. Despite my pains, I felt more in the groove.

Then there was this buzzing noise. It was like an annoying fly or mosquito: There it was, and suddenly it'd be gone, then I'd hear it again. It seemed to be getting closer.

Out of the corner of my eye, something moved overhead, just above the tree line: It was a small airplane, zipping back and forth.

Curious to see what the buzz was about, I tied the boat to a branch and got out. Leaving the boat and my belongings, I told myself I needed a break, that I *deserved* a break.

After climbing up the bank, through the shade of the trees and out onto a large open field, I suddenly realized where I was. It was funny 'cause I saw how only hours into my trip, there was the sense that I was far removed from civilization. But this was the radio-controlled aircraft field.

I'd driven by here dozens of times with my folks, in happier days. It was just off Woodley Avenue, and we'd only stopped in to see it just a couple times. I walked over to where the guys were fixing up their planes. One guy nodded at me while I watched him work. He made a gesture with his hand on his face, and I didn't know what he was doing until I reached up with my hand and felt dirt and realized that I must've had a speck of mud on my cheek. The guy smiled and went back to work.

I found a bathroom. When I got inside, I looked at myself in the mirror. I was shocked. I didn't just have a speck of mud but was speckled *all over*—tiny dots to big globs, from the mucking around. I didn't half mind it—it gave me an experienced look. Yeah, *now* we're talkin': *Dirt makes the boy!* Still, as I leaned over the sink and splashed clean water on my face and saw the dirt and grime come off, it also felt good to be refreshed, to get a break from my troubles. But once the mud came off, I saw how red I'd gotten. I dunked my whole head in the sink and turned it on full. An old-timer came in to take a pee and he gave me a double take, wondering why I was dripping wet. I couldn't blame the guy. I quietly made my exit.

There was a soda machine, and I rummaged through my pockets until I found some loose change to get a cold drink.

It was awesome—like I'd never had a soda before! It was so good I had to have another.

After meandering around the mini airfield, feeling more rejuvenated, I found a good spot to watch planes taking off and coming in for landings. I envied these planes flying around, so free up there in the air. It made me feel happy, like *I* was soaring, too. Things were starting to click. *This* was what I was after: A sense of feeling free, of abandon, was within reach.

I don't know how much time passed with me ogling the planes. I noticed some dads who were there with their boys, teaching them how to control these mechanical birds. Suddenly, a twang of jealousy rose up. Why couldn't I be like them? Wasn't this how dads and boys were supposed to be? Why did I feel so separated from this whole little ritual? Did I do something to make my dad the way he was or drive him away from me? My cynicism was creeping back in.

At a certain point I realized that the sun was weakening. The scorching midday rays were fading, turning slightly softer. It was a good time of day. Some of the people were starting to pack up and put all their gadgets and contraptions back in their cars and head home.

Home. Distance wise, it was nothing—*I* could've gone home, too. I could've left the canoe in the water, betting Zoe's family wouldn't even miss it. Or I could've gotten it later. I felt like I'd gone a great distance, but with the things that went wrong I'd barely traveled much at all—at least as the crow flies.

So *that* was depressing. But at the same time, I was surprised to feel so good. The water and the soda helped. And though tempted to return to the comforts of home, the stronger impulse went to the river. *I couldn't* just go back.

Screw comfort! How lame would it be to stop, just when I was starting to feel the air lift up my wings and carry me. But to where?

I tossed the empty soda cans in the bin and headed across the field. I found my way to the shade of the tree line, pausing to look at the airfield one last time.

Starting down the bank though, I heard a commotion at the river. It was a bunch of voices. They got louder. It was in Spanish. An argument. I picked up the pace—the sound was coming from where I'd left the boat.

When I got there, three guys were nearly coming to blows. I crept up to get a better look, hiding behind a few bushes. There were two guys on shore beside the boat, picking through my stuff—and there was that Ignazio guy, too! I wanted to jump out and yell at them, but something in me said to stay put.

Ignazio was cursing at them. They weren't paying him much attention though (after all, there were two of them, and they looked about five years older than him), but I could see they were bothered by him. He grabbed something out of their hands and threw it back in my boat. He got between them and the boat at one point and made like he was going to take them on. I decided to make my move.

I started talking loudly to myself, as if carrying on a conversation with someone nearby. I romped around, making a racket so they'd know someone was coming. I walked closer, shuffling my feet to make it sound like there were more people than me.

About twenty feet from them, I made like I suddenly saw them: "Hey, what are you guys doing!?" The two guys froze—not because they were scared of me, but because they were caught off guard. They didn't know what to make of the situation. The fact that there were two of us and two of them made them talk amongst themselves. One guy was holding my thermos and the other guy was holding my dad's Swiss Army knife.

They went from having the upper hand to feeling on the defensive (even with the knife). They pocketed the thermos and the knife as Ignazio lit into them again. I didn't understand a word of it, but I liked the sound of it.

They finally strolled away, whacking through the thick bushes until they found a meager path, which they took as they disappeared downriver amid the crackle of sticks and the occasional curse thrown at them. Ignazio also threw a few sticks and stones in their general direction, for good measure.

I turned to him. "Ignazio, right?" sticking out my hand. But he had his gaze fixed downriver. This was a different side to him: his survivor face.

"I hate them guys," he said. I dropped my hand.

"Hey, I owe you one—again."

"Sorry, I could not save it all. Idiots!"

"*Muchas gracias*, dude—*seriously*. Thanks a bunch."

V. RATTLED

It wasn't long before those sodas at the airfield kicked in and nature was calling again.

So I excused myself from Ignazio and went off into the woods, looking for a private spot. I went about thirty or forty feet off the main path and looked around to make sure the coast was clear. I had started to pee when I heard an odd sound beside me that made me tighten up.

It sounded like one of those mariachi players shaking a pair of maracas. I reflexively tried to step away but froze in midstep, dribbling on my leg—something deep inside me instinctively just *knew*. As I slowly turned my face to the sound, I stared straight at a coiled-up rattlesnake, its eyes cold and detached.

I have no idea what kind of odd sound I must've eked out in response, but it was loud enough for Ignazio to hear. It felt like I was stuck in this way for five minutes (though it was probably only a few seconds) before hearing him approach, calling out: "You okay? Hey, you okay?"

After a few moments, out of the corner of my eye a paddle came into view, moving toward the snake slowly, and the snake turned to it, as if to pick a different fight. But it didn't strike.

To my surprise, it allowed itself to be lifted gently. It even coiled itself willingly, it seemed, around the paddle. I could see Ignazio carefully walking away, delicately holding the other end of the paddle. He calmly went over to a tree branch and let the snake slither onto it, where it stayed, curled up, camouflaged, barely moving a single muscle.

I was shaking as I tried to move again.

I zipped up my fly. Ignazio returned: "You a lucky guy."

I couldn't get the words out, but nodded humbly, putting my hand on his shoulder to steady myself, feeling lightheaded.

He left me alone momentarily to calm down and collect my thoughts. But I didn't like being in the brush just then, so I quickly followed after him.

We chilled a bit, skipping stones and killing time. Once he saw I was calmed down, he teased me about the incident. He went on and on about how funny it was: Me there with my own "snake" in hand (actually, he called it *gusano*, a worm), facing that big rattler.

"Yeah, yeah, *real* funny, dude." But I had to admit, it was. The guy should've paid me for all the entertainment I'd just provided. I could already see him telling that story to others for years afterward. After a while though, my stomach got angry at me again. The snake incident only sped up my metabolism. I had to get *some*thing to eat.

I offered to give him a ride in the boat so we could look for food. At the least there had to be fruit trees in the area that we could scavenge. Rather, he suggested we get some dinner handouts at a camping place he knew of, where his friends hung out. That sounded better than foraging for mealy fruit.

So we got in the boat and took off. The more distance we got from that damned snake, the better I felt. I decided I'd turn over a new leaf with this guy. He seemed okay after all. And, of course, him saving my ass didn't hurt his ratings either. Despite my having treated him poorly, I was pleasantly surprised to find him so forgiving.

As we paddled downriver to this supposed cookout rendezvous, I felt like I'd been given a second chance, in a cosmic way. I don't know if I could've died from a snake bite like that, but I felt fortunate not to have to found out the hard way.

It didn't take Ignazio long to start chipping away at my new lease on life and my confidence. He started in on my acting recklessly: being out here in the first place, at my age, when I didn't know a practical thing about taking care of myself. Then he'd flip it around and get me for being overly cautious, too, suggesting I was homophobic and racist, based on how I behaved and things I'd said.

With the language, we somehow frankensteined it together, with both of us using a mash-up of Spanglish. He went on about how I was so untrusting and how that stood to get in the way of allowing God to work his magic in my life.

"Whoa! Hold on." Was he really going to play the God card?

"Oh great," I thought. See, me and religion don't exactly see eye-to-eye. I know it's part of that whole cynical point of view, but even as a kid it seemed obvious that religion has probably created as many horrors in the world as it has done good—and that's just Christianity, not to mention groups like Al Qaida or the Taliban, and who knows what else is out there, always for the sake of a higher cause: all for God!

I know I should be more thankful, but I hate it when people hand everything over to God, like mindless, obedient robots. I don't like how especially athletes make a big show of God helping them hit a home run or make a touchdown. Seriously!? How totally self-centered. Even if there were a God, are we supposed to believe he'd have enough time to be hanging out keeping tabs on sports?

So although the guy possibly saved my life, I wasn't going to sit back and listen to a zealot's sermon. Fortunately, he didn't harp on it for long. He made a few counter judgments about me having "no faith, no how" and how that "never does any good," and only led to being lost and set on "putting things down" instead of contributing anything constructive or positive to the world. What about the Mother Theresas and MLKs of the world? Without any sense of structured religion, he said, we'd be *worse* off, "no better than animals."

I said I didn't think that was bad, since animals don't tend to kill their own kind. In the end, we agreed to disagree—neither of us was going to budge.

At one point he mentioned his wife and baby son back in Guatemala—even pulled out a few pictures and showed me.

"Aren't you a bit young to be having kids?" I asked, taking a look at his even-younger wife, and his infant son.

"I am twenty. My wife, she is nineteen."

Wow, I thought about what it'd be like if I became a dad within the next couple years—no way, not prepared for that! Suddenly twenty seemed so old, so mysterious, so over the hill. I mean, we shared the same generation, but we were worlds apart in so many other ways.

"But after having a kid, how can you just up and leave your family?" I said. "Isn't that sort of cruel?"

He didn't seem to take it personally. "*Depende* if you mean cruel for short *tiempo* or long *tiempo*."

"Huh?"

"Where I am from, you learn what are *los límites*—what are your *posibilidades* or not, *para la vida*."

"For life?"

"*Si*. Not possible to fly high. Maybe I can work *la tierra*, the land, *por la familia*, or move to city, work in factory, but still not get much pay. I want more for me, my wife, *mi hijo*. So I come here. Yes, maybe it seems cruel *now*; but if I stay there, then maybe it's cruel for long time. So what to do? I come north."

After talking for a while, with the sun again having dimmed a notch, we came around a bend in the river and saw a concrete bridge up ahead, with occasional cars passing over it.

It turned out these were actually two side by side bridges, huge blocks of concrete made to withstand flooding, maybe forty yards long, that held up the bridge span, each covered with graffiti from the ground up to ten to fifteen feet (as far as a person could reach with a ladder and an aerosol can). I could read some of the words but not all—maybe they marked territory or were art or something else entirely. A few people walked around beneath the bridges on the west riverbank.

As we got closer, I could see more guys, maybe ten, poking out their heads, looking at us, and still others who centered around a fire inside one of those big oil drums. Spread around the area were a few makeshift tentlike tarps, with clothes draped over the lines.

It was just shy of sundown, and there was a lot of contrast between the red-orange light gleaming off the water, the shimmering trees, the bright top of the bridge, and the passing cars, and then the shadowed underside of the bridge. I'd probably driven over that bridge hundreds of times and never imagined this amount of life right under it.

"These are your amigos?"

"Friends is maybe too much, but *si*, I know many."

Then, beyond the bridge, I saw something else: the Sepulveda Dam. It has the weight and stature of a giant UFO. I'd seen it before in passing but never from this angle, and never in the context of having to interact with it. Yikes. It's not an ugly structure, at least as far as concrete monstrosities go. It's maybe fifty to one hundred feet tall, made of glistening concrete, spreading out across the floodplain for a half mile or more. It was once used as a massive, futuristic prison in *Escape From New York*.

As we pulled up to the encampment, Iggie got out his bucket of carp and brought it with us—our "ticket" to dinner, he said. Up the bank there seemed to be about twenty more guys who came out of nowhere. They were Hispanic and mostly in their twenties or thirties, it seemed. And guess who was among them? Those two dudes who walked off with my stuff!

"Hey!" I blurted under my breath to Ignazio.

"I know, I know," he says. "Don't point. Ignore. They don't hurt. They just look for stuff—like, how you say ... *el zopilote* ... birds that eat extras."

"What, like a scavenger?"

"Yes. I don't like them, too, but we must mix. Sorry."

I looked at the guys. This wasn't in the plan. I turned to Ignazio: "I feel like I'm the only person invited to a party who didn't get the message that it wasn't a costume party."

"*Por que*, because you the solo Gringo?"

"No. Well, maybe. Yeah."

"*No gusto* being *la minoria*, the minority?"

"So?"

"*Bienvenido a mi mundo*," he said. "Don't worry. You stay close with me."

The guys I met were friendly enough. They slapped each other on the back and smiled as they chatted, trading the day's stories. For a bunch of guys who were practically living on the streets, they had a surprising amount of gold in their mouths. I figured that if they pooled together and sold their fillings, they could buy a nice house in the Palisades.

I could tell from their body language that they didn't exactly like Ignazio bringing me. There were little comments being spoken in hushed Spanish as they passed near us. And then there were the two guys we had met before. They were keeping an eye on me but pretending not to be obvious. You didn't need a PhD in Spanish to tell they were making fun of Ignazio. It started to piss me off. Ignazio grabbed me by the arm and pulled me through the crowd.

Through a few conversations, I pieced together that the two guys at the canoe were named Hector and Jorge. With a better view of them now, I could see that I was only about an inch or so smaller than them. I guessed they were maybe twenty-five-ish. They were pretty dark-skinned, too, like Ignazio, and I wondered if he knew them from back in Guatemala. They each had little knickknack scars—not too much but enough to give them a hardened look (and the tattoos didn't hurt the look either). They weren't really bulked up or anything, but still, I wouldn't want to get into a fight with either one. Like Ignazio said, I tried my best to steer clear, and they didn't seem eager to talk to me anyway.

Taking a stroll, I went down to the river and around to an open area above the bridge, near the roadway. With the lights of passing cars, I caught a glimpse of candles and other stuff together on the ground. I went over and squatted close, the dim candlelight joined by the moonlight. It looked like three makeshift graves. Two sticks tied at its junction formed a cross that was stuck in the ground. There were three of them in a line. There were a few scattered bunches of dried-up flowers shoved into broken beer bottles or strewn about each memorial and a few mementos on each grave, too. Notes written in Spanish had small rocks on top to keep them from blowing away. It reminded me of something out of an old Western. I doubted there were actual bodies there, but it was still creepy. I returned to the gathering beneath the bridge.

So, where was this supposed food that Ignazio was talking about? He'd been so busy talking that he nearly forgot he hadn't eaten. Then he brought me over to where the fire was and where more than a few of them were drinking out of paper bags. You'll never guess what they were eating: fish. And I knew what kind it was, too; definitely *not* salmon or mahi-mahi. No, thanks. I was getting pretty hungry, but I knew I couldn't eat any of it.

One look from Ignazio and I could tell he knew what I was thinking. I could already tell he was a pretty intuitive guy, and he could read me easily. He pulled me aside and I said I was ready to go. He said he understood it was awkward and ushered me back to the fire and pointed me to some rice and beans that were in a big pan. Any other day, I'd pass up plain rice and beans. He grabbed something that resembled an old 49er tin cup and slapped a few big spoonfuls into it; it felt like a scene out of the Depression. I chowed it down real fast but tried to pace myself, like I wasn't so desperately hungry.

After I ate, Ignazio walked me back toward the canoe. The serving I got was good, but it wasn't exactly a buffet. Still, the hunger was under control for now.

He said he was going to stay longer. He pointed me to a barely visible tent across and upriver a bit, telling me I could set up my tent next to his area or use his makeshift tent. Most of these guys, he said, would sleep on rollouts under the bridges; he said he preferred the independence of his own area. Or maybe he wasn't fully welcome there.

So I got in the boat and, standing, paddled slowly to the other side. I felt like that creepy dude of the Underworld—Sharon? Charon?—who led people across the river Styx. With the murky water ahead of me and the flames leaping out of that oil drum behind me and the people partying on and on into the night, it was surreal and otherworldly. This wasn't *me*. I blinked and pinched myself to make sure this was still my life. I probably wasn't more than five miles from home. Oh my God—my dad would go absolutely nuts if he saw me here!

When I got to Ignazio's tent area across the river, I tied the canoe to a branch, got out my flashlight and my tent, and trudged up the slippery bank. It was hard to set up the damn tent in the dark. During the day it would've been a challenge for one person; at night, it was near impossible if you'd never set one up before. But I decided this was one of those nonnegotiable things. Tempted to drop it and hop into Ignazio's tent—which was basically a sheet of plastic tied to trees and bushes, with a sleeping mat underneath it—I decided that wouldn't set the right tone to end the first day of my trip. So I stuck with it; it wasn't perfect, but once it was up it was supersweet to be inside: my little cocoon. I went back out and got my half-wet sleeping bag and most everything else, wondering if Hector and Jorge would try to snatch anything else during the night. I didn't think so, now that we'd faced them again in a different context, but why take the chance.

I was exhausted. Then again, after grappling with the tent, I was also wired. Except for the distant yahoos, it felt real quiet. And though I'd been alone for most of the day, it seemed like this was the first time there was a moment to just think. I'd been in constant action-and-reaction mode.

"Fine," I thought. "I'm in over my head." But I figured that I could still do this thing (blocking out the gash in my leg, the hole in my boat, and—oh yeah—that big, fat rattlesnake).

For kicks, before going to bed, I lit off a few of the fire-crackers I'd brought—to the delight of the guys across the river, who cheered. I watched as the smoke drifted low over the moonlit river. It looked cool, even oddly beautiful.

Back in my tent, I thought about home, both Mom's and Dad's. And I knew that when Ignazio came back and was lying in his own tent, he'd be thinking about his own home, too. I thought about how much I'd been longing for familiar comforts, and I saw how much I'd taken them for granted.

I dozed off ...

Next thing I remember was a hazy image of Ignazio sticking his flashlit head into my tent and offering me another portion of rice and beans. Half awake, I remember mumbling a bit, then sitting up, eating for what felt like ten seconds.

"Gracias, man, thanks a lot, mmm," I think I said before flopping over and passing out again.

And what a deep sweet sleep it was!

Until ...

VI. THE RAID

Somewhere in the wee hours, outside our tents, there was a loud ruckus. I mustered the energy to stick my head out of the flap. Sirens, yelling, English, Spanish, running, megaphones, mayhem, and blaring lights cutting through the darkness. I was fairly certain I was awake, though it seemed so strange to have been a dream.

Ignazio was up, too, already out of his tent. He stood there surveying the scene.

I saw a helicopter overhead, circling, shining its light all around the bridges where those guys were or had been.

"We go, *now!*" said Ignazio.

"What's going on?!"

"ICE!"

"What?"

"I explain later!"

In the bustle of activity, I spied a bunch of white vehicles, like vans and buses and SUVs. I stood there, totally stunned.

"Come on!" he urged. "This is not TV!"

I was already dressed, so I quickly gathered a few valuables I'd put aside before I slept. Then I emerged from the tent and looked back at the bridges. Ignazio handed me a pair of binoculars.

A line of bulky guys dressed in dark blue with printed white writing on their backs were making their way across the bridge to our side of the river, as a bunch of the Hispanic guys ran from beneath the bridge's undersides, up and down the riverbanks, across the bridge, and down the road toward the dam, the woods, or wherever they could find cover. People scrambled in all directions, yelling. There was no way the helicopter spotlight could cover all this chaos.

A couple of guys got chased, put face down, and hand-cuffed. Others were being herded onto buses that had no real windows—at least nothing you could see through. When uniformed dudes started to fan out and search our side of the river, then come in our direction, I snapped out of it and found my legs again.

We ran off in the same basic direction. Before long though, we got separated. I could hear them getting closer, with their flashlights shining toward us, sweeping through the underbrush like hound dogs.

I thought: Why am I running? I haven't done anything wrong. Are these uniformed guys friend or foe? How did it happen that one night I'm sleeping comfortably at home in my bed and the next night I'm tearing through the woods at four a.m.? In the end, I had a hunch it wouldn't be good for me to get rounded up with these other guys. But maybe I should just stop and talk to one of them. But everything was happening so quickly! I didn't know what these guys were capable of, so I didn't want to take a chance on getting shot or stun-gunned or anything close to painful. I hadn't bargained for *that*. It's hard, it turns out, to run and think straight at the same time.

Already winded, I stopped to look around. A couple of the flashlights were closing in. I thought I saw Ignazio in the dark on a path to run into one of the guys with a flashlight. I couldn't let him get caught. I ran to where both he and the other guy were coming together at an intersection. I ducked in the brush and waited. Ignazio flew by me, but I didn't dare speak up—the other guy was like fifteen feet behind him and closing. When that guy came running past me, I just stuck out my foot.

He hit it, went flying, and landed hard. I heard him groaning and cursing. I saw the other lights nearby approaching. I booked it around the guy on the ground and sped off in the direction that Ignazio had run.

After another few minutes of running, I stopped, totally gassed. I would've just given up when I felt a hand on my shoulder and someone pushing me to the ground. I thought I was a goner.

"Hey, wait," I blurted. "I'm—"

"Ssh!" whispered Ignazio.

He pulled a dark cloth over us, and we lay still, trying not to breathe. I heard voices and the crackling of sticks in the woods coming real close, like they might step on us. It was only a matter of time before they discovered us.

But then there was a crackly call on their radio or whatever. Gradually, the footsteps and voices subsided.

Little by little, like a snail testing its surroundings when it comes out of its shell, we emerged. First, we popped our heads out, glad to get some air. Later, we took off the cover entirely (which, I saw from the moonlight, turned out to be only a sheet of plastic).

We started walking again, farther away from the bridges. But we hadn't taken more than ten steps before we heard, "Two over there!" Flashlights beamed back in our direction again.

"Follow me!" said Ignazio.

We ran through the bushes, getting cut up as the large grasses and tree canopies whipped against our faces.

We arrived at a place where I heard trickling water. There was an opening in the woods where a creek flowed down and into the river. The flashlights—maybe four of them—were farther behind but still coming. Ignazio pulled me along, "Almost. Hurry!"

He led me toward a concrete sewer opening near the creek, with a trickle of water coming out of it. The voices were getting louder. I could faintly see the entrance.

"Are you nuts? I'm not going in there!"

"Trust me, *está bien*."

The flashlights weren't more than fifty feet away now.

We hustled into the pipe, about five feet in diameter, and scurried down it. Our hands and feet were on either side of the water that ran through the bottom. We did a quick right turn into a recessed area off the main pipe stem and crouched and waited.

After a short while, the voices were at the pipe entrance. At one point we saw a shaft of light shining straight up the main pipe, but they couldn't see us—only a couple of rats scurrying away from the light, about six feet from where we were. Still, if they'd walked in about twenty feet or so, that would've been the end of us.

Since those guys seemed determined to do a thorough roundup, we were in no hurry to get up and go, so we hunkered down for a longer wait this time.

As we did, Ignazio explained that ICE stood for Immigration and Customs Enforcement. I seemed to recall something on the local news about these guys once raiding a sweatshop in Reseda. But I never thought I'd be on the other end of something like this.

"Um, so, you're an illegal?"

"*Si*, if you say so."

"Yeah, but what do *you* say?"

"*Primera*, I am persona. Aliens, from space. I am undocumented. Yes, and I am a visitor. Okay?"

"Whatever."

"No *whatever*."

"It's all just words, isn't it? Visitor, immigrant, alien, undocumented."

"Maybe it look like just words to you. Maybe this is just a *curiosidad* ..."

"Curiosity?"

"*Si*. But this is *my life*. Words matter. They hurt. It makes a difference to *me*."

"All right, jeez!" I kept digging myself a deeper hole. If it wasn't one thing, it was another—so many politically correct landmines! I kept quiet for a while though, thinking about what he said.

"I tripped that guy, you know. Back there."

"I know."

"That's not good."

"He will be okay."

"He went down hard though."

"These guys are tough. Don't worry."

We were quiet for a while. Then: "Where did you say you go in your boat?"

"I don't think I said. To Long Beach."

"Long Beach?!" he laughed. "A beach? Around *here*?"

"Yeah, a beach, but no. It's far away. Like, fifty miles. At the Pacific Ocean."

"Oh, come on, man!"

"No, for real."

He didn't speak for a while. We listened to the percussive scuffling of rats in the next pipe. "Sorry I get you into this," he offered. "But you do not get caught. You are fast. Nice!" he said, slapping me on the back. "Cold?"

"Yeah. I guess I am." I thought it must be the temperature, but I realized it wasn't even so chilly. I was just plain scared, I had to admit. Maybe even in shock. Why was I putting myself through this? The heat, the cold. How did I imagine any of this would be a good idea? What did it *prove* anyway—that I'm capable of getting in trouble *away* from home, too?

To hell with it. I should just cut my losses and head home—this was *insane*! Adventure was one thing, but I'd clearly crossed a line. I might've hurt someone.

I argued back and forth with myself, thinking of our earlier conversation in the day and how he thought I was totally unprepared for being out on this kind of trip. Finally

I confessed out loud, "You know, maybe you're right: maybe I *don't* have what it takes. Maybe I don't belong, you know, out here."

He mulled this over for a few seconds. "You're throwing the towel?"

"You said it yourself, that I was reckless to even be out here, right?"

"*Si*, but only if you don't know what you doing. Don't worry, you be okay." But I could hear his displeasure, even in the pitch black.

"What's that supposed to mean?"

"*Nada.* You're out of here."

"Hey, you suggested I was too ... too coddled, then you encourage just the opposite. You're making fun of me for wanting to go home?"

"No, no, *amigo*. That's *your* decision. Do what *you* want."

"See? You're angry. That's not helpful. I didn't *do* anything. You're the one who got me into trouble."

"Me?! You were, *como se dice?* Wrong place, wrong time."

More long silence, then ...

"You're right," I said, realizing I had blamed him for what had happened. "I'm sorry—*lo siento. Si?*"

There was a long pause.

"*No es nada.* Don't worry."

Long silence again. Somewhere in the darkness of the sewer system, a creature was running amok, chewing on a bone or something. It sounded bigger than a rat—maybe a possum or raccoon?

I shivered again. Somehow, as if to block out the image (and the prospect that I'd be there all night in this cement hole), I clenched my eyes shut real tight and curled up in a ball, rocking back and forth, trying to think of anything but rats.

My eyelids got super heavy.

Next thing I knew it was barely beginning to get light out. As my eyes adjusted, I saw I was back in my tent. So, everything that happened with the raid was just a bad dream? No way. Beside me was Ignazio, sprawled out, fast asleep. How did he end up in my tent? I sat up and unzipped a tent flap, peeked out.

We were at the opening in the woods near to where that sewer pipe emptied into the river. I crawled out into the predawn light. I stood up beside the tent. Birds were calling out like crazy; I didn't speak the language but liked the sound of it.

I walked down to the river and looked upstream, downstream. Nothing. Nobody. All the trash that came together at this little confluence was surreal: rusty shopping carts embedded like fossils; random flotsam like stuffed animals, dolls, baseballs; and in the branches overhead, white plastic bags blowing in the breeze, stopping at what seemed to be the high-water mark, about fifteen feet up.

I remembered being chased and seeing Ignazio being chased by a guy, by one of the agents. And I pushed him, or tripped him, when they came by—oh my God, I hurt one of them! I did, yes, but to *protect* Ignazio, right? Oh, shit. What have I done? I'm like, that's gotta be against the *law*. Was it also resisting arrest? But I hadn't done anything at that point, I mean, *wrong*. I remember hiding in the cement pipe and being afraid. Oh yeah, *rats*! I did a quick check of my fingers to see if a big ol' rat hadn't chewed off any of them: eight fingers and a couple of thumbs—check.

But the rest was fuzzy.

A faint path ran alongside the river. I needed answers. Being careful to watch the ground for early riser rattlers, I made enough noise to let them know I was coming but not so much as to draw attention from anyone else.

I came to a clearing and saw the two concrete bridges where everything went down. Every now and then I could see a car pass over the bridge, but not many. I was pretty sure there was no one left over there but felt like I should approach with extreme caution anyway.

I found Ignazio's old tent, which was trashed and spread flat across the ground. The canoe was still tied up as I'd left it. I hopped in and paddled down and across to the other bank, to the site beneath the bridge.

As I got close, I could see it was a mess.

I beached the canoe and trudged warily up the riverbank. There were crazy footprints going in every direction—all kinds of different sizes and types of shoes and boots, with markings that showed a history of movement: skid marks, crisscrossing tracks, beer bottles and cigarettes littering the whole area. There were a few used-up flares still sticking out of the mud. I even found one sandal that fit my foot well enough, so I cleaned it off and used it to replace the shoe I'd lost.

All the plastic makeshift structures that had been there were torn down. Suddenly, movement. I ducked down, surprised 'cause I hadn't heard anyone talking. When I popped my head up, I was staring directly at a coyote.

Cool, I thought. It looked like a dog at first. But it had that feral look about it—about *her*, it seemed to me—like an American dingo or something that roamed, uncontrolled.

She'd found leftovers from the night. The oil barrel had been tipped over, and the fire was mostly doused. Black and gray ashes trickled down to the water in tiny black and gray canyons. There were a few stray smoldering embers. The coyote scavenged the food remains, probably some of that fish.

The coyote noticed me. She measured me as a threat. And vice versa. I didn't feel threatened exactly, but it crossed my mind that maybe I *should've* felt more on guard. One on one, I was bigger, but what if she was traveling in a pack? She went about her business but still kept an eye on me.

My curiosity satisfied, I backtracked to the boat. The coyote scurried to the edge of the muddy plateau overlooking the river. She looked sort of skinny yet somehow majestic in the dawn light. Maybe she could be my new spirit animal (coyotes would be *much* cooler than carp). If so, was she protecting me or just tracking her next meal? It'd really suck to get eaten by your special animal.

Paddling away, I sort of nodded at the coyote, like we had an understanding and a connection now. But she stared indifferently back at me before trotting into the brush. Oh well.

The orange dawn sunlight hit the back of the dam, about a half mile downriver. High up in the dam's central watchtower, there seemed to be a single light on. Was somebody up there, looking out, monitoring everything in the sprawling floodplain?

I paddled back upriver, thinking where to go next. Or was I calling it quits? Having gone back and forth on it, I couldn't remember what I'd even decided. Was I packing it up and cutting my losses? *But hell, I'm still only in Encino!* But if it was quits, then how embarrassing would *that* be? I imagined myself sitting across from Ian and Zoe, trying to explain why I quit on Day Two. I tried to imagine the looks on their faces—and I didn't like what I saw: pity, loser, quitter, a fail, big time. I imagined trying to explain to my dad about what happened; that *certainly* wouldn't go over well. Mom would understand, but she'd feel deeply deceived and would remind me of it forever after. Apart from them, would *I* be able to live with my*self*? An old line I'd heard somewhere haunted me: "You won't regret the things you did half as much as you'll regret the things you *didn't* do."

But wait—I snapped out of my obsessing over my situation: This was about more than all that now. That was so petty, really—this wasn't just a choice any more. For all I knew, this place was now considered a crime scene. Would the agents or the police come back later this morning to reassess the site? Was I, were *we, on the run?* Were we *wanted?!* I had to get back to Ignazio. We had to leave immediately— what was I even thinking?! There was no going back *now*, no way! No ifs, ands, or buts.

I paddled hard as ever, trying not to zigzag.

I peeked my head into the tent. He was still asleep. I made noise.

"Dude, wake up!" He groaned. "Hey, c'mon. *Vamanos.* We can't stay here."

Finally he stirred, struggling to unglue his eyes. The guy looked like hell.

"*Que?* Oh, hey," he mumbled, rubbing his eyes and stretching. I watched a couple of egrets perched on the other bank, gazing down into the water, hunting for breakfast. It made me hungry. "What, *esta problema?*"

"Look, I think I messed up. When I tripped or pushed that guy, you know, who was chasing you. I could be in serious trouble with, like, the law. It's maybe a federal crime. I have to keep moving, pushing on. And you *should* join me. I'm asking you, dude: join me."

This seemed to catch him off guard. He started to speak, then stopped. "But you say you are done."

"Well, I can't. I just can't go back. Not now."

"I see," he said, hesitating, thinking. "But I can't just go on a vacation, see? I need work. I send money home. I must. For you, maybe this is fun, but ..."

"It's not *fun!* Okay, I'm serious, I *swear.*"

"Well, iz not really choice for me. That is a luxury I do not have."

"Well," I stammered, my mind calculating, making a plan. "I'll ... I'll *pay* you then."

"What?"

"Yeah, I will. What do you need? What's your, uh, rate or whatever?"

"You can't pay me."

"Why not?"

"You're a kid. And you don't have the money."

"I can get it."

"Really?" he eyed me skeptically. "So you be my employer?"

"Yeah, why not?

"It does not feel right," he hedged. "You, *mi jefe*."

"Hey, money is money. You said that's what *you* needed. Now you're backing out. Where else were you going to work today anyway, huh? You'd rather what, wait out in front of Home Depot all day and hope you get something? This is guaranteed already—and you just woke up. Besides, this will be much more fun than any work you'll ever find."

He was quiet for a while. Then he looked me in the eye, "It would be seventy dollars a day. You can do that?"

I gulped, thinking. "Uh, sure, no problem."

"Where you get the money?"

"That's *my* problem. Are you in or out? I've got to get going. *Please*, I can't do this alone, and I'm not goin' home. I can't."

He stared hard at me.

"Fine," he said, rolling his eyes and crossing himself. "But you're not my boss or anything like that, just because you pay me."

"Fine. I don't wanna boss anyone around anyway."

"So you need a *companero de viaje*," he said, sort of poetically.

"A what?"

"A travel companion. Besides, I need a new place to go. Iz not safe here no more. If I go south, maybe I keep going, and go home, too. *Esto es loco!*"

"Huh? Why?"

"After all this traveling," he admitted, "maybe this whole El Norte trip iz *estúpido*. Like I chase clouds. Maybe, when I say you are not prepared, I mean *me*. But like you, I think I know everything. You say 'no one go on the river.' *Perfecto.* You go south, I go south." He paused, poking a stick firmly in the ground.

He went on, "Back home, we say: Person born a flowerpot never leaves porch. I think I am afraid of being flowerpot. Now I think: Maybe is not so bad. Maybe I run from myself. Maybe I am scared to be a father. I don't know. Maybe, maybe, maybe."

Apart from the new father part, I could relate.

"Deal," he said, extending his hand.

"Deal," I said, shaking it.

We both were a bit stunned for a second. Then he looked up at me, real straight, hopping up to his feet. "Well come on, *amigo*! Like you say, Let's go! *Andale, andele!*"

I smiled for a change. "*Como se dice*: bon voyage?"

"*Buen viaje.*"

"*Buen viaje,*" I repeated. "Sweet. Okay, then let's do this."

VII. POINT OF NO RETURN

We folded up my tent and brought it with us as we retraced my tracks from earlier that morning, then headed back to the bridges as Ignazio filled me in on what happened the previous night.

"Sometime after you sleep," he began, "the helicopter, it disappear, and flashlights and voices, they go away. Then buses go, all cars go. I wrap you in my poncho and drag you out. I lay you on the ground. Then I go back and get your tent. Mine is no good. I set it up, put you in. You don't remember?"

"Very little."

We came upon his mangled tent. Without talking much, we cleaned it up, folded it, and stored it with the rest of the gear in the boat. Across the river, in the tall woods beside the freeway, we could see some smoke faintly billowing up against the blue sky. It looked like a small brush fire.

When it came to getting back in the boat, there was the question of who was going to steer and who was going to be in the front. He wanted to be in the back and said that was only fair, given that he was more experienced.

But despite the little time I had been in that boat, I'd gotten used to steering, whether it was me alone or me and Ian. I'm not saying I was good at it, but yeah, I preferred it. Maybe it was a control thing. Ian never cared one way or the other. Steering had given me a taste of being in command, of being the captain of my own ship, no matter how small that ship was. Now, along comes this guy, playing the seniority card.

"Okay, but what do you know about boats anyway?" I argued.

"Lots. We have many more rivers than you have here. And cleaner. You?"

"Look, it's my boat, so I should get first choice."

"Your boat? ¿De *verdad*? You bought this yourself?"

"Well, okay, so I don't *own* the boat. But that's beside the point."

"Is it? If I am in front, the boat is too heavy there. No good."

"Yeah, but if you're in the back, then it'll be too heavy in back."

There was an awkward silence.

"Fine," I muttered. "You start in back—but only because you're my guest. But we'll trade off, right?"

"Right," he said as he jumped excitedly into the back of the boat.

We started paddling downriver again, along a canopy of cottonwoods, with fluffy, floating seeds that silently snowed down on us.

"Where'd you learn to paddle a boat anyway?" I asked. "You're pretty good."

"You Americans aren't best at *everything*. We had a river where I grow up, the Rio Chixoy. Lots of very, very nice rivers in Guatemala, nicer than this one, for sure. But we make the most of what God give us, eh?"

God again. Jeezus! Whatever.

The nearby fire had picked up its pace. Fire trucks could be here before too long. This time of year, it felt like fires were as common as traffic jams.

As we paddled, I told him about my encounter with the coyote. He told me that in most native cultures, coyotes were clowns and tricksters, but also shape-shifters. He said there was an area called Los Coyotes back in Guatemala, and that native folks rarely killed coyotes around there because of the beliefs, like that they accompanied the first man and first woman into the world. In their story, the coyote brings with it seeds of life to grow and spread around the world. But other tribes, he said, believed coyotes bring death, not in our sense; rather, the death that makes way for new beginnings—more like the seasons giving way to one another. He said coyotes were way-makers—playful, resourceful, and intelligent. I liked the sound of that: *way-makers.* Yeah, I wanted some of that!

But then he got real quiet for a bit.

"What?"

"Well, then again, there are human coyotes, too." He launched into a story about crossing the deserts of northern Mexico, led by a coyote—the guy who gets large sums to take desperate travelers across the border. Often, he said, they don't care for the people they smuggle.

"The guy, he never tell us his real name," Ignazio continued. "He say we call him Johnny. He yell at people and talk to us like we are dogs. Three people die from the heat— 115 degree—and very little water. He just wants money. I start to dig holes to bury the bodies, but he pulls out his gun and won't let me do it. He say it slows us down. They are left to rot in the sun. Hector and Jorge join our group in Mexicali, and *even they* don't like the guy. This coyote, he does not want to be close to us, but he must travel with us. It is business, even if these are people's *lives.* He stays alone. The only good thing is he get us here; some of them disappear, run away with the money."

He spoke about how Hector and Jorge, after entering the U.S., ended up in his smaller group. He told how they'd both caused trouble, stealing stuff and making life tough on the others in the group.

"They think they're the new coyotes. They look up to coyote as the big man. Now that they are here, they think they just push everyone around."

"Then why do you stay with them?"

"We cross together. You never forgot those people. We *had* to get along and watch out for all to survive. We are on the same side. They are up here," he said, pointing to his head. "We have a connection, for good or bad. But still, I look for reasons to go a different way. They probably stay near here. I need to go, too. I think this is the right time to leave them."

"Well then, good riddance, eh?"

"Yeah," he nodded, as the bridges faded behind us. The fire had definitely grown and had quickly moved from the sparse riverside vegetation into the woods, with a lot more, blacker smoke, just as the first fire engines showed up.

As the water got shallower and the air smokier, our boat skidded into sandbars. It wasn't long before we were amazed to be face to face with the dam.

In the center, at the bottom, there are about five square-shaped tunnels (Zoe had noted on the map that they were sluice gates). It's through these holes that water flows when the area above the dam needs to be drained; or if needed, the gates can be closed off to hold back water. Above those gates is a tower that looks like the main operational room where the chief honcho probably sits. For all we knew there was a whole crew up there, like in an air traffic control tower. It had the feel of a fortress, a massive barrier to halt anything besides water that might entertain the foolish notion of going beyond this point of no return. Maybe through the gates there were giant turbines that chewed everything up into tiny pieces and spit them out the other side. We didn't see that in our reconnaissance maps, but that didn't mean they, or another unknown danger, weren't lurking there.

We pulled the boat to the side of the river where there was shade and more places to hide.

"How are we gonna get around or over that?" I said. "If we carry the boat around the ends (if there even *are* ends), then there's probably barbed wire fences or something, and we'd end up coming back here again."

"Maybe, maybe not," Ignazio said calmly, thinking it over. "Why not go—*pfssht*—direct, in?"

"Oh, come on. It can't be that easy. You think they'd allow people to go in there?!"

He shrugged, squinting. "Well, let's see."

I didn't have a better plan, so I went with it.

We stashed the boat in the bushes, climbed up the riverside concrete slope and walked down a maintenance-vehicle path until we hit a small creek flowing into the main river.

We stepped over a few rocks and climbed a dirt hill on the other side. We lay there on our bellies and got a better view of the bottom-center part of the dam.

It was good that we were closer, but we were looking at it from a side angle.

"It looks light," he claimed. "But can't see what is on the other side."

"I can't either. It's got to be a trap. You can't just expect to march through it."

"Why not? You're are a *pesimista*, you know."

"You barely know me."

"Sometimes, when you *don't* know someone, it make it more easy to *see* them."

"That makes no sense. Look, I'm just saying it may seem easy, but ..."

"Excuses. See? You see reasons *porqué* not to do things. You don't think why something *will* work. And that's how you look at everything."

"No, it's called being realistic."

"Pfssht, *derecha!*"

I contemplated his plan. "You're talking frontal assault. Charge right into the fiery gates of Mordor, past 10,000 Orcs?!" He looked confused. "Never mind—I'm only saying, you have a death wish or something?"

"No—not when your reasons are just excuses."

"Yeah, that's easy to say, but they also sometimes keep you alive, too. *Now* who's the reckless one?" I paused and tried to see it from his point of view. "Okay, so if we did go for it, and make it, what if someone sees us, like from the tower, and calls it in to the police, or worse?"

"We say we didn't know it was not okay. So far we do no wrong."

"What about, like, trespassing?"

"No signs. Nothing say 'Keep Out,' *si?*"

I looked out and squinted. "I don't think so, but ..."

"Try these," he said, picking up the binoculars.

I grabbed them and looked.

"Well, I don't see any turbines or anything in those gates," I said. "But I suppose they could shut them at any point and crush us like ants. But no signs posted, I guess. Huh, maybe you're right."

I handed him back the binoculars and he took another look. "So, we good to go, no?"

"Wait," I said. "What if something happens and we have to run, and we get split up? Where's our emergency meeting spot?"

"Back under bridge?" he proposed.

I glanced back and saw that the whole area around the bridges was being taken over by a cloud of gray smoke. "Uh, no. Let's just stick together, no matter what." He nodded. "You ready?" He nodded.

We backtracked to the boat, psyching ourselves up for a run right into the belly of the beast.

So getting through that damn dam would be a straight-ahead charge—out in the open, guns blazing, running the amphibious assault vehicle as fast as possible until you can find something, anything, to use for cover.

Because the water spread out in the area before the dam, the main channel got increasingly shallow. We had to get out and grab the ropes tied to the front and back of the boat, and walk beside it. We kept to the side of the river to be as discreet as possible.

Where another creek came in, there was more water, so that helped. We gave the nod and hopped in the boat, each keeping a leg out so we could push ourselves off the rocks and scurry swiftly toward the target.

With the imposing, colossal wall and its cryptic tower, I half expected machine-gun fire to come screaming out of the few openings that we could see. I imagined enemy aircraft suddenly dropping from the skies, crisscrossing and strafing us mercilessly as we moved closer. But there was none of that.

We got to within a hundred yards of the dam.

Ignazio got edgy. He whispered how it reminded him of approaching the U.S. border. He started talking about it, maybe to calm his own nerves. He recalled how the tension in their ragtag group was ratcheted up by the deaths of his three *compadres* from the crossing and the actions of his coyote.

"As we approach the border, we are like a herd of sheep. We have to believe in our coyote, not because we trust him but because we need him. We take turns watching him, always make sure that when we sleep we have one person awake so he don't run—take our money, leave us out in nowhere, lost. If that happen, we would not know how to move ahead or how to get back where we come from. We would die. I imagine the border to be a big wall with barbed wire on top, armed men patrol, round people up, ship them back home. In the end, it wasn't like that. Suddenly, coyote announces: 'Here we are, welcome to America.' At first, we think he tries to fool us. After the distance we come, how could *this* be the big border? In the end, there was no real border. Nothing unusual. More like an imaginary line."

We got to within seventy-five yards of the dam.

I thought of the barriers that I'd dealt with so far: the stuff with Ian and my folks, making preparations, getting on the river, the ledges, the heat, the hunger, rattlesnakes, raids—it seemed a small miracle to me to get this far. I had to smile as I realized I was doing what I'd set out to do: have an adventure, test myself, shake things up, start to make my own choices. It wasn't like I suddenly had the answers, but there was a feeling of being connected to something larger than myself. It didn't seem important whether I could say what it was exactly. But I felt it. And it felt good, felt right. I had to admit I was thirsty for all this. *Just keep going and don't give up* seemed half the battle, I thought.

We got to within fifty yards of the dam.

Ignazio said he was thinking about his wife and kid again. He told me that when his wife was pregnant and fearful of giving birth, he reminded her of the story of Jonah and the Whale, from the Bible. He got her to imagine their child being like Jonah, who found the way out, and that their unborn child had that same wisdom and would find the way. He told her that at times like those, you needed faith to see you through, and that you needed to reach deep inside yourself to find it, surrender to it, and let it guide you. He said that helped her find peace and inner strength, despite her fears (and his comparison of her to the whale). He said that was what it was like to find God—the surrender that happens when you get swallowed by the whale. He said getting to the U.S. required that same faith, like the Israelites wandering in the desert. The same for finding a new home in America. And he told me he had faith that, on the other side of the dam, were opportunities for both of us that we didn't know existed.

Now, I liked the idea, but I couldn't say that I shared his faith. I'd just call that wishful thinking. This guy's whole faith thing was foreign to me, like something out of another time and place.

We got to within twenty-five yards of the dam.

I thought back to my home, too. I had the feeling that I was either running *to* something or running *from* something. I saw how my life so far had been about resistance, creating big dramas, constantly feeding that little voice inside me, that person who liked to go against things, mostly for the sake of having something to press against. I realized how much time and energy I devoted to all those battles. I got tired thinking of the ways I kept that up. Parents and teachers paled in comparison to this figure, this thing, this constant voice, this alien *in me* who dictated every thought and action, even put me down all the time! If the trip ended now, and I took nothing else back with me, it would be that I had to corner this dude, set new ground rules, and start getting some control over him.

Finally, we arrived at the dam. So far, nobody else showed up.

The water narrowed and got a bit deeper as it funneled through the sluice gates, giving us enough volume to float the boat through. Each of the gates was maybe thirty feet long, ten feet high, and five feet wide. It was darker in the sluices themselves, which made the other side appear brighter; we couldn't see fully through yet. It felt like what you always hear about heading for the light at the end of the tunnel.

As we caught the current, it took hold of us and turned us backward, channeling us through one of the gates.

Once inside and floating through, we looked up and admired the bird nests along the top corners of the sluices. At first we thought they were bat nests, but then we saw birds—swallows, I think—flitting and soaring around. They seemed surprised by our presence (they don't seem to get many visitors). It was amazing to see how, even in a place that you'd never imagine life could exist, there it was, doing fine, even thriving.

Vague shapes began to emerge on the other side of the dam. The police—waiting for us in their squad cars? More of ICE—with their white van, preparing to take us away? The Wicked Witch herself, descended from the tower, surrounded by her monkey minions of doom?

We squinted hard to see what was in store for us.

I looked back one last time to see the riverside woods now engulfed by twenty-foot flames, whipping around in circles like whirling dervishes. The smoke both drew attention to this whole area, but it also cloaked us in cover, enabling us to slip away, unnoticed, amid millions of people.

Section 3

You can read a river up to a point, but there are deeper, darker undercurrents you can't fathom.

— Sam Hawkins, February 1, 2016

i. CONCRETE CANYON

It's not that we were disappointed exactly. But the drama we'd created around the dam didn't pan out. Which was good. After the sluice of darkness, when our eyes adjusted, we saw that there were no standing armies, no archenemies waiting for us. No authorities at all. Rather, a bland, square, sun-bleached concrete canyon extended into the distance, with a slim sheet of gently meandering shallow water draped across a flat, concrete bottom.

Vertical walls now stood like sentries, to the left and right, about twenty-five-feet high and fifty feet apart, topped off with fencing and barbed wire and with a walking path just on the other side of it.

The water was shallow enough that we had to get out and walk beside the boat. As we sloshed through the water, I looked over at Ignazio to gauge his mood. He was actually smiling despite this less-than-glamorous trek down the river. But he seemed to take it in stride.

He just looked back at me, winked, and assured me, "*Poco a poco*: Long Beach."

We glanced back at the tower atop the dam that was starting to fade into the distance—still amazed that still no one seemed to be up there. This whole giant structure and no one home?

Whatever. We put it behind us.

Up ahead we could see that the water shifted to the left side of the river, and farther downriver we could see it meander back to the right again. We looked at each other, not entirely sure what to do. We had no idea how long this stretch might go, but it seemed foolish to keep walking if we could find a better way to get through it. We figured the bottom wasn't built to be exactly flat, but we didn't know quite why. It had the effect of creating more depth on one side and then the other side, so we could at least get in the boat and float.

But it was tricky. We had to anticipate the shifting bottom and water depth, then steer the boat away from the shallows. Scraping our way from time to time, it was a lot of trial and error.

We traded off so that I was in the back. As we went along, we developed a system where Ignazio would call out: "Shallow right!" or "Shallow left!" and I'd then steer us over to the deeper parts. Sometimes he'd stick his paddle down into the water and measure the depth with the flat part of the paddle, calling out the blade height: "*cuarto paleta,*" "*medio paleta,*" or "*complete paleta.*"

Once we started to be able to read the water better, we didn't have to think as much about how to navigate, and we started looking around and relaxing more. Ignazio's shouting gave way to simple pointing and gesturing. At least as far as navigating went, our minds were starting to think as one, and that was sort of cool—almost like we knew what we were doing, or at least we began to feel in sync.

Despite the gazillion tons of concrete, it still felt and acted like a river—albeit an unusual one. It felt like the open road, or maybe more like a wet highway cutting through urban terrain.

At one point, Ignazio, with his gaze fixed down into the river and scanning for shallows, spotted something moving. We dangled our feet over the side of the boat and pressed down until the boat slowly stopped. We walked back, criss-crossing until we found what he spotted: a fish. But it wasn't just any type of fish. It was exotic looking—like someone had scooped it out of their tropical Amazon fish aquarium. It had dramatic black and greenish stripes across it and freakish fins that jutted out from the back, which spread out like a sail. I'd never seen anything like it. It was smaller than the carp, but much more mysterious. Here, in this most unlikely of places, was such a weird thing, far from home, just tossed in here and expected to survive. I couldn't imagine what it ate, but there was something here that it must've liked or was suited for. All we could do was scratch our heads and marvel at how it got here—then again, anyone who saw me and Ignazio out there would've been wondering the same thing.

Eventually, we got back in the boat and kept on going, down the winding river. We had barely seen any other people. Every now and then on either side, though, you could make out the heads of walkers, joggers, or bicyclists going parallel to us, beyond a hedge or in between scattered trees. But now, up ahead, was a footbridge where it looked like someone was walking a couple of dogs across.

As we approached, we could see it was a lady with two golden retrievers. She was surprised. And when her dogs took off after a squirrel, her shoulder nearly got separated. The dogs forced her to move on, but she kept stealing a few last looks at us while she tried to figure out what we were up to as she got yanked away.

Another hundred yards brought us to a second overpass, with cars stuck in traffic on the bridge. As we approached, we could see the drivers doing double takes at us when they glanced in our direction, waiting for the light to change. A few passengers rolled down their windows, stuck out their heads, and craned their necks. I could swear a couple of them were honking for us (but it might've just been cars honking at other cars ahead of them). Dream on.

We passed under that bridge, too, and kept on going. After another few football field lengths of floating, we got a better view of the bike paths alongside the river. Up ahead, a group of kids were there at the sides, leaning over the fence, waving at us, shouting excitedly.

"What are you doing?" shouted one of them.

I thought a bit, then shouted back: "Just hanging out."

"But where are you *going*?" another said.

"We go to Long Beach!!" Ignazio declared proudly.

For some reason, that cracked them up.

"Yeah, well good luck with *that!*" said one of the older ones.

We didn't know if they were mocking us or what. Anyway, they chased us for a while, giggling and carrying on, before giving up. They whistled after us and waved goodbye.

We agreed that it sort of felt like a parade, with us being the entertainment—a weird Rose Bowl float, plodding along with spectators alongside the route. Ignazio said he liked that idea 'cause it made him feel welcomed, which was something he hadn't experienced much since he'd been in the States.

We cruised farther, talking about how, if we kept up this steady, leisurely pace, we might actually get to Long Beach by evening.

Everything seemed fine until, in the distance, we saw a maintenance crew beside a dump truck, right there inside the flat riverbed, with the few inches of water flowing right past their wheels. As we coasted up to and were nearly beside them, the guys elbowed each other and pointed at us, thinking that it was pretty amusing. They were a mostly Hispanic crew, so Ignazio exchanged a few back-and-forths with them in Spanish.

But there was one other guy—a white guy in the truck, with the air-conditioning probably blasting, talking on his cell phone. I figured he was the supervisor. By the time he'd noticed us, we were beginning to pass their group. He hopped out of the truck and followed after us, trying to flag us down. He said something into his phone, then put it in his pocket so he could lecture us.

"Hey! You're not supposed to be in here. What are you *doing!?*"

I told Ignazio to speak to him in Spanish, because I didn't want to talk with him. I shrugged and pretended like I didn't understand, trying to look like a dimwitted simpleton (which wasn't much of a stretch).

"You two! Stop! Hey, I said *stop!!*"

This time I gestured like I couldn't hear him. He was madly dialing his phone, looking all perturbed and red-faced. He slipped and fell on his ass. As we picked up the pace, we could hear him shouting:

"Yeah, a couple of kids in a canoe, in trouble, going down the channel. We're at Moorpark and ..."

We put our backs into it, without trying to look like we were escaping, going as fast as we could.

So there we were, drifting along. We'd dodged our first bullet in this stretch, and since we'd been working pretty hard up to that point, we decided we had some time to chew the fat and catch up a bit. We eased up a little.

"Ignazio, say, d'you mind if I call you, uh, Iggie?"

"Why?"

"I dunno, it just came to me. I mean, if I need to get your attention, it'd be good to have something shorter. Four syllables is a lot."

"Syllables?"

"Oh. Ig-na-zi-o."

He pondered this for a second. "Iz too much for you? I can call you Fred?"

"No. You can't call me that unless it's connected to my name, see? That's how nicknames work."

"Well, like what, for you?"

"Oh, I don't know. It has to be like, Sammy, or Slammy, or Slam, or maybe a straightforward Wham-Bam-Thank-You-Sam. I don't know, anything catchy."

"Catchy?"

"Never mind."

"I wonder," he said, switching the subject. "If I get work on a crew like back there."

"You'd *want* that?"

"Sure. Why not?"

"Because it's lousy work, just picking up other people's stuff."

"I don't care. Hey, it is work. Better than no work."

"Yeah, but you can do better. Besides you're getting paid to do *this*."

"I believe that when I see *dinero*, in hand." He thought, trying to make sense of this. "I don't care about better. Not now. After. How much you think it pay?"

"It looks legit and all, so probably minimum wage. About seven or eight bucks an hour."

He looked confused. "Buck?" Then he remembered: "Ah, *dinero, dolár*."

"Yeah, something like that."

"I take that! Niiice. Let me see, one day, maybe $60," he said. "That's what I get in a week—a *good* week—back home."

"But what do you really wanna do?"

"I don't know. Does it matter? I make money for family. I do not care how. Coyotes collect from me and my family."

Now it was time for *me* to pause and look confused. "I see. So ...?"

"Sure. What's wrong?"

"Well, nothing. But, I mean, you come to this country, you can be anything you want. That's the whole point, you can dream big, right? You could, I don't know, start a business or something?"

"Me? Come on, Schlammy Boy?" he said with a wink.

"See? There you go. That sounded all right. So, anyway …"

There was a sound. A motor. Iggie looked at me and I could see he heard it, too. We both looked around. There was something coming closer, but we couldn't see it. The sound seemed like it was coming from all over, like a disembodied voice, but it was strangely mechanical. A drill, or a giant lawnmower, or maybe a leaf blower or what *was* it!?

Then I saw it. It came low over the tree line, moving steadily up the river.

"Quick!" I looked around frantically. "Come on!"

He had a fearful look in his eyes, 'cause he knew something was going on, but he still didn't see what I saw.

"Look!" I pointed at a helicopter heading our way.

We were stuck out in the middle of a long, straight stretch. There was nowhere to hide. Up ahead, another few hundred yards, we could see the next bridge crossing the river. And behind us, the nearest one was a hundred or so yards away, but we'd have to go against the current to reach it. We were trapped, literally boxed into this concrete canyon.

We both winced and froze as it flew over, as if that would somehow make us so small and unobtrusive that we wouldn't be seen. When the sound started to subside, we opened our eyes and could see the helicopter moving beyond us. We breathed a sigh of relief.

Until …

It began to veer to the right and started circling back around. It was close enough that I could see two guys up in the cockpit.

Without saying a word, we both bolted out of the boat. "Over this way!" I shouted. We started pulling the canoe over to the side where the chopper was coming from. If we could only get over to the vertical wall, it would barely shield us from the chopper's view.

When we got there, we braced against the wall.

The helicopter swooped right back over and kept circling when it didn't find the spot it expected to find us at. But pretty soon it would be on the other side of the river again and would get a clear view of us. Fortunately, there was a higher line of trees on the opposite side, and for a few critical seconds the chopper was out of sight.

Then I saw our chance. Downstream, about thirty yards on the opposite side was an indentation in the wall, a shadowy little rectangular nook where water flowed out into the river from a pipe we couldn't yet see. If we could only get over there.

Iggie saw it, too. With the chopper nearly over the tree line, we scrambled across the river without a second to spare. Hell, they might've seen us this time. We couldn't be sure.

We booked along the wall, and as I looked back to see the chopper starting its turn, we arrived at the indentation, which acted like a small concrete cave. We pulled the boat into it, backing it up into the shadows as much as possible, then stayed still as we watched the chopper fly back and forth along the opposite side. If we hadn't found this spot, that would've been the end for us. These guys were close enough that we could read LAPD on the side of the chopper.

ICE. LAPD. They were likely sharing info and acting jointly, I bet. Didn't they have better things to do than chase a couple of kids?

It flew by again. Still, we didn't dare move, at least not until it passed us for good. We stuck our heads out to assess the situation. We could hear the chopper circling around again, spiraling a bit higher now. It came over the river again, then made another turn. It came through one more time before it made a big sweeping turn and kept on going upriver.

"Phew! That was close, eh?" It got my adrenaline going, big time.

But one look at Iggie and I saw it actually made him nauseous. He looked like he'd seen a ghost. He was crossing himself and muttering a prayer. It struck me how he must've felt. Worse-case scenario for me: If I got caught, I'd end up back at home with maybe a fine (for my parents) and a slap on the wrist or elsewhere if my dad found out (for me). Possible, but unlikely: They'd connect me as the one who tripped that agent—but it was increasingly unlikely they could prove that, the more time and distance that passed. My folks would go nuts and I'd be grounded, but then life would go back to normal. Worse-case scenario for him: the beginning of a whole long degrading deportation. So much for finding his family a home or sending them much-needed money. He'd have to face the coyote without prospects for paying off his debt back home. So much for dreams. So much for his family's future plan.

"Nice work, Iggie," I eked out, my voice echoing off the concrete chamber and disappearing down the long tunnel to nowhere. "It'll be okay."

He nodded and looked back at me, sweat dripping down his forehead. "I thought you say there are no people on the river."

"Okay, well, maybe a *few*."

After fifteen minutes or so we craned our necks again and peered around.

The coast was clear. We brought the boat out and crept back in it and skirted along the side of the river, no longer waving at every person we met. We knew we had to be more cautious, more invisible. We understood that we might not be as lucky to find a hiding place like this if we needed one again.

ii. THE NARROW CHANNEL

We pondered how long we'd be stuck in the boxy canyon. The exhilaration of being on the open road—albeit a watery one—was replaced with a creeping sense of claustrophobia.

For starters, neither of us had much food. And after being chased this way and that, we sucked down the last traces of liquid in our water bottles. I joked with Iggie about how ironic it'd be if he'd survived nearly impenetrable deserts to come north only to die from lack of water on the L.A. River. Again, he didn't think it was so funny—maybe 'cause he'd known people who'd actually *died* in the desert. Duh.

As far as we could tell, the only way out of the canyon was by the few maintenance access roads that ran down into the river, but those routes were always closed off with big ol' padlocks on their gates. Apart from that, there were vertical steel rungs here and there that went up the sides to the fencing at the top.

We discussed one or the other of us going up and out, over the barbed wire, to resupply with food or drinks, but we figured it would draw too much attention. No, we were better off as aquatic lowriders, cruising through this interminable watery maze until we could find a normal way out. The more distance we put between us and the Sepulveda Basin, the less we'd be connected to that whole unfortunate incident the previous night. I knew from the maps I'd seen that it didn't go on like this too much longer but couldn't remember exactly how it went. And the maps I'd brought along were mostly drenched, making them virtually unreadable.

And then, as we were starting to feel a bit lightheaded and hungry and nagging at each other like a married couple, we saw something up ahead that drew us in. The water in the river started to narrow to a central channel that, as we approached, looked like it dropped off into nothingness. For all we knew, it was a waterfall.

Fifty feet of water across had become thirty feet, then twenty-five, then twenty.

The water funneled down and over an edge in the concrete and into some sort of horizontal monolith. We went from the problem of how to navigate back and forth in the shifting, deeper flow to how to stop in time to prevent our getting sucked into this thing.

Fifteen feet wide turned into ten feet.

We backpaddled as fast as we could, but we kept moving toward it. Without saying a word, we both started to lift a foot out of the boat, ready to jump ship and scamper away if necessary.

But as we approached, the boat gently skidded to a stop.

We got out, relieved that imminent disaster had been avoided. We pulled the boat over to a dry section and went to see what this was about.

It was a transition point where, for whatever engineering purpose, the water dropped into a narrow channel, then picked up speed as the funneled water disappeared in a dark line into the distance. This was the kind of thing you'd see if you glanced out your window driving over the river along the 101—the main freeway that cuts through the San Fernando Valley.

We didn't know what our strategy should be. We carried the boat about thirty feet past the cascading water and put it back down on the concrete. When we looked back at the cascade of water, we saw it wasn't the waterfall we'd imagined it was—enough to tip the boat forward into the channel but not enough to be dangerous.

We shrugged and went back to the boat. We placed it in the water where the current was moving swiftly but steadily. I held on to the boat while Ignazio got in; when he was set, I got in and the water started to move us along.

The water carried us without our having to paddle much at all. It was kinda cool. There was no more of the side-to-side thing. At the most, the paddling was only to steer a bit here and there, mainly to keep the boat from banging on the sides of the narrow concrete channel—sort of like a bobsled run. It widened out a tad more so that it was about six feet side to side—just enough to be able to paddle on both sides of the boat. And the water was deeper now, too. Iggie stuck his paddle in the water and shot back a wide smile and a measurement: "*complete paleta!*"

We were stoked. We must've been going at a pace of about eight to ten miles an hour. If things kept up at this rate, we could do easy distance, no sweat. We were ear to ear with grins. In addition to the free ride, it was a lot more private, too—instead of residential areas, these were the backs of industrial spaces, maybe movie studio lots, judging by the equipment. And the sides of the sunken channel hid us slightly, too.

Every now and then, we might see a guy working a forklift, fixing a mechanical thing, or spraying something down with a garden hose.

All was going smoothly, until ...

Iggie began pointing frantically to a bunch of frothy water up ahead.

We reached out beside us and put our hands on the concrete, feeling for a grip on something that would slow us down. There was nothing but flat concrete to slide our hands on. As we got closer to the frothy water, we stuck our paddles out and pressed them against the sides of the channel, hoping to at least slow ourselves down enough to bail and jump out. But we couldn't do it.

We looked on helplessly as we were forced toward a frothy bunch of fast-moving water. It was horrible feeling so helpless. We got as low in the boat as we could, to be less tippy, and braced ourselves.

Water suddenly came shooting into the channel from yet another channel, creating a bunch of waves that would likely tip us.

When the front of the left side of the boat hit the wave, the boat wanted to tip in the direction of the oncoming water. "Lean *away!*" I shouted, and Iggie shot a look back at me and saw me twisting my upper body as far as I could to the right. He added his weight in the nick of time—but then the boat was weighted too much to the right and we almost overcompensated ourselves right into the water. If it hadn't been for Iggie's hand finding the edge of the concrete for a split second, we would've gone over. Instead, our front and back ricocheted off each side like a bobsled and jarred us real good.

But by then we were riding over these waves—up, down, up, down—until it spit us out into the calmer (but now faster) water. We yelped at the exhilaration and the sudden safety of getting through it.

I chose this moment to ask him if he could swim. Up to this point it hadn't been an issue because the water itself wasn't swift enough to cause much trouble. But getting by in something like *this*, it couldn't hurt to know how to swim; in fact, it could be deadly if you *didn't* know.

"No. Sorry," he replied.

"For real?! You're kidding, right?"

"I wish," he said, crossing himself. "*Dios mío!*"

"Damn, dude. Why didn't you tell me?"

"I do not think to run into stuff like this. I think we are lucky to find *any* water, especially in summer. Why do you not tell me iz like this?"

"Well, hell, I didn't know this was here either! It's not like there are signs or anything."

"But you say you have maps."

"Yeah, well, I guess they're neither dry enough nor detailed enough. Gimme a break, there's only so much you can see from space!"

He looked as worried as I felt. Finally, something we could both agree on!

We stowed away our anxieties for the time being, kicking back and letting the lazy river carry us, each of us flailing in the turbulence of our own thoughts and insecurities.

For lack of anything better to do, we mucked around and razzed each other every chance we got.

Nothing was sacred. When I poked at him about being so pious and holier than thou, he'd razz me back about being faithless and without a compass to guide me. When I put my devil's advocate hat on and called on him to justify coming to the country illegally, he'd get me back with how we illegally came to the New World and stole it from the Indians, then the Spanish. When I needled him about leaving his wife and kid back home, he'd counter with me deceiving my parents with lies. I hated the way he argued—it was too freakin' rational and balanced!

Then again, maybe it was the tension of nearly getting caught, or blindsided, or maimed along the way, and we both had a lot to vent about. Maybe it was the sun, beating down on us, cooking our brains, playing tricks on our minds— it didn't matter if I wore my hat or not or if I slapped on sunscreen; the sun or the heat always found a way to get in there. Maybe there was a full moon pulling on us from somewhere out in space, making us both salty as hell behind all the pleasantries of that deceptive blue sky. Maybe one of those freakish Santa Ana devil winds was starting to blow and getting into our heads, making us demented.

It felt like with everything I tried to say, he just kept throwing shade on me—but not the kind I really needed. The really annoying kind. It went something like:

"Don't forget that *you* agreed to join *me* on this," I'd say. "So stop complaining about the lack of planning. I did the legwork, practically googled my fingers to the bone."

"And you think iz easy to cross deserts," he'd say, "then to get in trouble or sent back because *you* do not do your homework? That's so typical."

"Typical?! Of what?"

"How you assume things. How you can be *so* casual, *so* comfortable, because you can *afford* to la-la-la and be that way. But me ..."

"Yeah, meanwhile, *you're* the only one working hard. I guess *we're* just lazy, self-centered, and spoiled."

"Hey, you say it, I don't."

"Yeah, well people say you're lazy by leeching off *us*, like a parasite, when you should create your *own* jobs instead of taking other people's jobs. Maybe look at what could be done back home first instead of running away just to avoid facing your problems. I mean, that's pretty lazy, self-centered, and spoiled, too, you know!"

"You think we come here if not desperate?! You just do not get ... how *could* you know what it is like to have these gangs control everything, *todo*, and have to pay them—and pay and pay—just because. Not to kill you, or someone you love, or ..."

"Hey, we have gangs here, too. That's not a reason to just come into another country."

"Iz different. The police, government, they do not help. They make worse. Everyone pays. You cannot imagine how corrupt it is, what it is like, every day, to live with helplessness, everything out of control."

We both thought we knew a lot more than the other guy—so again, we at least agreed on *one* thing.

But what we didn't know was that around the next bend there was an overpass. And coming down from the overpass was a piling. And the piling was planted smack in the middle of the narrow channel. And the middle of the channel suddenly splits in two around it, creating a situation where, if you don't hit it perfectly and you get turned one little bit at the wrong angle, it can seriously mess you up.

Which is, of course, what happened.

I remember seeing Ignazio's mouth open wide for his next argument, then I saw the piling come into focus beyond him.

I pointed, weakly. He turned. He freaked out.

We had no more than about ten seconds this time to prepare. It wasn't anywhere near enough. The piling was like a huge junk magnet, with the force of the water drawing everything to it, which rapidly included us.

We tried to backpaddle. All in vain. I tried to steer us to the side channel to the left, and we almost made it. But the junk against the piling made a gnarly boil of water that pushed up from below, and when the front of the boat hit that, it turned us to the side so that we went smashing into the wall of the channel, the left side of the boat tipping upstream, and we went over quicker than I could yell, "Help!"

Everything became a blur underwater. The only thing that was clear to me was that I was definitely in the water. Opening my eyes, it was dark, and I felt the force of the water washing over me, moving me around like a plastic bag. I didn't know which way was up. I was scared but also surprised I had time to think actual thoughts. I flashed the image of when Ian and I sank the boat up in the basin. These weren't long thoughts, just passing blips sort of out of time altogether. Was my short life passing before me?

I needed to do something. *My leg was caught somehow, and I couldn't move it.* I tried to sit up against the force of the water, to deal with what was going on with my leg, but it was too powerful. Instead, I reached out beside me and found a large stick to grab hold of. I was cold and felt my strength leaving me. But then my fear of dying right then and there shot me full of adrenaline, enabling me to pull myself up, little by little. I could feel my fingers, hands, and arms coming out of the water and, finally, my head.

I gasped for air, looking around wildly, like a panicky horse caught in a flood. Then I started pulling again, up the flotsam on the piling, but my leg was still awkwardly pinned by the canoe, which was partially submerged. I could only pull up so far—and I didn't know how long I could hold on.

Up to that point it was like the audio track had been turned off. But little by little I became aware that Ignazio was yelling at me. He had somehow managed to drag or pull himself out of the water and up onto the concrete. He was trying to work the canoe loose by kicking the end that was sticking up. Even in my compromised position, I could see it was pointless. Then I saw him take a few steps back, run forward, and leap onto the top of the flotsam above me on the piling.

He dropped himself down, looking frazzled, and followed my leg down toward where it met with the canoe. I could feel my stomach muscles giving up as I started to slide down into the water again. I knew from the look on his face that he saw this, too. He knew he didn't have much time left. He couldn't both prop me up and free my leg at the same time.

He looked at me, trying to reassure me, but I could see through him—it was hard to tell who was more scared. Then he took a big breath and went down into the murky water. I could feel him pull himself along my leg, moving downward, feeling around the foot, assessing the problem. Then he started yanking on my foot, twisting it back and forth. The foot was mostly numb, but I kept feeling a sharp pain.

After about thirty seconds, he surfaced again.

"Turn to the side! When I hold the foot, let go, turn *that* way, yes? I think I can get it!"

"Don't go back under! You can't swim!" I said. "There's gotta be another way. Are you crazy?!"

"I don't need to swim, just hold on. Trust me!"

Trust me. This was one argument I knew he'd win. Trust—again, not my strong suit. But I wasn't exactly in a great bargaining position. I looked into his eyes like I hadn't done with anyone, including my folks, probably since I was a baby. Totally dependent on this person to survive, I nodded to him. My heart was pumping in my ears. I gathered a big breath of air, let go of the flotsam and sank back into the water.

It went dark again.

I could feel him climbing down my leg and working the foot while I did what he said: With my last strength I turned so that the water was pummeling my back. I wriggled my foot, though I could barely feel my leg now, let alone do what he told me to do.

After a dull pain, miraculously ...

There was the sensation of floating. It was like those reports from surfers who have an encounter with a shark, and they recall not feeling the shark biting off their leg, only an odd feeling below, then being released from its grip.

I bobbed to the surface, gasping for air, and saw that I was indeed moving along in the water. I looked back upriver to see Ignazio, downstream from the trapped boat, still holding to the piling, smiling, giving me a thumbs-up.

As I floated along, I was surprised that I could now touch bottom. It was real slippery though. There was still nothing to hold onto. I could sort of push off the bottom with my good leg and scoot over to the side of the narrow channel and reach out with my arms and slide them along the concrete, getting them scraped up as I did this. Combined with pressing downward, I was able to slowly skid to an awkward stop, more or less. Too tired to pull myself completely out, I could at least keep myself from being washed farther downstream.

I put my head down on the warm concrete and rested—a cold, wet piece of pulverized meat. I saw that a few of the firecrackers we'd brought had somehow made it up and onto the concrete; I could faintly smell the wet sulfur. They were drying, too. I closed my eyes.

Next thing I knew, Ignazio was tugging on me from the back of my shirt. Then he grabbed at my belt and hoisted me up like I was a drenched sleeping bag. It wasn't pretty, but he managed to do it. Again, I lay there, sprawled out, thankful for the heat of the sun on my shivering, cut-up body.

After the incident with the piling, and all our prior nagging, we didn't have much use for words. Ignazio wandered around in a daze and I limped pretty badly, both of us trying to gather our belongings, most having washed downstream.

Bit by bit, we dried off. In the open air it didn't take long.

The boat itself was more problematic. Water is freakin' heavy; and *moving* water is worse.

That canoe was totally wedged. The only way it was coming out was if we could use the force of the water against itself. I had an idea. I undid my rope belt and tied a loop around the part of the boat that was sticking up. Then we grabbed the line and pulled the boat toward the side of the river, allowing the water to catch more of the rest of the boat. It worked. Boom! Like it was hit by a cannonball, the lower end of the boat lurched forward with the help of a ton of water. The canoe uttered a primal groan along with my own painful yelp, then scraped painfully along the concrete and finally shot out the other side. The sudden shifting and change in water pressure had pushed the boat up so that more of it crested the edge of the narrow channel. Only then were we able to bail out more water, turn the canoe over, and empty the water out of it.

After that, with the boat high and dry, I retrieved my rope and redid it as a belt again.

We truly needed a siesta. We dragged ourselves under the overturned canoe, enjoying the shade until we both fell fast asleep.

X

Eventually, our stomachs woke us up and urged us onward. Plus, sleeping or not, we couldn't stay out in that exposed hot area for very long. Again, no need for words. We put what we had back in the boat. We readied our paddles and prepped the lines on either end of the boat. We gingerly placed the boat in the water and held it snug against the concrete. I got in first, in front. My leg still hurt, but was slightly better with the rest. When I was set, I nodded and Iggie got in. We let go of the side and started moving with the current.

This time around, we spent less time goofing and debating stuff and more time scanning the water's horizon far ahead, being diligent, looking for any kind of unexpected obstacles so that we didn't have to go through another ordeal like the one we just dealt with. I knew cats had nine lives, but I wasn't sure how many lives teens were entitled to.

Thankful that we'd dodged another disaster, we spent a good while cruising down this lazy river stretch, gathering our strength again. At one point we passed by some real beautiful hanging gardens—with red and white flowers trailing down the walls like a long curtain down the vertical sides. The scenery changed, slowly but steadily. There was nothing as challenging in this section compared to what we'd gone through, and so we cruised down the narrow channel and sometimes scooted down a few small drops of a couple feet or so, but those were pretty manageable and even fun. And sometimes we ran into a wash coming in from the left, from where the mountains drain, but we knew what to look out for now—leaning away from the incoming water in order to maneuver through them better.

We started talking again, lightly at first. We progressed from pointing and grunts to phrases and from phrases to actual sentences and so on to a fairly normal conversation again. It was as if we had to relearn how to talk to each other, but it was much more calm and respectful now.

I guessed there's nothing quite like a hairy situation and a brush with death to humble and bond two people and get their priorities straight. And if I was honest, I had to admit that he was rubbing off on me. I also felt a lot more aware of all the stuff he had to deal with—why he came north and what things were like from his perspective. It wasn't as black and white as I had wanted to believe.

Eventually, that stretch ended in a whisper as the narrow channel terminated at one of those horizontal aquatic monoliths again, but this time it spilled out onto a flat, wide concrete expanse—even wider than before. We saw some of our gear that had floated down and collected at this end of the line. We gathered it up: the fishing rod (tangled in a float cushion), the old military canteen, a few plastic bottles of nearly empty Gatorade, the plastic compass, and one last dry plastic bag of firecrackers.

Here the river widened, double or triple the width of how it was after we first shot through the dam—now it was about fifty yards wide, all flat concrete on the bottom, though the sides turned into the angled concrete inclines that we saw just before the dam. It wasn't going to be possible to stay in the boat and expect to move at all. It was maybe only three or four inches deep. We needed a couple more inches to make a go of it. We looked up at the sunny SoCal sky and there wasn't a chance of rainy help from above.

So we got out and started sloshing through the water, walking beside the quietly floating boat through these shallows, amid the yipping and yapping of a bunch of those black-and-white birds with pointy beaks and red, stilted legs.

iii. STENGEL & CO.

We trudged along like that for maybe a mile or two, me hobbling along like Quasimodo with my bum leg before looking at each other and having the same thought: If this is all there is, we're outta there—too much of a slog to be worth the effort. We would've consulted our river maps at that point had they not been consumed by the river itself.

Then, far up ahead, as if seeing a mirage, we saw a large bridge with a shady underpass. It sort of wavered in the distance, like in those Western movies when the parched cowboy sees the hazy oasis. We could swear that we saw a flashing silvery thing under its dark cover, like a fish flitting around.

Real or imagined, it put some life into our tired steps. Gradually we got closer to the bridge, to within a hundred yards.

And it wasn't a bit too soon either. Somewhere over the riverbank's horizon we heard that all-too-familiar *schwhoop-schwhoop-schwoop* of another helicopter. And again we were sitting ducks out in the wide expanse of concrete. We made a watery mad dash for the dark comfort and protection that the bridge promised us.

A hundred yards may not seem like much, but it felt like forever. We got soaked as we ran through the shallow water, sometimes tripping, dragging ourselves back up again, until we were nearly there.

Before we reached our cover, I glanced up at the bridge and saw the perfect black silhouette of one of those furtive, hunched birds with the beady red eyes that I'd seen along the way.

Finally we made it beneath the bridge and collapsed beside the boat. And the helicopter flew by, low enough that I could read that this one was an L.A. County chopper. It circled the area a few times, high over this stretch of the river before turning and disappearing downriver.

It took our eyes a while to adjust to the sudden darkness under the bridge. First we heard things. And felt things. And not good things.

"Whattchadoin' 'ere, boys?" said a deep, dull voice.

"Huh? Who's there?" I said, feeling someone jab me in the chest with the tips of their fingers.

"Ze question iz: Vat iz your beezness?" said the jabber.

"Neveryamind 'im," said the deep voice. "I says da questions, and da question is: Whattchadoin' 'ere?"

I saw the vague outline of a hulking guy. Scratch that, make it two guys. Another, shorter. They came slowly into view like those old Polaroid pictures. I lifted my hands to my eyes and rubbed them, but someone smacked my hands back down. I lowered my hands to my waist.

"Vee'll tell you ven to move, vat to move, and ven to move 'em. Got it?" said the little one, with a cackle-like snicker. "Okay, *move!!*"

That startled us. We jumped back and these jerks chuckled.

"See now, that warn't so hard, wuz it?" the big guy said.

"Yes, 'ow difficult can zis be, *pignon?*" said the short guy, who seemed to be in his thirties and had dark hair.

The tall guy, more like fortyish, had eyes a bit too close together and eyebrows that merged like there was a moth stuck to his brow. He didn't strike me as the smartest guy I'd ever met—but hey, maybe his looks were deceiving. He was grinning and his teeth were kinda messed up, like we'd interrupted him from snacking on a bicycle chain. The other guy was much shorter, and he looked like he had a bruise on his cheek, like maybe he'd been in a fight or fallen down stairs recently. He was the damn jabber, short but strong. When I caught his eyes, I thought they looked sort of tortured, like those self-portraits I'd seen of Van Gogh. In fact, he had some sort of a European accent—maybe Italian or French.

"Youz there," the short guy threatened. "Did you not hear vat I ..."

"Lay off, you idiots," came a disembodied third voice.

A third guy sauntered up casually from behind.

"Pay no attention to Tweedle-dweeb and Tweedle-dumbass here," he said, then turned to the other guys. "Didn't anyone ever teach you how to treat a guest?"

They stood there, suddenly docile, looking down.

"Where you boys from?"

"We're ...," I thought of how to portray Iggie. I didn't know how he liked to be introduced, so I offered: "We're from Canoga Park, up in the Valley."

He studied us for a few seconds, as if measuring what I'd said.

"And what's with the boat?"

"Oh, we're just going downriver. Having some fun, that's all. We don't mean to bother you guys. We're passing through."

"Really? We don't get too many boaters 'round here. How far you goin'?" he countered.

"Oh, we don't know for sure. A ways. We wanted to see where the river would take us."

"River?!" chimed in the short guy. "Zis thing? Are you shi—"

He cut himself off and looked up sheepishly at the alpha dude. There was a long pause.

"So, how is it anyway, upriver from here? Are you with a larger group?" said the leader guy.

"Oh, no sir."

"So no Boy Scouts? Youth group? Not with the media, are you? Anybody else coming through like you? Anyone know you're here?"

We both shook our heads.

"For shits and giggles then, eh?"

"Something like that, yes, sir."

He turned back to his minions. "See how sweet that sounds? Sir. You two could learn a few manners from this kid." Then he turned back to me, grinning, and sort of whispered: "That'll get you far, son. Keep it up." He looked over at Iggie. "What's with him. He a mute?"

"Oh, no. He's just shy. Say something Iggie."

"How do you do?" Iggie replied, as if reading from a language book.

The two other guys cracked up.

"All right, all right, you knuckleheads. You guys oughta talk—you're not exactly fresh out of grammar school! You'll have to excuse my crass colleagues here. They've got the manners of a couple of baboons. So, you're out on this voyage, in it for the long haul, come what may, eh? Looking for adventure, whatever comes your way and all that?"

"Yeah, I guess you could say so," I said.

"Well," he said, glancing over at the other two minions, "I respect that. You've got vision." He turned back to his cronies again, "See, that's a lot more than you two can say for yourselves."

The tall guy grumbled unhappily. Although he looked a good six inches taller than the alpha dude and a foot more than the short guy, he seemed to know better than to talk back. Maybe he wasn't the sharpest knife in the drawer, but he was at least smart enough to know his place—more than you could say for the short guy.

Long pause.

"Well, hell, I don't see anything wrong here, d'you fellas?" he said to his buddies before turning back to us. "You understand that we had to check you out, don'tcha?"

"Oh, sure. Can't be too careful," I parroted.

"See now, you dolts," he said, "the boy is more mature at his age than the lot of you combined."

They grumbled again, giving me the stink eye whenever the top dude wasn't looking. But neither spoke—they stood there and took it.

"Well, now that we got that settled, I don't suppose either of you would be thirsty?"

"Oh, are you kidding?!" I exclaimed.

"Well?" he said, turning to the short guy, "where are your manners? *Garcon!* Fetch these weary travelers some ice-cold ones: Coke? Pepsi? Sprite? Dr. Pepper?"

Iggie and I exchanged glances. "Are you pulling our legs?"

"Not at all. You passed muster, boys. Come on in: Mi casa, su casa." I looked over at Iggie. "My house is your house," he uttered softly.

"Ah, so he *does* speak!" the main guy gushed. "That's okay, boy, don't be shy. I had a feeling you'd know that one." He winked at Iggie then turned back to me. "What, you think that because we live like trolls beneath this bridge that we throw all semblance of class, style, and amenities out the window? Not a chance! Here, let me show you around while these guys prep a couple drinks. Get them a few appetizers, too, but not too much—I don't want to spoil their appetites before the buffet."

"Buffet?!" I didn't hold out much hope of warming up to the two other guys, but I liked this one guy. He was cool.

"You'll join us for dinner, won't you? It's the least you can do, to help break the monotony here. Put yourself in my position." He elbowed me in the ribs, rolling his eyes in the direction of his associates. I knew it was important to keep in this guy's good graces, so we didn't have to deal with the other two.

I looked around. I couldn't believe it. In this rundown old bit of infrastructure that was covered top to bottom with graffiti, three hammocks hung. And other ropes for, I imagined, getting in and out of the hammocks. A few small, ancient radios were suspended in midair, blaring out meager, tinny sounds. Nearby on the ground were a couple of couches that looked like they'd been washed downriver but which had brand new pillows doing their best to cover up that fact. There were sun-bleached, small coffee tables with ashtrays spilling over with cigarettes. As far as I could tell, there were a few distinct spaces: a sleeping area, a living room area, and a kitchen area. Totally awesome! It was a kid's perfect hangout: There were hockey sticks, dartboards, boxing bags, hanging plants, blacklight posters, even a pair of fencing swords and masks. Not your typical homeless guys. How'd they get all this random stuff? And why bring it down *here*? Whatever—I could get used to this kind of living!

"Wow," I said wide-eyed, "this is some place you got here!" Already I could swear that the pain in my leg was starting to fade away as our prospects started looking up.

"Glad you like it, son. Now you see why we had to give you the third degree," grinned the lead guy. "No offense, but we don't want just anyone knowin' about this. We'd be overrun and then we'd have to move along. And we don't fancy carryin' this stuff out of here. It took a good while to gather it and set it up like this in the first place."

"No, no, we get it. That's cool. Iggie, looks like we found ourselves a home away from home, huh?"

Ignazio smiled tightly. "Yes, very, very nice."

The two minions came back with a couple ice-cold sodas, three beers, and an assortment of noshy stuff: pretzels, nuts, BBQ potato chips, and chocolate bars. I felt like I'd died and gone to kid heaven.

"Here's to you, then," said the leader, raising his beer. Everyone toasted with their drinks. "So, either of you got names?"

"Oh, I'm sorry. I'm Sam. And this is Ignazio."

"This blubbering, lumbering gentleman here's Lance, and our sharp-tongued Euro-compatriot is Jean-Paul. And I'm Stengel. To our illustrious and intrepid travelers. Cheers and happy trails!"

I'd never been toasted to before. It felt good.

iV. HOME AWAY FROM HOME

We chilled and chatted with the guys, sitting around on old wooden industrial spools that doubled as living room chairs.

Relieved to have found a few creature comforts out in the middle of nowhere, it never occurred to me that you could have it both ways: domestic bliss *and* adventure. I may have felt relief, but Ignazio was edgy. When the others had gone away for a few minutes to get stuff from the kitchen area, he leaned over slightly and whispered, "These guys, no good. *No quieren Latinos.*"

"Don't be so paranoid—you're too harsh. Remember when you felt I judged you too quickly? Well, you can't blame me now for giving them the benefit of the doubt, can you?"

"No, but, I just ..."

Jean-Paul and Lance strolled back over and loitered near us, chatting between themselves. Then they showed us around the place some more. These guys not only had cool digs in the living areas, but they also took me to an awesome place out in the open that they claimed was a makeshift shooting range.

"You wansta see sumthin' cool?" said Lance, looking at Ignazio.

"Sure," blurted Ignazio, trying his best to change his attitude.

"Now you are talking, *el hombre*," said Jean-Paul. "Ovah zis wayz."

I'd always wanted to shoot stuff. Mom never let me get anywhere near guns, even BB guns or plastic guns, even sticks pointed at a kid like it *was* a gun. These guys had tons to shoot at in the junk that piled up in the river or whatever they wanted to bring in here.

Their current target was an old-style broken TV set up on a milk crate. On top was perched a beaten-up soda can.

"The family that shoots together, stays together," said Stengel as he sauntered up to the rest of us. He seemed to have a knack for appearing out of nowhere. "Go on now, step right up. Five bucks to the first man who can shoot that can off the TV."

"Steps aside, ever'one," said Lance, grabbing the gun. He took the rifle, slowly aimed it, and as he squeezed the trigger, Stengel walked by and nudged him. The shot fired but the can stayed put. "Hey, dat's not fair!"

"Oh, quit whinin', ya big baby," said Stengel. "Who's next?"

Jean-Paul jumped in and grabbed the rifle, making a big show of it, as Iggie whispered to me. "That is a real gun."

"What, like a BB gun?"

"No. The kind with bullets," he said.

Jean-Paul was trying a fancy way of shooting, with the rifle resting on his other forearm. I could see the jittery rifle barrel moving all over the place. It didn't help that he was already pretty buzzed from drinking.

He fired and missed and cursed.

Ignazio whispered again to me: "These guys are *loco!*"

"Ah, zis piece of junk," cursed Jean-Paul. "Ze sight, eez way off."

"*You're* way off," chuckled Stengel. "Come on now, which of you two will give it a go?"

"Go ahead, Iggie. You want to?"

"No, you go," he replied.

"Oh, come on, man," Stengel said to Ignazio. "Be a man. You'll be insultin' us if you don't."

"Sorry," Iggie muttered. "I do not mean to. It is ..."

"Suit yourself," said Stengel. "But know that shooting prepares you for life. You prepare and position yourself, you aim for a clear goal, you learn to be calm and patient in the face of activity swirlin' around you. It gives you a tool that can take down anything on this planet that's a threat to you. You prepare to let go. That's what it's about. You release the trigger. Shebang! Like shootin', life is mostly about the calculation *leadin' up to* action. The action itself is practically a done deal and happens in an instant. You execute, that's all—and wild, explosive shit happens." Then he turned to me, "Go on. Give it a try."

There was a certain sense to what he was saying, and something very seductive about shooting a gun.

"Really?"

"Sure. Everyone who comes here has to try it. Think of it as a common courtesy and a rite of passage."

"Well, in that case, I don't mind if I do."

I turned and saw Jean-Paul holding out the rifle. I'd never seen one up close before, except back at Zoe's garage. "Whoa!" I coughed, trying to act casual.

This thing looked like more than a BB gun, and probably was more powerful than a .22, too, I figured.

I reached out and grasped it, being careful not to get anywhere near the trigger. It was heavy. It felt cool. I slowly raised it up, toward the TV, setting my sight on the can.

"Release da triggah," chanted Lance.

"Releez ze trigger," repeated Jean-Paul, like a litany of sorts.

"Re-lease! Re-lease! Re-lease!!" they chanted as Stengel urged them on.

I pointed the rifle in the air as I took a few steps forward, so that everyone was behind me. I lowered the rifle and pointed it at the can again. I just hoped the bullet wouldn't shoot right through it and ricochet up and end up lodged in someone's head somewhere far away in L.A.

I pulled the trigger. When I looked up, I saw that I'd pegged the outer edge of the can and the force had spun it around and knocked it off the TV.

"Woo-hoo!" shrieked Stengel.

"Doh, beginnah's luck," grumbled Lance.

Jean-Paul dismissed it with the wave of a hand.

"Now, go for the TV," whispered Stengel in my ear.

I loved that it was a TV—somehow it felt right, as if the stuff it spews out deserved punishment: all the schlock, the late-night infomercials, the endless cable ads. I aimed again, lowering the sight to the center of the TV and fired off three times, straight into the screen. After the second bullet, the screen completely shattered, and I could see the electronic guts starting to show themselves. Four more shots blew the shit out of the back and sides, scattering parts all around and into the water. When I stopped, it was so quiet you could hear the broken parts settling inside the remains of the TV.

I had to admit it felt pretty damn good.

"I think we found ourselves the right man for the job. Eh, boys?"

They nodded and seemed genuinely impressed.

Handing the gun back to Stengel, I savored the smoky smell of the shooting range area and strolled back over to the kitchen. Stengel patted me on the back and handed me five dollars.

"Hey, I promised it, so here y'go. Fair is fair."

We ended up helping out with the dinner preparations, right there under the bridge, in their makeshift kitchen area. It was one of those summer days that stretched the daylight way into the evening hours.

I couldn't stand the suspense—the food smelled *so* good. They cooked on a rickety Coleman stove, but it did the job.

And they had a decent-sized cooler filled with ice. I have no idea where they got the food—it looked like good-quality stuff, like you'd find at Albertson's or Whole Foods, and that didn't exactly fit with these guys.

We peeled potatoes, chopped veggies and meat, and told them stories about how we'd managed to get to where they were. Ignazio loosened up a bit, as did Jean-Paul and Lance. Shooting together did seem to help break the ice.

All the while, Lance made use of one of those butterfly knives, though it looked too small for the guy's size. He flipped it, without much success for his sausage-like fingers. He dropped it frequently, and sometimes he'd nick himself with the blade, then mutter a curse. I realized this was what we'd seen from a distance: the glimmer of Lance's knife occasionally reflecting a beam of sunlight, acting like a tiny beacon to the darkness of the bridge's underside.

I noticed that Stengel had gone elsewhere but didn't see where until I happened to see him sitting up near the underside of the bridge, atop an extension of one the bridge pilings. His eyes were shut but his mouth, which was moving as if he was praying, reciting something, or just plain talking out loud to himself. Regardless, I remember thinking he sort of commanded this authority, as if operating in a realm where his thoughts and focus were oriented to higher matters.

When we finally sat down to eat, I still didn't know exactly what it was that we were eating. It tasted like chicken (doesn't it always?) but was different. They joked about various delicacies that it might be: "Grilled egret," smirked Jean-Paul. "Coyote cube steak," added Lance proudly.

I didn't inquire too much. Who cares where it came from, as long as it didn't come out of the river. I was up for it. I can remember a handful of truly great meals that I've had in my limited number of years, and this was definitely one of them.

V. 'CRAZY MAKING'

So I found out a thing or two about the motley trio.

Based on our dinnertime conversation, it sounded like they shifted from place to place, depending on whatever they seemed to be up to at the time. From the look of the place and a few loose, drunken comments that they'd been under the bridge the last few months, it didn't seem like they stayed in any one place too long. They also kept mentioning something about "the yard" (which I gathered was an abandoned railroad yard) as another place they'd once hung out. And they mentioned "the penthouse," too, evidently the top floor of an abandoned office building. Anyway, they went on about the girls they brought to these places.

After dinner, the conversation shifted to their agenda for the evening. I was surprised to hear they had one. It seemed like they had all the time in the world and no other commitments. I longed to be in such a world. These guys didn't have to do a damn thing if they didn't want to. That was a big slice of real freedom. Stengel was, like, my new idol, the fun uncle. He said it like it was: raw, unfiltered and brutally honest—not like most adults.

"Well, whatever's on the agenda," I interjected to the group, "I hope it's not too ambitious, 'cause I am sooo beat."

They observed me for a second, then turned awkwardly to Stengel. He simply stared out into space. Finally, taking his sweet time, he spoke up.

"After all this, we assumed you gentlemen would be joinin' us. I mean, you guys are the guests of honor. It'd be the right thing to do. We try to accomplish a few things here, too, nomadic though we may be. That's just how we roll. Besides, you won't want to miss out on *this*. It's totally boyish fun. Right up your alley, I promise you. You'll get a second wind, don't worry. It's a real kick in the pants."

Stengel was the kind of guy who presented things in a way that made it awfully hard to turn down. He had that charm. Or charisma. Something magnetic-like.

"Well, what is it you had in mind?" I asked.

"Eet's 'ard to exsplain, ain't it, J.P.?" said Lance. "They'z like field trips."

"But ze important szing: iz like noszing else," Jean-Paul added. "Very *je ne sais pas*: liberating. *Liberté!* Do you veesh to be free?"

"Well, I suppose," I stammered, looking over at Iggie.

"Okay," he shrugged.

"We aim for that kind of simplicity," added Stengel. "When the world goes to hell, you've got to figure out how to get busy and take it to the man before the man sticks it to you. But you're too young to appreciate how tough it can be when the world disappoints. You haven't been cheated out of things, disillusioned, you haven't been smacked in the teeth, you haven't been *down*. See?"

"Oh," said Ignazio, "you never know."

"Well, sure, it's relative: pain and suffering. I'm not tryin' to patronize you, my friends. Kids get enough of that from all sides. I get it. But the point is, what we've got to offer—what's on the special agenda tonight—is a vent, a cleansing ceremony of sorts, a chance to clear the air and get things off your chest, out of your head, your heart—your choice. You're gonna love it."

"But what is *it*?" I asked.

"It's whatever it is that's holding you back or down or getting in your way. We go 'crazy-making.'"

"Crazy-making?" I liked the sound of it.

Iggie did not. "*Loco que?*"

"That's right," explained Stengel. "We go on excursions. Like Lance says, it's hard to explain. You have to experience it. Trust me, it's great—we insist."

I felt awkward, as all eyes were on me. I darted a look over at Ignazio, who suddenly didn't look so at ease. Even if Iggie didn't want to go, the polite thing for me to do was to go. After all, what could be the harm? We're only going along for the ride. Sure, we were tired. But how often would we get a chance to go out on the town? In fact, when I thought about it, I couldn't believe I was even hesitating. Wasn't this what I wanted: the ability to shape my own destiny, to do something out-of-the-box crazy, something disruptive for a change, to get dirty, to cut loose? And *my* choice. It was fitting we'd run into these guys. Who cared what they did to get by? Not my business—*don't ask, don't tell*—so we just sat there, sipping sodas.

"We're in," I said, barely glancing over at Iggie. "Of *course* we're in. Wouldn't miss it."

Stengel put his hand on my shoulder, gave me a wink, and said, "See now, good things happen when you let go of these reservations floatin' around your brain and just open your mind and pull the trigger. Like I said. Think of it as your comin' of age ceremony, where you become men. We'll take off a bit after sundown. Lance, go get the car. Jean-Paul, get the gear." Then he turned to us: "Come on now, boys. Finish up and put your stuff away. We'll be outta here soon enough."

We waited a while for Lance and Jean-Paul to round up their stuff.

"How far does he gotta go to get it?" I asked later as we waited by the side of the road, on one end of the bridge.

"Far enough," replied Stengel, in his typically cryptic manner.

Judging by the time, I figured Lance must've been parked at least a half mile away, maybe more. Finally he zoomed up in an '80s-era black Camaro with tinted windows. Wicked! Stengel gestured for me and Iggie to get in first, in the back, which we did.

Stengel nestled in the passenger seat while Jean-Paul sat with us.

Lance had evidently picked up beer on his way to getting the car. Before long, they were drinking and carrying on. "Gettin' loose" is what Stengel called it.

I didn't really care that Stengel and Jean-Paul drank, but I wasn't feeling so great about Lance drinking while driving. I'd been around alcohol plenty, but never where the driver was openly drinking—even my dad didn't do that. Something told me though, that my commenting on the fact wasn't going to change anything. So, like a good boy, I kept my mouth shut, just hoping we'd get to our destination soon.

We drove up all kinds of winding roads, somewhere in or near the Hollywood Hills, I figured—one of those dark and craggy canyons that seem to go on forever, the kind where you imagine if one of these highlanders took the time and effort to get up to their house, they wouldn't have much reason to ever come back down to the flats, the lowlands, the social marshes, and mingle with the masses. At these altitudes, it was peaceful and quiet. It was an odd combo of rural along with the periodic gargantuan estate. With the elevation gain came an increasing number of BMWs, Mercedes, and Jaguars. The lights of the Valley twinkled below.

At a certain point it got more wooded and secluded. It seemed we were looping around and narrowing in on a couple blocks. Stengel and Lance were muttering back and forth. The radio was mixed with equal parts static and very bad heavy metal bands.

On one particularly dark, narrow lane, Lance clicked off the lights and we pulled onto a long and winding small road or driveway. The moon was full, so we could pretty much see where we were going. There were few other houses in the whole area. The house up ahead was fancy, with a modern look that seemed somewhat out of place here, in what felt like the rural countryside again.

We didn't drive all the way up to the house; rather, they barely managed to turn the car around and park it in a turnoff in the woods, fifty yards or so away from the house.

Stengel reached over and turned off the radio.

Wow, silence. I didn't realize how loud it had been along the way.

Stengel turned around and grinned. There was something changed about him, something about the look in his eyes that made me wary of him. His pupils seemed dilated. Did he take a drug, or was he just excited, or was it something else entirely?

"Okay. Ground rules," declared Stengel. "Number one: Merry mayhem."

"Merry mayhem!" the other two barked in unison.

"Number two: no lights; only the holy blacklight." He held up a bare purple bulb in his hand. And Number three: Pull the trigger." The minions repeated after him. "Pull the trigger!" "Number four: Make yer mark." They droned after him again. "And Number five: Have a helluva time!"

They began a rhythmic, dog-like woof—though still in hushed tones.

I nodded in consent (though we didn't have a clue what it all meant). Iggie wore a blank look on his face, and he crossed himself as he got out of the car last.

Stengel was right: I wasn't tired any more. When we got up near the house, Jean-Paul split off and headed around back. As my eyes adjusted, I could see the lights of some other ritzy houses dotting the woods and a creek or ravine that ran through the canyon. In the front gardens, there was a large wraparound pond with those big Japanese fish in them—koi, I think. I realized they're like carp cousins, just with much brighter, fancier colors. Somewhere not so far away was the sound of running water—I imagined it to be a waterfall coming out of the pond, probably snaked its way down to the creek and, in due time, out to the river.

After a couple minutes of waiting, the front door clicked and then swung silently open, revealing a grinning Jean-Paul. Iggie and I entered last, walking up and in like on a pirate's plank.

Inside, Stengel unscrewed a regular light bulb from a lamp in the middle of the room. He replaced it with his blacklight bulb.

As I walked around I could see it was, indeed, one of those swanky modern homes like in a fancy magazine, where everything had its place and nothing was out of line. Jean-Paul and Lance went into one of the bathrooms carrying a bag of stuff.

"Whose house is this?" I said.

"You wouldn't know him," Stengel replied.

"A friend?" said Iggie.

"You're going to prank him?" I added.

"In a way, yes. I do know him. I've done business with him. Up to a point."

"Oh, okay," I concluded, still not understanding much better.

"Look, let's cut to the chase and admit he's a real asshole, shall we?" said Stengel. "The evening is young, but time is ticking by. The guy screwed me over. Thought he owned me, but we'll show him." He addressed the room as if it were the same as the guy, "Who owns who *now*, asshole?"

"Well, um," Iggie started but didn't get far.

"Trust me: This guy actually believes that he deserves everything he's got— all this that you see. But he doesn't. He's one of these mucky-mucks, and see, these types let everyone else, the have-nots, work their asses off for them. And guys like him get all the credit. He decides who advances and who stays behind. He's a runt though. But since he believes he deserves what he gets, we'll give it to him. We'll give it to him, and he'll get a lesson in what it feels like to take it. Got it? You don't have anything against a little tit for tat, do you, fellas?"

I shook my head, not 100 percent sure what I was agreeing to. Ignazio had opened his mouth and was about to raise a fuss when ...

"Great! Then let the wild rumpus begin!" said Stengel. "Pull the trigger!!!"

And with that, Jean-Paul and Lance emerged from the bathroom wearing some sort of goopy liquid on their faces that gave them a ghastly look when it caught the black light. They let out these muted war cries, like demented Indians, and whooped around the room; they even had the liquid on their teeth, giving them a creepy skeletal look. Lance carried a set of golf clubs that he must've gotten from the guy's bedroom. He let them flop and jangle in the middle of the room, and he and Jean-Paul selected a few clubs. They went around looking for anything that seemed fun to take a whack at and found plenty: porcelain teacups, paperweights, wine glasses, etc. That kept them plenty busy. As they did this, Stengel had found a mirror and was starting to draw on his face with a glow-in-the-dark pen, giving himself these oversized bug eyes and a big clown's smile superimposed over his regular mouth; for good measure, he added a pair of vampire fangs.

Lance walked over to a piece of art that was the sculpted bust of a Greek figure. He started talking to it like it was a real person talking back to him, like they were having it out, and it escalated, "Oh, yeah?" he yelled, "You wanna piece a me?" He got in the statue's face, "I'll take a piece a you, buddy!" and then "Fore!" He finally took his golf club and whacked the figure upside the head. The sculpture cracked at the neck and the whole head got decapitated and fell through a six-foot-long glass coffee tabletop. I just about had a heart attack. I glanced at Iggie and he looked ill.

Then Lance dripped the red glow liquid on top of the headless statue, letting it roll down and over the neck and onto the torso, giving it a bizarre bleeding look.

Meanwhile, Jean-Paul had taken out his own knife (a big, fat one—like a bowie knife, I think—maybe ten inches long) and was cutting big Xs through the canvases of fancy artworks, sofas, and the appliance cords (after unplugging them).

Stengel had brought in a ladder and, over the fireplace, scrawled messages on the walls, like: "Let the Royal Runt-ass Begin" and "Merry Mayhem and the Black Light Special" and "Pull the Trigger." Once that was done, he turned and put the bottle up against his groin and pretended to be peeing on everything, leaving his neon mark wherever he went: liquid squirting out the tube and onto a lamp, over the couch, onto the Oriental rugs. And when he came down he still ran around like a rabid dog, raising his leg and peeing on the floor with the black light liquid, against the walls and big glass windows, howling all the while. Then he went into the kitchen where he sprayed it over their stove and into the pots on the stovetop.

Jean-Paul opened the fridge and swept a whole shelf full of food into a pillowcase; and whatever didn't make it spilled or broke onto the floor.

Things went on like this for what seemed like an hour but was probably just ten minutes or so. I was getting real nervous that a police car would come screaming up the entranceway. I wanted to call the police myself.

At one point, after a whole lot of damage was already done, Stengel came up to me and Ignazio, who were obviously dumbstruck and paralyzed by the whole thing. We didn't think it would come to *this*. Stengel held what seemed to be two spiffy glass vases. He handed each of us a vase— Chinese, as far as I could tell.

"On the count of three," Stengel said, with Lance and Jean-Paul pausing to look on.

"C'mon," shouted Lance, "where's yer fightin' spirit, boyz? Think of it like breakin' bread together. This'll be our lil' communion."

"Yez," added Jean-Paul, "you do not vant to be—how do you say?—pusszies."

Stengel cocked his head and stared at us with his reptilian eyes.

"One," they shouted.

I didn't want to do this, but I didn't know what choice I had. These guys were a lot bigger and stronger than either of us. I looked over at Ignazio, sussing him out—I was sure he was thinking the exact same things.

"Two," they shouted as I raised the vase.

I figured that the fate of these vases was sealed already. If we didn't break them, they'd break 'em (maybe along with *our* heads). We only stood to get in trouble with these guys— to lose credibility and their trust—and, mostly, I just didn't want to take that chance.

"Threee!"

I hesitated a second, then tossed mine unenthusiastically to the ground. It's true, if I'm honest, it *was* sort of liberating to bust something like that. Everything in me knew it wasn't right, but there was also something in me that got into it, way deep down. For a few seconds, it all seemed trivial—all this material stuff we accumulate, and for what? (At least that's how I rationalized it.) In the end, it was only a couple of vases, probably like a thousand other knockoffs, and besides, someone would get every penny back with insurance. There were maybe ten thousand more where they came from.

But when I looked over at Iggie, I had a sick feeling in my stomach. He didn't throw his vase. He stood there cradling it in his hands. In fact, he carefully, even defiantly, put it back on the stand.

They heckled him.

"Wuss!" "Douchebag!" "Faggot!" "Spic!"

"Hey, come on, guys," I interjected. "Cut him some slack."

"I'll cut 'im all right," said Lance, approaching with his flashy little knife, then stopping short to cut up a lampshade. "Ah, jus' kiddin'! But you'ze still a pussy!"

Something caught Stengel's eye. Out the front window, a car was coming up the street. He shushed everyone and we froze. The headlights shone on the woods nearby and cut across our house before moving on. Stengel watched it go but didn't like what he saw.

"It's a wrap party!" he announced.

They started gathering up their stuff. They were pretty quick and professional about it, pausing to take care of a few finishing touches.

Stengel strolled around the beautiful koi pond out front, pouring a big box of laundry detergent into the pond as he danced along the edge of it. The fish jumped at it like it was food, making big splashes in the water. "That's right, come on, little fishies. Come to daddy—suckers!"

After emptying the entire box, he took to netting a few with the skimmer net, then flinging them across the entryway floor like he was playing shuffleboard. They flopped around, gasping for water. I looked back at the pond and already a few koi were floating on the surface. The sudsy water moved slowly toward the waterfall.

Jean-Paul was nearly out the door before he said, "Almost forgot, vill catch up in one sec. I must drop my uh, how do you say, calling card on zee meeztah room bedz."

We scurried toward the front door as he made for the bedrooms.

On the way, I noticed the one vase was still standing, intact, on the pedestal. It stood in stark contrast to the broken, chaotic mess throughout the room. It was the one Ignazio put back.

Jean-Paul pocketed a few valuables as he ran from the bedroom, then shouted back, "All eez clear!"

"You'z a sick man, J.P.!" echoed Lance.

We tore back to the car and waited until Jean-Paul and Lance came hustling down the path, with Jean-Paul pulling up his pants as he staggered, wiping his ass with a white towel, then draping it over the bushes that led up to the house.

Finally he reached the car, opened the door and jumped in the driver's seat. He stank like, well, you know.

We waited for a couple of minutes until there was absolutely no trace of any lights going either direction on the main road. Then Lance eased the car out of park, not using lights until we'd gotten back on the main road, and even then not until we saw another car approaching in the distance. When the car passed, then he'd turn them back off again. He used the moon like a big flashlight, to guide himself, lunatic that he was.

VI. THE SPOILS

The guys were more quiet on the way home, at least during the long and winding ride out of the hills. Jean-Paul insisted on keeping the radio tuned halfway between stations (any two), creating a distorted white noise mix, with a hint of music or voices—like he was some sort of deejay of chaos.

"Oh, find a decent station, would ya?!" Stengel directed Jean-Paul, who sat in the center of the front seat, between himself and Lance.

After Stengel sifted through the items in the pillowcases, he turned around to us and declared: "To the victor go the spoils, boys. I want you to be the first to pick out something from the grab bag. Go on." He held out a pillowcase full of booty.

"Oh, that's all right," I stammered, trying to distance us from what had just taken place. "We didn't do much. It was your doing. You guys take it."

"You know," Stengel continued, "in certain cultures it's considered an insult to refuse an offer like this. Sometimes you gotta eat the monkey brain, the lamb's eye, the whatever. That's doin' the proper thing."

"Well, I'm sorry, but that's too kind of an offer. Besides, we're trying to go without a lot of stuff, you know, instead of gathering things that'll weigh us down on our trip."

"Is that right?" he cut me off. "Well, listen up guys, looks like we got ourselves a couple of simple-living types. Too good to get your hands dirty? Hey, I said, knock off that radio! Too good to reap? Not man 'nough to take responsibility for your actions."

Lance harrumphed and eyed us stupidly in the rear-view mirror. Jean-Paul looked back at us, all smug now, then returned to fiddling with his music in an even more annoying, dissonant way. Stengel sighed and quietly observed Jean-Paul and shook his head. Then, in one quick motion, he drove his right fist into the radio, smashing it to pieces, and followed it with a quick jab of his shardy, bloody fist up and into Jean-Paul's nose. He reeled back and reflexively tried to hold his nose, but Stengel was too quick as he grabbed Jean-Paul firmly by the windpipe with his other hand. Jean-Paul wheezed, pleading with his eyes for the pain to stop.

"That, as I said, is *really* annoying."

Stengel then turned to me, "See now, kid. I'm just tryin' to train you in how to get by in the real world. It isn't always pretty"—indicating Jean-Paul, who was turning blue. "Besides, a man's got to cover his basics: roof over the head, food in the stomach, keep the ol' dignity in check."

He finally released Jean-Paul, who gasped and clutched his throat.

"Even if he's a rambler."

I gulped. "I see."

"Ah, but do you *really?*" he said, reaching out with the pillowcase booty again. He reminded me of my first dentist who allowed me to pick from a treasure chest, smiling all the while—before drilling my first cavity. This time around, I didn't refuse. I picked out something, which turned out to be a woman's broach, with real (or real fake) diamonds on it.

Ignazio reached in and came out with a boy's high school ring.

"Now *that* wasn't so hard, was it?" We shook our heads obediently, as he continued. "You know, pirates of old were actually pretty democratic. They'd take a ship and its riches and divide it up according to contracts that were prearranged before they ever took to the seas. And they'd vote for a captain and elect a quartermaster. It was this type of system that predated and influenced modern democratic governments. That's the kind of ship we run around here, too: a tight one but an equitable one. That's why I *insist* that you take a share: It's for the sake of fairness and keeping with tradition. It's for the team that you take one. Otherwise, the whole social order comes tumbling down. And we wouldn't want that, would we?"

It was painfully clear Stengel wasn't the type to be messed with. Disregarded or crossed—he'd bide his time and then, one day, he'd strike. He reminded me of those crocodiles that are known to stalk large prey for weeks—quietly observing, noting patterns of movement—so that by the time it made its move, the fate of the victim was already sealed.

I thought back to the ransacked house. Stengel kept up a monologue about how the guy was a jerk who deserved what just came to him. I didn't believe him; then again, maybe the jerky guy with the mod home was a pedophile, or a wife beater, or one of those super-rich white-collar criminals screwing everybody over.

Sure, there was the thing about the vase, and I knew I'd catch hell from Ignazio later on, but whatever—the deed was done. I had to remind myself not to totally cave to the pressure of these guys, even if they seemed to feed on fear, snacking regularly. Stengel had a way about him that was disarming, for sure. But he also had this twisted charm, too, which was hard to resist. And who was I to judge him anyway? Who knew what hardships or traumas he'd been through. What if he was a vet who'd fought for the country and suffered from a post-traumatic syndrome or whatever and had been forgotten and become embittered? In the end, there was no way to know how he might've suffered under that guy with the fancy house.

We made a pit stop on the way home. It was one of those dubious roach motels. We picked up some lady the guys knew. She reeked of cigarettes and liquor as she staggered into the car, straight onto Stengel's lap. Turns out she went by the name of Daisy; but she definitely didn't smell like one! She seemed way too skinny to me—a jittery, high-strung squirrel. She chattered on and on, all the way home. I was afraid Stengel would hit her, too.

Lance dropped us off near the bridge, then disappeared to wherever it was that he kept the car.

The rest of us slipped and stumbled down the concrete incline to beneath the bridge again.

Jean-Paul got us set up with a makeshift tent, but he was only doing it 'cause Stengel made him do it. He seemed to resent being a servant to two kids, especially now with his messed-up face. I probably would've felt the same. Whenever Stengel wasn't around, he fumed and cussed, so we steered clear of the guy.

After we were squared away, the three of us traipsed back to the fire that was already going nicely. Stengel drank from a liquor bottle they'd taken from the house, and he'd pour some on the fire and it would roar, and he'd laugh hysterically. And they'd yell along with it.

It was there that Stengel took up his Satanic pulpit and laid out his personal philosophy. He worked himself up into a frenzy. His eyes were more lit up now. It was hard to tell if this was from the alcohol or if he was dipping into something else more powerful that got him juiced up. I suspected the latter, since he seemed to be another person entirely from the guy I thought I'd met earlier. Or maybe he was excited from the gal he'd picked up. Beats me.

"What you got to get is that there's a war coming. And I'm not talking terrorists. Yeah, they're out to get us, too, but that's just a battle, the latest *distraction*. These dry runs, like tonight, are training grounds for when the shit *really* hits the fan. We've got to test our mettle, before it's too late. We've got to get our heavy mettle on. That's what'll protect us, what'll keep America strong.

"But don't kid yourself, kids, our very foundations are at stake! We've got to redouble our efforts. We've got to shore up our defenses. Little by little, the real America is being diluted. Sure, the Blacks and the spics (no offense, my friend) are part of that, but they're not the real problem. It's the gooks and Chinks we've got to worry about. Ever wonder why they're always at the front of the class? 'Cause we're already so in debt to them. They *own* us, fellas. We're their bitches. A smarmy bunch of ants, they are. And it's only the beginning of the New Order. The deck's being reshuffled, and we've been dealt the joker.

"America may be going down the tubes, but we aren't going down without a fight. It's gonna be a balls-out affair. It's gonna be the shit. It's gonna be nasty. See, they aren't stupid. They've been around for millennia. They play a patient, long game. They've been taking their sweet yellow time, waiting for us to make our mistakes: extending ourselves in a couple of wars, going into deep debt with them, fighting amongst ourselves, indulging in decadence, greed, and corruption. Face it, we're not a democracy anymore. I don't know what else that makes us, all I know is that voting and the democracy of old doesn't amount to a hill of beans any more. It's a sham—all bought and paid for. Special interests own us from the inside, and on the outside, it's them. We are screwed!"

I'll spare you the rest—not that Stengel did. He totally went off, but in between his racist stuff and his other rants there was some stuff that sort of made sense. He was mad about things I'd heard my dad bring up, too—but they each said it in their own ways. Stengel had no trouble speaking his mind. I'd already believed most people were hypocrites who never said what they truly felt. I swore I wouldn't be one of those nice-but-cowardly types, and I respected that Stengel didn't bow to peer pressure, no matter how unhinged anyone thought he was.

But I could still see the look in Ignazio's eyes. With the stuff he'd dealt with in the U.S. already, I doubted if he'd yet run into the likes of Stengel. He isn't the image you conjure up when you're thinking of a better life up in El Norte. At one point Stengel turned to Ignazio.

"I don't want you to be afraid, my friend," Stengel admitted to him at one point. "You and me at least share *some* white blood, way back when, with the spics. And although you've been sneaking into our country, the larger truth is that, when the time comes, we're going to need you to match them, mano-a-mano. Otherwise, none of us will stand a chance. There's just too god damn many of them. Billions! We've got to prepare for the endgame. We've got to get our strategy together. And in the meantime, we practice our dry runs, on the individual level, until the signal comes and everything goes down."

Ignazio was enormously patient. What else could he do though? He let Stengel rant and wail on anything and everything. Iggie didn't seem to take it personally, but that didn't mean he was comfortable with it either.

With Stengel talking the way he did, we forgot about how tired we were. We were awake by then all right. As Stengel wound down, the fire started to die out, too, as if they were intertwined—there was something elemental about the two of them, and I couldn't tell which led and which took the lead from the other. And Daisy kept tugging at him, though he kept shooing her away until she got pissy and staggered off to their tent. That didn't bother him a bit; on the contrary, it freed him to preach without restraint, into the wee hours.

Toward the end of it, as he got more drunk and started to lose that filter we have that keeps us from blurting out what's truly on our minds, I could swear he said stuff like:

"We're going into business together, boys, seal it with blood, these ties: business, personal, if they're going to stick, require sacrifice. Tomorrow night, yeah, on the morrow, we'll christen it. Let the trumpets blow! We'll go wilding, make tonight look like child's play. You wanna be men, right? Well, you'll see, you'll be *the* man, men. It's a war out there, but nobody's saying nothin' about it, 'cause we've become indentured servants, *their* slaves already, our debt, their gain. It's us and the Chinese, man. The endgame is comin', like humans and cockroaches, the new war of the superpowers, but when we find our sacrifice and take him to the altar, he'll scream and holler—they always do—but you've got to be strong and just do it. Maybe cap one of 'em, 'cause if we don't start standin' up to them, then how can we expect our lame-ass government to do anything?! We'd be as hypocritical, no, we ratchet it up, we hatchet 'em up. You and me, we can't be blood brothers, son, without drawing some blood, am I right?"

I didn't know what to make of all that rambling but nodded so it could be over quicker. One look over at Ignazio, though, made it clear I wasn't mishearing what Stengel was saying.

And when Stengel stood and glared at us, I could only eke out a lame "Hell yeah!" (I needed to say *something* so he wouldn't think we were totally freaked out.)

I thought he'd go till dawn, but the guy turned out to be mortal after all. His voice started to fade in and out, and his eyes glazed over—like a parent trying to read a story to their kid but fighting a losing battle. Either that or he finally surrendered to the notion of hopping in the sack with that flaky flower child, Daisy.

In the distance we could hear them grunt and squeal, dying out to the sound of Stengel's unbelievably loud snoring. Even asleep he kept us on edge, with his abrupt changes in breathing, occasionally blurting out things in his sleep.

Later, as Jean-Paul and Lance stumbled to their communal abode, Iggie and I went back to ours.

After we both got settled in—without saying a word—we knew the other guy couldn't fall asleep without discussing the night. We knew we needed a plan for how we'd ever get away from these guys and back on our quest.

VII. MAKING A BREAK

Ignazio finally broke the night's silence.

"What are you *thinking*, man?!" he said as he began to cut into me, as I'd imagined.

"Look, I know—"

"No, you *don't*," he whisper-yelled at me. "You think this is funny, entertaining, or something?! You don't know what you do. These guys, like my coyote, they don't joke. I watch you. I keep my mouth shut. But when you do what they want, you are no better!"

"Look, I was trying to shield you, to make them not have to worry about us."

"*Mierda!* You are afraid to stand up for what is right! You have no *cojones*. You are chicken."

"Oh, come on. It wasn't like that."

"You're *loco*, like them, sick. This country, these people, sick-sick-sick. Are you blind? They don't want to hear from *me*. Maybe they have no more patience for me than Chinese. Whatever they say, to them we are *all* brown. The only reason they do not get rid of me is because we are together. On my own, I am dead man."

"You're being a little paranoid, don't you think? I mean, okay, so these guys are whacked out, and they vandalized stuff, but, well, whatever happened to your faith in people?"

"But they are evil, that's different."

"Whatever happened to your 'he who is without sin can throw the first stone' or however it goes? We've *all* messed up, big time, in our own ways."

"Faith does not mean you turn your brain off, or your heart, or that you shut your eyes and be like Nazis. What they do to that house, with *your* help, they could do next to *your* house."

"But they were just letting off steam," I shrugged. "Guys do that sometimes."

"*Really?!*"

"Ssh! It was bad, okay, but that doesn't make them murderers."

"No. You're blind! You are hypnotized with him. Didn't you see their tattoos?"

"Well, yeah, so what? A lot of people get tattoos."

"Yeah, but not *those* kinds. Jean-Paul and Lance, when they change, I see prison tattoos—there is a difference. *Los carteles* in Mexico, the same look: rough edges, no color. They do not plan to go back there either. People like that, they have *boleto de ida*—one-way tickets. Stengel, he is more careful to not show his."

If he was right then my gut instincts were way wrong, and I just didn't want to admit that. "Yeah, but what if you're wrong and you misjudge them? What if you see only one side of things, and maybe you know nothing about the other side?"

"If I am wrong and we are far away, then *no hay problema*—except maybe we hurt their feelings. Who cares? And if I'm right and we're far away, then *no hay problema*. They have no feelings to hurt. Plus, if that is the situation, then it may save us. But if we keep going like this, they get rid of *us*. Or we become like them. Better for us to go."

"What do you mean? What are we supposed to do, just up and leave?"

"Yes! *Y rápidamente*, understand?"

"In the middle of the night?! I can barely see you in front of me, let alone out there. Now who's *loco*? We barely know where we *are*. What, we walk away? We take the boat? We steal their car?"

"We take the boat, we—what are the words?—go with the flow. They will be glad if we go. We are a burden for them. We should not have stayed. They don't like us."

"Hey, speak for yourself."

"So, you *want* to stay?! Sam, *por favor*. If you have no conscience, then at least use your brain!" He gave up a big sigh, searching for a new angle. I knew he had a few good points, but I honestly thought he was being melodramatic. But then, what he said next hit me hard. "What do you think Stengel meant, at the end, when he say they, maybe cap one of 'em'"?

I remember hearing that he said that, but I didn't think *too* much about it. "I don't know," I said, "give him a hat or something?"

I could hear the exasperation in Iggie's breathing.

"No! *¿De verdad? Shoot* him, you fool. Put a *bullet*—a cap—in someone."

"Hold on, come on, you think they want to *shoot* someone?"

"Yes. Maybe."

"*I* don't know."

"Like they do tonight with the *jarrón*, the vases. As a loyalty test. A blood oath—*juramento*. I don't know. I don't care. I just want to be away from here. I cannot wait. If you will not come, I go, just me."

That shut me up for a while. "I need to think."

"Fine," he replied. "You think, for a change."

Ouch. I closed my eyes and retraced the night. I went to that place deep inside myself to see what it had to say. I thought again about the stuff Iggie was accusing these guys of, and back to when we first met them and how they behaved during the day. Then there was the mess we'd made of that guy's house. And Stengel punching Jean-Paul. This wasn't *me*. I mean, yes, I *was* involved. In the end though, it struck me that Iggie was right. I don't know how I missed it so badly.

But I felt strangely bound to Stengel, like I was sort of hypnotized or something. Maybe I simply felt indebted to him for how welcoming he'd been (at first). Maybe I didn't want to believe all that was just another illusion, that I could be so easily suckered and manipulated.

I thought to myself: *Adults are okay—until they're not, then they go bad.*

I saw how, through my silence, and breaking even one thing in that house, I was terribly guilty. I felt ashamed. Given my all my supposedly new freedoms, I was failing out here on my own. *This* was how I wanted to define myself?!

But if we tried to leave and got caught, I still worried about what he might do, what he was capable of doing. It didn't look good for leaving *or* sticking around. If we didn't leave soon, as in *that* night, when would we get a next chance? Finally, from that place deep inside my conscience, a shout came back with one simple word: Leave!!!

"Fine," I whispered. "We go. We just can't get *caught* going. How do we pull this off?"

"Pull *off?*"

"Do it. What's the plan, man?"

It was like he'd been waiting the whole night to tell me.

"Ah, *si,*" he smiled for the first time since he'd arrived at this place. "It is like this ..."

The next thing I knew we had tiptoed out of our tent. We scoped out who was asleep by the sound of their snoring and gathered only what was absolutely necessary. We got to the boat, our little hearts pounding like crazy—*vaboom, vabooom, vaboom*—as we scurried under the moonlight.

The trick was how to get the boat and equipment on its way without making a racket. We were prepared to sacrifice the tent—too risky to try to pack it up. We'd have to come up with another solution for camping out later.

When we got to the boat, we could see that someone had made an effort to tie it up real good with a length of old nylon rope that looked as if it'd been river flotsam itself. In the moonlight, it was hard to tell if the boat had been tied up with extra knots or if whoever had tied it up simply didn't have a clue about tying knots.

Either way, we whispered back and forth until we concluded that the only way we could free the boat would be to cut it loose. But neither of us had a knife. I told Iggie that I'd get one from the kitchen and for him to find and gather up the paddles and life preservers.

It seemed like it took fifteen minutes just to creep over to the kitchen area; it was about forty feet away. But I knew there was lots of junk on the ground—bottles, garbage, and the occasional chair to be careful of. So there I was, feeling my way around the kitchen area, trying to remember where I'd seen sharp objects. It struck me how there was something so fundamentally wrong about looking for sharp objects in the dark. I couldn't find *anything*. Valuable time was slipping by. I didn't know what to do.

Suddenly, there was rustling behind me. It was Jean-Paul, coming out of his tent, with a tiny light spilling out. I was certain he must've heard me. Still, I crouched down and froze. He didn't come for me, but he did walk over toward Iggie. I thought we were done for. I could only hope that Iggie didn't call out to him thinking that he was me.

Something caught my eye—a glimmer coming from Jean-Paul's tent. It was his big knife, reflecting in the moonlight; he'd put it aside for the night. I figured we could borrow it.

I stepped quickly but carefully over to the glimmer, then stopped for a sec as I heard him peeing into the river. I had to act fast. I reached into the tent, through the flap, and snatched his knife. I must've taken too long, 'cause I could already hear Jean-Paul stumbling and shuffling his way back toward me. I had to time it just right. Luckily, Jean-Paul was grumbling and cussing under his breath, so that helped with the noise factor. As he came around one side of the tent, I slinked around the other side. He didn't waste any time flopping back inside the tent, and he couldn't bother with zipping up the flap either.

I held my breath for what seemed like forever, his face being just inches from mine. Finally, his breathing got heavy again and his snoring became ridiculously loud. Time for me to make my move.

I went over to Iggie, who was hiding behind the canoe. I showed him the knife, and he seemed impressed, especially since he knew where it came from. That knife wasn't so big, but it was sharp—coming from the kind of guy who has a lot of time to do things like sharpen blades. It cut easily through that nylon rope. After we freed the boat, we flipped it faceup and gently put the paddles in it. One false move could wake everyone.

I thought about whether or not I should keep the knife. I knew they'd be pissed at us once they realized we'd snuck out on them and didn't want to give them any extra incentive to chase us down. So although I liked having a cool knife to mess with, I decided it'd be wiser to leave it for Jean-Paul. I could've put it back around his tent and he probably would've thought that it had fallen out when he went to pee. But there was something satisfying about leaving it stuck in the middle of the bull's-eye that they used for target practice on the shooting range. It would be like our signature, to show we were there—sort of like how Jean-Paul marked that guy's house, leaving his "calling card" on the guy's bed. There was something fitting about us leaving our own message, to restore some balance.

We carried the boat downriver for a bit so it wouldn't scrape loudly against a rock or concrete and wake everyone.

Eventually we lowered it into the water and rested for a few minutes, in silence, listening to the sounds of the wee hours. But when we got set to go, we could tell it was still too shallow to jump in. So we just held onto the ropes at both ends and schlepped along in the water, trying not to make any loud splashing.

It felt like we did that half the night; then again, everything we did that night felt like it lasted much longer than usual. Staying up late was what I always wanted to be able to do; but now that we were actually doing it, I couldn't wait to get back to sleep. So much for getting what you ask for. Sometimes I could swear I even fell asleep while walking.

As the water level got a bit higher, we took turns walking while the other person sat sideways, sort of half-assed in the boat, feet sticking out, hunched over on the seat, getting a brief catnap before switching again later.

After what seemed an eternity, the water got up to our knees and we both got into the boat and let ourselves float downriver.

I remember forcing my eyes open at one point, enough to see that the sun was just beginning to come up. We'd gotten stopped on a rock, and we just sat there like zombies. It was sort of cool 'cause we were surrounded by a lot of shrubs and trees in the riverbed itself. I nudged Iggie, and he saw what I saw. There were islands in the middle of the river. I thought it was a dream.

But we headed for one of the islands with thick plants that looked like giant bamboo growing up out of it.

When we got there, we hauled the boat up and out of the river, found some tall grasses and bamboo thickets, flopped the boat over in it, and tore off wisps of cottonwood and willow branches to cover ourselves with. We laid a rusty old shopping cart on top, and a spattering of flotsam, to complete the natural effect.

Then we crawled under the canoe and instantly fell asleep.

Section 4

Rivers give and rivers take, so if you can't go with the flow or you don't know your way around them, just steer clear.

— Sam Hawkins, February 14, 2016

i. FREEDOM

It was still mostly dark, and all was quiet as could be.

I looked around—or tried to anyway. Above, some trees were blowing lightly against a dimly starry sky. I tried to make out a constellation, but there must've been too much city light and lingering smog for a constellation to stand a chance.

Nearby was the barely visible, shiny blade of a paddle, reflecting light from some distant source—same with the gray white of my sneaker and Ignazio's teeth as he slept. It must've been nearly dawn, or I wouldn't have been able to see a trace of anything at all.

I shut my eyes again and opened my ears. There was a mournful cooing sound from a bird somewhere. At that hour, when sound seemed to travel so far, I couldn't tell how near or far away it was—it could've been ten feet or maybe a mile. There was the steady trickle of water not just from one direction but from everywhere. It was relaxing and nearly lulled me back to sleep. But I wanted to hear more, so I forced myself to stay awake. Something sped by in the distance. There were about a dozen of these sounds, and I figured there must be a road nearby and that these were passing vehicles.

I opened my eyes. Already it seemed like the light was changing. I closed my eyes again.

I focused on the smells. *That* smell. The one that followed us: the river smell. I think it's processed water. It's not horrible, but it's not quite inviting either. You have to smell it to know it. I've been up north to the Kern—a typical, natural river—and I don't remember it smelling like this. I've been to the Colorado and the Rio Grande—same thing. I was on the Mississippi once, too. Those rivers smell, well, like the air itself. Or it's more that they just *don't* smell like anything extra—only nature, plain and simple.

Anyways, I heard a stray voice in the distance, blurting out something, like someone was speaking to people in a dream.

I looked around again and could make out silhouettes: our boat, a bamboo-like plant, a shopping cart. Were my eyes adjusting or was the sun coming up? With the light taking on a reddish glow against the dewy spider webs of power lines, I calculated where east must be. Judging by the direction of the faint shadows, I got my bearings.

I got up, feeling my sore muscles. Wow—I didn't know how many miles we'd trudged and floated in the wee hours, but it must've been a lot.

Walking through the tall grass, up the mound of grass-covered dirt, I surveyed this bizarre new world. We were on an island perhaps, one covered in thick bushes and trees, maybe fifty feet wide. It must've been another of the soft-bottom stretches. On each side the concrete banks extended away and up at an angle. I thought I heard something smack the surface of the water. I saw the expanding ripple of what must've been a fish. Then, as my eyes darted around, in a pool of water I saw one of these graceful snowy egrets, its impeccable white making a stand against all the early morning gray.

As I stumbled around, it felt like people had vacated the whole planet and we were the only survivors. It felt calm. I wasn't used to being comfortable with stillness, as if it was a thing in and of itself. I guess I'd always thought of silence as whatever's left over when nothing is really happening. But it wasn't so dull and empty or boring at all; it was surprisingly full of stuff: sounds, sights, smells, touch, taste, thoughts, feelings—it was actually very active.

The fish reminded me that we still had my dad's old fishing rod strapped to the canoe, so I doubled back to find it, compelled for some reason to try it out. After tracking it down, I dug around for a worm, hooked one and tossed my line in the water. I wasn't much of a fisherman, but if I was going to try my hand at it, now was the time. I tossed the line toward the area where I'd heard the fish splash, propped up the rod in the fork of a tree, and waited.

And waited.

And waited some more.

My notion about being the last human on earth faded along with the morning cover slowly burning away. In the distance was the dim outline of what looked like the Emerald City—skyscrapers shooting magically up into the air. Elsewhere, there were the outlines of freeway signs and I realized that's where the passing cars were zipping past. I could see that one of the roads crossed over the river, the marble of the bridge lighting up from the sun, just like that egret, contrasting with the grayness of Oz hovering over it all.

A feeling washed over me: like I somehow belonged there. It was like one of those déjà vu things—like it had already been written, as if it were the most natural thing in the world. Unglued from time and my normal sensibilities, here I was, covered in streaks of grime, separated from my accustomed comforts, and yet it didn't seem to matter. I just felt like a creature—equal parts animal and human—and that, somehow, felt like enough.

I saw how outside of me my usual concerns were; I'd always imagined the world spinning around me, so this was a shocker. For the first time I saw how silly my puny view of the world was. Maybe I was cracking up—having an existential crisis or whatever. In my normal mind I knew I chose this river to go on this trip, but at that moment it felt like *it* chose *me*. And then it didn't seem to be an *it* so much as a *she*. But that was crazy, right?

Speaking of *she* though, I imagined that Zoe would probably be sleeping right about then. I wished she was with me, though I'd have spared her the rattlesnakes and raids, the near-drowning, and psychos, but right here it was different. In my head I said a few kind words about her and imagined sending them her way: They floated up and through the hazy, smoky summer ether of La-La Land, traveled along the river herself, up to the Valley, back through the big dam and up to her neighborhood. The thoughts arrived at her backyard, rose up to her bedroom window, and went in, over to her bed, to her ears, and into her mind while she slept soundly. But when she woke she'd know that I'd been there in some way, had communicated these thoughts to her, for whatever they were worth.

I took in a deep breath and let out a long sigh. It dawned on me that it was moments like these that I'd been searching for. This was a perfect slice of life no one could take away. I felt proud that I'd gotten myself to it, even if it meant a certain amount of undoing, of unraveling, and, yes, plenty of mistakes. Maybe mistakes are okay, in their own way. And, come whatever, I vowed to be okay with it.

Bring it on.

Just then, the line on the fishing rod began to move ...

ii. THE EASY LIFE

The rod itself became dislodged and was moving toward the water in fits and starts, catching on sticks and stones. I started shouting for Ignazio. I couldn't imagine, in this abandoned and neglected river, what else could be on the other end of the line. You hear stories on the news about the unlikely places in Florida, or even in the Chicago River, where rogue alligators or big pythons show up. It was far-fetched, but that's what crossed my mind; I couldn't rule it out.

Ignazio came stumbling up near me, bleary-eyed. As his eyes cleared he stood there and watched me foolishly chase after the line. And when I caught up to it, he watched me pulling on it, slipping, struggling to keep my balance despite the loose sand and uneven, slippery rocks. He rubbed his eyes to make sure this was actually happening.

"*¿Qué pasa*, Sam? What do you have?"

"I don't know! It's ..."

He came up to me and gave a hand. Together we pulled on the line.

We reeled it in. It wasn't a paint bucket. It wasn't a beer cooler. As it got near, a big black tail flapped at the surface and splashed—once, twice, a third time. We saw its head pop out of the water. It had a mustache-whisker thing on its face.

"I think it's, like, a catfish!" I squealed with delight, and as we pulled it in farther, that's what it was.

We heaved it up onto land and the three of us collapsed there, panting and heaving for air. It must've been about two feet long. I felt bad for the poor thing and suggested we unhook it and throw it back. But Ignazio said as long as we'd caught it, we'd be crazy to throw it back.

"We should not waste it. What else we eat? We leave everything behind!"

"Yeah, we're back on our own again," I had to admit. "No more freebies."

"Free bees?"

"Handouts, something for nothing, stuff for free."

"Well then," he chirped, "let's make breakfast!"

He gently slid his hand along the fish's back, up to a point behind the head and placed it against the ground. "Get a rock," he directed. He firmly held the fish. I selected a nearby rock and lifted it up. I preferred my fish without guts—filleted, sanitized, and processed into neat packages. But I knew I had to do this, to not be a hypocrite, to not always leave it to others to do the dirty work. I took a deep breath and brought my hand down swiftly—I whacked that fish hard on the back of the head. It never saw it coming and was knocked out cold.

"Breakfast is served," he said, grinning up at me. "Not bad, for a gringo."

I realized it had been more than a day since I'd last seen him smile, which was a lot for such an upbeat, optimistic guy.

"Uh, sure," slightly stunned, as if someone had knocked *me* on the head.

We went back to the canoe and our makeshift campsite, gathering wood for a fire as we walked. We couldn't get away with a fire at night because of the attention it'd draw; but during the day it was okay. Ignazio took me through the process of gutting and preparing the catfish. We set up a metal shopping cart over the fire, propping up the corners of the cart with a couple of plastic milk crates. I found that trusty old flip lighter. Finally I could put it to good use. The fire started up pretty fast since the wood probably hadn't been rained on for five or six months. We cooked the fish on the grid that formed the side of the shopping cart. After our effort, no matter how unsanitary our methods, there was no way we weren't eating that thing. Besides, as we grilled it, the surprisingly good smell started to outweigh the gross factor. And by the time it was fully cooked, I rationalized that I'd rather get sick than appear wimpy and spoiled to Ignazio. It was a matter of pride and honor—or at least avoidance of shame.

So as the sun rose on downtown L.A., and with the birds cruising up and down the river, we sat there in our humble campsite and ate that catfish. Along the bike path, we saw a few early risers: joggers, dog walkers, bicyclists, homeless.

"Look," Ignazio pointed out, "*gato grande.*" He pointed at a big circular cap on the end of a sewer pipe on the side of the river. It had two pointy hinges on the top side that someone had spray-painted to make a couple of pointy ears; below it, on the round part, there was a cat's face with whiskers. Ignazio told me about the dozen or so stray cats that they took care of at their house in Guatemala, as well as stories about the mysterious jaguars in the jungles back home.

After breakfast we did an inventory of our possessions. It was quick since we'd lost so much. What we didn't lose after we tipped over got left behind when we parted with Stengel & Co. What we had was pretty much to be found when we reached our fingers into our pockets: my lighter, $14.63 in wet bills and dirty coins, a partly crushed pair of sunglasses, a tattered and moldy bandana, and a couple flattened cheese sticks. Iggie had once read the actual story of Robinson Crusoe, so he started telling it to me. We imagined how we were like Crusoe when he first ended up on his island. Iggie didn't know about the show *Lost*, so I got him up to speed on that island, too, and its adventures. Stoked with these images, we went on a scavenger hunt to stock up on supplies for the next leg of our journey.

Fortunately, there was plenty of river flotsam to consider for additional trip items. We gathered up a bunch of balls—baseballs, softballs, footballs, soccer balls that had found their way into the river—and tossed them around, then added them to our collection. We found a plastic T. rex dinosaur toy and decided to make it our boat mascot. We stuck him in the front, like one of those carved maidens on the bow of a sailing ship. We also found a few plastic utensils and washed them with sand and water so we didn't have to eat like Neanderthals. Same with a couple of plastic cups. It was gross, but it wouldn't kill us; bit by bit, my standards were definitely being lowered.

We found a rusty old serrated bread knife and used it to carve the ends of a few bamboo-like shafts. (Zoe called them *arundo*—fastest growing plant on earth, like four inches a day!) We decided to make spears, because, well, we were in the thick of it and that's what boys do. Who knew—they might come in handy.

I felt enormously liberated—maybe more than I'd ever been before. Was this what kids did all day before the Web?

Our chief acquisition, though, was an old tin full of damp tobacco and an old pipe that were abandoned or lost. We were pretty fascinated by it. Neither of us had used one before, and only he had ever smoked a cigarette. We decided that since the opportunity arose we should take advantage of it. It took us awhile to clean it and get it going. When we finally lit it, however, neither of us actually wanted to smoke it—it was more about the idea, the wrongness of it and how it was so connected to the antiworld of adults. After taking turns coughing our lungs out, realizing that you're not supposed to inhale, we got better at puffin' and pushin' out the smoke. Still, we both ended up a bit ill. I liked the ritual of it more than the taste—we imagined that would grow on us over time, but we didn't care enough about our newfound vice to invest the time and energy needed to build up a bad habit.

We were sitting there smoking when we heard a loud splash and commotion beside one riverbank. We hurried over, snuck up close, and peered through the thicket. Talk about wildlife. I'll be damned if there wasn't a big naked homeless woman flopping around in the water, taking a bath. Now, I'd barely seen a live naked woman before (except my mom) or a virtual one (on the Web), so seeing *this* woman as one of my first encounters was a rather alarming example to see up close and personal. She must've weighed about 300 pounds! At first we thought she was naked 'cause she was sure no one was around, but she didn't react at all when a dog walker came down near the river and passed right by her. We figured she was simply gone in the head. Must be nice, at least in some ways—feeling that free to do whatever. Taking her sweet time, she eventually started to get dressed and we went on our way.

iii. WORD ON THE STREET

We were exploring the south end of another island downstream from our own humble one when we vaguely overheard a conversation. So we snuck up to a line of thick undergrowth, as quiet as we could. What we saw surprised us.

There was a sandy open space beneath a few big syca-more trees. And in that open space was a full-on bed, with mattress and frame but only a ragtag sleeping bag on top. I couldn't imagine how it got out there—it was like it fell out of the sky. And off to one side of the bed was an old wooden dresser, on top of which was a boom box that was playing old-timey music. Above the dresser, hanging from one of the tree's limbs, were a few shirts drying. Elsewhere there was a small kitchen table with a couple of chairs. There was a campfire shaped by a circle of stones and a hobo-like coffee percolator resting on the coals. A bunch of pots and pans hung from tree limbs; and at the foot of the trees near a fire circle of rocks was neatly stacked wood. In the distance, at the edge of the clearing, there seemed to be a shopping cart full of someone's stuff—I guess it was for when the person wanted to go mobile. Down by the water itself there was a colorful hammock strung between two trees.

The guy who lived here, who looked Vietnamese or Cambodian or something like that, was talking to a couple of cops. We could only hear bits and pieces. We snuck up closer, then froze when one of the cops glanced our way for a second before going back to his business.

We heard them talking about a body. Someone had found it yesterday. They asked him if he'd seen anything unusual going on. It seemed like they sort of knew this guy they spoke with. Then we heard that it was the body of a Korean dude. And word on the street, according to the police network, was that foul play was suspected. When we heard that, I looked over at Ignazio, and he shot me a bug-eyed look back: Stengel!

Of course, we couldn't be sure. We debated in whispers about coming right out and telling our story to these guys. But a few things stood in our way: 1) It might connect us to the crazy-making night; 2) Ignazio could get exposed and deported; 3) the trip would probably have to end right then and there; and 4) we had no proof against Stengel & Co.

We'd never seen them hurt anyone, just trash a guy's house. And Stengel maybe had some violent potential, but it hardly amounted to murder. We *wanted* to believe it—at least I did, in a twisted way, for all the drama and excitement. When I got home, I could say I'd run into this fugitive, a real, live one. That'd be cool.

So we decided to keep quiet, though our imaginations were getting the best of us. But that didn't last long. Just as the cops were wrapping up their interrogation, and while Iggie and I were going over the pros and cons again, I got so tense that the branch I'd been holding onto snapped in half. We held our collective breath. We tried to make ourselves as small as possible. The beat cop definitely heard it. His hand instinctually went to his holster. He slowly scanned the brush. He sauntered over toward us, his eyes searching, scanning, then smoothly unclasping and extracting his revolver. He headed for a spot about twenty feet away. Phew!

Sweating now, I felt the beating of my heartbeat up in my neck. The cop got to our line of undergrowth, stepped into it, and looked around. We crouched down farther. He walked toward us. He kicked around, steadily combing the area until he was nearly on top of us. He was so close we didn't dare look up; instead, we stared down into the dirt and listened for his footsteps to be walking elsewhere, and listened, and—

"All right, let's see those hands, slowly!" came the stern, flat voice.

We did as he asked.

"Get to your knees and keep the hands where I can see 'em." We did so, no questions asked.

"Now put 'em behind your heads, stand, and turn around to face me."

We did. He came closer and gave us the once-over. He lightened up a bit once he saw we were boys, more or less.

"So," said the cop, "what are you doing out here?"

"Just playing around, sir," I said respectfully. "We didn't mean any harm. We were catchin' frogs and crayfish and stuff when ..."

"When what?" he urged.

"When we saw you guys," I answered, "and wanted to know what was going on."

He eyed Ignazio: "And you? You live around here?"

It would've been awkward for me to answer for Iggie, like I'd done at other times. When Iggie realized this, he came out with a few lines:

"I live over there,"

"What, Lincoln Heights?"

Iggie thought for a second, then nodded obediently.

"And you?"

I pointed to the other side of the river.

"You boys know you're not supposed to be in here, don't you? There have been drownings—boys like you get in over their heads. I could cite you for loitering, you understand?"

"No. I mean, yes, we didn't know, sir," I said. "We've seen a lot of people down here." It slipped out before I had a chance to retract it.

"Is that so?" he noted. "How far d'you go along here?"

"Oh, we've been upriver some, not so much downriver," I said.

The guy reached into his coat pocket. He pulled out a sheet of paper, unfolded it.

"Ever seen a guy who looked like this?"

He turned the sketch drawing around so it faced us.

My mouth went dry, and I got the chills. It was everything I could do not to cough.

Playing it cool (at least I *imagined* that I did), I squinted and looked over the picture, taking my time, then cocking my head a few times, stalling, to find a way to swallow again and speak half normally.

I looked at Iggie, who kept a good poker face, shrugged, and shook his head sadly, like he was a dull and stupid person, careful not to give more info than he needed to divulge.

I tried to mirror him: "Nope. Sorry."

But the back of my mind was screaming: *It was Stengel!*

"Did this guy do that?!" I eked out, trying to control my wavering voice.

"We don't know, kid," he admitted. "But he's been seen around the river a few times. There are a lot of transients who come down here. Do your folks know where you are?"

Finally, a question I could answer honestly. "Nah. We're just exploring."

"Well take my word for it, this guy isn't messing around, so steer clear. I grew up in the neighborhood, too—you can get into serious trouble down here, so you both need to get on out and head home. Understand?"

We nodded. But he must've thought we weren't quite sure enough. So, to drive home the lesson, he pulled out another couple of pictures.

"In case you don't believe me, take a look at these."

The photos showed a dead Asian dude lying facedown (his head turned unnaturally to the side), with lacerations like letters across the back of his neck and upper back. As we looked closer we could make out the words Made in China carved into the poor guy's skin.

"Wow," said Ignazio weakly.

"Got it?" the cop said.

We nodded. "Oh, yes sir, we'll be headin' on home."

"Good," he said, inspecting our faces one more time. "Have a nice day then."

We turned and meandered silently through the homeless guy's bedroom set.

"Nice place you got, fella!" I said. He watched us go, looking a bit in shock himself, blinking, thinking about those pictures, too, not pleased at the sudden influx of visitors and disturbing news.

We trudged upriver again, finding our way over to the riverbank. We climbed up the sloping sides and plodded along the bike path for a while.

"*Que es!?*" Ignazio said, "That was close, man."

"Holy—"

Ignazio shook his head and looked at me like he told me so. And he *had*.

We walked along silently for a while. Then we pieced together the events of the past two days to see if we could make sense of it all, but after a while it only seemed like a bunch of nonsense.

iV. OUT OF THE FRYING PAN

After some random wandering and mulling things over, we circled back around to our humble campsite. We were fairly sure the cops had moved on.

We were both pretty quiet. After a little while we ventured a block or so away from the river and found a convenience store where we splurged on a couple sodas with the damp cash and stray coins we had scrounged. We returned to our campsite and figured that, with the news, our time on the river was coming to an end, whether we liked it or not. This was a whole other league, a new level of crazy that neither of us had bargained for.

Despite talking it over, we were still dumbfounded, considering the new information from the police. We poked at the fire's smoldering embers. I lit up that pipe again and we both took a few more puffs.

"Here," he said, pulling something from his pocket. "For you." It was some kind of woven bracelet. "I make it for you."

It was a combination of strips of plants, or maybe a long vine, put together with random pieces of colorful cloth bound with twine.

"This is awesome. Thanks so much. So, we call this, like, a friendship bracelet?"

He nodded and smiled as he tied it on my wrist.

"That's really cool. That means a lot to me."

We sat in silence for a while.

"What are you thinking about?" I asked.

"Oh, the pictures we see. And home. I see a dead body one time. My father and me hunt in the mountains. We come to a river and there is this guy, dead, at the edge of water. Two holes in his back, shot, and I think he must be so cold. I feel so sad for him. I remember I want to cover him with my jacket. And I start to, but my father pulls me away."

For me, the pics reminded me of that stuff my mom said. It occurred to me that death is, like, the ultimate alienation. It's freakish. But on the most basic level, it's as natural as it gets. I mean, we know death is never too far from us, but we distance ourselves from it until it's something totally foreign. Okay so maybe *this* kind of death that Iggie saw was exceptional. But in the end, death is death, however it happens.

So I put the same question to Ignazio that Mom had asked me and Ian. I didn't have much patience for it then, but it was on my mind:

"Say, do you ever feel alienated?"

"*Qué?*"

"Alienated. Like everything is out of place, wrong," I said. "Like you're having one of those out-of-body experiences, but the body is ... the rest of the human race or you're a stranger to your own self, like you're fighting your brain or maybe your own heart."

He shifted uncomfortably, sighed, and said, "Yes, I think I see: '*El sentimiento de alienación, o distanciamiento.*' Something like this?"

"Yeah. I guess. Or like when we were at that house with Stengel, and you say to yourself: 'This isn't *me*. I don't belong here.'"

"*Sí*, like what I tell you last night!"

"Yeah, yeah, I know. I should've been myself. But that's easier for you—you've lived longer. It's hard, man, when you don't know who you are yet."

There was a silence again. "I should be myself? Yes. Right now, I should hold *mi hijo* in my arms. I should walk in front of our house, on the edge of *el bosque, con el sol*, the sun, going down behind *las hermosas colinas*, the beautiful hills, the evening breeze, it is warm, and the face of my wife is perfect, like a painting, and I talk to *mi hijo*, I tell him stories about *El Norte* and all the things I do, or stories from my parents and grandparents."

"And where are they now? Your parents."

"At rest." I cocked my head. "They die when I was sixteen."

"How? They could only be what, maybe forty-five?"

"Yes. It's a long story. My father was a police officer. They fight the drugs, cartels. I lose an uncle and two cousins, too."

"I'm sorry."

"When you lose your parents, you feel this alienated," he said. "When the most secure, *sólido* parts of your life— that bring you into being—*cuando se evaporan*, everything disappears, feels temporary, like just passing through. It is confusing. You never really get used to it, but we keep moving, like the river, we survive, we do what we do—we do for them. When they die, I think I want to have family as quickly as possible, to fill the emptiness, to fix home. So I do. It gives me faith, hope again."

"More? It seems like it would lead you *away* from it, no?"

"No. When you lose so much, where else you turn? Alcohol? Drugs? Maybe, but iz not for me."

I had to process this for a bit. In my cynical brain, it didn't add up.

"But doesn't that just make you *lose* faith in things— even in God—for allowing horrible things to happen to good people? Didn't you feel like he took these things *from* you?"

"Sure, for a while. But when you are ready to look at life again, *Dios mío*, God wants to help us back out, out of that alienation."

I was quiet. Then I admitted: "Sometimes I wish I had your faith, Iggie. I really do. It definitely seems like it makes everything simpler. But I just don't feel it."

"It's always there, Sam, waiting for you to take it."

"I have to leave it, I'm afraid. I'd feel like I'd be giving in, sort of handing over my brain, to go blindly on faith. Sorry, doesn't seem right for me."

"Blind? Faith is not blind. There is wisdom in it. It leads. There is intelligence. That is why you are lost. *Soy serio.* That is why you have to do crazy shit like this trip."

"You're one to talk. You gave up family to come here."

"No. I did not give up. I just put on hold. But I need to try this possibility right now."

"Me, too. Look, I'm just sayin' it seems like it lets you off the hook too easily, like you don't have to think anymore, and you accept everything as it is. Okay, maybe not blind, but you accept that and then you can cover over the truths that aren't so black and white."

"But that's just it, Sam: Why keep searching for truths when the answer is right in front of you? And there's only one truth: Jesus."

Stalemate.

We both sat with that for a while, stewing, each of us thinking about home as the evening temperature cooled mercifully. Our debate would sometimes flare up again as we'd try to convince the other he was wrong. We switched from one uncomfortable topic to the next.

In light of the police incident, we inevitably came around to the events of the prior night (which I could sense had been smoldering) and the whole crazy-making incident. He started laying into me again. It was a sore point that we'd brushed under the rug; it put us both on edge and in bad moods.

I think we both felt frustrated and powerless to do anything under those other circumstances. He kept riding me about going along with Stengel, Jean-Paul, and Lance, and it always came back around to *how could I have acted the way I did?*

"I know, I know! Look, I did one stupid thing. Can't you gimme a break?"

"No, *you* look. Look at yourself. You need to understand before you do stuff like that. Because if you do, then you are no better than them. Are you a monster?"

"No, c'mon, you know me."

"Do I? I am not sure, if that iz what you can do, then yes, I see *you*. You were. *bajo su hechizo*—under his spell. And I do not mean as an excuse. You think it iz funny to be a pirate for a night? You think it iz fun to be a man, but a man like *that*? Well, man or boy, how does it feel now?!"

"How many times do I have to say I'm sorry? Can we move on already?"

"It iz not enough to say sorry to put it behind you. It's about *arrepentimiento*, contrition, *real* contrition, in your heart, *con Deo*, and not doing shit like that, ever again, because now you see what that does to people."

All I could do was hang my head and let him vent. I hated that he was so right *and* so righteous about it all, like he never made mistakes. I wondered if he was so angry at me because, at some point, maybe he'd done a lot of stupid stuff that he regretted. Did I deserve all the misdirected self-anger? How was that fair? It irked me also because, for the first time, he felt more like a parent to me than a friend, and I resented that.

But most of all, regardless of whatever else he might be bringing to the argument, I had to admit, I was angry and disappointed in myself. Here I'd had an opportunity, a first real chance to break from my parents and establish my identity—and *that* was how I chose to act?!

It was too bad, too, 'cause the day had started out so well, so carefree—one of the best. How quickly things can change. Now, by night, I felt so low, so bad.

As sunset hit, we were both feeling down and didn't feel much like talking about what to do next. Maybe there wasn't anything to do about it. All we could agree about was to sleep on it and discuss our options again in the morning.

So we got up and put away a few things, neither one of us wanting to speak much. We took our obligatory pees and ambled over to our quasi-tent. I lifted back the cardboard flap and nearly had a heart attack:

"It's so damn touching, isn't it, boys?" said an all-too-familiar voice, followed by snickering that surrounded the tent.

Stengel and his cronies!

V. iNTO THE FiRE

They posted a guy outside our tent, guarding us the whole dreadful night long. We fretted and tossed and turned and cursed ourselves for not getting far enough away while we had the chance.

Whoever said *you can't be too careful* was probably spinning in their grave right about then.

When I woke the next morning there was a really intense red sky beaming down on us—so much that I thought maybe there was a fire on one of the nearby hillsides. After all, we were getting close to fire season. It was surreal enough that I entertained the thought I was still dreaming. I'd never seen anything quite like it.

I recalled the achingly long previous night, being forced to sit and take in all the bile that Stengel, Jean-Paul, and Lance filled our ears with. They were less drunk or stoned, but their views were the same, which answered our question about whether it was because they were simply high on something.

Jean-Paul was the watchdog at that early hour, and it looked like he'd been watching the sky with interest, too. When he saw me staring at it, he coughed up a ditty: "Red sky at night is da sailor'z delight; red sky in da mornin', sailorz take zee warnin'."

I couldn't tell if he'd made that up or heard it some-where else. Either way, it was creepy. I convinced myself he was doing it to get on my nerves.

Lance awoke and, before long, Stengel was up and about, too. They picked up where they left off. That next day they kept us on a short leash, our arms bound with a lot of duct tape, just in case.

We didn't know what they intended for us, but we weren't optimistic about what it would be. The hours clicked by, about as thrilling as a bug stuck in a jar of honey. All we could do was think about escaping while watching the sky turn, gradually, from that blood red to dark frothy clouds and now cooler. We figured that if they wanted to off us, they'd have done it during the night, under the cover of darkness. Even so, the anxiety alone was killing us.

Again they gave us the harangue about how disappointed they were in us, after they'd "made a considerable invest-ment in your futures." Things like: "Sammy boy, I hadn't pegged you for a quitter, a cut an' runner, a flip-floppin' turncoat backstabber."

What was there to say? On the one side, Iggie would call me a dirtbag for trying to find an in with these guys; on the other side, these maniacs called me a traitor. It was lose-lose all over again.

"I told you," I started with Stengel, but when his eyes widened and his nostrils flared I decided to change course. "That is, with all due respect, we didn't say nothing to anyone. I swear. Ignazio will back me up. We looked at a few pictures a cop showed us but we didn't say a thing 'cause we didn't know nothing about it. Honest. I swear."

Then they separated us, presumably so they could play a game of bad cop/worse cop. Stengel stayed with me while

Jean-Paul took Iggie away to where he couldn't hear us. They figured, I guess, that one of us would slip up with our story. That was the only good thing about our predicament: Apart from continuing on our way and talking with the police, we hadn't done anything against these guys. And talking to the police wasn't our idea—we simply got caught.

"So," I asked, "who were those guys anyway?"

"Which ones yous talkin' 'bout?" said Lance.

"Oh, what does it matter?" replied Stengel. "Cops are with the Feds. If you've seen one cop you've seen 'em all: a bunch of lazy do-nothings sucking on Uncle Sam's teats! Government is one big cult. Bunch of followers, parasites. They sit around sipping on their cushy union jobs and pensions while the rest of us got to be out there in the trenches, trying to save the damn country from the mongrel hordes. I thought you could see that. But you're just like them—more concerned about your own skin, in getting back to your creature comforts, than battling demons. This is an epic, cosmic fight, fellas. And while we're out there fighting, the bosses and playmakers are in D.C. digging us deeper into debt to Yu-Know-Hu and his prophets of the coming doom! You boys are not helping the cause; and if you're not helping, then you're in the way. And that's the hard, cold truth."

"Well, what do you want us to do?" I asked. "We're only a couple of teenagers."

"I told you: You can talk and talk, but until I see you back it up with guts, with blood of the lion, then you're history to me. I take no prisoners. 'Cause when you've fallen that low, you're dead to me anyway, Sammy boy. At that point, you're a sleepwalker, just one more zombie clogging up the system. You're the husk on a cob of corn, see? And there's nothing to do with a husk but to shuck it. 'Cause it's only gonna get deader and deader and deader. Is that what you wanna be? Dead?"

What could I say to that? I had to convince him somehow that I still had some bad in me, to buy time to maybe get seen by those officers, or someone who'd spot our group and see something fishy about us down in the river and would call 911.

"No, sir. I get it."

"Well, let's see if there's a speck of truth in that, or if you're just handing me another load of BS.

"What I'm gonna do though, since I'm such an understanding guy, is to give you one more chance to prove yourselves. After that, god help you, boys. Fair enough?"

I nodded. I had to make another deal with the devil but without knowing the terms. It didn't leave me feeling particularly comforted.

Jean-Paul, and Ignazio returned. I'm sure he'd been grilling Ignazio. I could see Iggie looked more than a bit spooked.

Then Lance stayed with the two of us while Stengel and Jean-Paul went off to chat. They must've taken a good half hour to discuss our situation. Judging by the sun trying to poke through the angry-lookin' clouds, I thought it was about three o'clock in the afternoon.

When they finished their evil tribunal, Lance headed off to another part of the island. Stengel went over to Ignazio and sat down across from him, like they were going to do a staring contest. Jean-Paul came over to me and sat down beside me. He pulled out his oversized knife, grabbed a nearby stick, and quietly began to whittle.

Eventually, Lance came back—and he wasn't alone.

In front of him was an Asian dude in his twenties or so, hands behind his back, mouth gagged, being pushed along by Lance. The guy was tripping and falling. When they got to the rest of us, I could see the poor guy's eyes racing wildly. I didn't want to think about how they found him, what they must've put him through already to get him here, and what they planned to do with him now. Then again, I didn't much want to dwell on what they might do to us either.

"Stop yer squirmin' 'n' carryin' on, ya stupid wretch!" yammered Lance, trying to shake the guy into calming down. Lance grabbed him by the shoulders and rattled until the guy stopped mumbling.

We were soon shuffled over to a part of the island that was even more remote. There was no way to see in or out now. When we got there, they tossed the guy down on the sand, and everyone pushed in toward him and formed a circle. Jean-Paul ripped off the duct tape from the guy's mouth. He opened his mouth to shout, but Jean-Paul shut it quick enough with a backhand smack. The guy fell to his knees, his head bowed, bleeding into the sand. It got real uncomfortable, real fast.

The guy was trying to say a lot of things, but it was more incomprehensible with a fat lip and blood in his mouth. I couldn't say for sure, but my sense was that this guy didn't speak much, if any, English. It was just as well, 'cause nothing he could say was going to sway these guys one bit. So he could at least save his breath.

Stengel had stepped away for a few minutes, and when he came back he was decked out in black ash smudged across his face, like he was a commando or had come back from an Ash Wednesday ceremony that had gotten out of hand. He looked like some sort of drug-induced Amazon shaman.

The other guys chimed in, jokingly chanting in their twisted way: *Ah-oo-gah! Ah-oo-gah!*

Something told me, like with the crazy-making, they'd been through this sick little ritual before.

Stengel ascended the throne (basically, a stump) behind the guy, who was slumped at his feet, muttering, praying. The twisted chanting ceased, replaced by the sound of the wind that had picked up and was whipping the trees and bushes all around us. The clouds looked like big gray anvils, climbing impossibly high in the sky. The temperature continued to drop.

Stengel gestured for me to come forward. I did. Lance positioned me so that I faced the Asian guy. I locked eyes and there were, like, a thousand thoughts that shot between him and me, none of them relaxing.

Stengel began: "We are gathered here today to witness the deliverance of this wretch, No Name, by this lad, Sammy boy. Out of the earth are we born and back to the earth we shall return. The fools and naysayers who drool with lies in their posh circles, their elite penthouses, I am ashamed to call them my countrymen. We are the New Minutemen, astronauts of the New Dawn. To separate the chaff from the wheat is a simple act. There is reaping and sowing—and I assure you: This is not the time for planting, my friends. But with God by our side, and more holy days like this one, we will win the war. In the cauldron of the apocalypse, there is no other master but Thyself. And there is no other lord than our God, the wrathful God, who on this day of days demands his holy sacrifice."

Stengel nodded to Jean-Paul, who stepped up and cut me loose from the duct tape, then he grabbed my hand and put his knife in it. "I am vatchin' you, boy. You vill do zis if you know what eez good for you." And then Jean-Paul stepped back again, to rejoin his spot in the procession.

"My son," Stengel bellowed over the wind, "are you prepared to prove yourself in this, your holiest hour?"

I looked over at Ignazio, pausing for as long as I thought I could get away with it. I knew that he was urging me to not go along yet again. Of course, I didn't want to do their bidding either, but I had a plan, so I simply and obediently answered, "I am."

I was no James Bond, but I might at least get a shot at taking one of them down and causing enough of a distraction that Iggie might seize the opportunity to escape. As long as I had the knife, I had more leverage than without it. In that moment, that's all that mattered. I wasn't under the delusion that I could force them to do a damn thing, but I had to at least try to screw up their plan. It was probably too late for me, but I owed it to Iggie for getting him into this mess.

In that instant I realized what sacrifice and selflessness was about. I knew then that I might use my very life, my physical self, to save another. This was what they meant when they said: Would you take a bullet for someone? I mean, at the time it was all just reflexive; only when I thought back about it later did I understand that, even in such a short amount of time that I knew him, Iggie was already a true friend.

I knew they weren't going to let me go, ever, after they had me finish this guy. I was *already* in deep enough. My mind was racing—this could seriously be *it*. It was really real yet also surreal. All I could think of was, wow, what a short ride my life amounted to—a lame kiddie roller coaster that went around a few times and came to an abrupt and unsatisfying halt when the ride ended.

"Approach and prepare!" commanded Stengel.

Stengel went into a ritual movement thing. As he did, I took note of where Lance and Jean-Paul were standing. I had a shot at Lance. Or maybe I could get a kick in the groin on Jean-Paul. Stengel was out of reach. I could summon and channel every bit of karate lessons I'd ever had.

By the time Stengel snapped out of his trance, it was starting to rain. He looked down at me. I looked at the Asian dude, his bulgy eyes ogling me. Ignazio stared at me, too, wondering what I was thinking.

"Let Operation Sacrificial Slam begin!" roared Stengel.

I raised the knife over the poor guy and hesitated, summoning my strength. Then I thrust it forward—at Lance!

I figured I had a good chance at hitting my mark but, dull as he was, I guess he'd been in enough knife fights that his instincts kicked in and he reflexively dodged it at the last second.

"Get 'im!" Lance shouted to Jean-Paul, as he toppled backward.

I tried to run. But when Jean-Paul came at me from the other direction, I was so off balance that I couldn't even get in a solid kick at him before he'd grabbed me and knocked me around a few times until I nearly passed out.

"You stupid, *stupid* sonovabeech!"

VI. THE SACRIFICE

I don't mean to attach too much significance to stuff that occurs naturally. I'm not like that. Maybe it was all the hanging out I'd done with Ignazio and his talk of faith and God and that whole thing. But whatever you want to call it—a higher power, fate, or just dumb luck or plain old-fashioned weather—all I know is that I never experienced a time it played out quite the way it did on that particular day.

I'm sure that Ignazio, if he were still with us today, would've called it an act of God.

So there we were: goners, history, toast. When Iggie and I started on our quest, I imagined lots, but I didn't plan on being the next victim of some sicko psycho killer. Stengel glared down at us with his usual cold-blooded warmth. He wasn't the kind of person to hedge on decisions, like, "Should I kill these people today or spare them?" Guys like him aren't known for being wishy-washy, they don't care about the same things that real flesh-and-blood people do. They exist in parallel universes, though on the surface they mostly look and act like the rest of us.

"Sammy boy. I thought you had potential. But I guess this is your destiny. God works in mysterious ways. You would've grown up and become another poor soul who doesn't get it. They cloud your vision with ivory towers and social niceties until you'll forget about the warning ol' Stengel gave you: the standoff, the cauldron of the apocalypse. Look at it this way: It would've been a lot more painful for you to spend time growing up only to get cut down by the mongrels. You'll be a mercy killing—like Abraham's son when God asked Abraham to sacrifice the kid as a testament to his faith. I like you, boy, so I don't mind doing that *for* you, sending you ahead as a messenger."

"Thanks," I responded matter-of-factly. "That's so considerate of you." One of the perks of nearly being dead is that you get to freely speak your mind and everyone just accepts it. I didn't care anymore. If this was it for me and my puny life, then I was going out with my head held high and my sarcasm intact.

"Now don't be a smart-ass, son, or killing you might become a pleasure."

I remember that he had his arms outstretched when he said that. And ever so slightly, he blinked quickly, as if distracted for a millisecond. He rubbed his fingers, then brought one of his hands to his mouth and tasted it: rain. He looked up and, apart from his psychosis, his ragged, near-dreadful head of long hair, his intense green eyes and chiseled face, and his upward gaze, I had to admit that he bore a resemblance to Jesus himself—or maybe just someone who'd turned, like Vader or Lucifer, to the dark side.

He ratcheted up his speech and began his demented countdown.

"By this water and blood, under the remission of mankind's sins, do we offer up these sacrifices to the cause."

The rain started coming down harder.

"For the race of races cometh, when the Asian hordes will rise up and take over—save the chosen ones—who will answer the call to Armageddon."

The water began to rise. Around us, random objects that had been lying on the ground were met by the rising water. For a split second I had the sensation that I was in the middle of a magician's levitation trick.

"And on this glorious day we send these young men unto you, oh Lord of brimstone and fury, for they are not worthy of the taking up of arms and fighting for your new dawn."

The water crept up my leg. At first I thought I was only sinking down into the muddy ground, but when I looked down I saw that wasn't the case. At the side of the river there were those drainpipes small, medium, and large—spilling water into the river in steadily increasing amounts.

"Clean away our sins of leniency, of ignorance to the truth, of slothfulness and harden our hearts that we may do the deeds you have asked us to do, the hard work necessary to redeem the world through the shedding of blood, our remission, for without this we are nothing, and the prophecy remains unfulfilled."

The rain was coming down in sheets now, as the wind picked up and the sky turned a purplish-gray color. The water level was above my knee and rising—I couldn't believe how fast it was coming up. In the distance, lightning flashed, and we heard the unmistakable rumble of thunder. All kinds of objects were floating and not swirling around in circles but headed in a single direction: down!

Stengel steadied himself despite the water pushing against him. I could feel Jean-Paul slipping a bit behind me and saw Lance struggling to keep his footing, too, as he traded nervous glances with Jean-Paul, neither one wanting to be the first to cut off Stengel in the middle of his demonic sermon even under these circumstances.

"Uh, boss," Lance finally stammered, barely audible.

"Your ways are mysterious, oh Lord, but we hear you, we heed your call, the bells of war are ringing, tolling for thee, and sweet to our ears they are, for the time is nigh and your anger is high, for they have not heeded your warnings, and they shall pay with their lives."

"Pardon, *excusez-moi*, Stengel, sir, vee have a problem."

Stengel opened his eyes fully and for a moment seemed to snap out of his trance, but still, his glazed eyes never ceased that look. He sloshed toward us, then slipped and was carried for a few feet by the water's current. He caught a tree branch and pulled himself back up to a standing position, but by then the water was up above his waist. He stepped toward me with the knife, ready to do his brutal baptism—ready to toss me aside like all the other stray bodies in La-La Land to be swallowed up forever by the growing fury of the river, matched only by Stengel's.

Jean-Paul wasted no time in grabbing the hair on the back of my head and yanking my head back, exposing the nakedness of my neck, "Do it now!" he begged. The more water that came streaming downriver, the more the vegetation got bent low. I imagined that at least Jean-Paul felt more and more exposed, too, and that someone looking on from the sides of the river or one of the nearby houses could now see what was happening. Normally, that might be true, but I was pretty sure that the rain sent normal people scattering elsewhere. With the rain, there would be no one strolling by to see us and save the day.

"Take this scallywag unto your Kingdom, his soul gutted and cleansed for deliverance unto You. Make him true to your word."

I closed my eyes and thought about home and about Mom and Dad; my room, my friends seemed to flash in my mind like they always said it did just before you died. I saw Ian and Zoe and a few of the other kids and teachers from school. The rain smacked me in the face, and it made me open my eyes one last time to both see the world in a fresh new way and also say a big farewell to it. How much of the world I took for granted! I was sure I was crying, but it was hard to tell in the rain.

When I blinked and looked upriver, out at the wide expanse before me, with the dark mountains in the distance,

I couldn't believe what I saw. I figured that I was hallucinating. "Maybe," I thought, "it means I've already been killed, and this is a cozy last-wish vision." From over the last of the tree line that was being overrun by the water came this large white object (in my feverish state of mind, I swear, the first thing I thought was: "Moby Dick!"). It must've been all that talk of fury and wrath that summoned it from the depths of my consciousness.

An old refrigerator, its door ajar and barely hanging on to the rest, full of murky water, was coming straight for the bunch of us, giving the appearance of a giant hinged jaw as it bobbed and undulated up and down.

Not seeing it coming, Stengel reached out with his hand and raised the knife. Even with the wind I could smell his nasty breath and, as he dipped me back toward the water in some sort of inverse baptism *out* of this life, I could feel the blade on my neck slightly colder than the water itself.

"Into Thy hands I commend this spirit!"

VII. WILLIWAW

All at once, his sermon came to an abrupt halt as the fridge broadsided him hard, catching him squarely in the back and plowing into the rest of us.

We lurched downstream, each person fending for himself. That fridge couldn't have been going more than ten miles per hour or so, but there was no give to it: It was definitely an irresistible force.

It busted into us and sent us spilling, like in slow motion, in all directions. At first, Jean-Paul tried to keep a hold on me, but self-preservation was a stronger impulse than murder. The first thing I did was duck under the water and swim downward, trying to pull him under with me. After that, he wasn't too fond of holding onto me. I didn't know if he could swim or not, but I guessed that was as good of a thing to try as anything else.

And so Jean-Paul let go. I surfaced about ten feet away from him and maybe five feet from Stengel. He didn't seem too fazed, and he still had that sick smile on his face, stuck in rapture mode. But he reassessed the situation. Lance and Ignazio had become separated, too, with both floating down beside us. Stengel knew he couldn't let us get away.

The water was now about halfway up the concrete banks. I couldn't believe how fast it was filling up. It couldn't have been more than ten minutes since it started raining!

Stengel could swim well enough. He didn't come at me, but he stayed close. Keeping as much distance from him as I could, I scanned the surface for the others while bobbing along. My feet hit objects beneath me as we moved steadily up and down in the powerful, rolling waves. I saw Jean-Paul and Lance struggling to stay atop the water, frantically trying out objects to hold on to. Lance, especially, had trouble—his mass was an advantage on land, but in water he just had too much weight to keep afloat. Ignazio, too, was in a similarly dangerous predicament though, with the green fleece of his jacket going in and out of visibility. I flashed back to upriver, when he first mentioned he couldn't swim.

Iggie went under, then came up again gasping for air, shouting my name. He was maybe twenty-five feet away and getting farther every second. A ratty old soccer ball floated nearby me, so I swam over to get it, but Stengel followed in my direction, too. I yelled at Ignazio to hang on, but he was barely keeping his head up.

The rain was really dumping, almost like hail, the water now about two-thirds of the way up the riverbanks. We must've been moving at about twenty miles an hour. Everything was suddenly moving so fast. I couldn't believe it. I saw bridge overpasses in the distance, but the next thing I knew we'd gone under them and quickly left them behind.

As good of a swimmer as I was, I was no match for the force of the water. I was getting tired, especially as, more and more, the mysterious, heavy undercurrents pulled me down, twirling me around—toying with me, it seemed. I might as well have been a rowboat in a huge Pacific swell.

I turned just in time to see Stengel nearly closed in on me, his knife raised again as he tried to swim with the one hand. I took a stroke away from him as he took a jab at me, all the while keeping the soccer ball ahead of me. He missed. When I judged I had enough of a safe distance from Stengel, I yelled to Ignazio.

"Hold on, Iggie!!"

In an instant he saw me (but I don't know if he heard me) and he knew what I was up to as I raised the ball in my arm, like this was a demented game of moving water polo. He was about thirty or forty feet away now, but I aimed carefully and chucked it so it would hit ahead of him. It wasn't a bad throw at all; it made it to maybe five feet away from him but off to the side.

He eyed the ball but still he couldn't quite reach it. He splashed around again, and when he did I could see he was holding onto stuff but nothing substantial. He must've known it, too. At a certain point he made a second lunge for the ball. I think he touched it that time, but in the touching it moved farther away, then farther still with another touch. But with the rain I couldn't see so well.

I thought I saw Iggie go under, with his hand reaching into the air, as if still feeling around for that damn ball that could've saved his life.

That was the last image I had of him.

I never felt so completely helpless. Even if I could've somehow gotten over near him, it would've been impossible to keep him afloat, assuming I could've found him somehow in those black currents aiming to bring everything and everyone down with them.

I yelled out for him again and looked eagerly for him to pop up downstream. But that never happened.

At a certain point I became aware that it was only me now. Something dark kicked in, inside *me*. I didn't have time to make peace for poor Ignazio but resolved to live if for no reason than to get back at these guys for bringing about this tragedy.

Instead of just observing how Jean-Paul and Lance were struggling, I really *wanted* them to go under now. I was willing them to it. It didn't take much.

It wasn't long before Lance, coughing up that dark water, sputtered to keep more air in his lungs than water.

"Boss!" Lance begged and gurgled. "Helf! J-P! P-leeze! Ghl ... gh ..."

One, two, three times he went under after hitting a giant set of waves. I wasn't ten feet away from him, and I saw the whites of his eyes as they lolled, looking for something, someone, to deliver him from his imminent death. His eyes fell on me, and he knew I would do nothing for him. I remember thinking he was already a dead man. It was like I could see his eyes recollecting his wretched life—all in a millisecond—and finding nothing worthy of fighting for. It was like he gave up and allowed himself to sink into the abyss.

And then there were three of us.

I looked around, more determined than ever to outlast these two demons.

The water was now about three-quarters of the way up the banks and moving faster still, maybe now thirty miles an hour. Up ahead, it almost looked like we were going to hit the bridge overpasses themselves.

I noticed downriver that there was a big ol' sewer outlet still above the level of the water, pumping water into the river. It looked like, around it, some of the water was pooling and swirling, creating a giant eddy. It didn't look like much, but there was nothing else to take a chance on. I'd been struggling to keep my head above water the whole time, but now I put my head down in the water and began to swim for it with my remaining strength.

I looked up to gauge where I was headed. Pretending I was back home at the neighborhood public pool in the Valley, swimming laps, trying to go faster with each length, I tried to shut out everything else—I didn't have much choice: I could feel that I'd kicked into overdrive, tapping into an extra reservoir of energy.

As I got closer I could see that the sewer outlet was covered with a bunch of vertical steel rebar that had lots of garbage attached to it, some of which was dangling out into the river. An old garden hose that'd got stuck to those bars was waving around in the river like the tail of a snake.

I *had* to get it. If I missed, that'd be my last chance. The river was just too tiring to fight any more.

As I approached, I was sure I'd overshot it all. But then I caught a glimpse of the green end of the hose up ahead, popping up and writhing.

I muscled my way with a few last strokes and grabbed the last foot of the garden hose and began pulling myself up it, inch by agonizing inch. It seemed like forever to go ten feet against the current of water barreling out of the pipe.

When I got up to the opening, it was incredible to finally hold onto the grate—something *solid*!

I rested there, clinging, paralyzed with fear and shock.

The sound of guys yelling to one another snapped me out of my exhausted daze. Over my shoulder was both Jean-Paul and Stengel, also pulling their way up the same garden hose. At first I tried to untie it to send them downriver, but it was pointless; there was no way I could undo it. I looked around for something jagged to cut it with, tried a few things, but they were useless, too. If I'd had more energy and time, I would've climbed up to the top of the pipe and pulled myself over the lip of the edge to safety. But these guys were right on my tail now. I had little choice but to squeeze through the bars of the grate to escape them.

I looked into the darkness of the pipe and eyed the biggest opening in the grate (a couple of bent bars) that was above the water line. I made for it, and when I got there, I squeezed through it—almost. Just as I was on the other side, a hand grabbed me by the ankle. It was Jean-Paul. Little by little, he was pulling himself up along my pants leg as I slid back toward him, my leg sticking back out the other side of the bars. And the more I slid back, the better grip he got on me, forcing me down into the water. He had a grin on his face now, but I meant to knock it off his ugly face.

When my head fought its way back above the surface, I cocked my free leg and let go a fierce kick that caught him right upside the nose. He yelped and let go of my leg. I then scrambled to put distance between us. But it wasn't long before he was squeezing through the grating, too.

After the grating, there was a vertical chamber—it looked like an area to clean out the junk that got caught down here. Somehow, thankfully, there were steel rungs embedded in the concrete sides, going up and out of this hellhole. I could see a couple of holes of white light at the top, two weird eyes staring down at me, pitifully. I told myself that if I could only make it fifteen more feet up, that'd be enough.

But again that damn hand grabbed me! Jean-Paul must've made it through the grating. I had nothing left, no reserve of strength to draw from.

But then, inexplicably, he had a weird, troubled look on his face. And his grip began to weaken. I couldn't figure out what was happening, until ...

I saw Stengel coming up and over the back of Jean-Paul, pulling his own knife out, then digging it back into Jean-Paul again, higher up his back, and climbing up by that terrible handhold. He then repeated the process over again until he was just a couple of feet from me, glaring at me with his soulless pupils.

As Jean-Paul's eyes became listless and distant, Stengel grabbed him by the shoulders and cast him off without the slightest remorse. Jean-Paul fell, hit the gushing water in the big pipe, and floated down about twenty feet and got stuck against the rebar grating, his arms and legs jumbled as the water rushed over him—an awkward moment, even for a dead guy. His body stuck out against a big flash of lightning behind him, grotesquely highlighting his lifelessness.

Stengel caught his breath as he looked back to see this, too, not wanting to miss his sick piece of artwork framed neatly against the backdrop of the still-raging tempest of the river. The water must've been licking the very tops of the riverbanks by now, 'cause there wasn't much air left, even in the big pipe below us. The part of the grate that we'd clawed our way through was now mostly submerged, too.

Stengel looked up at me, as calm and collected as could be, but I kicked at his devilish face like I did with Jean-Paul. This time my foot was so terribly feeble though. Still, the slow, stealthy way he moved gave me a sliver of time to scurry a few feet away from him.

The guy was built for ruthless moments like this. It was bare-bones survival, and he was hell-bent on being the sole survivor by taking out all others, one by one.

I was right in assuming that this vertical hole was where crews must've climbed down to access and clean out the grate, 'cause I saw that, straight up above, those lights I'd seen were the familiar holes of a manhole cover.

Stengel saw this, too, and started gaining on me again, closing in like a spider that senses the stranded, helpless insect in its web. He could smell my imminent death, and he apparently loved drawing out every last second of his sadistic chase.

When I got to the top of the rungs, I was so frantic that I hit my head smack on the underside of the manhole cover. I was trapped. I could feel how heavy it was, and now, as I struggled to push it up and off, Stengel had me by the calf. It was like the bastard had planned it this way—to give me hope of getting this far, nearly out, only to nab me in the end.

Game over.

I braced for the worst.

But as I did, I felt something with my hand. Some sort of stick, attached vertically along the steel rungs?! I didn't ask questions. It just happened to be there: dumb luck. I seized it, and as Stengel crept up the next rung of the ladder, he got his knife ready again.

I could feel in my hand that this was a construction or cleaning tool—a rake? a broom?—that had been stored there for maintenance people coming down into the chamber to do their work.

Stengel had me with the one hand on my thigh and took the knife from his teeth and raised the knife with his other hand.

"Sammy boy, you could've been among the chosen. I'd wanted to deliver you up, but now I'll have to bring you down instead! No guts, no glory. Now, down you go."

"You first!" I shouted.

A jolt of adrenaline came to me from somewhere, somehow. I jabbed at him hard with the stick. It wasn't that the blow was so strong, but it struck its mark. It caught him smack in the eye socket and he let out an awful yell. His hands came to his face in agony, and when he did he had nothing to hold on with. By the time he realized this and reached out for me again, I followed with a kick to his shoulder blade that sent him backwards, off the ladder and down.

I remember him falling, peeling off the ladder rung, and dropping into the swiftly moving water, sucked underwater toward the same fate he'd sent his crony to. I wasn't about to stick around and see exactly what happened to him; it was inevitable.

Survival instinct sent me upward. I pushed awkwardly against the manhole cover with my head and shoulders. The cover slid slowly off to one side, inch by inch, but enough to get my hand through. I slid it farther to the side. There was a streetlight right there, and it shone down into the depths of the chamber. I clawed my way out, then looked back down one final time.

I'll be damned if Stengel wasn't still holding onto the very last rung of the ladder. I saw his head pop up, and I'd swear he saw me up there, silhouetted against the light. The water was gushing through the pipe, and I had no idea how anyone could still hold on against *that*. It didn't make sense.

But it was too much even for Stengel. In the end, he was human, too, and no match for the surging power of the water. I saw his hand finally ripped from the rung as he got sucked down the pipe and let out a final yell, and then ... no more.

Angrily and superstitiously, I threw a few random, nearby objects down the hole for good measure, as if to put a few last nails in his lousy coffin. Like it made a difference! Then I slid the manhole cover back in its place.

I would've smiled except that every muscle in my body felt so exhausted that even the muscles I needed to smile couldn't deliver. I crawled, trying to stand and walk, not sure where to go, what to do, or how to do it.

I think I only staggered away in my mind; for all I knew, I collapsed right then and there on the manhole cover. Either way, it didn't matter—already soaked to the bone, I got cleansed, through and through, by the torrential rain.

It wasn't long before I simply passed out.

Section 5

Enigmatic eddies carry you upstream, buoying you and providing safe haven to recover yourself.

— Sam Hawkins, February 21, 2016

i. LOST

Feeling something nibbling at my ear, I woke.

No idea how much time had passed. It was no longer raining, but I felt the wet heaviness of my clothes. Shivering uncontrollably, I tried hard to open my eyes, but could barely see a sliver of light through my squinty slits. Bit by bit, it looked like mid to late morning.

There was that ear thing again—more jabbing. Ouch!

I reached up to my head with my aching right arm and felt around my ear. Something was moving there. I tried to raise my neck to see what it was: something black—and a weird clicking sound. Jab, jab, then like a bite. By the time I got a good look, I saw I was being pecked at and picked on by a bunch of crows.

It's a shock to realize that you've fallen so far, so fast, from the top of the food chain. Those creepy black T. rexes hopped around my carcass, squawking and fighting over me. Trying to wave them away, I was weak as could be and less threatening than a stupid scarecrow. Every muscle hurt.

A quick body inventory showed wriggling of fingers and toes—good. And there seemed to be no other major body parts missing.

Peck, peck, peck. I waved them off again, getting pissed and feeling the anger well up in me, giving me energy. I nearly snatched one of those birds with my hand. I don't doubt I'd have wrung its neck or crushed it against the pavement.

They tilted their heads curiously. They weren't likely accustomed to bodies rising from the dead. They took a few more hops nearer, waiting for me to keel over and finally die. But instead I got to my knees, stared them down, raised my arms as best I could, and uttered a half-assed yell.

Even though it wasn't much, they got the idea and flew off for deader meat.

I rustled up my creaky body: slowly raising my torso and precariously balancing it over my lower half, rising up until I was standing again. It took a few minutes. The world was spinning. I had a massive headache. I was parched.

A quick, blurry survey of my surroundings revealed some sort of tiny park. I could see the expanse of the river close by, but not the water level. The fact that it wasn't cresting at the height of the nearby bridge gave me the assurance that it had subsided.

There was a homeless guy sleeping on a bench, wrapped in a blanket, completely still. I wondered why the crows picked me over him.

I shuffled out of the park, toward the river, occasionally stopping to pick up and inspect things that had washed up in the storm. I meandered, stunned.

And then it hit me: *Ignazio!*

My mind raced. I started to remember, wanting badly to believe it was all a dream. I searched my mind for another possible misunderstanding, but there was a deep dread inside that told me otherwise.

I *couldn't* have lost a friend—I'd only just found him.

The events of yesterday came rushing back in disjointed bits and pieces. The images were certainly not *my* life. *I* lived a quiet existence in an all-American L.A. suburb. But this was insane.

I reran my last image of Iggie: his bobbing head, taking on water—"Sam! Help!!"—with a hand waving above the surface of powerful waves of rapids, then him splashing at the surface, then no more.

Rationally, I knew what that combination spelled; irrationally, I needed to trick myself into hoping, to search for him. I wondered if I was a bit beside myself, and if so, what that did to my memory. When I spied stuff from the storm that triggered a connection to him—a shirt, a hat, a soccer ball, a plastic bag with something written in Spanish—my brain automatically jumped to the possibility that he was somehow around. Then I'd realize that the object wasn't in any way his and that it was hoping against all odds.

I wandered for miles down one side of the river, then trekked through the green areas where a lot of debris was caught up in the trees and smaller plants. Hopping from island to island, looking for any flotsam that might be a clue, none of it made sense and it felt like I was moving in spiraling circles, trying to will time to reverse itself, looking for a wormhole to a world with Iggie in it.

I ended up where we had our campsite before the storm hit. It was barely recognizable. It might as well have been a tornado that had touched down along the river, 'cause the tree limbs were broken or twisted, with junk everywhere. Tree trunks were split from the force of the water.

How bizarre it was that, just yesterday, we'd had so much fun right in this same spot. It didn't make any sense that we might not ever enjoy it again together. I always thought that, if tested, I'd be able to deal with a lot, but I discovered I had a hard time wrapping my head around death. This wasn't like you see in movies—this was real, very matter-of-fact, cold, sad, final, and uncompromising.

Picking up one of the shards of sticks, I started to lightly smack the end of it in the palm of my hand while sifting through the events that led me to this point.

As I puttered around that area in a fog, a bazillion questions streamed through my mind: What's the point of living if it ends so quickly and pointlessly, and without dignity? Why make choices when everything seems to be, in the end, dictated by forces larger than our puny selves? How's it possible to act normal when you find yourself in a world that too often seems upside down? Where's the justice in a world where guys like the coyotes live off others and have it easy while guys like Ignazio struggle every inch of the way only to meet up with an unfair fate? If a person doesn't live by a specific faith, how is he supposed to keep faith in the world, and in people?

I had to stop myself. Was I going crazy? Or was this perfectly normal, given what I'd been through? There was no one, nothing, to measure myself by. Sometimes asking questions makes stuff make sense, but sometimes it only makes you feel more lost and anxious.

Looking down, I was startled by something. I guess I hadn't been aware of how long I'd been there, anxiously pondering, but it must've been a while. I'd worked up a gash in the palm of my hand from scraping the sharp edge of that wooden shard against my flesh—so much so that it had started bleeding and without me feeling a thing!

Why, when a person is already hurt, would they create more pain? Why would a kid like me do self-destructive things to himself? Pretty messed up!

It hit me hard that I needed help. *This* was the time to call it off. I thought of the trouble I'd get in. But then a big wave of shame washed over me. Was I so stupid and callous that I only worried about whether *I'd* get in *trouble?!* That was so ... so self-centered, so small-minded. What would *Iggie* want? That's what I should've been asking. The truth was that I couldn't just bring him back. Wouldn't he have *wanted* me to continue and finish what we'd begun and that anything shy of that would dishonor him? I jabbed the stick again into my hand, as if to teach myself a lesson.

It was like I stepped out of myself and had little else but hatred for the old me. The only thing I knew for certain was that I was seriously messed up and didn't trust my own ability to make good decisions.

I thought that, maybe, whatever doesn't kill you makes you stranger.

I wandered back up the other side of the river, finding lots to look at but not what I was actually looking for: nothing at all, nothing that mattered, nothing I wanted.

I didn't think about much else. I couldn't. I was like a dog trying again and again to pick up a scent where there was none. I must've searched every square foot of those few miles downriver, and there was no sign of him.

As the sun crept up to high noon and my mind finally dried out some and became slightly more rational, I had to face it: He was gone. I'd barely met the guy a couple days ago, but I felt that I'd known him for much, much longer. I couldn't exactly say that I knew him well, but I already considered him a real friend. It never happens that way with me. But just as quickly as he entered my life, he exited it.

I thought about his family and wondered if they sensed what I knew. I began to set my mind on ways to honor his passing. I'd never been to an actual funeral. I didn't know about that, but I'd seen it enough in movies to know about buddies paying homage to fallen comrades.

I saw one of those big pipes that empties into the river and the heavy grated metal door where a graffiti artist had painted a cat's face on it. I remembered how Iggie had a fondness for cats, so I figured this would be a fitting place to honor him—right in front of that steel pipe cover.

He'd once told me that there were about a dozen stray cats that roamed around his family's house and how he gave them regular handouts. I figured the painted cat could sort of watch over him, or his spirit, or whatever.

So I started hauling things up from the river below, stuff to make a small memorial on the flat concrete landing. I hauled and stacked river rocks and found a candle that was encased in partially broken glass that was painted with the image of a saint. Since he was Catholic, I hoped that'd be appropriate. I put rocks around that and made it the center-piece. It was a shrine, of sorts.

I sat there for a while, thinking of what to do next. I considered putting the friendship bracelet that he'd given me onto the stash of objects on the altar but decided to keep that for myself—after all, it was the only thing I still possessed that had touched his hands, so I didn't feel like parting with it.

This was enough. It was respectful. It was done well. It somehow felt right.

When everything was set, I used a Bic lighter I'd found to light the candle. I made a small fire, too, composed of found stuff, and lit that. It took a while.

Then, feeling my own mortality strongly by then, I took out the tobacco pipe from a plastic bag in one of my pockets. It was damp, but I was finally able to light it. I took a puff, thinking in twisted logic that doing a small activity we'd shared might bring me closer to him. It didn't. It made me cough violently and nearly throw up—and I missed him even more. After a couple of lousy attempts, I snuffed out the pipe and got on with the ceremony.

Though I've never been a churchgoing type, I knelt there and spoke the best words I could summon. I think it's pretty safe to say I prayed more at that time than I'd done my whole life.

I won't bore you with everything I said or thought, 'cause it was pretty personal. I'll only say that I cursed myself for bringing him along on this trip. But I also gave thanks for having met him and for the things he'd taught me in the short time I'd known him. I wished peace for his spirit and his family and for them to find the security that he'd been trying to provide. Sappy stuff like that. I somehow bumbled through it all, sometimes talking aloud like a crazy person. I remembered that hefty homeless woman bathing in the river and how she no longer knew, or cared, what anyone thought; suddenly, I wasn't so different from her. It was wave after wave of sobs, like I was barfing emotions.

I'd certainly never experienced anything quite like that. It scared me how much I felt, especially from being accustomed to thinking that I didn't ever feel much. It made me think that maybe my mom was right: I'd become so distanced from myself that I didn't know that there was stuff in my heart and mind that I was totally clueless about. Identifying emotions—not my strong suit.

Anyways, after that, drying my eyes, I noticed a stray cat had wandered nearby and set up a perch on the concrete ledge overlooking me and the memorial. I liked that. In my sadness I felt comforted. You know that I'm not one to attach a lot of meaning to things like that, but you can bet that, at least in this case I believed there was something more to this cat showing up than mere coincidence. I *had* to believe—I didn't have anything else to hold onto.

So I sat there silently with my cats, one actual and the painted one on the sewer grate, watching the small funeral pyre fade. When it was done, I scooped up the ashes and took them down to the river.

I knelt and released the ashes into the river.

Sitting there on the hot concrete, I figured that I'd let simple, raw fate make the next decision for what to do. I rummaged through my pockets for a coin and finally found an old quarter.

"Heads I stay and continue. Tails I cut my losses and go home."

I shut my eyes. I flipped the coin.

I heard it hit, then roll back downhill, behind me. I opened my eyes slightly and followed it until it rolled over to and bumped against a pair of shoes.

The coin was then stepped on by one of those shoes, which smacked itself down on top of the coin as a voice called out my name.

It turned out to be a familiar voice.

ii. FOUND

I looked up at the figure but could only see a hazy silhouette against the sun.

Squinting, then looking back down, I studied the feet.

It wasn't the cops or rangers or anyone else like that, 'cause they'd've had shiny black boots. There was something about these shoes, but I still couldn't place them. And the damn person didn't say anything—were they messing with me? Meanwhile, I waited at the shoe owner's mercy for the foot to be lifted so I could glimpse at the coin and know whether I'd be staying or going.

But then, with a single gesture, that foot flicked the coin off into the river and the coin landed with a *plunk* in the water. It happened so fast I didn't have time to protest.

I started to get upset as I looked back at the figure again, and my eyes began to adjust. I could barely make out the silhouette now. Then I could barely believe my eyes.

"Ian?!"

I slowly got up and faced him. I gently patted him on the shoulders, making sure that he wouldn't evaporate. He seemed solid enough—*not* a phantom. I pawed at him like he was a lifeless mannequin. I'm pretty sure I startled him by doing this, 'cause he had a concerned look in his eyes. Then, as if I were blind, my hands found their way to his face, and he backed off and held up his hands.

"Whoa, dude! What the—," he blurted.

"It's okay, I have to be ..."

"Sssh, Sam, it's *me*. C'mon, snap out of it—you're freaking me out."

"Ian, really? I—"

I staggered forward and gave him a big bear hug that went on, I'm sure, way too long.

"It's been a few days, dude, not like decades."

"See, that's just it though," I said, gradually finding words. "Time stretched way out, Ian. It feels like I left the neighborhood about a month ago. You won't believe, never mind, it's ... later. I'm a mess, man, I *am*, I know, out of whack—you gotta help me. I ..."

I got so worked up that I felt weak in the knees, trying to hold onto him again—like a boxer in the eleventh round who's been knocked silly—but he just stepped back, steadied me, and looked me hard in the eyes. I had to sit down. I found a nearby rock. I was practically hyperventilating.

"Hey, relax. Everything is going to be okay," he said, looking around anxiously, as though everything was decidedly un-okay (Ian never was good at acting). "I'll go get help."

"No!"

"Okay, okay."

It felt good to sit. After calming down and to refresh myself a bit more, I reached down to the water beside me and splashed it on my face. That felt good. But when I looked back at Ian, his face had sort of gone slack.

"What?"

"Don't put that stuff," he said, "your skin might melt off your face! What *happened* to you?" His eyes fell on my cut-up palm. "Ew, that's nasty! You can't just put a cut like that in this kind of water. What are you thinking? Didn't you ever hear of germs?"

"Well sure, I, but—"

I recalled that I used to be a bit squeamish about the water, touching it at all. Now, it wasn't that I was under the delusion that it was bubbling up from a pristine artisan spring, but somehow I just didn't care one way or the other.

Ian circled around me, thinking hard about something. When he returned, he said to me straight: "Are you, you know, right in the head? I mean, seriously, Sam."

"No, I'm *not*. But now that you're here I feel better. You can't imagine what's happened, Ian. I swear," but then I started to hyperventilate again.

"That's okay, save your breath."

I was glad I didn't have to go back over it right then, 'cause I didn't know if I could handle that quite yet. I knew, in time though, it would all come out. There was this gap between me and Ian, and I didn't know how to close it and have things be like they'd always been. Maybe that was no longer possible.

"What's happening back home?" I mustered, struggling.

"Well," he began, straining to think back a few days. "First I couldn't believe you'd actually gone. I wanted to find you, but there were things my parents had me doing, so I didn't get down to the river until it was too late that day you left. And I didn't know where to find you."

"I probably wasn't as far as you thought," I countered.

"I tried to go about my regular routine," he said, "but I got obsessed with what you were possibly doing down here. I tried to imagine what you were seeing."

"Well, what did you imagine?"

"I don't know. Something more."

"But there was! I swear. There was the raid, and the helicopters, and our boat got wrapped around a piling. I nearly *drowned*! I swear, if it hadn't been for Ig—"

"For?"

"For a bit of luck," I eked out, "I would've been a goner."

"You tipped?"

I nodded, and as the memories of that day rose up in my mind, I suddenly got silent on him. I shifted uncomfortably and shot the questioning back at him.

"And my mom?"

"Everything is fine so far. She called once to check in. It was good I was there."

"So what happened?"

"Well, you're a much better liar than I could ever hope to be. I didn't know what I was going to tell her. Then I thought: What would Sam do? So I got creative: I told her a long sob story about how we were having a great time and you begging for another two more days for the sleepover, with it being summer and all. I figured that she'd nix it immediately, but she must've had a lot of stuff going on. She asked to speak to you, but I told her you were in the bathroom."

"You did well, Ian. A real pro."

"Oh, and then I called your dad, too, to be sure he wasn't expecting you anytime soon either. I left him a message—I didn't want to have to try to explain things to him either."

"So it's all good?"

"Yeah, but then there was that huge storm everyone was tracking on the news, and I got real worried about you, Sam. They were talking about the freak hundred-year storm. I was dying inside, because I couldn't tell a soul. Finally, I went to Zoe's place, and we talked it over. She confessed she'd been thinking a lot about you, too."

"Really?"

"Oh yeah. So, next thing I know it's raining like crazy, like they said. And then we heard about those two bodies they found."

"What two bodies?"

"You know. The two drowned guys, just two random homeless dudes, nobodies—you must've heard by now. No? Never mind. So anyway ..."

I didn't hear a word he said after that. My mind went off: Ignazio? Stengel? Jean-Paul? Lance? The Asian sacrificial dude?

"So, like I said," Ian finished, "it's been on the news."

"I need to know the names, faces," I said. "These are people's lives, don't you see? They're not just these faceless, homeless people!"

"Hey, easy Sam, I—"

"Look, find me a picture of those guys. I think, I think, I might've known them."

"What?!" he stared. "Seriously? That's cool."

I stopped and glared at him. "Cool?! Someone dies and it's *cool?!*"

"Well, no, I ..."

"Someone loses a husband, or a son, a kid loses a father, or maybe that's someone's brother—it's personal. How can you even ... Do you realize how sick that is?!"

"Okay, okay. How would I know though, dude?"

"I don't know. *Think* about it, engage your brain, have a little sympathy. Is that expecting too much?!"

"Hey, I'm sorry," he said, seeming contrite enough, but also confused. Then he had an idea. "Hey. Come on. I know where we can find pictures of those guys."

iii. SOMEBODIES

So we walked over to a place Ian had seen on the way down to the river. I didn't much like the idea of going outside the bounds of the river, but I didn't know what else to do to get answers. Going around and around in circles, getting nowhere, wasn't working out so well for me.

On the way I tried to distract myself and snap out of my depression by deflecting questions: "How'd you get down here anyway, Ian?"

He said he'd asked his older brother to give him a ride in his pickup truck and to help him out with a few things—no questions asked. He owed Ian a favor.

He told me about him and Zoe trying to calculate and triangulate where I might've been by then, using online maps to work out a rudimentary algorithm. Using that formula, he had his brother go to that pinpointed place and then crisscross the major downtown bridges. Ian decided to get dropped off and try his luck on foot, north of downtown, in the Frogtown section. That was where the algorithm indicated a 47 percent chance of finding me.

He told me a few other things, but I was tuned out and mesmerized by seeing civilization again (if you can call it that). The dirt and filth—what a mess—wasn't much different than inside the riverbed.

I was having a hard time wrapping my head around feeling so removed from it all by being in river mode and feeling so alone lately, and meanwhile there were tens of thousands of people—millions—all around me. I stared dumbly at people. None of it seemed to add up right.

We ended up two blocks away from the river, and upriver a mile or so.

It was a ragtag Internet cafe. We walked into the space that was dotted with computer terminals, and other people using their laptops. Ian went and paid for a chunk of time, and we sat down and got online.

We googled the storm and the search for bodies.

If Ian had noticed, he would've spotted me looking away, not really wanting to see what I knew was going to pop up on the screen. I felt detached from everything that came up—all the hooks to lure eyeballs to this or that site and sell something that someone didn't need in the first place. It was already a distant world to me. Any second though, it might not seem so virtual and would connect with the all too real.

I tried to take an unnoticeable big breath, but it wasn't very convincing.

"Ah," he said, "here we go." He saw that I'd turned away from the screen.

Swiveling my chair, I saw a news link he'd found. There were clips of the storm battering L.A. intercut with weather graphics, then images of what the river looked like when it was running high and fast. It showed fire department rescue vehicles and, later, a body in a sheet, face covered, carried on a stretcher. Then they cut to photos, mug shots:

Lance, and an anonymous person, described as a man, his face and body torn badly, dark hair, estimated to be in his twenties or thirties, possibly Hispanic or Asian. There wasn't a clear close-up picture. They said this person would need further testing and investigation to see if the two men were associated with one another.

The news reporter spoke about the one being a petty crook who'd done time and was believed to have been on the run from authorities when the storm broke. Then the news segment ended abruptly.

"That's it?" I said.

"What do you mean?"

"That's what they found? Just these two guys?"

"Well, yeah. I mean, that's all I heard about. Am I missing something?"

"No one else?"

"Not that I know of. Why?"

"Try more searches, see what else you can dig up. Please."

And so he did. But if Ian couldn't find something online, then it wasn't out there. He knew his way around the Web.

So we left the place and started walking back toward the river and, then downriver, trying a different route on the return.

"Look, Sam, you got to level with me. It's not good for you. You're leaving me out of the loop. And for what? I came here to find you. I came here to *help* you—if you needed it—so stop dancing around this thing and let me have it straight."

I thought about it for a short while. He was right. He'd cornered me, and that was good. I knew I could always rely on Ian. I wasn't sure why I was being so miserly with everything that happened. I guess I felt this gap, like he couldn't relate to what I'd been through, so why bother? But that wasn't fair to him to assume he couldn't get it. Besides, friends share, for better or for worse, and I was certainly the worse for it.

I began to catch him up on the important stuff: meeting Ignazio and going through the rest of the basin; me nearly getting bitten by that rattler; our escape after the ICE raid; almost drowning in the narrow channel; meeting up with Stengel's bunch and then slipping away in the dead of night only to get caught again downriver. And, of course, the events leading up to and around the big storm.

It felt good to get the truth out. *Why do I keep so much inside?* I could see that my nervous condition made more sense to him now. To some degree at least, he got what I'd been through, and he also got my sadness about losing Ignazio. He didn't judge me either (maybe that was what I feared most—being judged for Iggie's death). I told him how I wasn't so surprised to learn the full story about Lance. I told him about Stengel and Jean-Paul. No one in L.A. except me seemed to know the actual death toll from the storm. It made sense that they hadn't yet found Stengel's and Jean-Paul's bodies, pressed there against the rebar gate. But they would before too long.

Bodies have a way of telling the living where they are.

But by the time we got back to the river, after reliving those tales, I was worn out. It was like retelling it took its toll on me again. Suddenly I didn't feel so well.

Ian put his arm around me, "Come on, bud. Let's find a nice shady place for you." He gave me the rest of his canteen of water, too, and I chugged it down in no time.

Just as Ian found a suitably shady spot back on one of the islands, I started getting the chills—and that was with the temperature outside hovering around 100 degrees by now; in my own body, probably 101 or 102. I imagined it somehow had to do with the things I'd been dealing with, psychologically, though I guess it could've been an actual infection, too, with all the junk in the river.

He untied the jacket that was around his waist and draped it over me, pouring a bit of water over my forehead. Then he lifted up my feet and rested them on a couple of rocks. He noticed the gash in my leg.

"Gross! What happened? Your leg's messed up."

"Yeah, I cut it on ...," I tried to gesture, but I was too weak. And in gesturing, he saw the cuts on the inside of my palm, too.

"Jeez, Sam—now how'd you get *that*? What else is going on, dude?" All I could do was shrug.

"I dunno, Ian. I don't know. What's happening to me? Am I dying?"

"Well, hell, Sam, I think you're maybe in shock. And sick on top of it. Take a nap for now. You've been going at it awfully hard."

"But—"

"I'm serious! Easy, man. Don't worry—the river will still be here. But no more washing in this stuff. Don't put it anywhere near your mouth. You don't know where it's been."

"Yeah, but—"

"Just a short rest, a little siesta. Doesn't have to be for long. Trust me."

"The boat!" I sat up. "Zoe's boat, I think it's gone."

"Sssh. Boats like that, you can find them anywhere. That's enough for now, dude, shhh."

Somehow, finally, I felt the fatigue and the heat catch up to me again. I surrendered and let go.

But in my restless dreams, it was only Iggie who was on my mind. I wasn't about to let myself sweep these things neatly under a rug—all these events, and people. I tossed and turned, and tossed again, and again ...

iv. RUNNING THE GAUNTLET

I'm not sure how long I was out. As tired as I still felt, another day could easily have passed. But the light was still bright.

Somehow I managed a position on all fours. Then, with a feeble stretch, I stood up, unsteadily.

Ian was crouched beside a boat. A kayak. Yellow. Two-seater. Shorter than the canoe. It said MalibuTwo on the side.

"What the hell?!" I mumbled.

"I called in another favor from my brother. He gave me the ride down here. We took a visit over to the sporting goods store and rented it. It's a three-day rental."

I looked him over and cracked a pained smile. "And I've been here that whole time?" He nodded.

"Okay, but what are you going to *do* with it? 'Cause I'm not long for this river—no way, I've got to—"

"Wait a second," he said. "You're coming with me. Of course."

"Uh, I don't think so. I've had enough," I told him. "You have no idea. You said so yourself. I'm a wreck, and you're right. I don't belong here anymore. I'm done, dude."

"But I just got this thing."

"Well, you'll have to un-get it. Take it back."

"No."

"No?"

"That's right."

"Then what're you gonna do with it?"

"What *we're* going to do," he insisted.

"Uh, are you deaf, dude?"

"You've got unfinished business, Sam."

"And how would *you* know that?"

"Here, tie off this line to that branch, would you?" he said, as he handed me a rope for the front of the boat.

As we talked, I mindlessly fastened the rope. "Where do you want to get to anyway?"

"Well, Long Beach, of course. Where else?"

"*Now* you wanna go? Why? Why didn't you come *before?*"

"Oh, is that what this is about? Well, I'm here now," he responded.

"I don't know," I thought, finding myself getting angry. "Maybe if you hadn't backed out things might've turned out differently!"

"Yeah, but that's a cop-out, Sam, and you know it. You can't blame me for whatever happened down here. You wanted to grow up, and fast, to go on this thing regardless. Remember? Well then, take responsibility for it. You can't choose your freedom and then blame others for whatever happens when you finally get it. That's not fair—say, adjust that seat, would you?"

I started adjusting the nylon straps on the back seat of the kayak.

"Look," he continued. "While you were snoozing I realized something: If you give up now, none of what you told me, and have been through, will make any sense. It'll mess you up. That's what happens to vets and others who've been through heavy stuff. You've got to finish what you started, go the distance, otherwise you'll be haunted by it the rest of your life—and for boys our age, you're looking at a long, long time. Do you want to be known as the boy who got halfway down the river? Who lived *half* a dream?"

"It's no longer a dream though, Ian, it's become a nightmare. What's the point of going the distance if, at the end, you're dead? Or somewhere along the line the cost becomes too high? Then it's all in vain. Maybe it's just about vanity. What good is a win like that if—I mean, doesn't that defeat the whole purpose?"

"Well, I don't know. Honestly. But why not turn it back into a dream? A good one, that is. Salvage it. Make it happen and make it a success on new terms. Don't let other things rule you. Isn't that what you tried to teach me to begin with? The Sam I know isn't a quitter. I got your letter in the mail. Plus, there's another side of you, something real, that's coming through."

I was intrigued, but then frustrated again. "Look, Ian, if I'm honest with myself though, I don't know if I understand any more than when I started."

"I can't say for sure, Sam. I don't know. I just feel like it's important that you push through."

Ian wasn't usually so direct, so candid, so philosophical. He was pretty convincing. The truth was that I didn't have a clue what I'd do back home either. Sure, I could chill the rest of the summer, but he was right. I'd be thinking back about these insane summer days, wishing for this or that, having regrets. But by then it'd be too late. I'd be kicking myself for giving up on this whacked-out river cruise, despite everything that happened. I had to continue to put aside my own wishes for comfort and security and peace of mind, to do this for Ignazio if not for myself. If it had been me who'd died, I was pretty sure Iggie would've continued on with *me* and my spirit in mind.

I remembered when we first learned about the Greek gods in school, especially Odysseus. All his adventures—*he* wouldn't have turned back, no matter how many horrible tragedies his crew endured. He didn't have that luxury. He was in it to the end, however that played out. It was his fate, they'd say. And *this* journey felt like mine, as twisted as it had become.

There was something that kept pulling me downriver, something that still promised hope in the midst of all the disappointment, doubts, destruction, death, and meaninglessness. I don't know what you call that; I only knew it was pretty damn compelling, in a weird way.

Damn. Ian got me.

"So?" he nudged.

"Since when did you become so good at exploiting people's weaknesses?"

He shrugged and smirked. "As a younger brother, I've had a lot of practice."

He handed me a lifejacket. "Are we in it to the end, or what?"

I nodded, thinking of our late-night penny poker games. *In for a penny, in for a buck.*

I sighed, put on the jacket, and snapped the clips.

"Piss and vinegar!" I said, feeling more clearheaded.

He smiled. "Now you're talking."

And with that we sealed our pact with a secret handshake and swore:

"To Long Beach or bust!"

We gathered up our stuff, silently and in sync. We loaded it on the kayak and strapped it down. When everything was in order, we nodded at each other.

We pushed the boat out into the mild current. I held the boat while he got in the bow. When he was settled, I sat down and swung my legs around and put them into the kayak. The boat found the current once again and started taking us downriver.

The kayak fit both of us pretty well as we sat atop it and paddled. It was nearly as spacious as the canoe, only not as deep. It was a good way to go since it was slightly shorter and, especially with the rocks to maneuver around, it was easier. Also, it turns out that plastic is a lot more forgiving with rocks than the aluminum of that canoe.

As we paddled along, avoiding unseen obstacles just under the surface, we got into a groove. Since we already knew each other real well, it was like we both could tell what the other guy wanted.

It wasn't long before we found ourselves toward the tail end of the Elysian Valley. I knew it 'cause I recognized where Dodger Stadium was from going to games there with Dad. The stadium's ravine hung over the steep hill that descended to the river, high on the hillside to our right. That meant we were approaching the 110 Freeway overpass that comes from Pasadena (over toward the San Gabriel mountain range).

Round about then, after going over a few last chutes and ledges, the river changed dramatically again. The greenery ended abruptly, the water got shallow, and the sound of traffic and trains came into the foreground.

We glided up to a spot where the narrow channel began again. There was cool graffiti painted on the concrete sides of the river—one that looked like red cave paintings and another that was, like, a freaky-looking clown girl who was crying (probably for the river).

We could see that the current picked up as the water funneled toward the center, into the narrow channel before us and into the distance. Fortunately, it was also shallow right there, so we got out and pulled the boat a bit across wet concrete, then got back in and prepared to drop in and go.

We hesitated, looking back at the lush, wild area we'd just come through. It was a shame to have to leave this stretch of the river behind. Ahead, it was wall-to-wall concrete, and increasingly wider, with only that sliver of water running steadily through it. The future looked terribly barren, industrial, and foreboding.

In the back of my mind I searched for Ignazio one last time. We had good memories of hanging out on these islands that we were about to leave behind. I took a deep breath and wiped away tears, trying not to let Ian see me.

When Ian and I scouted the river online with Zoe, *this* was where the lower half of the river began. From here on out, like after the Sepulveda Dam, it would again be hard to get out once we committed ourselves to it. Another one of those key points of no return.

We hesitated. It was a weird feeling—not altogether bad, sort of thick with the musky scent of fate. It felt heavy.

We scooted the boat to the tipping point so that it was teetering on the edge of the narrow channel. Ian looked back at me one more time; I nodded. We gave the boat a couple collective scoots and launched ourselves straight down and into the lazy river again.

As the water surrounded us and pulled us along, we coasted, turning back one last time to see the green of the Elysian Valley fading out of view.

We didn't paddle much at all. We were too astonished as we stared, stunned at all the city activity. Trains screeched and ka-lunked on both sides of the river, sometimes crossing right over us on a steel-truss railroad bridge. Cars on other bridges flitted back and forth above us, like annoying ants.

I remembered from studying the river that on the left up ahead there would soon be a creek—the Arroyo Seco—that joined the river. That spot was supposedly the original settlement of Los Angeles—where it was so beautiful back then (with tall oaks, sycamores, willows, and fruit trees, and fresh, clear, flowing water in the middle of summer) that Spanish explorers couldn't pass up putting down roots and building the original pueblo that would grow to become gigantic, sprawling Los Angeles.

The 110 Freeway runs parallel to that creek, and when we passed under that freeway, off to the left was a gaping thirty-foot hole in the concrete, strewn with garbage, and an anemic trickle of water flowing from it. Twenty or so feet up these walls were pipes sticking out, leaving behind rusty streaks and surreal colors from chemical horror houses, dripping into the river.

"Civilization, eh?" remembering the vow I made when I first started out. "Hold on a sec, Ian. I need a few minutes."

We gradually managed to stop ourselves. I climbed out and jogged over to the pipe that was the worst pollution offender. I gathered up whatever I could shove into the pipe to stop the stuff from coming out. I went crazy on it, shoving about ten feet of garbage into the end, pushing it deeper into the pipe with a broken broomstick. I felt like I was loading one of those old-time muskets—a very large one. I put all my anger and sadness into the task.

It was my hope that the whole thing would back up with the toxic sludge, so whoever did this would get the message. And in case the message wasn't clear enough, I took out a half-used can of spray paint I found nearby and scrawled on the wall: F*CK THIS SH*T!

Then I hustled back to the boat, where Ian quickly nodded and smirked, "Nice work."

I kept squinting, trying to envision the time when things looked beautiful on this spot. The original environment was nearly impossible to picture from the landscape we were going through. Gone was the lush river valley that the original explorers thought was so awesome; here was a concrete monstrosity, the infrastructural rear end of the city and downtown core butted up against the river as tightly as they could build it.

Anyway, we unhitched ourselves and floated unceremoniously past this historic spot.

We kept on going, deeper into the giant industrial no-man's-land. Just when we thought the river couldn't get any bigger, we entered an area that broadened into a concrete canyon at least two hundred feet wide across the bottom, with sides that sloped up and outward another few hundred feet before bumping against fences with barbed wire on top, on both sides, beyond which were more trains and tracks. At the top, the river span looked more like four hundred feet.

It felt like a fake amusement park version of the Grand Canyon.

As we traveled deeper down and into the belly of the beast, I had to admit there was a curious beauty to it. I put my cynicism aside long enough to notice there was a string of white marble bridges in the distance that were pretty damn spectacular. As we got closer, floating beneath them in silence, each seemed distinctive, and yet there was a pearly connectedness to the bunch of them. You look at those and you start to think there's still hope yet for this city. But it was like no one else in the world could appreciate these bridges for how magnificent they were, 'cause no one in their right mind could see them from our particular angle, which seemed to me and Ian as the best possible way to ever see them. We felt lucky, like this was a special screening, set up just for us.

Angelenos didn't seem to appreciate what they had right here under their noses, as they passed over it so busily each day.

We kept on going, our spirits lifting slightly as we put still more distance between us and the sad, tragic events on that last stretch of the river. Still, though the river distracted me for a time, I was haunted by what happened to Iggie.

Later on we approached an area where a few people were gathered. To the right, below one of the bridges, was an access tunnel that emptied out onto the river.

As we got closer we could see that the tunnel was big enough to drive a truck through. And if I recalled from Zoe's research, people *did* drive through it from time to time for film shoots on this part of the river. With all its flat concrete, it was perfect for car races and big sci-fi sets.

The few homeless guys who were hanging out around that access tunnel suddenly noticed us. They watched us pass, like we were a ghost ship.

One of them cried out, "Hey there! Whatcha doin', cowboys!?"

And Ian shouted back, "Yeah, man, it's the Wild West!"

"Where ya goin'?!" one of them asked.

"Tijuana!" Ian declared.

That broke them up. "Niiiice! Alriiiiight! You go, boyz!" another said.

Then one of them did a crazy dance and chased after us for a bit until he got too tired to keep up. He paused to cough his lungs out. As he recovered, he lit up a cigarette as he watched us. Gradually, we fixed our gaze again downriver.

We cruised beneath a few more bridges.

Sometimes I got the sense that people were watching from somewhere above, waiting to ambush us.

At one point we passed by a bunch of taggers who were working along the inclined riverbanks on a giant swath of graffiti that was the biggest you ever saw—with letters that were maybe a hundred feet high.

A few of the taggers noticed us, but they were too busy with their own projects to care.

The white marble bridges eventually ended, replaced by another industrial stretch with vertical walls about sixty-feet tall, highest yet. It was there the narrow divided in two smaller, parallel channels with a flat concrete median in between. We couldn't figure exactly what purpose that served, except maybe to slow down the current as the river made a big curve to the east. The water got ankle deep again, and so we had to wade through it for a mile or so beside our kayak.

As we did, coming from the other direction were large schools of carp—maybe a dozen at a time—swimming upriver. They were a foot or two long and passed so close that we sometimes reached out and touched them on their backs.

The concrete walls gradually scaled back to form the angled concrete riverbanks with a flat concrete bottom about a hundred feet wide, split by the narrow channel itself again.

And way up ahead on the river, the industrial rear end of the city continued. We saw little specks moving in and around the river channel, accompanied by distant popping sounds.

Cool, someone else was shooting off firecrackers.

V. THE FEUD

Of course, as we cruised closer into that area, those popping sounds turned out to be gunshots.

We saw two groups of guys squared off against one another—Black guys, as far as I could tell—with just the river dividing them. They hid behind random objects—everything from sofas to burned-out cars that littered the channel. It was suddenly total chaos, a war zone. Once in a while, one of them would poke his head out to fire at the other guys across the way.

It must be paintball—but I didn't see any paint.

If a person had landed from another planet—which I kinda *had*—it would've seemed that a single group had somehow turned on one another and was trying to kill its own members. The only thing that seemed different, from one side to the other, was that each side wore different color bandanas.

The day seemed too sunny for cold-blooded murder. But what did I know? I was just a naive kid from the Valley. What were we thinking to push on and come down here? How stupid of us!

These guys meant business. And yet, there was a casualness, or simple recklessness, that made it feel like it wasn't that big of a deal to them. Scared us shitless though.

And the nearer we got the more I didn't want any part of it. Our boat inched closer regardless. We tried to reach out and stop, but the current was too strong and there wasn't much to hold on to except that flat slimy cement beside the narrow channel. Neither of us could get a good grip. Damn algae! We pressed down hard on the sides with our hands and skinned them. We tried with the paddles, and that helped, but still we kept moving forward, only slightly more slowly. We were coming up on one guy who was nearest upstream, and we worried that once he spotted us, he might mistake us for the enemy (whoever that was exactly, we weren't sure).

I had to make a jump for it, but I didn't want to yell out to Ian. So I gathered up my nerve and gave myself a countdown to jump. I took a couple deep breaths and made an awkward leap for the horizontal side of the narrow channel.

As I pushed off though, the kayak moved away from me, and I dropped my paddle in the water and it drifted away downstream. I fell and barely held to the side of the channel, scraping my forearms again. The boat kept going and my elbows and forearms hurt like hell. With my lower half in the water, I could feel the bottom of the channel and so I pushed off, ending up rolling over the edge. With the guy straight ahead, and Ian looking back at me in panic mode, I didn't have much time before Ian was right up next to the guy. If anyone was going to get shot, Ian would be first. I scrambled to my feet and chased after the kayak.

We were close to the guy with the gun now; fortunately, he hadn't yet seen us. So I was practically tiptoeing by the time I grabbed the straps on the end of the kayak and stopped the boat. As soon as I did that, Ian braced himself then quickly hopped out and grabbed the strap on the other end of the boat. Without saying a word, we both lifted the boat out of the water and made an awkward beeline across the flat concrete.

We looked up. There was one of those drainpipe outlets with the steel grate covers surrounded by two vertical sides of concrete, about our height, and a flat bottom. This one had its pipe grate propped open with a stick.

We hustled up the angled concrete riverbank and into the relative safety of this outpost. With all the gunfire, we might as well have been in a place like Fallujah or Kandahar.

Exhausted, with our hearts pounding, we plopped the kayak down on the ground and collapsed on top of it.

We stayed like that, heaving and catching our breath, for a minute or two.

The silence was broken by a voice, a female one, with a bit of an echo in it but no one in sight.

"Well now," it said. We whipped our heads around, searching. "Look what thuh cat dragged in!"

With all the gunshots, I thought I was starting to hear things.

I looked left, I looked right, I looked right behind me—nothing. I looked at Ian, thinking maybe he was doing a cruel ventriloquism bit and playing games with my feeble mind. But he had the same freaked-out look that I did.

"Ovuh here, ya damn nitwits!"

I followed the voice to the drainpipe but still didn't see anything. I got up slowly, walked past Ian, and inched my way toward the dark hole of the pipe where the stick propped it open. As I got up close to it and let my eyes adjust, I saw some movement. I stopped.

First one foot (a ragged boot) jutted out into the light, then a second foot. I stepped backed. Out came a leg (jeans, tight and ripped), and then another leg. The half-visible figure scooted to the edge of the pipe, its upper half still not visible, though I swore I could see a pair of eyes.

Then the figure leaned forward. It was a girl, roughly my age. No wonder I couldn't see her—her dark black skin melded perfectly with the pitch blackness of the pipe. On top of that she had on a ragged black T-shirt.

"Whatcha starin' at?"

"Nothing," I stammered awkwardly, carefully, not knowing whose side she was on. "Um, I'm Sam. And this is Ian. We're neutral."

A gutsy laugh answered back from the darkness.

"Neutral? Funny, white boy. I'm Tawnya. Don'tcha know no better than tuh be comin' in here where there's wars goin' on an' niggahs gettin' shot?"

"We were ... we didn't mean to," I blurted nervously.

"Yeah, yeah, I saw yer whole sad entry there," she said, leaning forward, slightly out of the pipe now. "An' lemme tell ya, you guys crack me up! That's about the stupidest thing I ever saw." Turning to Ian, she added, "And what are you, deaf?"

"Er, no, ma'am."

"Ma'am!?"

"Sorry."

"*You're* sorry. *Ma'am?* Jeez! Do I look like your mama? Do I look like some middle-aged housewife? At first I wasn't sure if you guys were really brave or just dumb. Then when I saw your jump-outta-thuh-boat routine, I knew which you wuz, fer sure. So, whatcha gonna do now?"

"We don't know," I said. "It depends on what's going on here. It's not like we planned on running into this. So, what is *this* anyway?"

She leaned out farther until we could get a good view of her. She was pretty, small, with a real skinny, graceful neck, a flattop Afro, and sort of muscular in general, sinewy, like a rock climber or someone who did long-distance track and field. You could see her six-pack peeking out from under her cut-off T-shirt. "You stumbled onto some nasty turf, that's what. This is a favorite shootin' gallery for the Crips and Bloods. Don't mind them too much—they just like to shoot shit up. They ain't tryin' to kill one another, least not today. It's sort of a way tuh unload, you know, literally."

"I'll say," said Ian.

Two guys appeared, just then breathing heavily, holding pistols. As they stepped closer, we saw one was the guy we nearly ran into with our kayak. It looked like they'd come running up the embankment to find shelter in our nook, too. As they did, a few bullets whizzed overhead or ricocheted off something, somewhere.

Ian and I hit the ground. After a few seconds, we peeked up to find the two guys and the girl staring at us, incredulous.

"Who the fuck are they?" said the one guy to Tawnya.

"Beats me," she said.

"Well, what the fuck are they doin' in our spot?"

She shrugged. He turned to us.

"You're in our spot, muthafuckers!"

"Sorry," I said.

"Yeah, that's fine," Ian added, "because it turns out we were just leaving."

"It's a big accident that we ended up here," I tried to explain.

"You bettah believe it!" one of the guys said. "And if you don't get lost you're gonna have an even biggah accident. Like, I cap you right here!"

He raised his pistol and waived it haphazardly in our general direction.

"Lay off, Jojo. I'll get rid of 'em."

"Yeah, take these damn crackers out back an' get rid of 'em."

"Uh," said Ian, "no need for any of that. We can show ourselves out" as we stood up and scrambled to leave.

Ping-pang went the shots. We hit the ground again, covering our heads like dorks.

All three of them seemed to think this was hysterically funny.

"Well, what're you waitin' for now!" the one guy continued. "Didn't I just say to get the fuck outta here?"

"Yeah, but," we argued, raising our heads, "bullets."

Ptang!

We buried our heads again.

"Oh, come on, you pussies!" the guy said, fully standing up. "They don't mean nothin'. Are you waitin' for a fuckin' invitation?!" He reached his gun over the lip of the bunker and, not really aiming, fired off a few rounds.

"Come on, you guys," the girl said to us. "Grow a pair an' follow me." She looked at the boat. "Pull that thing into thuh hole afta us," indicating the pipe.

The two guys leaned out of the fort and fired off a couple more shots toward the other side of the river. And a few shots came back but far off the mark.

We didn't want to stick around to see what might happen next. It was well enough that Tawnya was willing to get us out of there fast. We had to trust her. She seemed pretty cool. Then again, I remembered how I thought Stengel was pretty cool at first, too, so I reminded myself to be more careful when it came to the issue of trusting people or not.

She led us into the pipe tunnel, then lit up her lighter so we could see. She directed us to pull the boat in behind us, like a giant cork plugging up the neck of a wine bottle. She told Ian to close the metal door behind him.

"Now, follow me."

We did as instructed, not wanting to go back, but then again we didn't want to go forward into even deeper darkness either.

But what choice did we have? We were between a rock and a few thousand tons of concrete. We had to put our lives in the hands of someone we'd known for less than ten minutes.

VI. THE PAD

We eventually popped up out of another manhole cover, like a bizarre family of urban groundhogs.

Tawnya seemed to know the area well, jumping across or through the city's pitfalls, here and there: broken glass, railroad tracks, potholes, jagged holes in fences, rabid junkyard watchdogs, semitrucks, and dilapidated buildings reeking of the morning-after vomit of industry run amok.

Turns out she was headed for one of those dilapidated buildings, sort of parallel to the river, maybe a quarter mile or so off of it. But it felt like longer than that, being that it was practically an obstacle course.

After our embarrassing exit from the river, neither of us wanted to be shown up by this girl and have to stop and rest—she seemed to expect us to keep up. She climbed a metal downspout and jumped over a fence. We followed awkwardly. She squeezed through two sheets of a sliding metal door. We followed, panting. We ended up at a warehouse with long rows of workstations and abandoned equipment.

"What the heck is *this*?" Ian asked.

"Some kinda garment factory," she said. "Sweatshop."

"You come here a lot?" he said.

"Is that supposed tuh be a pickup line?" Ian looked a bit stunned. "Just kiddin'. Relax, kid."

We walked down the main aisle and wove our way through a few barren workstations. "I try not tuh be here too much. Not unless I have to. But it's been a big help more than a few times."

We entered a side room off the main area and paused. It didn't seem to lead anywhere else.

"Where to now?" I asked. "Where are you taking us, anyway?"

"Up."

She climbed a rickety wooden ladder with a couple missing rungs, up to a second floor—not wanting to be outdone, we followed. Then she walked us up a questionable flight of stairs to a doorway, unlatched it, and stepped onto a long, flat, asphalt roof. There was an awesome view of the downtown buildings like I'd never seen before. Looking around again, I spied the river maybe a half mile away. In the one direction, the slim, winding strip of river veered up toward the mountains to the north and east. In the opposite direction, it snaked downstream and disappeared into the barren concrete plains. Somewhere that way, to the south, was Long Beach.

"Wow, cool!" I said. "You could fit a whole football field on top of this building!

"Hey," she replied, "not so loud."

"Why? Seems like there's no one around for miles."

Tawnya shook her head, trying to be patient with me. "*Seems* that way, sure, but you'd be surprised: There's a lot goes on down here, jus' not the kinda shit that's visible. This is where pretty boys like y'all get your overpriced clothing and shoes made. This is where they make the parts for yer fancy cars when ya get a ding or something. This is where they butcher and process and pack thuh food you eat at those highbrow restaurants ya go to, and where they dump extra shit that went into makin' it all. Out into the wash and to the ocean."

Ian and I were sort of dumbfounded. Still, she was making a lot of generalizations, so I had to speak up:

"What makes you so sure you know our habits anyway?"

"I don't. I'm just shittin' you." She paused, then shot back: "But I'm right, aren't I? Come on, admit it," getting in my face and Ian's, opening her eyes real wide. "I'm just shittin' you again. Uh huh. I thought so."

"Yeah, well," I grasped for a timely comeback but ended up with something lame. "There's stuff that's made up in the Valley that you probably buy and use, too, you know."

"Really?!" she laughed. "That's all ya got? Duh. Come on, boys, let's go back downstairs."

So we opened the rooftop door and leveled down a floor.

On the second floor, she led us through another door. "Welcome to the pad," she proudly explained.

There were a couple of medium-sized rooms that looked like they were once maybe manager offices. I suppose it helped to be in a smaller space, to contain the vastness of industry that surrounded them. There were signs that this room had been inhabited more than a few times since the demise of the company. Tawnya took us over to what looked like a large executive's balcony. She'd somehow made a BBQ grill that was repurposed from an old stainless steel industrial sink, then fitted with some grating on top. She showed us how to put wood into the base of the dual sinks to get the whole thing heated up and functioning as either a BBQ on the one side or all-purpose stove on the other.

"Cool," said Ian.

"Glad you like it, 'cause I'm nominatin' you as cook tonight."

"Huh? Uh, sure. As long as you know I'm a lousy cook," he said, looking around. "But with what food?"

Tawnya walked us back inside and over to a closet door. She opened it up. Inside were a bunch of dried goods: cereal, rice, bags of pasta, potatoes, onions—stuff like salt, pepper, sugar, and spices, even bars of chocolate. Also, there were a few shelves of canned goods, like corn, baked beans, tuna, and salmon.

"Think you can find somethin' to use?"

"Yeah, I guess."

She reached in and lifted a few items that didn't look so fresh and pitched them in the nearby trash. As she did, we saw that tons of little black ants had found whatever it was and swarmed all over it. She followed the line of ants from the pantry and traced it outside of that room and along another wall. It was like someone had taken a black marker and drawn on the walls. Several lines of constantly working little ants converged. Their numbers seemed infinite. The lines stretched across the walls and disappeared into several holes in the exterior wall.

"Damn ants. Ya gotta make sure you close up everything tight. You leave a crumb out and them ants will be on it in no time. Got it?"

We nodded.

"I'll come back and clean this up in a sec," she added.

"What do you do for water?" asked Ian.

"Water? Gottcha covered. Come on," she said.

She walked us over to another wall where there was an old spigot. She turned it on, and after a short delay and odd sounds, a trickle of dubious water came out. "There, that oughta do ya. Boil any water ya plan on usin'." Ian looked overwhelmed. "Well, whatcha waitin' for, fella? Eighty-six the hunger an' get that order up!"

Ian took a deep breath, then snapped out of his trance, went over to the closet pantry, and started digging for ingredients.

Tawnya walked me into another room that was some sort of crash pad. There were things like old beanbag chairs, sofas, blankets, and a couple of mattresses spread across the dusty floor.

"Jeez, who sleeps here?" I asked.

"Depends. Whoever needs it most."

"You?"

"Sometimes, more than I like tuh admit."

"All night?"

"Well, yeah. Why *not*? Unless you think it's better tuh get up an' leave in the middle of the night."

"Well, I mean, what about your parents?" I asked.

"My *parents*?! Oh, I see, like dinner around the family table, sittin' on the sofa together watchin' *Friends* reruns on our flatscreen TV? Ha! My dad died a couple years ago. My mom's not much there on a lot of levels. She got her own problems; she don't know when I come or go—might as well be on another planet, I s'pose. An' it's probably better that way. That's not a sob story, just an FYI."

"Oh, I'll bet she cares," said Ian.

"Nice try, but that's a losin' bet, pal. Trust me. I mean, sure, deep down, somewhere in there. But ya don't gotta be polite. Look, that's how it is. It's not totally bad—I've had tuh learn to take care of myself. No need tuh put a shine on shit. But hey, speakin' of which, how 'bout gettin' this place tidied up, wouldya? Everybody's gotta pitch in—the rules here are that ya gotta protect the pad and earn yer room and board. Fair 'nough?"

I nodded, surprised at how organized she was with this place. It was like a bare-bones, off-the-grid bed and breakfast, run by this kid. Which was pretty awesome to me, at least the independence part.

So I started cleaning up. At one point I turned to ask her a question, but she'd already moved on—tending to another part of her home away from home, which to her was probably more like a real home anyway.

After tidying up and unrolling a couple of sleeping pads for the night, I went back out to the balcony to see what was cooking. With some effort, and the smell of food, it was starting to feel kind of cozy in there.

Tawnya and I had fun ragging on Ian about how he cooked—or rather, his utter lack of cooking skills. Tawnya thought he was pulling her leg to get out of the work. And while we hung out and razzed him, we learned a lot more about Tawnya, like that she had two brothers with the Crips gang, in a "set" called GangstaSouth, or G-South (wearing blue), and a cousin and a sister-in-law with a set in the Bloods (mostly red stuff) called Nation710, or N-710. She talked about her dad, and the bad shit she'd done herself with the gangs, and why they did what they did, and how they communicated with hand signals and graffiti, and why it was okay by her in some ways because of the family-like support it gave her, and wrong by her in other ways at the same time.

All evening—through dinner and hanging around the BBQ fire afterward, through S'mores we made after roasting marshmallows on barbeque skewers, and into the night—we talked on and on, with no topic off-limits. It was a relief not to have to keep up facades; we didn't need to prop ourselves up with the usual BS we put out there to look good or seem cool as teens. We were okay with who we were and got to know each other on a deeper level.

Tawnya referred to herself as a contrarian, which is another way of saying that whatever everyone else does, she tried to do the exact opposite. She said that bothers a lot of people, but that she doesn't care. I'd never met a contrarian.

Like whenever everyone around her likes a certain singer, she goes out of her way to dislike that singer, even if she secretly likes them. She went out of her way to buy things that were out of season—which applied to everything else she did, from the food she ate (nothing seasonal, like pumpkin pie around Halloween) to personal fashion (only what was *out* of style at the time) to her larger life choices. She made a home at the pad but was always sure, in a minute's notice, to be able to up and leave—she said she kept a stash of supplies for if that time ever came. And while most of her friends talked down school, she was privately taking online courses at Santa Monica Community College and getting her high school equivalency degree. She said she wanted to be something, someday, that no one around her seemed to want: a computer scientist—you know, programming and all that.

Ian and I developed a lot of respect for her. In a surprising way, beyond our backgrounds that were clearly different, we identified with her: the way she forged her own identity, her attitude about independence, and her hatred of the status quo, injustice, meanness, and waste. She was pretty deep for someone our age. She definitely felt like someone who was aware of a shit-ton of stuff that most adults didn't even know about.

We talked about our trek downriver, and then everything and anything else we felt like: music, race, adults, downtown, suburbia, and sex.

At one point we noticed that she'd fallen asleep. She was doing a cute little snoring thing, and we cracked up listening to her. We tried to wake her by tickling her face and feet with a couple of pigeon feathers we found on the floor.

She'd sometimes mumble, "Szknock it off!" which would make us howl even more. But mostly she was a rock-hard sleeper, so we gave up trying.

We rolled her over onto a blanket and grabbed the ends and carried her into the sleeping room and put her down gently on the most comfortable of the mattresses.

We were sad to think that no one was going to miss this girl, this daughter, that night—someone with such character, spirit, and sense of humor. We realized we'd both miss her after we parted ways the next day. But tonight was tonight and, being teens, we're at our best when we're living in the moment and don't get too far ahead of ourselves.

Ian and I eventually curled up on our rollouts and passed out into a deep sleep.

VII. THE NEIGHBORS

But for all the relative calm and comfort of the prior evening, I grappled with alarming dreams, as if my mind was a few steps ahead of me. It always seems like whenever I got to a place of balance, peace, and simple fun, my mind always got back to the task of roasting my brain, churning things over, stirring stuff up, waking me up with the latest anxiety.

I sat up in a sweat, trying to remember the dream that was torturing me. Something about Ignazio. The details were fuzzy, but I remember feeling haunted by the notion that I dared to laugh and carry on, pretending that nothing extraordinary had happened the last few days.

I vaguely recalled the part of the actual dream where I was back at that ransacked house, with Stengel, Jean-Paul, and Lance. But this time I'm alone there, and I'm anxious because the place is a complete mess and I have the sense that I did it myself and was about to be blamed. They're all staring at me, like, shocked and all judgy. I looked for Iggie in the rooms but couldn't find him. In a bathroom, I tried to splash water on myself to wake up, and I washed my hands, but they never got cleaner. The water spilled over the edge of the sink and the whole room was filling up with water, no matter what I did. In the mirror I caught flashes of Iggie in the bathtub; he was a horrible blue color, and his eyes were bloodshot, and he moaned while rocking back and forth. I heard the distant sirens of police cars winding their way up the canyon road. The room filled up with water and all objects started to rise.

Only when a pillow hit me upside the head did I snap out of it. Ian was grinning across the room, proud of his direct shot. I threw it back at him but was hit from another side. Tawnya was sitting up in her sleeping bag, also pleased with her marksmanship.

"Come on, you guys, I'm beat!"

Eventually, we got up, threw on our same stinky old clothes, and shuffled over to the pantry closet to rummage for breakfast. We brought it all out on the balcony.

It was already another scorcher of a day, with clear skies and the sun well above the smoggy horizon. There was the river again, steady as always, sucking water from the whole state and elsewhere.

Since we didn't have stuff like milk or eggs, we heated up water in a pot on top of the stove and fixed ourselves instant oatmeal with dried apricots and apples on top, with some brown sugar.

"So, what're we doin' today, guys?" said Tawnya.

Ian and I looked at each other awkwardly. We didn't imagine that she'd want to keep hanging with us. Neither of us minded, we simply hadn't planned on it. Ian and I had talked about going back to the river before any of the gangs got going, so we could push on toward our goal.

"Oh, I see," said Tawnya. "Ya got places to go and people tuh meet." We bowed our heads in acknowledgement.

She didn't dwell on it. She set about getting us restocked with food and water and other supplies we badly needed to continue.

"Are you sure our kayak is safe where we left it?" Ian asked.

"Sure I'm sure," she replied.

"Okay. But we've still got to get a replacement paddle," he continued, "for the one that got washed away when we ran out of the river yesterday."

"I s'pose you boyz think there's a convenient REI around here somewhere, don't ya? Why not rent another, eh?"

"No, we *know*," said Ian. "We'll have to either find or make something from around here."

"Well, good luck on *that*," Tawnya shot back. "Maybe you can make one outta old bricks or glob together broken pieces of asphalt or ..."

"All right, fine. The challenge is on," I declared. "First to find a workable replacement wins bragging rights."

"But wait," Ian stopped us. "We should check on the kayak."

"Yeah," I admitted, "what's the point of searching for a new paddle if the kayak is gone?"

"Gone?" she laughed. "Even if someone here found it, they wouldn't know what the hell to do with it." She looked at our anxious faces. "Oh, all right, we'll swing by there again if you need to."

So we shoveled down the rest of our breakfast and went downstairs.

We squeezed out the metal sliding doors, and she led us a different way back to the river.

It was real quiet, a ghost town, back at the river. The stuff from the previous day's battle was spread over the whole place, including bullet casings that littered the area.

We made our way over to the tunnel where the kayak should've been. We opened up the grate. It was safe and sound—hadn't moved an inch, like she said.

Satisfied, we started wandering back toward the pad. Before we left the river, we passed another of those pipes with something oozing out of it. Again, I got angry and paused to bend the rusty end of the tin pipe by hammering it with an even stronger steel rod. Ian and Tawnya helped, too. After we were done and had plugged the pipe with other junk, we started walking away from the river. It wouldn't solve L.A.'s pollution problems, but at least it left the place better than how we'd found it.

Near the top of the concrete riverbank, something caught my eye. Wrapped around the top of a pole was a wet piece of cloth. It was a lot like Ignazio's green fleece jacket.

"What's all that?" she asked.

"Oh, nothing," trying to move on. But then it came back to me again and got to me. Out of nowhere I started spewing tears again, beyond my control, overwhelmed by the stupid piece of green cloth. I went over to it, and it was only a torn piece of something that looked like his jacket.

I was amazed at how the slightest reminder could still trigger such an effect. They sort of hovered, silently patting me on the back.

Eventually, I pulled myself together and we moved on. But it was a reminder for me about how much was still unsettled, despite thinking I'd somehow moved on. Yeah, right—dream on.

We fanned out to search the area and find ourselves a substitute paddle. We agreed to meet up again in a half hour. Ian and I didn't admit it, but the idea of wandering around this foreign turf spooked us. Inside the pad, we were at least contained by Tawnya's safety net. But out on the postapocalyptic streets of L.A., anything could happen.

We each headed down different alleys, not far from our own building. Mine smelled faintly like mold, paint, engine oil, and urine. My eyes scanned the sides of the buildings, cordoned off with fencing.

From inside one lot, a couple of pit bulls came charging out, high-fived the fence, and carried on like they wanted a piece of my hot steamy guts.

I kept going, but it was pretty much a dead end—marked only by leftover homeless bedding, splayed-out cardboard, and empty liquor bottles. Retracing my steps from that alley, I walked down the street for a couple blocks and selected another alley to explore.

Again, I got to the end of it without much to salvage. As I was walking back out though, I heard a noise, stopped, and listened. The sound was hushed mumblings and whispers. Finally, beyond the fence I spied a small, open vent.

I climbed up the chain-link fence and the sound grew slightly louder when my head was up at its level. No, I wasn't imagining it—there *were* murmured voices coming out of there, but I still couldn't distinguish any words. The chatter didn't sound like English. I delicately pushed aside some razor wire and climbed down the other side, walking over to the building, and looking around for a way to get up to the vent. Whenever I moved I swore I could hear the mumbling grow quieter, but I couldn't be sure. I found a few old milk crates and stacked them up against the building, beneath the window. I climbed up.

Before I peered inside through the slits, the smell hit me. It was a combo of sweat, body odor, bleach, and poop. I'd never smelled anything quite like it. It was seriously nasty.

What I saw was shocking, too.

It was a room about thirty feet by thirty feet, and twenty feet tall, with bodies spread out over it—maybe fifty or so. They were stretched out in all kinds of ways. Some were leaning on one another, some seemed to be under others, and some were leaning against the walls. It was bizarre. I wondered what the gathering was for. There only seemed to be one door in or out of the room, but nobody left or entered. It was a very generic-looking room, with no notable features besides peeling paint that made a few irregular shapes on the walls and a few flickering fluorescent lights.

The people seemed like they were from seemingly everywhere, ethnically, and I understood why I couldn't make out any of the words. Mostly Asian and Hispanic. I put my ear against the vent, but I couldn't distinguish the languages very well. It was chaos, a sad mess down there.

There wasn't a smile in the whole bunch, and with the conditions being what they were, I couldn't say I blamed them. I thought about calling out but decided to keep my mouth shut. This wasn't my home turf, so I might get into trouble before knowing exactly what was happening. Tawnya would know what to do.

Just then I could've sworn that one lady across the room could see me peeking through the vent. Her eyes became unglazed, and she craned her neck forward, as if to determine whether or not I was real. As she elbowed the guy next to her and pointed, I decided it'd be best to disappear. Whomever she was nudging probably thought she was imagining something. Poor woman.

As I walked away and retraced my steps, the voices fading. I looked at my watch and realized I'd better book it if I intended to meet up with Ian and Tawnya at our appointed time.

VIII. THE BOOTY

For all her talk, Tawnya didn't have much to show: a street parking sign that had been bent over and snapped off. It would be hard to paddle with it, especially with the sharp shards at the severed end.

Ian had already strung together a bizarre bunch of flotsam that he'd found. It didn't look like any kayak paddle I'd ever seen, but very Ian-esque—bits of sheet metal to form the blade of the paddle, with a good amount of duct tape, on what seemed to be an old garden rake. It was sorta sleek and cool (if you squinted).

They turned to me and my unmistakable empty-handedness. I told them what I'd seen. Ian thought I was joking to cover up the fact that I didn't have anything to offer. She scanned my face and had a sense I was telling the truth.

So they followed me. I took them back down the alley, over the fence, and up the crates.

They saw what I was talking about.

When we got back to the pad, we hung out on the balcony, catching our breath, discussing the situation.

"What the hell was that?" said Ian finally.

"What the hell do ya think?" she replied. But both Ian and I wore a couple of blank looks on our faces. "Oh, come on, you guys are so damn naïve! Get real. Ya think that's some sorta AA meeting or Tuppuhwear party? Or what, a very unusual sports bar? Dudes! Get with the program—this is the *twenty-first* century. Can you pick up the pace? Don't you know traffickin' when you see it?"

"Trafficking?" said Ian. "Whoa. No way!"

"What else, dude? Duh," she replied.

Ian and I shrugged. She was right—even a sweatshop wouldn't keep so many people in a single room. Still, we simply couldn't conceive of it since it was something we'd never run into—way off our radar. But judging by her wide-eyed excitement, I wasn't convinced that she'd seen it firsthand herself either—even if she might've had a better sense about it than we did.

"Now," she went on, "I'm sorry to burst your innocent bubbles, boys, but we gotta get back there and do somethin'."

"Like what?" I said. "That's *so* over our heads. No way. We're on a different mission, and we didn't sign on for getting involved with ... sorry."

"Really?!" she bellowed. She pursed her lips at me and turned to Ian. He looked down at his shuffling, restless feet and emitted a feeble shrug.

"You're gonna leave them there and me here tuh deal with them? You know, that's sooo typical. Go back tuh yer cocoon. Go on yer little adventure. But that's messed up. Go on. Just know that it's 'cause you can *afford* tuh take no risks. I suppose that's your privilege though—pick an' choose what bothers you."

"Look, you don't know what we've been through," I said, starting to tear up again. "I'm done with looking for trouble. Last time I did, it ended badly. Very badly. So I'm sorry, but I'm out."

After that there was more than a bit of awkward silence. She just let it work its way in and under our skins until finally ...

"Ffffine," I said, kicking myself for being spineless. "Damn it!! We gotta do something. She's right." I looked at Ian. He sighed—he knew, too.

"What've we got to lose?" Ian said, trying to convince himself.

"Pretty much everything," I said.

"All right," Ian responded, "then it's settled."

"Thataboy!" she yelped, jumping up. "You won't regret it. Or you might, but whatever. You gotta do this—we *know* we gotta do this, right?"

We nodded reluctantly. So be it.

"Damn," she went on, marveling how "you live next to folks for a long time and you don't get a chance to get to know the neighbors. Now," she said as she paced a bit, playing drill sergeant. Finally, she dropped her role, smiled, grabbed us by the shoulders, and huddled up, blurting out, "So what's the plan?"

Ian and I looked again at each other. We thought for sure that *she* was the one with the plan.

The rest of that morning and into the afternoon we threw around various ideas until we could agree on the plan. Then we snacked and mulled things over and refined them more.

So much for our planned departure back to the river. But the river would always be there. It was reliable that way.

We chilled until evening. After it got dark, we prepared to make our move. We did some stealthy reconnaissance on the building. The first significant thing we noticed was a door at the front, from where a few people (not the types in that room) came and went. We counted two burly guys wearing shades, tattoos, and attitudes but didn't know if there were more inside. We needed to get a closer look. They didn't look like anyone I'd ever met before. These guys looked, well, rough. They made Ronnie McMasters look puny. They stomped around, making little head nods to one another, never cracking smiles, and sometimes exchanging things between hands and pockets. There was always at least one person keeping vigil out front, sometimes talking on his phone.

The back of the building had freight doors, but those were impenetrable and looked like they'd been sealed for a long time. Along the opposite side of the building from where that small window was, the other long side of the warehouse, were a few interesting options in terms of doors and windows. About halfway down that side was one window where we saw two other guys hanging out. We figured that was their main gathering place, which seemed to be an office. We dubbed this the lair.

"I've got to get a closer look," I said. "You guys watch my back."

I snuck up to the fence that ran along the property line with the adjacent warehouse. Conveniently, the fence was pulled up near there by some prior intruder, so I took advantage of that, then skulked along the side of the building until I got to the office window. I saw movement inside. I checked the ground nearby to make sure we wouldn't knock into anything, then moved in closer, to the lip of the window and peered in.

Three of the guys were in there, kicking back (one I recognized from out front). So I could remember them better, I gave them nicknames. The most massively muscular guy with a shaved head looked like he must've been a bouncer, so I tagged him as Bouncer Dude. Another guy was young, short, wide, and oafish, and always seemed to be the one in the recliner chair, so I labeled him Lazy Boy. The third guy was wiry and covered with the most tattoos, plus he sported freaky contact lenses that gave him a catty look. He was as skittish and chain-smoked through his rotten, jagged teeth. He became Circus Freak. That left one guy (at least that's what we figured) out front, the one who dressed stylishly and sported one of those Chicago gangster-style hats, so I named him Al Capone.

Four against three. The odds weren't great to start; still, we had the element of surprise and the cover of darkness.

Having done my research, I was about to turn back when I stopped. Circus Freak went over to the corner of the office. He stooped down. He lifted up several floorboards and reached into the hole. He pulled out a few bundles of money and tossed one each to his buddies and pocketed one for himself. Then he put back the floorboards and returned to his seat. The guys counted out the money.

I hustled back to where Ian and Tawnya were on lookout.

"See anything?" asked Ian.

"Definitely. But let's talk somewhere else."

We spent some time revisiting the river to stow the new paddle options and prepare our boat, just in case. We didn't know how long this whole operation might take, but Ian and I decided that as soon as it was done, whatever that meant, we'd be out of there and back on our way as fast as possible—we were running out of time. We talked about it with Tawnya, and she understood. She said her goodbyes to us right then and there, where we'd first met, in case we got separated somehow.

I cooked that night. It wasn't quite like the previous night. We had the evening's mission on our minds, and so it was hard to mask what was weighing on us. We tried to distract ourselves, but we kept coming back around to it.

"We need more time to scout out the place," I argued, reminding them about the stash and suggesting there could be a whole lot more about the place that we might not know.

"We don't know how desperate those people stuck in there are," she countered. "They look like they've been waitin' long enough. Imagine if it was you or someone in your family. What if someone in there is sick and dies *tonight*, and we don't act? How'd that be? Could ya live with that, huh?"

"All right. Jeez, can't you be wrong *sometimes*? You should be, like, a salesperson or something, a freakin' lawyer. I'm serious, Tawnya."

We waited anxiously for a while as we discussed contingency plans and went back over the details of our scheme.

We each killed time in our own ways. Then, around three a.m., we donned our spy gear; some dark fabrics on our heads and dabs of charcoal soot on our faces.

We headed downstairs and out into the night—ninjas that we now were.

iX. A LiTTLE SURPRISE

We went back around to the alley and checked in on the room where the people were kept, on the original side of the warehouse.

It was about the same as before, but with more people sleeping beneath the dim lights. It was hard to count how many of them there actually were now.

We snuck around the other, darker side of the building. We checked the front to see who was on guard duty: Circus Freak, smoking as usual, his orange cigarette tip pulsing like an evil little lighthouse, signaling people to stay away.

The blinds were down at the office window. We could barely peek in through one small hole; it looked like only two guys now—Bouncer Dude and Al Capone—were there. That left Lazy Boy unaccounted for.

After testing the windows and doors on that side, we knew there was no easy way in. We'd have to make our own way, according to phase 2: retrieve. We targeted a spot on that side of the building, near the room with all the people inside.

Ian had located a structural weakness in one part of the outside shell of the building, which was mostly made of corrugated metal sheets fastened with screws. It wasn't right at the room where the people were, but near enough, in a seemingly unused and blocked-off part of the building. We built our plan on the weakest-link theory, hoping that no one was using that section and assuming somehow that we could exploit that defect.

We did a quick check of the window on the opposite side of the building to make sure Lazy Boy wasn't in the holding pen dealing with his prisoners. Maybe he was outside their door; we still couldn't track down and confirm his presence. Damn. Then again, he could've been crashed out drunk somewhere else inside. We were going to have to take our chances with not knowing.

We made our way to the proposed point of entry, the flap in the metal that had come partially undone. We got out our bag and extracted a flashlight. Ian peeled back and held the flap as I shined the flashlight into the hole and Tawnya put additional pressure on the flap, causing it to snap out of another fastening. But it made a metallic *shpwang!* and we froze, listening for signs that anybody might've heard it. We waited for a minute, until a distant dog that we'd alarmed finally chilled out. We breathed a collective sigh and kept on going.

We stuck our heads through the hole to inspect the wall's infrastructure and yanked out insulation, then pushed aside wires. We felt for the hefty plumbing pipes and where the wooden two-by-four wall supports were positioned. Ian extracted the knife feature on his Swiss Army-ish gadget and marked the sheetrock in a few cuts. We listened for activity on the other side of the wall. Nothing. Ian scored it again, going over the three lines that would make a pet-sized door to crawl through.

When he was done, he nodded. I gave the sheetrock outline a swift smack with the heel of my foot. Once more and there was a slight cracking sound. I turned and raised my foot, then gave it a hearty kick on the third try. It broke open a hole—not quite an immaculate laser hole like they'd do in *Mission Impossible*, but it would do. We cleared away the broken pieces.

It was as dark inside as out but without the advantage of distant streetlights, skyscraper office lights, and moonlight.

Tawnya held the flashlight in her teeth and crawled in first. We saw her legs disappear like she was eaten by a giant beast. My heart was beating like crazy now—and we were just getting going! *Control yourself.* I took a few deep breaths to settle down.

After a couple minutes, she stuck her arm out and gave us the thumbs-up. We made our way in, one by one.

It was a big lofty space. We did our best not to trip over stuff and went to the wall that according to our calculations was one of the walls of the room where everyone was held. We put our ears against it and listened.

We double-checked our calculations, whispering back and forth until we could be sure we were at least 50 percent correct in our assumptions.

It was crunch time. We couldn't put it off any longer. We looked at one another, nodding.

Ian, our setup man, scored the sheetrock again. We heard murmuring on the other side. Again, a couple of pinpoint whacks and we were through. Sort of. It wasn't as easy this time. Beyond this wall was a real wall—that is, a brick wall we discovered the hard way. Great—*now* what?

We decided to keep to the plan and find a way through. This was simply a bump in the road. It was an old wall, and even if the folks on the inside couldn't get out, they didn't have the tools we had. Ian got out the heavy artillery: a couple of hammers and chisels. Fortunately, Tawnya had stashed away a few tools she found over the years and stored at the pad.

As we smacked against the brick and mortar, the folks in the room would be able to hear it, for sure. We had to move fast if this was going to work or bail and get the hell out.

It was a good thing that the wall was old, or we wouldn't have made it through. But it chipped and crumbled easily, and we made good progress, especially after we got the first brick to crack, which then allowed us to loosen the surrounding mortar, and to start knocking out bricks. One by one, like loose teeth, they fell out. Once through, we could hear the louder noises and voices coming from the other side.

But then there was yet another sheetrock wall! We weren't about to back down though. We didn't bother to score it. We just kicked the hell out of it.

When we finally broke through, and the sheetrock dust settled, the commotion was building to a dangerous level. When I looked into the room, with the sweat tumbling down my dusty brow, I couldn't see any people, just shapes scurrying back and forth.

Tawnya went first. Then Ian. Then me.

It felt like we'd landed on another planet. I think they thought we must be ghostly spirits, with all the sheetrock dust on us. Also, I'm sure it seemed unlikely to them that we'd be kids, a mysterious, doe-eyed youth rescue team.

It didn't last long though. A few of them turned quickly, hearing someone approaching from outside the door. Suddenly it was like they thought the same thing at the same time. There was no way you could plan something like it. They snapped into action, with some of them sitting against the hole in the wall, and others pretending to sleep up against the wall blockers. Another bunch came at us and pulled us into a corner, covered us with stray clothing and sat on us. They shushed us with their gesturing.

Next we heard a bunch of locks on the door being undone. Then heavy footsteps coming into the room.

"What the fuck is goin' on in here!? Stop yer chatterin'! If you don't shut the fuck up, we're gonna fuck you up! Understood?"

Followed by absolute quiet.

We heard boot steps strolling around the room. It seemed like two guys. We heard them stop over by the hole in the wall, surveying the heap of sleeping people. The guys continued, stopping right in front of us. We could feel the bunch of people lying against us and breathing heavily but trying not to show it. Then the shoes continued, circling a bit more, then pausing by the door.

"Knock it off! Got it?!"

The door slammed. Lock, lock, lock. Fading footsteps.

Slowly, quietly, the room returned to its normal awkwardness, but everyone kept real quiet.

Hobbling toward me was a one-eyed figure covered in makeshift bandages composed of filthy, blood-soaked cloths. Most of the facial skin was covered up, but I could see lots of cuts, bruises between the peeling cloth, with the dried blood underneath.

Then the figure started peeling back a few of the bandages that covered the other eye, but I protested, "What the hell, leave it. What are you—"

Despite the certain pain this person must've felt from doing this, he (or she) unleashed a fiendish, toothy grin. I looked closer. As the bandage over the other eye was pulled aside, I couldn't believe my eyes.

"*Ignazio!!?*"

X. GOING DEEPER

I've never fainted before, but that just about did it for me. If I didn't know there was an imminent threat to us, I seriously might've collapsed.

I started to give Ignazio—or his ghost (I still wasn't 100 percent sure)—a big bear hug, but then I realized that, in his condition, that might do him more harm than good. So we sort of fumbled our hands and forearms together and held onto each other for a few awkward seconds, with me putting my head on his hands and shedding a few tears onto them. He moaned, probably from the pain of my salty tears in his cuts, ending with a feeble utterance: "Sam, is that really you?"

"Si, Iggie. It's me. I could ask the same thing."

Ian and Tawnya were gently but insistently tugging on me. I nodded to Iggie. "Let's get outta here, mi amigo," and we snapped into motion.

We had to prevent a loud stampede to the exit. Tawnya was the first to get to the hole in the wall, where she backed herself against it and turned to face the overeager group. She raised her finger and demanded their focused attention. Which she got. I thought it was only Ian and me that she had wrapped around her finger, but I saw that she did this with everyone. She didn't wait for respect; she *commanded* it in every encounter. She then drew her finger to her lips, and the group relaxed momentarily breathing again and trusting her poise and leadership.

She pointed to Ian. He came to the exit, and she handed him the flashlight. He turned it back on, crouched, pulled himself quietly through the hole. After a short pause, he reached back through with his hand to give a thumbs-up. The group got it: This would be a smoothly managed operation, one by one.

Tawnya pointed at me, then pointed to the outside wall. I looked at Ignazio, reluctant to leave him even for a few seconds, 'cause in the back of my mind I thought he might just vanish again. But I knew my job. I scurried over to the hole and went through.

On the other side, Ian helped pull me out, then stand up. With him shining the light, I went over to the outside wall and snuck back out, to the fresh air, to be the helper at the exterior wall of sheet metal.

I looked around and saw the perennial smoke from Circus Freak's cigarette wafting around the front corner of the building, fifty yards away, caught against the streetlight at the front of the warehouse.

Along that same wall the slotted light shined through the blinds of the lair, about twenty-five yards away. I noticed that one of the windows was open, so I had to keep everyone quiet.

Crouching down to the hole in the outside shell, I whispered: "All clear!"

One by one, the evacuees started to emerge.

As they came out, I gestured for them to wait at the back of the building, where the sound wouldn't be an issue. But I didn't know what they understood exactly.

When I was lifting the metal flap to help people out though, I saw bandaged hands and a bit of fleece green sleeves on the other side guiding people to the outside. It hadn't been five minutes and already Ignazio had joined our group and was helping out. Since I'd met him he'd always had a sense of what needed to be done and was always able to jump in and do it. I'm pretty sure that in my whole short life I've never been so glad to see someone.

I was anxious about the people at the back of the building. There was an intermittent stream of them sent that way, but I had no idea what they did once they turned the corner. Would they bolt out onto the city streets? Were they waiting for one of us to lead them the rest of the way—and if so, to where?

We had a people-management problem on our hands that could unhinge our mission before it was completed. We must've already gotten thirty out of there, and they kept coming.

When I saw Ignazio come through the outer hole, I knew that was the tail end. I was sure he'd only come through when bringing up the rear of the captives. I must've sweated a quart of water, feeling that every sound was echoing off the walls of the alley and finding its way to the ears of the four thugs. By that point it must've been well past four a.m. The sun would be coming up before too long.

We had to keep going, or it would be for nothing. All it would take would be for Circus Freak to hear something and peek around the corner and see us scurrying around. From being on the offense, we were now in retreat, and that wasn't comforting. Being nearly free isn't the same thing as being actually free.

After Ignazio came Ian and finally Tawnya.

The four of us held onto one another and hobbled together to the back of the building. The pain was starting to catch up to Ignazio, so I put an arm around his shoulder and sort of half-carried him along.

When we stepped around the corner at the back of the warehouse, it was crazy. I expected that our newly freed group would be waiting there obediently. But they weren't satisfied with only a sip of freedom—they wanted it all and didn't want to wait. And who were we to stop them? We saw the backs of a few of them, the slower ones, finding their way back out into the metropolis after being cooped up for however many days, months, years it had been for each of them.

It felt like total anarchy, but it was probably best this way. We'd done our job. Besides, the truth was that it would've been hard to lead them anywhere else as a group.

"Bon voyage!" I uttered under my breath. It was like blowing on a bunch of dandelion seeds and watching them scatter, hoping they found their ultimate destination.

"Ya got that right," said Tawnya. "C'mon, let's get outta here."

"Where we go now?" said Iggie.

"We've got a place not so far from here," I told him.

We started out, but somehow my feet didn't move. In a few seconds, they turned.

"What is it?" Ian asked.

"I ... I've got one more thing to do," I said. "Look: If we stop now, we may have hurt them—it's like we crippled their ship or clipped their wings a bit—but they'll just move on, rebuild, and round up another bunch like those folks. We need a knockout blow, to disrupt them in a way that'll hit them where it hurts."

"The stash!" said Ian.

"Yeah," I said, irrationally emboldened by our success with freeing the group. "We know where it is. We can't let them keep it. I'm going back. I've at least got to check it out and see if it's possible. Tawnya, how 'bout you take Ignazio over to the pad and do something about his wounds?"

She nodded. I looked at Ian. He was scared to death. So was I.

"Don't even ask," he said. "I'm with you."

"All right, you two, but don't try tuh be heroes. Check it out, but nothin' stupid."

"Deal," I said, trying to sound confident. "We'll meet you back there as soon as we can."

Iggie pulled back the cloth from over his eye and gave me a look that was equal parts "Go get 'em, man!" and "You're a stupid fool!"

For a few seconds we watched them go, then Ian and I took off on our little bonus venture.

XI. THE STASH

We snuck back along the alley and paused beside the metal flap to listen and make sure there were no sounds coming from inside. We were certain that if we'd been found out we would've heard a whole lot of commotion in there by now.

We kept going, closing in on the lair's open window. When we got there, to get a good view, Ian clasped his hands together and I put a foot into his hands, and he lifted me up so I could look through a gap in the blinds. Once up there I got a good foothold onto the narrow window ledge, to study the scene.

Lazy Boy was there in his recliner—a sleeping, snoring troll. In the corner were those floorboards where the stash was kept. The window was slightly ajar, and no more locked than it was last time we were there. But even when we pulled it to its widest, it was too narrow for us to sneak through. Damn. Though Lazy Boy was doing plenty of deep and loud mouth breathing, our chances still weren't good for getting in there and past him any other way. I signaled for Ian to put me down.

"There's no way," I whispered. "We'll have to be satisfied with springing the people." We started to skulk away, back toward the rear of the building.

"Wait a sec," said Ian, turning. "Let's at least check around front again."

So we did, crouching and hustling under the window of the lair, then scurrying to the front of the building.

When we craned our necks around the corner out front, Bouncer Dude was there, pacing back and forth, slowly, steady as a pendulum.

"There's no way," Ian said.

Then I had a harebrained, totally suicidal idea.

"Are you sure about this?" he checked me after hearing it. "Wouldn't that only be stirring up a hornets' nest?"

"Yeah, but we've already stirred it up—they just don't *know* it yet. It's a matter of destroying the nest before they realize what's happened, which is going to happen before too long anyway."

"But what if there are more of them in there?"

"It's gotta be four or less."

"I'd give it good odds that it's just these four."

"Maybe. It depends on what the game is, and what's at stake. Betting lunch money is one thing; but for life or death, I'm not sure those are good numbers. I mean, there are no do-overs."

"Yeah, yeah," I said. "Look, at least this way we call the plays and keep it under *our* control—more or less. Come on. Remember: Go the distance."

Ian took a deep breath, then trotted back to the metal flap.

I peeked back at Bouncer Dude again. He was about to get a big surprise.

After a couple minutes, I heard it. Ian had by then crawled back inside the room and was making a whole lot of noise to wake up Lazy Boy—and the other two, wherever they were catching some shuteye.

Suddenly I could hear one guy yelling to the others. Bouncer Dude reached for his walkie-talkie and tried to hear what was going on inside. After a minute or so, he couldn't resist any longer. He gave up his post and ran inside.

This was my chance. If I didn't trail him now and closely, I'd never find my way to where I needed to go. But knowing I needed a way out of there, too, I grabbed a handful of gritty soil, shoved it in my left pocket, which I knew had a small hole in it, and ran after the guy.

The good thing about him being so big was that I could catch up to him, and he made a lot of noise. He lumbered down a hallway. I heard one of his pals calling for him, and I managed to duck out of sight before the two met up. It was Lazy Boy, holding a pistol. While they talked, I crouched and looked back down the hallway to make sure the gravel was doing its job. I could barely see a gritty trail disappearing into the distance, but more importantly I could feel it underfoot.

The two guys hustled away, toward the back of the building. I stopped at the hallway where Lazy Boy had met up with him. *That way to the stash!* But not yet. I followed after the guys. If the timing went wrong, it could very well mean that I'd suddenly come face to face with them.

I turned the corner and saw the door to the room, with a bunch of locks on it. I saw the four guys buzzing around, arguing, punching walls, blaming one another. I couldn't help but smile. They crouched down to look into the hole we'd made, so I tiptoed to the door as fast as possible.

As I grabbed the door and shut it, I caught a glimpse of their shocked faces before I sealed them in. Fumbling with the locks, I got the first lock latched before I felt a large thud on the other side of the door. By the inevitable second thump, I had locked the other two padlocks quickly, as the pounding increased.

"You're SO dead!" one of them said as I stepped away. "Open up or I'm gonna rip yer head off!!" You get the idea: not pleased with their new accommodations.

I was glad they thought to put on a bunch of locks, 'cause I didn't know how long this room could hold them. Even with them being big guys, it would be awhile before they could further open up any of those holes in the wall that we'd begun, especially without any tools—and being at least twice the size of any of us who had squeezed through that same hole.

I ran back down the hall, retracing my steps with the gritty help of the trail of dirt. I got to that junction where the two guys met up and went in the direction of the lair.

I took a few wrong turns, backed up again, and barged through the correct door.

I went straight to the corner of the office and the floorboards and started to pry them up. I reached down and grabbed a gym bag. I unzipped it. There were bundles of money. I flipped through it: I guessed about a hundred $100s per stack, and maybe two hundred or so bundles. I did a bit of quick math (finally, a real-life application): about $250,000! Sweet—that ought to hurt them plenty!

As I was about to cover the boards, I noticed another bag in the hole. It was a leather satchel, and I pulled that one out, too, revealing a bunch of brick-sized plastic bags with white powder in them. Flour? Confectioner's sugar? I didn't know for sure, but I seriously doubted those no-necks were bakers. Opium? Cocaine? Heroin? Whatever. I wanted to take away their toys, their capital, their ability to spread their particular brand of cancer in the world.

Far away, their muffled slamming pounded that door, again and again. Or was it my head, pounding away?

Either way: time to go. I covered up the floorboards, took the gym bag and the leather satchel, and went back to the main hallway. Then using the gravel trail as my guide, I made my way out of the labyrinth to fresh air again.

I picked up Ian along the side of the warehouse. He was a nervous wreck, trying to fortify the metal exterior wall we'd pried open.

"Come on! I'm about to have a heart attack!"

I put the satchel strap around his neck and shoulder. "I'll explain later."

I picked up the gym bag and we ran like crazy back to the pad.

Section 6

*When all is swirling within and around you,
find the resolve to stay calm, be smart and, above
all ... hold on for dear life.*

— Sam Hawkins, March 26, 2016

i. iNFiGHTiNG

It turns out that cash is heavy, but drugs are heavier. We had to rest every fifty yards or so to switch arms. By the time we got back to the pad we were exhausted mentally, physically, and emotionally. Sleep deprived to begin with, we were running on adrenaline, which didn't help us much to stay calm, cool, and collected.

When I went into the bathroom and saw myself in the mirror, my eyes looked crazed, with tiny cuts and scrapes on my dusty, sweaty face and all down my arms.

When I came back out, Tawnya and Ignazio were inspecting the loot in a state of awe. In fact, each of us in this new foursome stared, dumbstruck.

"Well *now* what?" said Ian.

"I could call in a few favors an' get us picked up in a van," said Tawnya, "but my phone's dead. Maybe I can run out an' try tuh find my cousin, an' he can ..."

"No," Ignazio interrupted, "no time! We must leave, from them *now*. Keep moving."

"Says who? Hey, we rescued your ass. Who is this guy anyway? Take a number an' get in line."

"No, you do not understand," he urged. "I *know* how they think. They are smarter than they look. They are connected."

"They're well-connected to a locked room right now," said Tawnya, "so they ain't goin' nowhere."

"No!" Ignazio insisted.

"Hey, watch your tone, buddy! Don't be shoutin' at me. That's disrespect, fella!"

"Look, I respect, yes," said Iggie, trying to contain his frustration, "when I keep you *alive!*"

"You keepin' *us* alive?! Chill, dude—we've got a plan an' we're doin' it, so calm down."

After an awkward pause, I jumped in: "Right. At least we *had* a plan. But this," I said, looking at the money and drugs, "is a game-changer."

"Yeah," added Ian. "I don't remember the old plan anymore, anyway."

"Sam," begged Iggie, "can we talk about this somewhere?"

"Don't worry, dude. No one knows 'bout this place. So, how *do* y'all know each other anyway? I think I missed thuh intros."

"Okay, okay," I said. "Everybody take a step back. We're on the same side here. Look, this is Ignazio. I met him upriver, we traveled together, got separated in the ... when I and he ... never mind. What *happened* anyway, Iggie?"

He looked around at the group impatiently, seeing that they wouldn't budge until they got the bigger picture of our relationship. He sighed, then hurried through it in order to get them to finally listen to him.

"There was a big storm. I ... I get lost in the water. I lose Sam. I kick with my feet, try to move to the side of the river. I can't. I keep going. Finally I hold onto a soccer ball, lose it, find it again. I knock into stuff, and I am pulled down. I hold on for my life. I find a big piece of wood to hold on to. I go under bridges, and when the water slow down, at a big curve, I kick to get to the side and hold on. I pull myself up, over, on to shore. I rest a long time. Later, I wake up there," nodding toward the other warehouse. Then he turned to me, and his eyes narrowed. "What take you so long, Sam?"

"What *took* me?"

"Yeah. What you do?"

"What are you *talking* about? I thought you were *dead*, man. I saw you go under. I lost it. I was out of my mind *loco!*"

"But you are not *sure*? You give up on me?"

"No. I mean, yes—but not after searching like, everywhere."

"Well, not *every*where, or you would find me, no? You leave me for dead."

"Oh, come on. No, I—"

"You like, 'Oh, well.' How could you, after what we go through?"

"But I didn't. I ... I did *everything* I could. Iggie, I swear. Anyone in their right mind would've thought that was it, that you were done. And I'm sorry, but I wasn't in my right mind."

"Do you call police?" he blurted angrily.

"Well, no," I hedged, "but since when would you want me to contact the police about you anyway?!"

"When it's *life or death!*"

"I was *sure* it was death. I couldn't do anything about that. Look, Iggie. I'm sorry. For whatever, for all of it. I did what I could. I didn't know what else to do."

"Forget it. I'm only another 'illegal' to you!"

"Hey, that's not fair, not true!"

"All right," said Ian. "Cut it out, you two."

But Iggie pressed on, stepping toward me. "You don't abandon friends!"

"I didn't abandon you, dude. I looked up and down for you!"

"It's true," said Ian.

"Who are *you*, anyway?" said Iggie to Ian.

"He's my friend," I said. "Leave him alone."

"I don't care," Iggie blurted. "I know what you do and what you do not do. I can see guilty in your eyes."

"Oh, you *know*, do you?"

"Yes, I know you enough," he said, stepping toward me.

"You *think* you know me," I replied, stepping toward him.

"Look, people," said Tawnya, getting in between us, trying to keep us back.

I faced Ignazio, the two of us were ready to go at it.

"You're out of line, dude," I said. "Back off!"

"Hey, don't touch me, girl!" Iggie snapped.

"*Girl?!* You keep actin' this way an' we'll drop your sorry ass next door again, see how you like bein' back there, ya ingrate."

"You think it is *funny?*" Ignazio said, stepping toward Tawnya. I cut him off and jumped in front of her.

"Don't take your shit out on her," I yelled at him. "Why are you being this way?"

"Why are you being the way *you* are being, eh?"

"Iggie, drop it, man. You're way overreacting."

"Am I?" he added, getting back in my face.

"Hey, I told you to step back, dude," warned Tawnya.

"Don't worry, Tawnya. I've got this. He's just upset."

"*Just* upset?" said Iggie. "You think you are a big boy? You are a spoiled little kid who never grows up!"

Then he shoved me. After all I'd done for him. What a jerk. That just made me shake with rage. I don't think I'd ever been so mad at someone before.

So I shoved him back. And he pushed me, wincing. And I pushed him back.

Then he grabbed me by the shirt and sort of clung to me 'cause he was still pretty weak.

Next thing I knew we were tumbling across the floor, neither of us really wanting to do damage but going through the motions. The others jumped into the fray quickly to hold us back.

Just then, from somewhere behind us, we heard a booming voice: "All right you pieces of shit! Knock it off!!"

ii. SNAGGED

We froze.

We craned our heads, stupidly, to see who it was, though we didn't need many guesses.

It was those four jerks from the human warehouse and a couple other cronies—two younger dudes dressed in black with black baseball caps, too, one facing forward, the other back. I figured these guys got called in to spring them. And none of them, now six total, looked happy to see us.

There was no time to waste. My mind scanned for exits, and I was sure the others were doing that, too. I didn't see a weapon or anything in their hands.

So I simply shouted, "Run!"

We scrambled for the doors and windows, fleeing for our lives. So much for a cohesive plan.

But as we did, and as I was approaching one of the doors, I turned as I ran to see one of Bouncer Dude's new cronies raise a pistol, aim in my direction and shoot.

Of course, it felt like slow motion after that. I always thought that was just a movie thing, but it really *did* feel that way.

There was the sensation that my leg wasn't cooperating, sort of like when it goes to sleep and loses that ability to support anything. In my mind I was headed out the door, but it was like my leg betrayed me. It awkwardly knocked into my other leg and somehow wasn't listening to my brain. Then came the pain, a laser-focused fire—a hot pain like no other. And only when I was about to hit the ground did it occur to me that maybe I'd been shot.

When I hit, I expected to be writhing like crazy, but not so much. Instead, I remember most that my vision started to go; it went white before it pulsed and returned again to relatively normal. I curled up and held the back of my leg. Then, my head sideways against the floor, I couldn't do a thing but watch the thugs, coming closer while the others ran. I remember that wet, warm, syrupy feeling down my leg, as if I'd peed, but knowing it was blood. As my mind raced, it seemed like ages until they got over to where I was.

So there I was, feeling my little life fading away (for all I knew I was bleeding out), stuck there, at the mercy of these Neanderthals. I felt myself being picked up roughly, and that brought the pain back a whole lot, like someone was sticking a tire iron into the wound and giving it a twist.

Seeing those guys up close wasn't pretty. The wiry, foul-smelling Circus Freak grabbed me by the shirt and pulled me up and into his face, as if he wasn't ugly enough at a distance. I nearly gagged from the mixture of tobacco, coffee, garlic, and cheap cologne.

"What were you thinking, punk!? Huh?" he said, shaking me. "You think you can outsmart *us*, you smart ass!?"

Bouncer Dude took out his cell phone and waved it, taunting and laughing at me. "You pay attention, or you pay in pain, kid. You think walls are gonna hold *us*? I thought your generation was supposed to be so tech-no-logical."

Circus Freak dropped me. Again, when I hit, the shooting pain in the leg came back with a vengeance.

"Tie 'em up," BouncerDude barked.

I was surprised to hear him say that. I assumed that the others had made it out. But as I turned I saw my friends had the same horrified looks. We were plopped onto a few chairs in the center of the room as they looked around for stuff to tie us up with.

Al Capone, still sporting his signature black fedora, came in from another room. He carried a bunch of old knotted clothesline. He began to cut lengths and tie us up, starting with Ignazio, who grimaced in pain from his other wounds. I had a hunch they were going to be particularly nasty with him since this was the second time they'd dealt with him.

Then they tied up the rest of us. Iggie was right about these guys: Let's just say they were thorough.

Still, when I caught Iggie's eye, it wasn't a mad look anymore—just a pitiful, pained one, like Mary on that statue with Jesus draped across her lap: the Pieta. There was a deep sadness to it all; no judgment, just resignation.

Next up was Ian. They tied him real snug. I don't know where these guys went to school for this type of stuff, but they were good at it. I imagine it was just a lot of on-the-job training. Ian didn't say much. He was smallish to begin with and now, in captivity, he looked even smaller.

Tawnya was the only one of us who still had a lot of fight in her. She spit, kicked, cursed, and stomped—until the guy who was wrangling her got tired of it and clocked her across the face with the back of his hand. After that she was real easy to tie up.

I thought back to Stengel and his guys and wondered who was worse: them or these guys. It was an awful close contest.

I saw something out of the corner of my eye: Ian had somehow gotten a cell phone out of a back pocket. *Wait—his cell phone?!* He'd have to explain why he had that but didn't tell me. Anyway, for now he was texting behind his back. It was impressive. My eyes met his and he gave me a knowing look. He slipped the phone back into his rear pocket.

Lazy Boy came in from the kitchen area and convened some sort of evil summit with the others, during which the guys were chuckling.

In the pantry he'd found one of those honey-bear plastic bottles. I had no idea what they were up to, but I didn't like the smirk on his whacked-out face.

Two of them went over to the wall where there was that very busy freeway of tiny black ants. There were easily thousands of them streaming along. Al Capone made a miniature exit ramp out of a line of honey. He then extended that line in our direction. He squeezed out a sinister detour and snaked it in our direction like it was gunpowder. He grinned as he came closer, until he made the line come right up to Ian's chair. Ian knew full well where he was going with this, and he started to sweat and squirm like crazy.

The guy dripped a bunch of the honey all over Ian. He worked his way up to Ian's head, making sure to pour a bit extra around his ears, nostrils, mouth, and eyes—basically, anywhere there was a hole or sensitive tissue. The bastard!

Already we could see the ants trudging along the super-highway of sweetness.

Then the guy went around making the line branch off and go to Tawnya. He took special pleasure in doing her up with the honey; it took on this extra edge of sexuality that was awkward and just plain wrong on so many levels. It was probably good that she wasn't awake for this part.

For me and Ignazio, they just sloppily covered us with the rest of the bottle.

The ants marched their way steadily toward all of us.

They got closer and closer, until they reached Ian's foot and started climbing up his leg. He started screaming and flailing. The more he did, the more these goons laughed. They were real proud of their twisted creativity.

The screaming seemed to wake up Tawnya as the ants made it over to her. She started yelling, too. The ants reached Ian's waist as he tried to shake them off. But it was no use. They made for his upper torso and aimed for his head.

Bouncer Dude and all his pals were having a great time, giggling and pointing idiotically.

Suddenly, out of nowhere, a loud blast broke through the commotion.

Everyone flinched and ducked. When our heads slowly popped back up, we turned to see ...

iii. TURNING THE TABLES

"**Z**oe!" I shouted.

She stood there like a sexy gunslinger from a Clint Eastwood movie. The smoke from her shotgun rose from the barrels, cut by the dusty dawn light streaming through the broken windows of the warehouse.

She was superhuman. Radiant.

"Keep your hands up, where I can shoot 'em," she sneered, with only a slight quiver in her voice.

Ka-chung—she reloaded.

"You made a big mistake, girlie!" said Bouncer Dude.

"We'll see. Now drop 'em." She went around pointing the shotgun at them until they laid down their weapons. Guns and knives clunked to the floor.

Lazy Boy started to step toward her. Creak, creak, testing her. "Hey," he said, "you don't owe these punks nothin'. A pretty thing like you, you don't wanna get messed up in all this. Wouldn't want you to get hurt or worse, would we? It's not too late to walk away."

"You done yet?" she said.

"I tell you what," said Al Capone, also inching toward her. "We'll let you walk away with more money than you can imagine. We'll do that for you, as a compromise out of this, uh, unfortunate situation."

"Careful, Zoe," I said.

I could see Bouncer Dude moving methodically toward a gun on the table.

"Uh, Zoe!" Ian winced, panicky, as the ants approached his neck.

"You wanna preserve your own skin," said Lazy Boy, "we'll give you this last chance to turn and run. Face it, you're outnumbered. You may have two barrels, but that doesn't quite cover all of us, now does it? Do the math."

Circus Freak was reaching toward his boot.

"I'll take my chances," said Zoe, her voice getting more strained with each exchange. "I'm not afraid to use this thing if I have to."

"Zoe, over here!" I shouted, as Bouncer Dude was nearly at the pistol on the table. She leveled the gun at him as the other two guys took another collective step toward her.

"Easy there, sweetie. You seem to be a sensible kid," Bouncer Dude added, talking her down. "I know you don't wanna hurt anyone, get blood on stuff."

"Shut up!" she blurted, looking rattled as she felt them encroaching. Behind her I could see Lazy Boy now preparing to lunge. I had been working on untying the rope they hadn't quite finished on me and managed to slip my hands out of it.

I maneuvered over near Bouncer Dude and snatched the pistol as he was about to grab it.

"See, the thing is," Lazy Boy said, taking another step forward until he was less than ten feet from her, "you bit off more than you can ha-*choo*."

And with the old fake-sneeze distraction, three of them lunged toward Zoe, and another blast rang out.

"Ewwwaaahhh!" yelped Lazy Boy, as the shrapnel against his thigh spun him a quarter of a turn around. He fell to the floor, clutching his leg and cursing.

She quickly reloaded and sent Al Capone reeling, too, with a grazed shot to his shoulder that knocked him to the ground.

And as Circus Freak pulled out a shiv from his boot and lunged for Zoe, I stuck out my foot and tripped him, and he fell flat on his face. He then scurried backward as Zoe turned toward him, reloaded, and pointed the barrels straight at him.

But Bouncer Dude took advantage of our focus on Zoe and grabbed Tawnya from behind, around her neck, and started to bring a knife to her throat. Fortunately, Tawnya had good reflexes and saw it coming. She butted him in the nose with the back of her skull, and he fell back, clutching his face. When he staggered inadvertently toward her, clutching his busted nose, she followed up with a substantial kick to his balls. He keeled over and a knife fell out of his hand and clanged across the floor. Tawnya swooped down and picked it up. She managed to quickly saw through the rope that bound her hands.

I went over and untied Ian too.

"You wanna piece of me?!" taunted Tawnya, standing over him. "Ya big baby. Well that's the only piece of me you'll get: my foot!" Then she smacked a few ants and turned to the group. "Would someone tell me what thuh hell is goin' on here?! How'z everybody findin' this place?"

"I've been texting with Zoe," confessed Ian, while madly swatting ants that made it up to and around his head.

"You're a bunch of sick dudes," said Tawnya, addressing the thugs. "I'm feelin' some tit for tat comin' on reeeeal strong. Whadayou guys think?"

We nodded.

"This rope sucks. There's duct tape in a drawer in thuh kitchen. Someone get it."

As Zoe kept the gun leveled on them, we helped each other get cleaned up as best and as quickly as we could.

Ian came back with a four-pack of duct tape.

We pitched in and taped the guys to the chairs, starting with their wrists, feet, and legs. And a strip or two across their mouths. We didn't waste one scrap of tape.

They were going nowhere fast. We remembered to gather their phones this time, promptly running them through the garbage disposal.

Tawnya disappeared into the pantry and rummaged loudly for fifteen seconds before emerging with a small backpack. We stared at her.

"What? A girl can't go nowhere without her to-go bag." We shrugged and gathered up a few of our belongings.

As we were nearly out the door, Tawnya turned and said, "Wait a sec, we can't waste the moment. Whatever happened to tit for tat, people?" She ran back, grabbed the honey bear, and turned their own sweet trick back on them.

We saw that the lines of ants were reassembling and beginning to head toward these guys with a vengeance. The disbelieving looks on their frightened faces were priceless as they pathetically failed to scoot away from the mass of approaching ants.

Iggie looked around the room and I heard him mutter under his breath, "*Poco a poco.*"

By the time we left the room, the swarms of blackness had reached most every person, and they just kept coming and coming.

iV. BEATING A RETREAT

With me being supported by Ian and Iggie, we hustled downstairs. Ignazio and Zoe carried the satchel of drugs and the money bag. Tawnya led the way. We ran out of the building and into the fresh air.

We paused to gather ourselves and talk about our next move. We realized there wouldn't be any quick getaway with me gimping along.

Since we didn't know how long our tape job would hold those no-necks, we were still pretty tense. Our cockiness led to them escaping once before, and we didn't need a repeat of that.

"You guys go on ahead," I told them. "Get the boat ready. I'll catch up as soon as I can."

"Right. Lemme get this straight. We leave ya here, we wait for you tuh crawl tuh us, then we take off? I don't think so. C'mon, folks, we need a solution."

Good thing we had Ian. Turns out he'd been holding out on me. Not only had he been in touch with Zoe ever since he'd arrived on the river, texting back and forth, but it turned out they'd worked *together* to track me down. In hindsight, it was good they cared enough to make a plan and find me, but I felt betrayed—like they didn't trust me. What else were they keeping from me? Or did they think I couldn't handle things in my fragile state of mind?

Finally, I couldn't stand it anymore. "Why didn't you tell me what you guys were up to?"

"Um, peeps, shouldn't we be gettin' a move on?" said Tawnya.

"See how it feels to be left out?" Iggie said to me.

"Look, Sam," said Ian, "I was going to tell you, but then all hell broke loose, and I had to be careful. I figured we might need a wild card. I didn't want to compromise you with that info. No offense."

"No *offense?!*" I blurted.

"Stop!" cried Zoe. "Are you guys insane? You have a death wish? This was a search and rescue mission. Let's get our act together and put distance between us and those apes or they'll be breathing down our necks again. And next time we may not get so lucky."

"Thuh girl's right," said Tawnya.

"But it must be a mile or so back to the boat," I said. "I'll never make it—at least not quickly."

"I've got something that'll get us there," said Ian. "My brother's been busy getting us set up."

I looked at Zoe, wondering if she knew what he was talking about, but she shrugged back.

Ian texted away on his phone as we hustled along as best we could.

Even though it was still a ways to get to the boat, it wasn't that far to get back to the river itself—maybe a quarter mile.

Tawnya had a great idea. She spotted a rusty old wheelbarrow sticking out of a pile of junk. It barely held together, but they dusted it off and put me into it. It wasn't long before we enjoyed the new, quicker pace of retreat.

Ian and Ignazio pushed as Tawnya and Zoe jogged alongside.

We rocked and rolled the last few blocks to the river.

After being cooped up in those warehouses over the last day or so, it was great to see the expanse of the river open up again and to glimpse that steady sliver of water running down the middle.

Ian led us to a near-empty lot right beside the river. There was random garbage everywhere.

"What're we doin' here?!" said Tawnya.

He walked us over to a plastic tarp that covered a lump on the ground.

"I called in a few favors from my brother."

He pulled back the tarp. It was Ian's electric bike, a skateboard, a pair of Rollerblades, and a scooter.

"What the," I asked, stunned.

"I told him to stash them here."

"Yeah, so?" Tawnya said. "How's this gonna help?"

"I'll show you," said Ian. "Okay, everyone, listen up ..."

Ian directed things. We helped get his contraption set up atop the flat part of the riverbank, facing down the concrete incline toward the river.

The e-bike went first. Ian planned to drive it, with me tucked in behind him, holding onto him. Three lines of ropes, with different lengths, were tied to the back of the bike and extended behind it.

On the first rope was Zoe, ready on her skateboard. On the second rope was Ignazio, on the scooter. And Tawnya was there at the end of the third rope, sporting the Rollerblades, hobbling around, and trying not to fall down.

"Grab your lines," Ian shouted as he got on the e-bike. I held tightly, imagining that this would end badly. I knew that Zoe was a good skateboarder, but I couldn't vouch for Iggie or Tawnya.

Ian accelerated slowly as the ropes became taut and the whole rig started to move. He fumbled a bit but somehow kept upright. Tawnya was squealing as she lurched, her ankles bent inward, but she somehow managed to avoid doing a faceplant. Poor Iggie had to be hurting, but he worked hard pretending it was fun.

We picked up speed as we went along the path.

"Hold tight. We're going in," announced Ian, as he veered over the edge and started down the angled concrete riverbank—not straight down, but at a slow angle.

"No-no-no-no!" shouted Tawnya.

"Not so fast, man!" shouted Ignazio.

"Sorry. Here we gooooo!" Ian yelled back.

"I'm gonna kill you, dude!" Tawnya yelled again.

It wasn't like we were going so fast, but ten miles per hour at that angle feels about like forty miles per hour on a flat section.

I looked back to see those guys barely managing to stay on, wobbling, trying to crouch as low as possible to keep their centers of gravity down, holding onto their vehicles for dear life.

We hit the bottom of the angled incline, and the bike heaved under the weight it was pulling. We straightened out on the flat concrete riverbed bottom, as Zoe, Tawnya, and Iggie miraculously made it without wiping out. After that, on the flats, it was easier.

We cruised along and put more distance between us and the goon squad.

After almost a mile or so, I recognized the river section where Ian and I got caught up in that crossfire the other day. Up the bank from there was the pipe we'd escaped to, where we first met Tawnya.

I looked back at her, cruising along more comfortably now, a big toothy smile lighting up her face. With the things we'd been through, it was hard for me to imagine that we'd only known each other for twenty-four hours or so. Time is weird that way.

Apart from the minor detail that I'd recently been shot (well, okay, grazed as it turned out) and that every time we hit a bump it hurt like hell, it was an awesome ride.

V. BACK ON BOARD

We arrived at the steel grate hatch that covered the pipe where the kayak was stored—at least we *hoped* it was still there, or our swift exit would be for nothing.

Ian eased up and put on the brakes. As he did, Zoe, Tawnya, and Iggie slowed until they stopped and flopped onto the concrete, exhausted but laughing.

We high-fived and hugged as if we'd won the Indianapolis 500. Sure, we'd done well, but no amount of distance from those jerks would be enough.

"Come on," I said. "Let's get this thing in the water and keep going."

"I don't know, Sam," said Ian. "I think we've got to get you to a hospital."

"A hospital?" I argued. "No, that's one of the first places they'd check. They could call around and make like they're my dad or something until they find where we'd checked in—then they'll check me out, permanently. No way, at least not around here."

"Yeah, but with a wound like that, you could be in serious trouble with infection. You can't be out here getting this water on it."

"Ian's right," added Tawnya. "It'll turn that leg somethin' nasty."

"Look, it's not going to fall off," I said. "It looks worse than it is. It's a risk we've got to take. Sorry."

"I've got an idea!" said Tawnya. "I know someone further down, a nurse in South Gate, a friend, who can help. It's on the way; we could meet up."

"Can you get a hold of them?" said Zoe.

"I dunno. Usually works thuh graveyard shift, so should be out by now. I'll check it out." Tawnya got on Zoe's phone and stepped away to make the call.

"Come on," said Ian. "Let's see if the boat is still where we left it."

He put his arm around me, and we headed uphill to the pipe.

"Let's just hope your leg doesn't fall off before you get it checked."

Iggie and Zoe joined us. They opened the metal grate and looked inside. They reached in the big pipe hole and pulled out the boat—but not the one I expected.

I looked at Ian, then back at a shiny dark green plastic canoe.

"If we're going to take everyone," he said, "then we need another boat. I asked my brother to rent one from the sporting goods store and drop it here."

He came through. This thing was much nicer than Zoe's aluminum wreck of a canoe. It looked like it was in pretty good shape, so we didn't have to worry about leaks every ten feet.

Then they pulled out the yellow double kayak, too, and lined it up so it was ready to slide down the concrete incline.

"Hey, what about the bike and skateboard and all this other stuff?" Zoe asked. "We can't fit all that in the boats."

"In the pipe," Ian said. "My brother knows to pick it up in his truck."

So we gathered up the electric bike, the skateboard, scooter, and Rollerblades, put them in the pipe and shut the grate.

Iggie and Zoe then got into the kayak. They scooted forward until the boat tipped and started moving down the angled concrete riverbank like a crazy amusement park log ride, but without the water, picking up speed and hitting the flat concrete bottom. They tipped over and toppled out, laughing hysterically—her more than him with all his wounds.

Ian and I weren't quite up to that, so we sent the canoe on its way, sliding down to the bottom. From there we all carried the two boats across the flat part and over to the narrow channel, where we began loading our stuff.

I hobbled over and tried to grab the satchel of drugs and was surprised again at the weight of it.

"Hey, someone gimme a hand. This stuff is heavy!" Then a fiendish idea occurred to me. "I don't want to be carrying this around. Besides, we could get in trouble with it in our possession. Why don't we just dump it?"

"What? That shit's valuable!" said Tawnya.

"Look, why should we lug their crap around?" I said. "We're not pack mules. And it's not like we're gonna sell it. It's got no real value for us. And if we get stopped by the police, trying to explain would only make big trouble. We're afraid to get rid of it because what, it's worth a lot of money? That's not a good reason. These are like blood diamonds. I say we dump it. Right here, right now."

"Yeah but, but," said Tawnya.

"On the street, maybe it's worth a lot; in the river, it's worth absolutely nothing. Simple economics, right?"

They looked at me like I'd lost it. Still, I didn't care. I shrugged. No one else felt strong enough that we needed to keep it, so that was that.

I reached into the satchel and pulled out one of the clear plastic bags, shaped and wrapped like a pound of coffee you'd find at a supermarket, but more dense. I ripped off the piece of tape at the top.

I held it over the river and bowed my head for melodramatic effect.

"Ashes to ashes, dust to dust, beginning to end, uh, good to go, we are gathered here today to ..."

"All right already!" said Zoe. "Either do it or don't, Sam!"

"Amen, 10-4, over and out," I concluded.

I took a deep breath and started to pour. Down it went, cascading into the river and out, someday, all the way to the Pacific!

The others got into it, too. One by one, each person reached into the sack and grabbed a bag, opened it, and dumped the drugs into the narrow channel in a somber ritual. It was probably fifteen or twenty bags.

It felt good—like we were cleaning up the city. We felt empowered and exhilarated by it. Except the wind would sometimes whip up and we'd get small pieces of it in our faces or hair, causing us to sneeze and freak out.

We brushed our hands off and took a moment to watch the last of the white powder trickle downstream.

"Okay now, *rapido*. Who goes where?" asked Iggie, looking anxiously at the sky and back toward the warehouses.

"For the canoe, let's put Sam in the middle," suggested Ian, "with Ignazio in the back and Zoe in front. Tawnya and I can take the kayak. Everyone good with that?"

We nodded.

"Don't get too far ahead of us though," I shouted. "We need to stick together."

"Let's go then, people," echoed Ian. "You heard him. Positions!" He put the money bag in the middle of the canoe, covered with a jacket.

We lowered the boats into the narrow channel and held them there. Zoe and Iggie helped me get into the middle of the canoe. They propped up my back real nice so that I was comfortable as could be. It felt wrong that they'd be working while I was resting, but I knew I didn't have much choice.

Ian and Tawnya looked awesome in the kayak, going in front of us. We were all set to go.

As Iggie and Zoe let go of the side of the narrow channel, the canoe started to move, too.

It wasn't long before we caught up to the speed of the current.

Our minds wandered as we quietly paddled downstream. The further we got from downtown, the more our worries about anyone trailing us gradually left our thoughts.

After a couple hours of this, and getting to talking again, we saw someone up ahead, right beside the river, waving a white cloth.

VI. PIT STOP

By that point we were conditioned to have a healthy dose of paranoia.

When we saw someone standing in our way up ahead, we immediately assumed the worst and braced for another encounter. Zoe felt around for where she stowed the shotgun, just in case. I imagined myself going Jackie Chan with a kayak paddle.

As we got closer, we could see that the figure was a man, Black and lean, with a big smile; he just stood there, his arms crossed, shaking his head. He didn't look intimidating, but we couldn't be too sure about anything, anymore. As we got closer still, the hairs on the back of my neck stood at attention, ready for something to suddenly go south.

Tawnya broke the ice by shouting: "Jaeden! 'Sup, man? Guys, that's my friend. Welcome tuh South Gate."

Ian and Tawnya scooted ahead, paddling harder until they got up close, then stopped paddling and held onto the sides of the narrow channel. They greeted Tawnya's friend and helped pull the boat out of the river.

As we approached, they grabbed our canoe, pulled us against the side of the narrow channel and, eventually, helped us out, too, before hoisting the canoe onto dry cement.

Her friend was sweet—kind, puppy-dog eyes with an easy smile and posture that signaled a quiet confidence. He was maybe in his late twenties or so. His eyes darted back and forth, observing Iggie swaddled in a mess of improvised bandages, like an old Egyptian mummy movie. And he saw that I was holding onto a bloody leg wound.

"What the hell have you been up to anyway?!" Jaeden said.

"Don't ask," said Tawnya.

"Look, Tawnya," he said getting a little anxious, "I've got to know what I'm dealing with here. We should really report this, whatever *this* is."

"No! This'z gotta be under thuh radar. Yeah? We need you. Sorry, but it's a long story an' we don't have time tuh go into it. We ain't goin' nowhere. No hospital, if that's what you're thinkin'. We've been through that possibility an' we ruled it out, for good reason, trust me."

"Yeah, but ..."

"No buts. These guys we're dealin' with, they're a real messed-up bunch. Now, follow your Hippopotamus oath an' get tuh work, wouldya, pleeeease?"

"*Hippocratic.* Fine." He sighed, grabbed his bag, and started to unzip it. "All right then, let's get to work."

He pulled his med kit toward himself, unzipped it, and started getting out a few items. He turned to Ignazio and gently started to inspect and carefully undo his makeshift bandages that were indeed looking a dubious rusty-brown color by then.

"How'd you get these wounds?" he asked. "And who did these bandages?"

"I don't know who did them—I was not awake," Iggie told him. "I scrape along concrete, hit sharp things in the water. I think I hit my head, too."

Jaeden paused a second as if to ask another question, then thought again, shook his head, and just focused on his work.

When he was done with Iggie, he turned to me: "Okay, now you. What do we have here?"

"Um," I thought about lying, but figured he'd know better. "A stray bullet. Grazed me, I think."

"Lovely. How about we gently peel back that bandage so I can see."

I did. He took one look, gave me the once-over again, and did a little *tsk, tsk* sound.

"Just, you know, wrong place at the wrong time."

"Uh-huh," said Jaeden flatly, "right."

He gave a knowing look over at Tawnya, but Tawnya beat him to it. "I know, I know, I'm gonna owe ya one."

"One?!" he coughed. "You're going to owe me about *five!*"

Jaeden set up a triage unit of his own, right then and there, out in this open, barren stretch of South L.A. The others helped by making a temporary shelter to shield us from the sun. He meticulously cleaned up Iggie and rewrapped him in sterile, proper stuff. By the time he was done, Iggie looked as cozy as Nefertiti.

After Jaeden learned where we were headed and realized he couldn't talk us off the river, he even put clear plastic around the bandages on Iggie's lower half to keep those wounds more protected from water.

He was super careful with me, too. After having to be constantly on alert these last bunch of days, it was nice to let down.

It got me thinking about the comforts of home. It was Monday, Fourth of July. I figured Mom would be home by evening. She'd be calling over to Ian's house to check in. I had no idea what they'd tell her or exactly how she'd react, but I knew it wouldn't be pretty. It was looking like we'd get to the estuary at least a day later than expected.

It also struck me that this whole *discovering myself* thing was like Columbus discovering America. That is, there were already a million people there by the time Columbus arrived; so for me, even though I was the only person I was hell-bent on finding, the "discovery" misses the point. The me I was trying so hard to find *had* always been there and *would* always be there—I just had to work out how to bring it forward, *relate* to it, and start *being* that.

"There you go," said Jaeden. "But you're going to need to get this taken care of for real, you hear? As in, within twenty-four hours—no more—and at a proper emergency room—far away, if I understand you right. Whatever, but just do it. Promise?"

I nodded. He was skeptical.

"Raise your right hand."

I did, begrudgingly. "I swear."

Then he finished touching up the others.

When he was done, he packed up his various goods and his mobile triage unit. He turned to the group of us and said, "Go on now. I didn't do this for nothing. Whatever it is you're up to that's just *so* important that it can't wait, well, get out of here, get it done and go home—and I say that with love and affection, by the way."

We thanked him and said our goodbyes. Tawnya walked him over to the side of the river and up the incline to a riverside dirt access road where Jaeden's car was parked. She had her to-go backpack with her and reached into it to pull out some money to offer him, but he didn't want to take it. After a bit of arguing, he finally took it and they hugged. Then Tawnya ran back down and over to us.

We worked together to return our boats to the narrow channel, got in, and went on our way.

Not far downriver, there was some guy who was biking along the bike path, up high but parallel to us. It's not that there was anything so unusual about him. I could've sworn I'd seen him a few times already, looking down at us as he paused on his bike occasionally along the way. He was probably just a homeless guy.

These are the kinds of constant questions you start to have once you get spooked—everything has an evil edge to it, suspicion becomes an everyday thing, around every corner: Ice cream trucks look like the perfect crime vehicles, two little old ladies crossing the street suddenly seem like a terrorist cell. Stuff like that'll drive you crazy. My body might've been temporarily mended, but my mind was fraying.

Anyway, I kept quiet about it, and we kept going.

We started seeing signs for Compton Creek and Del Amo Boulevard along riverside roads. It was right around there that we reached out our paddles and scraped them against the concrete beside us until we slowly stopped.

Zoe got out and held onto us. We pulled the boats out, with the intent to stretch our legs and maybe try to score some quick food at a nearby stand.

Again we walked across the flats and went up the incline.

It turns out Compton Creek wasn't one of those barren L.A. stretches at all. There were a lot of nice green plants along the bottom of it, with fairly clear water flowing out to the river. Not a lot of water, but still, it was at least something resembling a real creek. We couldn't find any food trucks or stands, so we didn't stick around. But it was good to see some life in the lower half of the river. Up in the Valley I'd heard the name Compton a lot, but this was nothing like what I'd imagined. There were egrets wandering around, searching for tiny fish snacks in the lush grasses—it was actually pretty damn sweet.

We hustled back to the boats, our minds suddenly fixed on our hunger. After hearing a few complaints, Tawnya reached into her backpack and pulled out a bunch of chocolate bars and passed them around.

"Like I said, people, always be prepared."

"No way!" yelped Ian.

It was starting to get darker by then, so we got out a few more supplies that we'd stashed in our pockets before we left the pad. It was hardly a smorgasbord, but we didn't care. We floated, noshed, and chatted as the sun set.

Our two motley boats made their way downriver, fighting a slight headwind as a thick chunk of black and gray clouds rolled in from the east. It gave me and Ignazio a scare though, thinking about the storm we'd endured. But on second look, we were much relieved—it was only a big warehouse fire somewhere nearby.

Either way, it divided the sky into a beautiful sunset to the west and north and a seriously heavy cloudy-smoky blob hovering over the southeast.

VII. SAM AND ZOE

There were so many unspoken things with me and Zoe
that had been building up since I'd left the Valley, and I
suspected it was time we dealt with them.

Of course, it wasn't like I was so conscious of that—or
somehow mature about these types of relationship things.
No way. This stuff only ever makes sense in hindsight. Still, I
had an inkling that we needed to start somewhere.

Ignazio paddled in the back of the boat, but after the
stuff he and I had been through I knew I didn't need to hide
anything from him.

"Hey, so, uh, big by the way—thanks for, um, saving our
asses back there," I started clumsily with Zoe.

"What else could I do, let you get devoured by a million
hungry ants?"

"Well yeah, there's that. But I mean: I would've come up
with *something*."

"Oh, really?" she said as she stopped paddling and turned
around to face me.

"Yeah, um, well, what I meant was, I got by. I ... on my
own, for a while."

"If you say so. You know, is it *so* important that you
always do things on your own? I mean, you traveled together
with Ignazio here, right? So, maybe you're good when you're

more like a team than, say, a captain of your own destiny and all that."

"Look, I get that you did what you felt you had to do, and I supported that," said Zoe. "But you, I don't know. Never mind ..."

"No, I *want* to know."

"No, you say that, but do you really?"

"Try me."

She paused, contemplating. "Okay. I thought there was maybe something between us, something *real*—and then you go away. Maybe we shouldn't have chased after you or cared what happened, 'cause maybe you're not the kind of person who can give back. Maybe that's too harsh, but maybe you're not capable. No offense. Maybe you're like, in chemistry, a molecule that can't attach to another; like you don't *bond*."

I could swear I felt the lower part of my spine turn inward and shrink—if I had a tail, it would've been tucked firmly in between my legs. Iggie started to shift uncomfortably in his seat.

"But, but," I stammered, trying to keep things quiet, as Ian turned from the kayak ahead of us to see what was going on, "how'd we go from being on the same side to *this*?"

"I don't know. You tell me," she complained, "how a person can be so detached, so distant."

"What are you talking about? With *you*, you mean? No, it's not like that. I'm saying we *agree*."

"But you know, the rest of world isn't that simple."

"I know," I said, increasingly not knowing what she meant.

"No, you're not saying that. And I *don't* agree."

"Huh?"

"Maybe that's all you feel."

"Well, yes."

"Well, make up your mind."

"Hey, hold on. Why are you, like, getting on me? I just wanted to thank you. And to catch up with you, and ..."

"No, I caught up to *you*. There was no you catching up to *me*."

"Well, technically, maybe yes—but I wanted to talk with you. I mean, here I *am*. Talking. I only wanted to connect."

"Okay, but are you just talk?"

"Well, huh? No, but what do *you* want? I thought of you, a *lot*. Just tell me what you want and—we don't need to go through all this."

"*All this?* First you say you want to talk, but then you throw it back at me, like I'm supposed to make the decisions, like you don't have a say. That's super passive. What do *you* want?"

"That's it. I'm trying to figure it out."

"Well if you have to think about it, then I'm out."

"Huh? What?"

"There, we just broke up," she declared. She let that sink in.

Iggie cleared his throat and started lightly whistling.

At first I was going to follow with the notion that I wasn't sure we were going out at that point, despite feeling close to her and the kiss back in the Valley, but I decided against that. I mean, I suspected that maybe we *were*. It felt like she was feeling hurt, like she thought I didn't care, so that response would only make her feel more insecure. Then I thought I'd ask her if she wanted to officially go out with me—you know, to be my girlfriend. But then she'd know that I had doubts about our status, though I had no doubts about whether I *wanted* to be with her—I *did*, for sure, even if this conversation with her was making me uncomfortable and making me doubt that. What did she *want*? And why all this when I had just gone out of my way to get on the same page with her?

Okay, calm down, Sam.

I was definitely overthinking. *Focus on the main thing:* I want her. She wants me. Ah, but which me? Maybe she already accepted me, period, rather than the me that I was trying so hard to convince her I'd become, to sell her on some kind of new me. It wasn't that she was rejecting me, maybe she was jealous of the whole trip, when all she wanted to know was, would I pursue her with the same amount of attention, passion, and determination as she did. Not something logical, something *definitive.* Like, emotionally. Right? What did I *believe*—that was *it.* She wanted the *why* of us. So I backed up and spoke to that.

"You can't break up with me."

"Of course I can," she said. "Are you trying to control me? Stalker."

"No, I'm only saying I don't agree. I don't, I'm *not okay* with that."

That gave her pause. For a split second, I felt like I had found a way in, that I might be on the right track.

"Well what's okay to you then?"

"What's okay to me is being with you. What's okay to me is both of us being able to live our lives and do what we want, and that we can do it *together*, like we are, right here, right now. What's okay to me is that you cared enough to track me down and fight for me, and ... and ... I just wish I could've been the one to rescue you. So I'm thankful and sorry, and—"

"Yeah?"

"I want to, you know—"

"No, what?"

"I want to be together."

She smiled. And with that smile, something in her melted away. And I remembered the Zoe that I'd originally fallen for. And I think she saw the *me* that she first liked, too. And it hit me how much effort I was using to convince her that I was worthy of her respect, when she already had that for me. It didn't mean that I really understood her; I figured I'd have a good long time to work on that. But most importantly, we both got to feeling we were okay, accepted, just as we were, at least between us.

I leaned toward her and pulled her to me and hugged her. I could feel her shaking slightly.

"Are you sure you want to be together? That's all I've wanted, all along." She stared me down.

"Yes," I said. "Are *you* sure?"

"I am."

We kissed. And kissed some more.

After a while Iggie chimed in, "Okay, guys, uh, get a yacht. You are rocking the boat. We will flip."

We kissed again, just to taunt him. He responded by splashing us lightly with his paddle.

"All right, all right," Zoe said, "That is so *not* sanitary."

As the moon rose, we eventually just stopped paddling and let the boats and the river carry us wherever it decided to take us. Fortunately, it had just one job: to get to the sea. So we sort of surrendered to that mission and trusted it would take us there, too.

Iggie found a comfortable spot to lie down (as much as possible, that is) in the back half of the boat. And Zoe and I lay there together, in each other's arms, in the front of the boat.

The air was warm, and all was good. I couldn't speak for the future, but at least for one perfect moment things felt right. I felt *at home*.

Section 7

THE MOUTH

Like it or not, for better or for worse,
the river will eventually spit you out.

— Sam Hawkins, June 15, 2016

i. iN THE THiCK oF iT

Somewhere in the wee hours, I woke—or so I thought. We were in the middle of thicker fog that felt heavy and oppressive. I pinched myself for a reality check; it seemed pretty real.

Despite my head resting on something hard, I was too tired to lift it. Instead, my focus switched to the pain in my leg, which was getting much worse now, even with the new dressing. If for whatever reason I needed to get out and run, I didn't know how well I could do it. My muscles felt knotted and tight, too. Then again, I thought maybe just my leg had gone to sleep and was having its own little nightmare, making it feel worse than it was.

We slowly and steadily floated along, catching hazy glimpses of random and bizarre things.

Passing a small overpass, a few bats flitted low over the water. Nearby on the concrete support of the bridge were spray-painted the words "Abandon all hope ye who enter here." What tagger would write something as old-fashioned as that? I tried not to let it rattle me, but it stuck.

Farther down, I caught sight of three stray pit bulls—one black, one brown, and one gray—who were devouring a large piece of meat beside the river. They looked up, pausing to give me the stink eye along with their blank, foamy grins, not entirely sure what to make of our passing flotilla. Fortunately, they were more interested in their meal, allowing us to pass without so much as a growl.

A homeless man (or perhaps it was a mannequin put there as a joke) stood still, wearing a hoodie and partially wrapped in a blanket. He was draped over a small caravan of shopping carts, as if he'd just fallen asleep while plodding along—or perhaps frozen in time as if a Santa Ana devil wind blew through here, causing everything to seize up and turn to stone. As we passed, the figure seemed to stare, first at me and then up at the sky. Nothing else in his body was moving—not a twitch, not a blink.

Then up ahead, somewhere in the thick of the mist, there was a truly awful screeching sound. As we got closer, the sound went right into me, piercing my bones. It was the high-pitched wail of two feral cats humping like crazy. The poor female had her little mouth wide open and was yelping that terrible cry.

Down another fifty yards or so, there was the carcass of a fish about two feet long, which looked like it'd been worked over by birds of prey. I could only think that the poor thing wasn't even allowed the dignity of sinking down and settling into the bottom and floating out to rest at sea. With the wall-to-wall concrete, he wasn't going anywhere.

And to top it off, there were bamboo sticks (or maybe just old brooms) with soccer balls, basketballs, and footballs stuck on the ends, partially deflated. Someone thought it'd be funny to draw on these and turn them into contorted faces. And around their stick-figure necks were blingy plastic medallions.

To the left, on the underside of one bridge was graffiti that said, Love; and on the right, Hate.

Eventually my brain called out "Enough!" and I had to shut my eyes and power down from this parade of creepiness.

I must've nodded off.

When I opened my eyes again, off to one side was a large pelican that opened an eye enough to monitor our passage.

He had a large fishing lure stuck through his lower beak, as if he'd gone out and gotten it pierced, for a Goth look.

Farther down, a pink plastic child's car, the kind where kids got inside and drove them, lay abandoned on the concrete like just another L.A. car crash.

A few minutes later, on a wire that crossed our path and stretched over the river's span above, there were a bunch of small shoes tied together by their laces and evidently tossed up and landed on the wire at different points. On the one hand they looked harmless enough, but on a deeper level it bugged me. Whatever happened to the kids who they used to belong to? Maybe it was just the chilly way they swayed and turned in the slight wind—something unholy about it.

This stretch took so much longer than I'd expected. On the map it was about twenty miles. It occurred to me that maybe we'd scraped the sides too much or that we got stuck on things in the night, only eventually getting loosened and continuing on our journey, but only after a long delay.

Somewhere after the creepy shoes, Ignazio went through the same rude awakening that I'd just completed. I didn't say anything to him, only nodded; and as he woke, he stared out at the city for a long time, too, mulling something over. Seeing me there watching him, he confessed:

"I should have died in the storm, you know? And I know I should give thanks to God. But I can't, Sam. When I go under, I think: This is it. Where is He now, *Dios mío*, my God? I understand no one is there to pull me out. I see the little speck I am. Maybe I have soul and a reason in life and still believe in God, but He's not who I imagine. He may be amazing, but He has his hands tied somehow. I think we are more alone than we want to believe."

"Yeah, you, me, and about seven billion others—if you call that alone. Hey, don't be so hard on yourself."

"I mean, it is up to *us*, and to each other. No one look down on us, pay us special attention, yes? Where I see God, now I see *vacio, espacio y infinito*—emptiness, space, infinity. I wonder if I am a bad person to make questions like this. Is it wrong for me to say this?"

"No, Iggie, you're not bad—you're good like no one else I ever met. All the trouble I got you into—you're a saint to be so understanding! But you seem more grounded now. It's like we swapped bodies, dude: If I'm honest, I have to say I picked up *some* of your faith, I think; you showed me how to believe in people, to cut through my defenses and at least some of my cynical bullshit. Hell, I even prayed, man. But I'm afraid I left you with a big bag of doubts—even though it's good to question things."

"What do you mean," he asked, "that you pick up faith?"

"Well, this whole trip makes me think that, when you peel back this layer, something *is* there, some sort of smarts—not a corny old guy sittin' in the clouds, but just, like, the source code for all things, which keeps going and is somehow self-learning and expanding, creating an infinite number of things. I mean, what if God died but his code lives on? Maybe that's why bad shit happens—it's all the glitches over time, it's outdated software. Maybe we seriously need an update for it to make more sense again, but there's no one around to write it, or fix it. So we're all a bit broken."

"Hmm," he muttered, mulling it over.

"I mean, look at how even at night light reaches us," I went on. "It's brilliant. Sure, maybe it's gotta bounce off stuff like the moon to get to us, but that, too, seems like a miracle, how it fits together. How the moon makes the tides, and how that affects life, no matter whether there are amoebas or dinosaurs or people crawling around the planet. It's totally wonderful and frustrating at the same time."

"Yes," he said. "So, you drop your burden?"

"What burden?"

"Like you say, your defenses that keep you away from being close with people. You open your heart, no need to be clever and put things down. *I* accept you because of what I see—in there," he said, pointing to my heart.

Wow. The guy was right. What he said hit me in the gut. Here I'd been living with myself for years and couldn't figure out what he figured out in less than a week!

"I think you're kinda right, Iggie. Maybe I'm taking this whole thing with Ronnie McMasters too personally. What if he's not picking on me but sort of *correcting* something that's sticking out in me, something he picks up that seems fake or wrong—and all along he's just trying, literally, in the way he knows best, to knock that out of me? If that's true, then I gotta face up to it, see what's there and put it behind me."

"Maybe. I don't know, Sam."

We chatted until dawn, rambling on and on, pondering the universe as the world slept around us. After our fight back at the warehouse, this was, I guess, our make-up session.

"I'm sorry I wasn't able to find you quicker, Iggie. I'm really sorry for all you had to go through, and how scared you must've been. To be honest, I *did* feel like I let you down."

"I'm sorry I attack you," he said. "That was not right."

"Hey, I had it coming. I got so lost in my own stuff."

"When those guys find me beside the river, I am too weak to fight back. They pick me up and take me to their place. I think they hurt me, maybe kill me. I feel so low. Then when they lock me up with others, I feel lucky to be alive and I have hope. But I also have time to see all my search in America is not worth much if I have to be away from family for so long. No matter what I can do here, in America, what is the purpose? More money? How much more? How it makes sense that I work so my family is better somewhere else? I work to have a kid, but is he one of many who never sees his father? *Mierda.* How quick to be American, already: I chase the dollar, but even if I make money there is a big cost for all that. I am not sure I want that now. I miss *mi familia* so much."

"Easy, man, you were just doing what you thought was right for your family. Cut yourself some slack. You're not the first guy to come here with the same plan, you know."

"I know. I just feel like an animal. Every day I'm afraid of being caught. That's no way to live—no *dignidad*. Dignity. But if I'm here or home, it feels like *las cosas importantes* is out of my control. Either I'm poor there and no opportunity, or it's work, work, work here and never enough, and no one will ever let me call this home. So no peace. Not enough just being. I lose my community. In Guatemala, community is *lo más importante*. And if I am honest, I forget *that*. That is more valuable than to live the American Dream and being millionaire here. But I think I need to come here to understand what I do *not* need."

"Well, don't give up *now*, after what you've been through. That would be crazy. You're a survivor, and you're going for something. Like all of us, you gotta figure out what it is for you. And maybe you just did."

"Yeah. Maybe."

"I was jealous of you, you know, for having such strong faith. I didn't like it at first, but I respect it now. You can do anything with that, when you have confidence. You taught me a lot, Iggie, and I'll never forget that no matter where we end up."

"I am happy for that, Sam."

There was a faint sound in the distance, like the snap of a stick.

We listened hard. Our ears pricked up, but we didn't hear anything else remarkable. Still, we whispered.

"I feel like I found something important. Do you think it's possible for someone to fall apart *and* come together, to sink *and* float, at the same time?"

He thought for a bit on this. "Well," he offered, "don't we do that all the time?"

"What do you mean?

"Our bodies. Your body. My body. They grow and die, no? Our little *células*, cells, they grow, others die—every day, all year. After seven years our old skin goes, like a snake, everything is new. All life, we change. And when we die, we make other things grow. On and on."

I liked how Iggie's brain worked. I'd really gotten used to him and I thought about what it'd be like to not have him around again. The end was coming, one way or another. I seized the moment 'cause I wasn't sure it'd come around again. "I like you, Iggie. Promise me something, would you?"

"Depends. *¿Qué es?*"

"Let's be *amigos*, like, for life."

"*Amigos for life?*" he said, making sure he heard me right. I nodded. "Sure. That'd be great. I want that."

We both stared out into the foggy night until our eyes got heavy again and we drifted back to sleep.

ii. ESTUARY

And so it was that we later woke yet again, this time one by one, each person groaning at the skanky smell that hovered over the surface of the water.

It turned out to be the gaseous mixture of the sickness and slime upriver that washed down every little nook and cranny of three mountain ranges that fed into the river. It was the smell of consumption and corruption; it reeked of decay and the funk of industry and personal waste.

Holding our noses, we carefully paddled through the muck and the fuzzy, foggy gloom that cover the top half of the riverbanks. We slid softly amid Arundo and cattails, getting a quick glimpse of something beyond the wider blanket of gray. With the narrow channel now ended, the river widened out and became more natural, at least on the bottom. Plants grew up and along the sides where the river met the angled concrete. Eventually, the stink faded away.

Since there was actual vegetation for a change, we figured this put us at or near the estuary, though we didn't know where it officially started. We didn't expect to see neon arrows pointing to it or anything like that.

For the most part we kept to ourselves, especially 'cause we could barely see anything. I thought more about the river, trying to imagine all the people who must've come the other direction, upriver, at some point. It seemed counterintuitive, but that must've been how a lot of places got settled. Large sailing boats coming from the oceans probably found a safe bay, then anchored in an estuary. In time, expeditions began to explore the interior, following the main watery artery, on a mission, most often, to either civilize, kill, or make dubious deals with the people who lived in those parts. I imagined these teams of men, overloaded in their boats with the seeds of destruction and expansion they were eager to spread. Maybe that's a cynical perspective, but whatever.

I thought about the coast ahead and how its predictable patterns of ebb and flow—and the consistency of waves, grinding it out through time with the help of the moon's pull—was fitting for the end of my little quest. The coast was more like home where you pretty much knew what to expect. Hell, you could look up a chart that could tell that the high tides tomorrow will be at 8:14 a.m. and 7:49 p.m. That's too regular, too like sliced bread, at odds with the part in me that wants something wilder, more random, and mysterious. That's what I've grown to appreciate about this river, no matter how lowly of a reputation it has. It seemed like the kinda place you could go down over and over, but each time it's got different things in store for you. It's always moving, changing, surprising.

"Well, keep lookin'!" a muted voice suddenly shouted in the foggy distance.

As if we weren't chilly enough already, we froze when we heard the rising chatter of voices. It was faint, but we could barely make out bits and pieces:

"Must've come through here—"

"Long Beach—"

"Try over there—"

None of us paddled; nobody dared whisper. After complaining about the fog, we were glad to have it now. We didn't recognize specific voices but knew it could only be the traffickers or their henchmen. Suddenly I wished we hadn't been so impulsive and self-righteous about getting rid of the drugs. Sure, we still had the money, but the drugs might've given us more leverage. *Stupid!*

A shot rang out.

We looked around. As far as we knew, we were still concealed, but we checked for damage.

None. Phew! Our hearts skipped a beat.

"Don't worry. They're just frustrated," Tawnya whispered, "maybe shootin' ducks or somethin'."

"Yeah or trying to flush *us* out, like ducks."

Apart from a few very careful whispers, we were mostly quiet. Only when we'd nearly floated into the shoreline did we do a few light strokes to keep us from making a louder thud against any rocks. The rocks might as well have been mines; it was nerve-racking—one mistake and we could've blown our position. Or the wind might've whisked away our protective shield and we'd end up suddenly face to face with them. They could be right there, squatting, waiting beside the river, like with duck blinds, until we made a wrong move, and then ...

Blang!! Another shot rang out, but now farther away.

After about ten minutes, we no longer heard anything alarming, so we started paddling again. We decided that we needed to get to Long Beach quicker than planned if we wanted to get to the arranged takeout spot while we still had the foggy cover.

Ian and Zoe had been texting since they woke up, with the last of their batteries. They'd worked out a plan through Ian and his brother with his old Dodge pickup truck, to meet us at the public parking lot near the fake lighthouse at Shoreline Park, at 10 a.m. That's in downtown Long Beach.

We not only had to be careful about ourselves, but we didn't want Ian's brother to get in trouble either for getting mixed up with us. But with these gangsters combing the whole waterfront area, if the timing wasn't right and the fog lifted early, we'd all be easy targets.

Without speaking a word, we leaned into the strokes and, blisters or not, we went as fast and as quietly as we could.

No turning back now—the only way out is through.

iii. BRIDGING THE GAP

We counted the number of bridges that we passed under, and Zoe looked them up on her map app: Pacific Coast Highway, Anaheim Street, West Shoreline.

In and around the PCH bridge (the westernmost highway in the country), we swore we heard those voices again. They must've been the lookouts. There had to be other groups of them in the area, too. If they were going to nab us, they knew that the bridges would be good vantage points, at least on a good day.

And so, with a wall of thick weather still cloaking the area, we stopped under each bridge to check out the next stretch. Only then did we make our next silent dash downriver. According to our calculations, we figured we were near our destination—one final bridge: Queens Way. Then the parking lot was supposed to be up a rocky embankment on the river's left.

We noticed that the angled concrete riverbanks were now replaced with large, stacked boulders, still coming out of the river at an angle, but ever so more natural-looking—it definitely seemed we were entering the final section near the ocean.

Barely making out the ominous shape of Queens Bridge, we also heard a bunch more voices. And there were two that we recognized in particular: Circus Freak and Bouncer Dude. And wherever those two were, Al Capone and Lazy Boy weren't far behind, even injured as they were.

We could've sworn we spied the figures of those two other dudes who joined the gang of thugs back at the pad—the younger ones dressed in all black.

Damn! Could we make it past that one last bridge? With the temperature rising, the fog was more wispy now; if we were in the wrong spot at the wrong time, we'd be goners. It just about broke our hearts, being so nearly home free, but not quite.

Maybe our ticket out (Ian's brother) would turn up dead and floating in San Pedro Bay even if we made it. Hopefully he had enough sense, if asked, to say something like, "Oh, I'm getting ready to go fishing" or "I come out here every morning to take a walk." You know, something dull and normal. I couldn't stand the idea of getting more people in trouble.

But first we had to worry about our own skins. We needed another plan—and fast! I had an idea. It was a long shot. It was a sort of a betting-the-farm kind of plan. I figured it was so idiotic that it just might work.

We huddled our two boats together. I told them the idea: "We paddle upstream and over to the other side. We set up the one boat to look like we're all in it—like, asleep, but under blankets. We load it up with the last of our firecrackers."

"Firecrackers?" said Tawnya.

"I think I know where Sam is headed with this," said Ian. "We stashed some away in bags for the ride. Most of them got wet, but we salvaged one last small bag."

"Anyway," I continued, "so we let that boat float away, as a distraction, see? Then we book back across and wait 'til the float is spotted by one of their sentries. Big fuss. They check it out. Meanwhile, we slink past the bridge on this near side, pick up our ride in the parking lot, and get out of Dodge—in the Dodge."

"Go Dodgers," said Ian wryly.

"That is it?" said Iggie.

"Hey," I said, "anybody got anything better?"

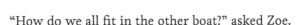

"How do we all fit in the other boat?" asked Zoe.

"Very carefully," I suggested. "I don't know. I didn't think of *everything*. Help me out."

"It'll be tippy, for sure," Ian said. "But you're right—it's better than no plan. I'm in."

"We do this then?" Iggie asked, looking around the group, incredulous.

No one stepped forward with anything else. Deal.

So we turned around and paddled upriver, back into the thicker part of the fog. Ian double-checked to see that we still had the money bag in the canoe and didn't accidentally put it in the kayak. Check.

Then we crossed the width of the river, maybe a hundred yards or so. When we got over there, we quickly began to set up our dummy decoy boat. We chose the kayak as decoy since the canoe was more versatile for storage, and just larger. We propped up whatever we could find to make the kayak look like there were bodies on board. Anything and everything—it was all hands on deck!

We were pleased with what we came up with. Ian added the icing on the cake: the last of our firecrackers, rigged with a long fuse he tied together from several shorter ones.

"Z'that it?" said Tawnya, watching him work.

"What do you mean?" said Ian.

"Those tiny-ass fireworks can barely be heard. We need this shit here." She reached into her to-go backpack and pulled out three substantially larger fireworks. "Nothing gets someone's attention like a few M-80s."

We all shrugged and smirked: *Why not?*

She set them in place on the kayak, adding under her breath, "Happy Birthday, America."

When we were set to paddle back across, we got settled as low as possible in the boat, to be less tippy. Then I pulled out my trusty old lighter, took a breath, said a quick prayer, and lit the fuse.

From that point on, we knew we had only about two, maybe three minutes, tops, to get in position on the other side of the river before it went off. We tried hard to stay in stroke with one another, for balance and to go as straight as possible.

We had nearly crossed back over to the other riverbank when we heard the first of the firecrackers, then the stirrings of commotion that our decoy caused.

"Here goes nothing," I said.

Voices shouted back and forth.

"Hey, over there—"

"I'll cover. Go check it out."

We could hear a bunch of boots clunking over toward the other end of the bridge. So far it was working as planned. The only problem was that they left one guy stationed on our side. Damn! Still, he was distracted, looking toward the other end of the bridge, hoping he'd get called off his post so he could be in on the action. We raised our paddles like we were at the starting line of an Olympic canoeing event.

The firecrackers seemed to work, and we were all set to seize the opportunity. As soon as the lone sentry looked toward the popping, we began paddling. My heart beat *thump-thump-thump*, in sync with our paddle strokes. I watched the sentry out of the corner of my eye—if he turned his head back, we were doomed.

Fortunately, the firecrackers were mistaken for gun shots, and the guys returned fire on the decoy, releasing a barrage of lead that certainly riddled the poor kayak. So much for our boat rental refund. The sentry kept his gaze turned away from us as we managed to glide under the bridge, unnoticed, in our overloaded boat. We kept on going out the other side, smiling in muted celebration.

It wasn't too much farther that we could make out the parking lot, with what looked like our hazy contact, Ian's brother, looking out from the shore atop the asphalt bluff, near that little lighthouse.

Behind us and on the other side, the racket continued until ...

"Hold fire!"

We stopped paddling. There was a dreadful silence.

Then—Boom! Ba-boom!! BOOM!!! The M-80s finally unleashed, allowing us the cover of noise to get away quicker. There was more firing, then another "Hold fire!" as they reassessed.

"It's a fake!! Quick, back across!"

We started paddling hard again. By the time we were nearly on shore, we could see them swarming all over the bridge, looking out, in every direction. We couldn't have been more than fifty yards from shore when we heard what seemed like a bullet skip off the rocks in front of us.

Then another. We could see Ian's brother in the parking lot, running for cover, back to his truck. I don't know how much Ian told him, but he understood that something was seriously going wrong here. His self-preservation instincts were telling him to get away fast. He seemed to understand that he had only a few key minutes or he was going to have a whole load of trouble swooping down on him. It wasn't thirty seconds before he was peeling away in his truck. Smart guy.

As for us, with the partially lifted fog, we had no choice but to head back out to the center of the estuary where the deeper, cooler water seemed to provide temporary shelter in its lingering patches of fog, or naval mist or whatever they call it. Our hideouts were fast becoming scarce.

The jig was up.

The chase was on.

iV. OVER AND UP

"I've got it!" I said, pointing across the river. "Over that way!"

"Is this gonna be as brilliant as your last idea?" said Tawnya. "'Cause if it is, I want out right now."

"Get out anytime you want," I said, "but until then, paddle like hell!"

"*Like* hell?" said Ian. "Too late—we're *in* it!"

"Hey, the plan got us past the bridge, didn't it?" I argued.

"Yeah, from the pot to the fire! Oh, *Dios*," grumbled Iggie.

"Let's just get to someplace safe before we DIE!" Ian shouted. "Is that too much to ask?! I'm too young for all this."

"Seriously, guys?!!" Zoe said. "Can't you stop talking and paddle!?"

We put our backs into it, finding an actual rhythm that sped us through the glassy water as I surveyed the horizon ahead.

"I know a hiding place," I urged.

"Yeah, right," said Tawnya, "we're in thuh middle of the freakin' bay!"

"Just head toward that misty patch over there. Come on! We're close. Row! And one, two ..."

As we leaned in and went for one of the last big patches with bullets whizzing into the water around us, we looked like a pathetic version of an Olympic rowing race—the five of us trying to move forward as we leaned from side to side, sometimes in sync and sometimes knocking paddles. It took serious concentration and constant counterbalancing to keep from tipping. If we capsized, we were history. We didn't know if those jerks had a boat, but we didn't doubt their resourcefulness; they'd have one soon enough if they wanted it. Plus, them carrying guns and having no problem killing people was definitely a major downside for us. So we breathed a sigh of relief when the bow of our tippy ship pierced the beginning of a misty patch and we were able to relax and catch our breath again.

We knew they were scurrying around nearby, an angry bunch of hornets who got their nest poked.

"Now what?" said Zoe, looking to me with eager eyes.

"We follow this to the other side," I said, making a few nautical calculations—like wetting my finger and feeling for the direction of the wind.

"You do not have a plan, do you?" said Iggie.

"*Sure* I do, at least up to a point. Ian, Zoe—you remember when we mapped out Long Beach to figure where we'd take out, right?"

They nodded. "Well, remember the debate over which side of the river to land on and why we chose that side back there?" They still didn't get it. "What was in the way, big time, on the other side?"

"The big transport cranes?" said Ian.

"No. I mean, yeah, but not them—"

Zoe's eye lit up. "The boat!"

In a flash, Ian recognized the plan. "Oh yeah, that ship!"

"Good, okay now: Think about the harbor from space, like a satellite, and help me get us pointed in that direction. Think of where we came from. On the count of three, point: One, two, three!"

Like rock, paper, scissors, we each pointed a slightly different direction. We seemed to be relatively on target—give

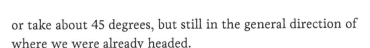

or take about 45 degrees, but still in the general direction of where we were already headed.

"Okay, we split the difference—that's our best bet." I moved my arm halfway between theirs, then they moved their arms toward mine. "Closer, a bit this way, got it! Stop." We pointed in the same direction. "Okay, set that course."

We started huffing it again.

Paddling for even a few minutes felt like twenty, as the occasional bullet whizzed past us. I thought back to the basin when Ian and I tossed pebbles and stones at helpless sticks in the river. I felt for those sticks right about now!

"This is ridiculous!" said Ian. "For all we know we're going in circles! We'll end up back at the bridge!"

"I know, I know! Go left," said Zoe.

"No," said Ian, "it's more to the right."

"No," I said, begging them to hold our course. "We've got to trust our instincts. Paddle evenly on both sides! It can't be much longer now! Keep going!! We can do it."

Another two minutes and the bullets had stopped; it was eerily quiet now. We didn't know what they were up to.

But finally, we came upon the most amazingly welcome sight.

"Whoa!" said Zoe, looking up in awe.

We were stunned. Towering above us, at least a hundred feet maybe, was the navy blue hull of a gigantic old ocean liner, the H.M.S. Queen Mary.

"What the fff—?!" said Tawnya, the only one able to utter actual sounds. Our mouths gaped open, as if seeing an alien spaceship. "And this is?"

"Our way out!" I exclaimed.

"Huh? How?"

Just then we lurched forward hard.

We had stopped looking at where our own boat was going. Zoe, Ian, and Tawnya toppled overboard, with me and Iggie barely managing to stay in the boat.

We looked up to see a mound of boulders, a long line of them, between us and the big boat. It extended in both directions and seemed to be a barrier—apparently to protect it from tsunamis, terrorists, and roaming packs of teenagers.

The last of the mist was disappearing—literally into thin air. I estimated our time.

"We've got less than ten minutes or so to get on board before we're totally exposed. Come on!"

"On *that*?!" said Tawnya. "I ain't goin' on that hunk a junk! Did I mention I'm scared of heights?"

"We don't have time for phobias," I said. "This is life or death."

"But *how*?" asked Ignazio.

I looked up, expecting to see an anchor smoothly descending from our side of the front of the ship, but there was only one on the side nearest land. *Damn.* My eyes followed the anchor down to a fence on the side of the river. That was our access. I pointed to the spot.

"We've got to get this boat up and over these rocks. Come on!" I said.

So we huffed the boat up and over, dropped it in the water and paddled over to the where the fence met the anchor, amidst tons of other boulders. The massive ship seemed like a huge beast tethered to the earth by these giant ropes.

I remember thinking: *The way out is up.*

We ditched the canoe riverside and climbed up to the fence. It turned out that it wasn't so much an anchor, as I'd expected, but a couple of massive ropes, each about a foot in diameter. They wouldn't be as easy to grab and climb, so I threw together a carabiner contraption that wrapped over the ropes with my own, much smaller belt rope. I put my makeshift harness so that a person could sit beneath the anchor ropes and shimmy up, pulling hand over hand. It would be difficult, but we had no choice.

I quickly hooked myself into it and began the long climb. "I'll send this back down for the next person."

The anchor ropes draped over a submarine that was docked beside the Queen Mary. I watched the sub come and go as I made good speed with my climbing. That was the easier part though, where the rope was more level. As the angle increased, every ten feet was increasingly harder.

I was about thirty feet from the top when I couldn't go any farther. I had to awkwardly pull myself over to the top sides of the anchor ropes, straddling them and scooting up the final length. I was hugging the ropes tightly by the time I got to the hole where the ropes went through the bow of the boat. I squeezed my way through.

I looked out, to the north; I could see all the way up to the Hollywood Hills—spectacular, except for the fact that the goon squad of cars must've spotted me and were driving fast, over the bridge that crossed where the river meets the bay, racing toward the ocean liner's dock and parking area.

Looking back at our group though, I could see how my original plan wouldn't work: to simply slide the contraption down the anchor ropes for the next person to use. It wasn't enough of a vertical drop, and there would be too much friction between the two types of rope. Plus, it would take much longer for each person than we had time for.

Crossing my arms to signal a no-go, I looked around for a solution. There was a regular rope, a long one, coiled on the deck beside me. I could lower that rope directly down and maybe hoist them up. But could I? It was our best bet under the circumstances.

I returned to the railing, waived my arms excitedly, pointed straight down, and began lowering the smaller rope from the anchor rope hole at the bow. I could see them make for the canoe again and head over to where the rope would meet the water.

I looked around for how I was going to pull them up. I wrapped the rope around a couple of pipes so that I'd be able to cinch them up easier, little by little. I looked over the railing to see that Ignazio was tying Tawnya, the lightest of the group, to the line. Great. When he signaled, I went to my rope and pulled like crazy, putting my legs against one of the poles, for leverage, reeling her up. It was tough, but in about a minute I was able to bring her up to the hole, where she climbed aboard.

I gave her a quick hug, untied her, and dropped the rope for the next person. Each person aboard made the process that much quicker as they helped to pull.

One by one, we brought them up. Iggie was last, making sure everyone before him had a secure harness.

Finally, as I could see a line of cars approaching the parking lot beside the Queen Mary, we hoisted Iggie up and onto the deck.

But our celebration was short-lived.

We didn't get more than a few seconds of rest when, from somewhere on the other side of the boat, we heard bursts of gunfire.

V. ALL HANDS ON DECK!

The deck was deserted. There were three huge smoke-stacks, with giant infrastructural gadgets sticking out of the deck elsewhere, and wires going one way or another, like an industrial spider web that kept it held together.

We hobbled over to the other side to see what all the racket was about. We found an extension ramp with a long cabin and tiny windows at the end of the ramp. We walked out on it, hoping to see what was going on below. We could see a couple cars screeching around in the parking lot, but that was about it.

The thugs were having it out with a few security guards. The guards had the protection of the ship, but the henchmen had the firepower. Most of the fighting was based around one of the bridges (or planks or whatever they're called) that connect the ship to the shore. The guards would poke their heads out from the massive steel openings and fire a few anemic shots from their puny revolvers, but it was no use. They might as well have had water pistols. The other guys had submachine guns and sprayed the opening with very unfriendly fire.

Then the fighting spread to one of the other doorways, creating two fronts to the attack. We thought we were safe at first, since our allies had the high ground, but those poor guys didn't know how to use their advantage (i.e., *shut the damn doors!*). At one point, as we were pointing and shouting, one of the roughnecks spotted us and turned his gun up high and sprayed gunfire at our lofty viewpoint, high up on the ship. We could hear the bullets pinging against the bulky enclosure, secured by a ton of hefty rivets. We felt sort of invincible, but then a few of the windows got shot out and we hit the deck.

"What do we do now?!" said Zoe.

"We're trapped!" said Ian. "We can't stay here!"

"Look, this boat is huge," I said, searching for a positive spin. "At least there are a lot more hiding places here on deck than out on the open water."

We tore across the length of the deck, our eyes darting around, looking for a small miracle that would provide the perfect hiding place.

"What about hiding in the smokestacks!" I offered.

Ian looked up at them, then stared me down. "Are you for real? They go down to the boilers. Think chimney. It's a long shaft. You'd fall and die."

"Look, I don't know how these things are put together. But okay."

"Maybe there!" Iggie said, pointing to a small lookout room atop a fifty-foot post coming out of the deck.

"No," argued Zoe, "if they see us there's no exit option. We'd be like a cat stuck up a tree. We've got to go down to other floors."

"But they'll be coming *up!*" said Ian, "Why would you want to go *toward* them?!"

"Because this whole deck is a dead end, dude. And this is the last place they spotted us, so they'll come here first."

"She is right," said Iggie. "They do not expect us to go *to* them. We take it to them. We have the surprise."

"Sounds good to me," said Tawnya. "We're outta time. I'm so outta here, too!"

Down we went—according to the unspoken consensus of the group, as judged by a show of feet stomping for the nearest stairway. Wounds aside, we practically flew down it.

We made it down two stairwells before we stopped and listened. We could hear muffled yelling down one of the hallways on the side of the boat nearest shore. I waved the group over to the other side, and everyone followed. It was a good move, 'cause no sooner did we go down one more level then we heard a couple of their guys burst through a door and end up right where we had first stopped to listen. Then they spread out in search of us.

We quietly ducked into a hallway one floor down and headed toward the middle of the ship. The place was completely deserted; it felt like a Victorian-era museum. The hallways had colorful, faded old carpets, with dark wood coming up from the floor and lighter wood toward the ceiling, with polished brass handrails along the hallways that seemed to draw a shiny golden line out to infinity. Along the sides were the individual rooms where people used to sleep. With the cushy carpeting underfoot, we could be a lot more quiet than the bunch of us rumbling down the metallic stairwells outside. That was a lucky break.

There was a whole lot of atmosphere to the place, but it was spooky, too. It had the feel of another world at another time, one that we didn't belong to and which we didn't know our way around—still, on the scale of problems, it would do just fine.

We were much more comfortable finding our way around a digital world with cell phones, computers, and the Web than we were in this lavish old hulk. In virtual spaces we worked buttons on our keypads and joysticks, and instantly transported to a new location. If you got killed, you got set back a bit and got the chance to start over. But there was an actual, real finality to this game we were now playing.

So after doing the long hallway to forever, we passed a few grand doors before looking back to see if anyone was following us. Nothing—so far so good. We pushed the doors open and entered.

It was a fantastic, huge ballroom with tall ceilings and chandeliers. It had a rectangular wood floor in the middle and ornate carpeting around it, with a few dozen round tables draped with white tablecloths and table settings scattered here and there. There were big velvet red curtains on a stage at the far end. The walls were a golden veneer. Dark wood panels led upward to sunlight streaming through old-fashioned, fancy skylights in the ceiling.

"This must've been ...," Zoe began.

"Hide!!!" Ian whispered to the group, looking toward the stage.

Without knowing what was going on, we scrambled for cover behind and under the nearest tables.

After a few long seconds, we heard muffled voices and yelling again. When I peeked out from a tablecloth, I had a good view of the stage. And just then, the curtains parted and one of the guys, his machine gun slung over his shoulder, surveyed the room. I popped my head back under the table curtain.

Everything was okay until ... *thunk*! One of our group—somebody at the next table—accidentally hit their head on the middle post.

The guy on stage turned his head and looked out, squinting to see against the glare of sunlight. Everything was quiet, until Iggie got our signals crossed; he thought the coast was clear and began moving again, starting to get out from under the table. I tried to shush him. There was a bunch of jostling at that table, and a glass on the table was rocking back and forth, and finally fell over and began to roll toward the edge of the table. It was going to crash and break and give us away, for sure. I made a crawling dash as it fell, in slow motion, from the edge of the table. Before it hit the ground, I reached out and caught it!!

Phew!

After an endless, awkward silence, the glass exploded in my hand. All hell broke loose. Machine gun fire ripped into our end of the room, putting bullet holes in the table-cloths and curtains and taking chunks out of the walls and carpets. The ricocheting bullets smashed through the ceiling windows, and broken glass rained down on us.

"Run!" I yelled as loud as I could.

Keeping low, we bolted for the doors. I transitioned from crawling to a crouched, gimpy running. One of the guys walked toward us between his waves of bullets while reloading his gun.

As the last of us left through the door, the bullets once again tore apart the old room, popping against the still-flapping, leathery doors, as we dove back into the temporary safety of the hallway.

We booked it, up a stairwell then quickly spiraled downward two levels and kept on going, down yet another hallway.

VI. POOLING TOGETHER

"**W**hat the hell, man!?" I said to Iggie, when we were able to duck in somewhere and catch our breath.

"I am sorry," said Ignazio, "but I get stuck."

"Well we're *all* stuck now!" said Tawnya. "Thanks a lot!"

"Hey, we're in this together," I warned. "Let's keep our heads! We've got enough to do with fighting *them*. We can *do* this, you guys. Look, that commotion will bring the cops. We've got to hold out long enough. If we can keep away from them long enough, we win."

"Psst," whispered Ian, "down here."

We saw him standing beside an even smaller set of stairs that led away from the main hallways and looked like it connected to back hallways that only the ship's staff would've known about.

It looked good to me. It seemed like maybe a storage area off the kitchen with easy access to the ballroom but also secret shortcuts elsewhere. We hustled through the spacious kitchen, contemplating the wonderful hiding spaces, but in the end we opted to keep moving.

"We've got to find one of those exit doors," said Zoe, "those metal planks leading outside!"

"No, they'll have someone posted at them for sure," said Ian.

"Well, we can't hide out forever," I said, frustrated.

"We keep moving," said Iggie. "They come. Quick, no time."

Clang, bang, step, step, step.

Someone was up above us on the same stairwell. We paused, hoping they wouldn't choose to level down. Fortunately, they stayed on that level and kept going. We had to be smarter and quieter.

We kept going, trying to get off the beaten pathways. We headed toward the front of the boat (at least where we thought it was). After a few more twists and turns, we found ourselves in a dark, eerie room. It was the kind of place where you could hear a drop of water falling from a pipe and hitting the ground. We passed under a dimly lit, fifty-foot-tall ceiling and smack onto the—whatever it was—even darker center of the space. In silence, we let our eyes adjust like an old Polaroid photo; we began to see that it was an empty swimming pool with the look of an Art Deco Aztec temple.

The pool was rectangular and painted a turquoise color, with mosaic tiles across the bottom. It was less than a hundred feet long and maybe a dozen feet deep on the one end. This wasn't a pool for kiddies to slowly wade into—here you jumped in and it was instantly deep. Around the top there were brass rails for people to hold onto. We were on the balcony level, looking down. The pool level had artsy, fake marble, fat pillars supporting the balcony level, wrapped with bright green seaweed-looking tiles. This was the creepiest public pool you ever saw.

"Wow! Cool!" said Tawnya.

"Yeah, wow, but no good places to hide in here," I argued.

"Come on," said Ian, "let's try the doors at the top of these stairs."

We went up an elegant, Aztec temple-style staircase. We saw the doors on either side and started toward them, but halfway up we heard a big steel door creak open from somewhere else in the room. A sliver of light pierced the darkness.

Two hulking guys came out of the shadows on the lower level—one on either side of the pool. By the steadiness of their steps, and the fact that our exit was cut off, they must've already heard or spotted us. They stepped forward with all the friendliness of a couple of hammerheads.

I whispered to Tawnya and Ian beside me: "Go up and check those doors. I'll go for that other door on the lower level."

As the guys approached, they reached down to their lower legs and pulled up their pants legs and unsheathed huge knives. Without missing a beat, they kept moving forward, tightening the noose around our collective necks.

Meanwhile, Iggie and Zoe checked the two doors above: "Locked!" she whispered.

As I fled for the door on the lower level, the guy on that side ran forward, causing me to back up, beneath the staircase. *Trapped.*

They skulked around the near corners of the pool and had me trapped at the end of it. They had the weapons, but we had the numbers. I saw it play out: They'd use me as the lure to get the others to surrender and come down, then they'd off us all and hide us somewhere in the room as they'd escape from the boat.

Right as they were close enough to grab me, I took a bunch of desperate swings to keep them at bay so the others might be able to slip out the sides and escape through the doors we came in by.

"Run!" I shouted to the others.

But they didn't. The thugs looked at one another and both stepped toward me again, reaching out.

As they did, I saw a shape above me, holding onto something and sliding down the nearby slide. It was Ian, holding an old lifeguarding pole with a hook on the end. As I ducked, the two guys looked up and saw it, but it was too late. The pole Ian held broadsided them, catching them at their chests.

The two guys put up their hands to try to block, but it put them off-balance. They tripped over their own feet and fell backward into the deep pit of the pool—down, down, and splat! They hit the ground hard.

Out. Cold.

The height may not have been lethal, but it was no mere headache either. If they came to, which was seriously doubtful any time soon, they'd still have to figure how to get up and out of the pool.

Proud of our collective little victory, we wasted no time scurrying back to the other side of the room, around to one of the unlocked doors, exited and continued on our way.

But to where? We couldn't say.

VII. A LAST STAND

Zoe took the lead now, checking around every corner, giving the rest of us the signal. Then the next person would go on ahead. And so on. Whoever was last watched our rear flank. It was amazing how, in the short time we were together on foot, we developed an unspoken system of acting in sync. We weren't exactly a commando team, but we were a team nonetheless.

We were getting closer to the outside walls—the hull. We got a glimpse of a portal opening with sweet natural light streaming in.

We snuck up to it and peeked out to assess the situation. As we imagined, the main access ramps were still covered: Two guards watched the entrances.

"Damn!" I growled. "We are sooo close."

We huddled to consider our options and didn't like any of them.

Zoe and Ignazio went to get a better look outside a nearby doorway.

It wasn't long before we heard a shout and then some bullets pinged off the side of the boat. They came running back in.

"Hurry," Iggie shouted, "they send guys! Come, I have a plan."

Iggie opened a door leading back into the ship. We entered a separate, darker room. I jammed the door behind us to slow anyone who tried to follow.

A few more shots rang out, outside the boat. Who was shooting now, we couldn't say. There was commotion outside, then a lot more shots fired.

We didn't stick around to wait for a written explanation. We hoped the gunshots were a sign that help might be on the way, might even come aboard. But we didn't know anything for certain except that if we stopped anywhere for too long, someone always seemed to catch up to us.

"Follow me," said Iggie. "I think I know a good place. All boats are the same."

We didn't know what he meant, but he seemed sure, so we went with it. So we ducked into a doorway and went down two more floors. Then we headed toward the *back* of the boat, through the lower intestine of this monster ship.

Down, down, down we went—a teen submarine on red alert, scrambling to avoid depth charges.

It wasn't because we thought it was the best way out, but because they were closing in on us. If we found a good place to hide, maybe they'd think we'd made it off the boat and would simply give up. It was lame, but it was a calculated hope.

I might've just been paranoid, but it felt like they were closing in on us, like they knew where to go next. Paranoid or not, we had to act fast.

"This way!" Iggie shouted, looking exhausted from carrying the extra weight of the money bag all this time now.

"No, this way!" Ian countered.

We were starting to panic and unravel, with everyone's nerves frayed and each having his or her own idea of where to go.

Eventually though, we ended up finding what Iggie seemed to be looking for: the old boiler room. *Ah, the motor is always at the back of boats.*

As we entered one by one through the thick steel doorway, we could see it was a perfect mess—like something out of one of those ocean liner disaster movies, a place with huge bolts, valves, levers, cables, pipes, wires, engines, you name it. Walkways snaked through the different rooms and cavernous spaces. They'd never think we'd be so stupid as to hide here, at the tail end, where there was no way out. *Would they?*

"Now hide!" Iggie said, gesturing to spread out.

I knew where he was going with this. "Find a good, dark spot where you can lie still and won't bump into anything," I added, giving a nod to Iggie. "This is it, guys. Got it?"

Judging by their looks, everyone seemed to be on the same page: our final stand.

The strangeness and finality of the situation put a claustrophobic dread in us. The place was such a trash pit that we were sure there was no way anyone could trace us to our hiding places.

Some of our gang hid high, others low. Zoe somehow found a spot on top of a big ol' duct. Others took the low road: Ian crawled beneath a giant horizontal cog, and then behind what appeared to be a turbine engine. The rest I couldn't see. I found a wall around the perimeter that was a façade to the actual hull itself; this made for a hidden corridor between the two, with a hole big enough to climb in and look through.

My sightlines to see danger coming were poor. But if needed, I could get around the perimeter of the room by using the corridor.

As we waited, in hiding, it occurred to me this was vaguely like our old neighborhood games of Kick the Can, where everyone would split up and find places to hide. Those were hot summer evenings in our neighborhood, when the sun never set, and it seemed like all of life would always be like that: totally carefree and fun. Except this new form of the game had much higher stakes and removed all the fun and carefree parts.

There was the door where we'd come in—a mass of steel with its own interlocking gears that somehow cranked shut (to make this chamber watertight in case there was flooding or explosions). That was the can, the goal, I figured.

Suddenly, I got that weird sense of *déjà vu*. It was bizarre. I somehow *knew* this scene.

Something brushed past me. My reflexes made me pull away, and as I did I thought I glimpsed something moving along the wall, but wasn't certain. A place like this could play terrible tricks on your imagination. *Get a grip.* Whatever happens, don't give away my position—that could jeopardize not only me but the whole group. Cockroaches, snakes, lions, tigers, bears—ghosts?—they'd have to take a number and get in line.

And then came the moment of truth.

Silently, they came for us through that solid but tiny door. It wasn't a good sign that there were so many of them: one, two, three, four, at least five, maybe more. Well, I told myself, five on five is at least a fair fight (except for their overwhelming firepower, of course).

And like us, they spread out. Assuming they'd somehow tracked us, we knew they were hoping for us to make a mistake, since there were too many places to search. And although we were kids, I didn't doubt they were a bit anxious, too, poking around in the dark, not knowing what they might stumble on.

They didn't do a particularly thorough search, but they did comb through most of the main routes. One of them stepped up onto a platform that put him close to seeing Zoe, but then he walked right past her as she remained perfectly still.

The longer we stayed quiet, the more likely they were to retreat and go looking somewhere else.

Then something happened that broke with the plan. Just when it looked like we'd outlasted them, something fell from the rafters and crashed on top of two guys who were looking around in the same area, prompting bullets to rip into the whole of the engine room—ricocheting off steel girders near the ceiling and then off the giant boilers. I know I wasn't the only one in our group to drop to the ground, cover my head and say a prayer.

Then the gunfire subsided.

That was no accident: One of us had made a calculated move. All we could do was to act on it and trust that the person knew what they were doing.

"Tony!? Eddy!?" a few voices called out.

Not hearing a response, a couple of them made their way over to where the ruckus happened. When they got over there, I saw that two guys got clobbered and were lying unconscious beneath a couple of fifty-five-gallon oil barrels. The guys who did the recon then retreated quickly back to the leader and murmured among themselves. Then they branched out and continued their search, leaving their fallen comrades unconscious or dead.

Three against five now. Much better odds. But we lost the element of surprise.

"Come out, come out, wherever you are," one guy said in a chilly voice, trying to unnerve us. He did a pretty convincing job, but we weren't going to give him the satisfaction of knowing that.

When I saw two of them on either side of where Ian was hidden, starting to poke under the cog, I decided that was too close for comfort. Besides, Ian didn't know that one of his feet was sticking out, and it was only a matter of time before they discovered him.

Since my position was fairly protected, and furthest from the exit door, I decided to distract them: I'd draw them out, then the rest of our group could flank them and sneak behind them and be freed. I didn't have a plan for how *I'd* get out but didn't see what other choice I had.

So I got up and started running along the perimeter corridor, creating as much noise as possible.

They fired again, in my direction. Then, when they realized they didn't know what the hell they were firing at, they stopped and began to follow my sounds. I was pleased with my cunning, until they were getting much too close.

I had the advantage, though, that I could see the three of them coming my way. I made noise in one area, then tiptoed to another area, made more noise, then tiptoed to yet another area and made still more noise. It gave the impression there were more of us than there were, to scare them, slow them down and confuse them.

There was no way around the fact that they were closing in on me. They had time on their side, and I had no real endgame apart from bluffing.

I'd have to retrace my steps, but one of their guys was nearly cutting off that exit route. I needed ...

CRASH! BANG! BOOM!

Our gang let loose with a cacophony of noises. I knew that, as I'd done for Ian, the rest of the gang was responding for my sake, to save my skin. These thugs had itchy trigger fingers, they were so jittery by then that they started firing again, everywhere. And when they did, I saw the opportunity I'd been waiting for: use the cover of the noise to race for the metal door.

It was a long way around, but I didn't mind as long as it got me out in one piece. It got me past the guy on the one side and a good ways back down the corridor from which I'd

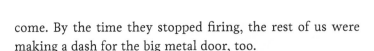

come. By the time they stopped firing, the rest of us were making a dash for the big metal door, too.

One of the crooks saw this and tried to alert the other two. They were determined to flush us out, but they still thought we were back where I made the fuss. Bad assumption. When they got up real close and kicked a hole through one of the rusty walls, rats came pouring through the hole by the hundreds, maybe thousands, running over the two terrified guys who were tripping and falling over each other to get out of there.

They raced for the same door as me, along with the third guy, accompanied by the hordes of squealing rats that were right behind them, freaked out, too, and wanting out. It was a close call as to who'd get there first: me or them. Our gang was assembled on the other side of the door, urging me on. Ian and Iggie, sensing that I wasn't going to beat them to it, grabbed a handful of stray items from the floor and started pelting the goons with them.

It worked. They reared back and fell down again—not expecting any of us to go on the offense with them.

I took the last ten steps or so to the door and jumped through it as my friends' hands pulled me the rest of the way. Then Ian and Iggie backed up, retreated through the door and struggled to shut it. They began turning the big cog on the door. It was almost shut when I saw one of the guys, through the small window connecting the two rooms, slam against the door, trying to force it open. But even a guy his size just bounced off the sturdy door. He fell to the floor. As he did, the rats came streaming past him, overwhelming him, causing him to yell horribly.

Despite the door being solid as could be, we could still hear their yells coming from the other side as the rats piled up on them, each group of creatures struggling in a panic to get out first.

We couldn't look. We stepped off to the side and gave a group hug. Then we realized it was still premature.

"This couldn't possibly be *all* of them," I said. "Come on! Up! To the light!"

Enough of the creepy underworlds. We went up a whole bunch of stairs, down a couple hallways, and back up another staircase. We braced ourselves for more hide and seek, but the boat felt much more empty and quiet. It must be a trap, we figured.

From time to time we'd encounter what seemed like the last of the thugs, who were on the run, having periodic shootouts with another group. We couldn't immediately understand what was going on or see who the other group was. We figured that maybe the security guards were taking back their turf, or maybe police had shown up by now.

But at one point, from a floor above, where we were catching our breath, we saw that a full-on SWAT team was sweeping through the boat, with bouts of sporadic but intense gunfire. At one point we paused to listen, as the SWATsters isolated and captured a few of the goon squad—those two guys in black with the baseball caps. The others, by then, must've been breaking ranks and fleeing as fast and far as they could—which wasn't much.

We could've come clean right then and walked up to the SWAT team and introduced ourselves, but I think we imagined that we, ourselves, might be considered perpetrators to a trigger-fingered marksman and shot dead accidentally. After all, it was the security guards in the boat who told us to stay away from the ship in the first place, so they might've reported us as terrorists or part of the same gang that attacked the ship and the security guards. From a distance, the SWAT guys saw targets—they'd shoot first and ask questions later.

So with a show of feet we decided not to make the direct appeal to the SWAT team—at least, not yet—and so we kept on going.

We found our way to the main deck, and finally, outside into the fresh air!

VIII. ABANDON SHIP

We reasoned that, as long as we could get away without getting into trouble, we should try it, just go for it and slip away quietly. With the no-necks either on the run or captured, this thing was a slam dunk—those jerks were about to get their due.

So we ran, smiling ear to ear, down the empty deck, practically flying from excitement.

We glanced over the parking lot side of the ship. The whole place was inundated with cop cars, fire trucks and ambulances. Overhead, a news chopper was arriving on the scene, taking turns circling with a police chopper. We ducked out of sight and let it pass overhead; we saw it circle back over the throngs assembled in the parking lot on shore beside the Queen Mary.

At that rate, we'd never get off the damn ship! We were ready to take our chances with the SWAT team again when I saw one last possibility: "A lifeboat! Check it out: we could lower it down and still make it back over to the other side of the bay, near our original take-out. C'mon, we can do it. Let's disappear. No one will know we were ever here. It's perfect."

I could tell that the group wasn't thrilled with the idea, but under the circumstances it made sense. Since no one resisted outright, we kept on going.

We made a beeline back across the top deck. I saw a few lifeboats dangling over the side and it hit me: *What if, sometimes, the way forward is straight down?*

I waved our group over and climbed into the first lifeboat, immediately starting to undo whatever ropes or cables I could make sense of. The rest of them came running up and fussed with the other lines, cranking and hoisting one thing or another. We'd get ourselves off the ship yet, if that was what it took.

Ian tossed the money bag into the boat. I positioned myself for the descent.

Suddenly though, the lifeboat lurched to one side as it dropped, then caught on something again. I got thrown pretty roughly and just about lost the bag of money over the side before I was able to grab it again.

"Keep cranking! Make the boat level!" I shouted.

"We're trying, man!" yelled Ian. "This freakin' thing hasn't been used in decades."

"Okay, that's good, right there," I said. "Hold it. Now, hop in."

"But how does it go?" said Zoe. "We can't steady it and jump in at the same time."

The news helicopter swooped the perimeter of the boat again, and we ducked for cover.

When it passed, we popped our heads up again.

"Come on," I shouted. "We can work it from inside the boat. Jump!"

They came out to the edge of the deck, with the lifeboat about five feet below them, tilted at a disturbing angle toward the ocean.

"All right," said Ian, preparing to jump, "here goes nothing: One ..."

Then the strangest thing happened.

I was pretty sure my mind was just overheated and prone to imagining stuff (yet again) from all we'd been through. Then when I realized there was no way I could've been dreaming,

I thought maybe post-traumatic stress had kicked in, causing me to see things. It's amazing how the brain tries to piece things together when there's stuff it doesn't want to see—and how it thinks all this in an instant.

Anyway, I saw *him* behind the others. He was crouched like a freaky gargoyle, hiding in one of those things on deck that that look like the bell of a tuba. He slithered down and out of it, and started running toward the railing, slow at first, then picking up speed. From my angle I lost sight of him for a second. Which is why I, I guess, I didn't—I couldn't—utter a word out loud to the others.

"Two ...," Ian continued.

Time slowed. Then he came into view again as I saw his face and upper torso rising over the shoulders of my friends as he vaulted past them. As the rest of his body came into view, his crazed face glared down at me, his eyes wide, his arms rising up like the wings of a big bat out of hell, his teeth bared, smiling that maniacal grin and falling directly toward me.

He was a specter from another world, a living, breathing Satan, coursing with bile in place of blood and bent on singling me out. There are moments, they say, where a person's hair can instantly go gray; it flashed in my mind that I might be the first teenager ever to experience that. I felt like my lungs forgot how to function, leaving me paralyzed.

I *was* helpless to keep him away. He *was there* though, swooping down on me, teetering, defenseless, in that stupid lifeboat, soon to be my deathboat. The irony of those final, precious seconds. If only we'd just turned ourselves in to the SWAT crew—what a colossal blunder!

His imminent boyslaughter was planned for the perfect moment of retribution; he must've been tracking us, hunting us, for a while.

Down he came. The last thought I had before he made contact with me was an expression I'd read somewhere: *By the time you spot a tiger, he's already seen you a hundred times.*

Circus Freak!!!

His knee met my chest. His outstretched hand was already reaching for the money bag. And when I toppled back against the side of the lifeboat, he came down on top of me and briefly knocked the air out of me. The lifeboat dropped under the sudden new weight.

There was a searing pain in my back, but nothing so bad as the horror of his face being right in front of me, whispering madness with that wretched breath: "You didn't think you'd seen the last of me, did ya, kid?" Then he paused a second before giving me a demented peck on my cheek, saying, "Kiss of death, m' boy. An' you're *it!*"

As terrified as I was, I was surprised by the fact that something primal erupted in me. Some kind of fight-or-flight survival reflex kicked in. My body spasmed in fear and delivered a burst of adrenaline. I pushed him and he flew off me and hit the side of the lifeboat, causing it to drop a few notches farther.

He had to make a quick choice to either let go of the money bag or fall overboard. He let go of the bag, but it only fell to the bottom of the lifeboat as he barely held onto the boat. Before he reached for the bag again, he looked up and saw my group preparing to pounce down on him, to help me. They needed the jump to be perfect or it would be an epic, deadly fall.

But Circus Freak leapt to the crank on the high side of the boat and released a lever, causing the boat to let out its line by about ten feet or so before it got snagged. In the process, as the boat swung, I grabbed hold of the side of the lifeboat and held on for dear life as the boat tipped to one side, the money bag landed beside me, and I snatched it as the ocean opened up below.

With the boat dangling almost vertically now and spinning out of control in circles, I could see my friends up above, unable to reach us. Circus Freak was there, climbing hand over hand toward me, then grabbing onto me, still smiling his dirty brown grin, pulling me down with his weight.

"What is he thinking!?" I thought. "This is suicide!" Surely he wasn't eager to fall, sending us both to instant death. "What would that accomplish, after stalking me the way he did?"

But he must've known something I didn't.

The grip of my legs weakened, and his kicks against my leg didn't stop. It was like he was chipping away at a big icicle, trying to crack it and watch it fall.

And after a few more well-placed kicks, I gave up.

Fall we did—down, down, down we went.

I was glad I was facing up, because I didn't want to see the surface of the water coming at me at terminal velocity which, from that height, we must've reached.

I could picture myself, bent at the waist, forming a falling V. At that moment I surrendered—I think I actually, physically, relaxed. After all, there was nothing else for me to do. Mine wasn't a long life, but apart from this last instant, it had been a pretty decent one. I guess that's what they mean by a person making their peace. After all the effort and hustle, that was my chance to say goodbye to the world. I took comfort in the fact that my friends were safe, far above me. I, alone, set out on this crazy trip, so it was only fair that I, alone, ended it this way.

The *thud* was like nothing else I'd ever felt. Although I was bent at the waist, the pressure on my back was incredible, taking most of my breath away.

The cold water took the rest of it away.

The only way I could've possibly caught a last quick breath was that our bodies made a little crater at the surface, from the impact, so I drew a final sip of air as we continued down into the water.

We couldn't have gone too far down, 'cause I remembered hearing about how a bullet, fired into water, doesn't penetrate as much as you'd think. Still, with everything blurry, jumbled together, and out of time, it felt like we sank, and sank, and sank.

The impact separated us temporarily. Circus Freak had somehow stripped the money bag from me and still held onto it, which I didn't care about right then. Between air and money, it's an easy decision for a body to make. I would've given a thousand of those money bags for a single breath, which it didn't seem like I was going to get, since Circus Freak kicked down at me, even underwater, to try to finish me off before he swam up for the surface.

I began to despair and give up. After all the struggle, the water seemed a fitting way to go—much better than death by fall or getting knifed or shot by one of his men. But in an instant, the injustice of him living and me dying hit me. It occurred to me that if I wasn't already dead from the fall, then why give up *now*? How stupid, pathetic, and passive was *that*?!

I looked around and saw that we were again near one of the huge anchor ropes that went way down into the water. I felt the belt rope that was still clipped at my side, and the carabiner on the end. I had one last-ditch, Hail Queen Mary of an idea: He wasn't about to let me get to the surface, so it was either him or me. I went on the offensive.

I looked up at the disappearing figure moving toward the light. I kicked hard and swam up, feeling the air starting to release from my lips—but I willed myself to clench them shut for ten more seconds. At the same time, I could see him struggling to get to the surface while clinging to the heavy bag of cash.

I undid my rope belt and looped one end around the enormous ship's rope one time, making sure it cinched upon the massive line. Then I swam upward, letting out my line as

I went. I held the other end of my rope. I got within five feet of Circus Freak, then four feet, then three feet, just about at the end of my line, I came up behind him, opened the carabiner and, just as my rope became taut ...

CLIP!!!

That familiar sound of high-pitched metal-on-metal was unmistakable, even underwater. It was a sweet sound to my ears, and I would've smiled right then except that I would've taken in water and foiled everything. I'd hooked the carabiner to his belt loop on the back of his pants.

There was confusion and panic in his face as I darted away from him and saw his now-desperate grasping. I continued to swim up as he faded behind me, his outstretched fingers clawing for me, for the surface. He tried to turn and undo what was keeping him down, but in turning his leg got twisted in the line and it only made it worse. He remained tethered there, his hands fumbling blindly at his lower back, trying to comprehend what happened to him.

He flailed some more, nearly undoing the latch on the carabiner. But nearly doesn't cut it. Finally, he swallowed his last breath.

The bag stayed gripped in his lower, still-clutched hand, somehow locked awkwardly beside him, with the stacks of money now cascading out of the money bag and down into the darkness. Circus Freak's other arm still reached up toward the surface, almost waving in the current, to the light and air he would never experience again.

I had about two seconds left myself.

With a single stroke of my arms and a final kick, I reached the surface. I felt the unbelievably wonderful holiness of the air but couldn't see a thing in the bright sunlight.

Time passed—I think. It could've been a second, ten minutes or two hours. Slowly, I began to feel the warmth of the sun on my frozen face.

iX. DEAD OR ALIVE

Or so I thought. I've learned that being truly certain is such a relative and fleeting thing.

Sure, I floated, but even dead things can float. I didn't seem able to move on my own; and I could swear I could think, but did that mean I was actually breathing? Maybe I broke bones in the fall and couldn't move. Still, an invisible force or some sort of physics kept me on the surface, at least for the time being.

Without a body, or at least a sensation of one, I was just consciousness. I remember that I began to monitor my body—the sensations of cold, of pain from wounds, the extreme fatigue, the taste of salt on my tongue, the sound and feel of breathing (or so I imagined). I seemed to have senses and saw snapshots of things, fuzzy stuff, but maybe they were just memories or illusions. I stared up at the blue sky.

Surrender, I thought to myself. *Up you go ...*

I sensed I was outside myself, as if rising over my calm, peaceful body, like a drone. There I was, floating face up, toward the sun, a slight smile in the corners of my mouth, and our gang there at the edge of the deck, way far away, looking and shouting and pointing.

What was happening to me?

And higher still I rose, above the ship now, swooping over the deck. Again higher, as I took in the wider view of vehicles zipping around the parking lot and the swirling chaos of emergency teams coming on and off the ship.

Rising farther, the circling helicopters buzzed around below, weaving invisible patterns in midair.

Stay down, part of me was thinking, calling to myself like an old friend.

It felt like coming home. A homecoming. *Home.*

Then a sensation came over me—not necessarily bad, just a tiny awareness, a pull or tug of sorts. It passed, replaced by an awareness of being part of something bigger than myself, that was drawing me closer, to something—what was it?—*inalienable*. I was a tiny atom in a vast body, but of what I couldn't say.

I was struck by the awareness of how I'd always thought the world revolved around *me*, and I was confronted with this overpowering, humbling but enchanting notion that I was so much smaller (and yet bigger) than I could've imagined. And that very knowledge was *huge*, was everything. *This* felt like true freedom.

I visualized bringing the thumb of my right hand to each of my fingertips. I commanded them to come together and create sparks each time they touched, sparks that lit up my whole body, like that Adam and God painting. *Wait—don't think of God, heaven, or anything like that.* But maybe that's a *good* thing.

What if I just shut up and stopped thinking so much?

But by now, of course, I looked around for the white light—and I half thought that'd be fine—but it was nowhere in sight. I looked around and suddenly felt like I was back again in my body, grounded, except in the ocean—so like, watered.

Again I tried to move my arms, to swim, but they felt like two large, limp noodles barely attached to my shoulders, floating beside me. I let the currents buoy me up and down, and the slight waves lapped against me.

More time passed, until ...

There was a nudge. Something hard and inhuman. Yet familiar. *Wood?*

"Hey!" a voice called to me. It didn't yell, but it was insistent: "Son."

I wasn't able to turn my neck but was barely able to roll my eyes in the general direction of the voice and force open my eyelids. A guy, a Black man, maybe in his sixties, held an oar pointed at me. It seemed he was in an old rowboat.

His face came closer. The end of the oar wedged under my armpit, and then he must've pulled me, 'cause I moved toward him and his hand gripped my upper arm. Pain shot through me, and I sort of gurgled, further waking up my feeble body.

"Sorry. Okay. Let's try this instead," the voice said. "C'mon, help me out."

As he grabbed me by my clothes at the chest and pulled me up, I tried to clutch the side of his boat with my cold, rigid, claw-like fingers. The edge of the boat was nearly at the water, and it looked like he was going to topple in, too. He sort of turned me over, then his other hand grabbed the back of my pants as he lifted me up and I flopped over, wincing, and into his boat.

I gazed up at him and eked out a smile, like a baby born into a whole new world. He smiled back, shaking his head: "I've caught a lot of fish. But you're the strangest yet, for sure!"

Instead of seeing the light though, everything faded to black.

EPILOGUE

When I opened my eyes, I saw flashing white lights like lightning and red lights whirring round and screaming sirens; there was the murmur of voices everywhere, and I felt that whooping wind. It was chaotic, but somehow safe.

I had the sensation of rising up again, but this time I understood it as being carried—passing through a crowd, strapped to some kind of board. Cameras were flashing. Off to one side there were blurry images of the Queen Mary and hypnotic helicopters hovering overhead, with warm winds and tiny grains of sand blowing hard on my face. The bug-eyed faces of random people passed before me. *Who were they, anyway?*

I shut my eyes and listened. That wonderful, crazy din of life—oddly comforting, despite the racket. I believe I felt both separate and at one with stuff at the same time if that's possible. Like I'm coming out of my body (and that's okay) or I'm coming back to the world (and that's okay).

I thought I heard my mom's voice talking to someone and turned my head slightly toward it. She grabbed me by the shoulders and brought her face close. I half-thought she was going to strangle me, so I tried to utter a preemptive, "Sorry," but it came out all faint, and she put her fingers against my lips.

"Sshh. My boy, my sweet, foolish boy. What've you done? It's okay, we'll get through this. Easy now."

Instead of throttling me, she burst into tears, draped herself over me, and hugged me tight—at least as much as possible with me lying flat on ... ah, *that* was it: a stretcher. Hot tears streaked out the sides of my eyes and ran down my temples and into my ears.

I hoped that my mom had it in her to forgive me. Maybe I permanently scarred her by acting the way I did; I don't know. I think I wanted her to understand that what I did wasn't directed at *her*—it wasn't a judgment or indictment of her mothering.

Later, at the hospital, I got a chance to go over the same forgiveness rituals with my dad. I'd like to say there was a happy ending there, but, well—negative. And I'd like to say there were at least realizations, and contrition, and a coming together of minds, or souls or whatever over time, but, well—sorry. In fact, it *was* sorry; it *never* happened. Let's just say it was messy. That was one of those things I couldn't quite fathom that summer: Despite all my cynicism in those days, it turned out I held onto an optimistic view of things over the long haul. Oh, well—nothing that years of therapy won't almost nearly fix.

Eventually I'd go home. But I wouldn't take that word lightly. *Home.* This didn't mean things were fine, only that I better understood its real value and, more than that, how it could take so many different forms and include so many more places than I ever thought possible. I had no idea I was connected to so many people. And at one point I realized home isn't defined or bound by brick or stucco but by relationships and love—it's dynamic and fluid, like a river. Duh.

Trust (and faith) is a funny thing: We assume it's a given. But it's so fragile. From big to small things, we need to trust, if nothing else so that we don't go crazy. We trust the planet to spin at an incredibly fast speed but in a way that stuff on it will stay put. We trust the guy driving toward us on the other side of the road isn't going to suddenly swerve and crash into us. We trust our bodies to do a million different things perfectly, without so much as a thank-you.

It was confirmed for me that trust begins, or ends, with keeping our word. I got better at that, only to slack off with it later, then ended up somewhere in the middle, I suppose, these days. We need people to be there for us when they say so—and we all need to be *that* kind of reliable person ourselves. 'Cause when trust breaks down, it's awfully hard to mend. All that to say: I've still got a lot of work cut out for myself. Anyway, sorry to rant, but you know me by now.

I saw my friends starting to assemble behind Mom. They rushed forward and surrounded me while the medics kept us moving along as a bunch. I could tell Ian, Tawnya, Iggie, and Zoe wanted to lay into me and razz me about a lot of stuff, but they held their tongues (at least for now). They were like these gorgeous creatures—angels, really—and I was in total awe of them.

We knew we'd be mulling over this whole escapade for a long, long time. No shortage of apologies. Crazy, reckless stuff. But at least we knew we'd be in the doghouse together, and there was no group I'd have wanted to share that dubious honor with than them.

Ian stepped up, "Hey congrats, man, you went the distance—to Long Beach or bust, eh?"

"To Long Beach *and* busted *up*," I whispered back. "Piss and vinegar, bud!"

"Absolutely. You take care. I'll see you back in the Valley. I think we take it easy the rest of the summer, yeah?"

I squinted at him, then blinked a few times in silent agreement.

Tawnya squeezed in, excitedly, trading places with Ian. "That was batshit insanity back there! You are freakin' nuts, boy. Don't you *ever*, *never*, not in *forever* do that again—least not with me along for the ride!"

I smiled and gave her a pained thumbs-up and a cheesy grin.

Then Iggie pushed his way through. He held my hand and bent down and whispered and prayed. "You do good, man, for a gringo. Serious, for all of us. Amigos for life— wherever we go, okay? *Lo entiendes, si?* We have a lot to talk about, yes?"

I squeezed his hand as hard as I could, "*Si, si,* for sure."

And as the medics started to shoo everyone away and slide me into the back of the ambulance, Zoe caught up and grabbed the side of the stretcher and stopped them for a sec. She looked hard at me, then planted a long kiss on my painfully dry, salty, cut-up lips. As always, she read my mind perfectly.

Through the end of that year, Ian, Zoe, Iggie, and I would sometimes get together with Tawnya, and we kept up those friendships through our senior year and beyond, more or less.

My friendship with Ian got tighter, and we're still close today.

It was harder to keep up the friendship with Tawnya, mostly because of the distance between where we lived. I mean, it *is* L.A. She officially enrolled at SMCC for a couple years, then transferred to UCLA. She landed a job on the East Coast, doing what she said she'd do someday, somehow: computer science—which is code for money. I was real happy for her and proud of her. Maybe I should've been more contrarian myself (oh well, too late). Anyways, her being on the East Coast made things tricky but not impossible.

Zoe and I stayed together our first two years at separate colleges. We had a good run, but distance and time and a few other issues did us in. Like they say, it was probably for

the best—that is, in this case it actually did save our friendship, I believe. Sometimes though, I wonder what would've
happened if we'd really gone for it. Mostly, I think it was
the right call. But *was* it really? See?! Damn, relationships are
freakin' hard! Anyway, she ended up using her design skills
to be an art director for some ad agency in Woodland Hills.
And with her knack for logistics, she did event planning for
a period, too.

And Ignazio, he stayed with us for a few months, doing
work around the neighborhood to save up enough money
to pay off his debts. A lot of neighbors got him loaded up
with work. He finally decided to return to his family around
Christmas of that same year—at least he said it would be
"just for a time." We lent him some extra money to give
him a fresh cushion of funds back home to start a business
or whatever. My mom and I drove across the border with
him and took a flight out of Tijuana. Even though he had
his Guatemalan passport with him, it turns out that while
everyone cares about your passport on the way into America
and Mexico, no one really cares much about your documen-
tation if you're leaving. So we flew down with him and spent
a week in Guatemala. We met his wife and son, of course,
and his whole extended family, and just about everyone
else in his small hillside community. And, of course, he
and I secretly discussed other adventures we wanted to do
someday. We were sure there was no border in the world
that could've keep us apart.

My mom and I returned to the States. She and I grew a
lot closer in that period after that trip and after her divorce
was finalized, when she was even more on her own.

But at some point after that, life just happened. Slowly.
Poco a poco, as Ignazio always said. One excuse or another
always came up that kept Iggie and me apart. Sure, we wrote
letters and emails, and I called every now and then, or wired
him some money when I had a little extra. He ended up

learning how to build or fix just about every part of a house you could imagine. And he evidently became sort of the unofficial neighborhood veterinarian, too, with dozens of animals, especially cats, that he kept an eye on. He told me he'd dealt with a blind capuchin monkey, a howler monkey that had lost its ability to howl, an armadillo that was partially crushed by a car, a fox that got burned, a white-nosed coatimundi, and even a one-legged quetzal bird.

But I guess it was hard for both of us. I didn't know what I could really offer by going south to visit him, what I would really *do* there. And he claimed that if he couldn't come north for good then it was simply too tough to always be reminded of that parallel life through me.

We sort of drifted from there. College, relationships, family—my dad's untimely passing (long story, don't ask). More recently, the humdrum workaday grind sort of wore me down. I guess that's just another reason why I've been in a funk lately. I mean: What happened to all the friends I had in college and before? We're all so spread out now.

Iggie was involved in an incident a few weeks back. I'm going down to visit him, finally, in a few days. But it really shouldn't get to the point where only a brush with death forces two friends together again. He said he refused to pay off some guys who wanted money to protect his house. That's not the kind of home security you want: Once you start, he says, you can't easily just get out of that racket. So they roughed him up pretty badly, and he ended up in the hospital. I didn't even hear about it until I got a call from his wife a couple days ago.

Regrets? Yeah, I've got plenty. Mainly that I should've just gone for it, in one way or another, when I had the chances. Angst? Yeah, check. But that's life, right?

To make a lasting change—either with ourselves or a larger cause—comes with a whole lot of collateral damage; there seems to be wreckage up and down that path. I'd also like to say good things happen when you go for it, but I can't totally stand behind that; maybe just a helluva lot *can happen*, for better *or* for worse, but it's up to us to push beyond our fears, one way or another. Then again, there's the flip side: Sometimes the consequence of *not* going for it costs you just as dearly. I guess that's what haunts me most. Anyway, *my* problem, not yours.

At the end of the day though, like they say, you gotta keep your crazy hopes and dreams alive, and your true friends close, and trust that the ends will justify the means it takes to get there. Jump in, go with the flow, and when it calls for it, paddle like hell.

For now though, I'm writing like hell, trying to put all this down on paper, to make sense of it all, hoping it'll reveal some magic beans to make everything—including me—whole again, or at least to find some peace of mind. At this point I'd certainly settle for simply some of that.

When they finally gurneyed me into the ambulance, our crew shouted out their last well-wishes. The medic hopped in. "That's enough excitement for now," she said as she closed the doors.

I wasn't about to argue. I shut my eyes and napped for what seemed like hours but turned out to be only five minutes or so. I know 'cause I looked out the small windows and saw us going back up and over one of the bridges that crossed the L.A. River. That beat traveling back across the bay in a damned canoe or lifeboat—what a hare-brained idea! At the time I promised myself to get my head examined, too, along with the rest of my body; as usual, I had no idea what I was getting myself into, how long *that* would actually take.

But somehow, through it all, I'd kept my word and done it—*we'd* done it. It wasn't pretty. It wasn't direct. And it wasn't anything close to how I imagined it. We do our best with what we've got, and in the end, that's all any of us can do—again and again and again.

END

ABOUT THE AUTHOR

George R. Wolfe is the founder of both *The LaLa Times*, dubbed *The Onion* for LA., and L.A. River Expeditions, a group that advocates for endangered rivers. His activist work has been featured in *The New York Times*, PBS, BBC, and in the documentary *Rock the Boat: Saving America's Wildest River*. Wolfe's first novel, *Blake's Bible*, was selected for the Jack Straw Writers Series, and several exhibitions. *Into the River of Angels* is Wolfe's second novel. He lives in Los Angeles with his wife, dog, and cat.

ABOUT THE PUBLISHER

The Sager Group was founded in 1984. In 2012 it was chartered as a multimedia content brand, with the intent of empowering those who create art—an umbrella beneath which makers can pursue, and profit from, their craft directly, without gatekeepers. TSG publishes books; ministers to artists and provides modest grants; and produces documentary, feature, and commercial films. By harnessing the means of production, The Sager Group helps artists help themselves. For more information, please see www.TheSagerGroup.net.

MORE BOOKS FROM THE SAGER GROUP

The Swamp: Deceit and Corruption in the CIA
An Elizabeth Petrov Thriller (Book 1)
by Jeff Grant

Chains of Nobility:
Brotherhood of the Mamluks (Book 1-3)
by Brad Graft

Meeting Mozart:
A Novel Drawn from the Secret Diaries of Lorenzo Da Ponte
by Howard Jay Smith

Death Came Swiftly:
A Novel About the Tay Bridge Disaster of 1879
by Bill Abrams

A Boy and His Dog in Hell: And Other Stories
by Mike Sager

Miss Havilland: A Novel
by Gay Daly

The Orphan's Daughter: A Novel
by Jan Cherubin

Lifeboat No. 8: Surviving the Titanic
by Elizabeth Kaye

Hunting Marlon Brando:
A True Story
by Mike Sager

See our entire library at TheSagerGroup.net

Artifex Te Adiuva

CPSIA information can be obtained
at www.ICGtesting.com
Printed in the USA
JSHW020344060523
41340JS00001B/3

9 781958 861028